STRANGER ON RHANNA

Christine Marion Fraser was born in Glasgow just after the war. At the age of ten she contracted a rare disease and has been in a wheelchair ever since.

A keen reader and storyteller, Christine started writing at the age of five and got the idea for *Rhanna*, the first novel in the popular series, while on holiday in the Hebrides. She has gone on to write six more volumes – *Rhanna at War*, *Children of Rhanna*, *Return to Rhanna*, *Song of Rhanna*, *Storm over Rhanna* and *Stranger on Rhanna*. She has also written three volumes of autobiography – *Blue Above the Chimneys*, *Roses Round the Door* and *Green Are My Mountains*, and four volumes in the successful *King's* Series – *King's Croft*, *King's Acre*, *King's Exile* and *King's Close*.

Christine Marion Fraser lives with her husband in Argyllshire.

CHRISTINE MARION FRASER

Stranger on Rhanna

Fontana
An Imprint of HarperCollins*Publishers*

Fontana
An Imprint of HarperCollins*Publishers*,
77–85 Fulham Palace Road,
Hammersmith, London W6 8JB

Special overseas edition 1993
This edition published by Fontana 1993
1 3 5 7 9 8 6 4 2

First published in Great Britain by
HarperCollins*Publishers* 1992

ISBN 0 00 647003 3

Set in Times

Printed in Great Britain by
HarperCollinsManufacturing Glasgow

For Andy 'Mahatmacoat' McKillop – the best.

Croft na Beinn

Aosdana Bay

RÙMHOR

Ben
Machrie

Fàilte

PORTVOYNACHAN

Loch
Sliach

gmhor

Bob's
Biggin

na Ard

An Cala

Mara Òran
Bay

S O U N D   O F   R H A N N A

Part One

SPRING 1967

Chapter One

Rachel stood at the door of An Cala and breathed deeply the scents of sea and machair that were borne to her on the fresh breezes of the early March day. Her dark eyes gazed out to the Sound of Rhanna where lively white sea horses leapt and pranced in foaming turbulence, and she thought how good it was to be back home on Rhanna, listening to the cries of the wheeling gulls and the wild surge of the ocean.

The rest of the world seemed so far away, especially her hectic world of endless concert tours that took her from one country to the next, where she was never still for a moment and there was never any time to pause and remember the people and places that were dear and familiar to her, but which were so very far removed from the bustle, the excitement and the adoring public that demanded so much of her time, her energy, her emotions . . .

Lately it had all become too much for her; she was drained, physically and mentally, and she hadn't made any objections when Jon, her husband, had suggested that she should take a long holiday.

'At least six months,' he had told her firmly. 'You are between tours and deserve a long spell away from it all. You could spend some time on Rhanna, then, if you would like, I'll take you some place where the sun shines all day and all we need to do is eat and sleep and find time for each other again.'

She thought about Jon. He was so good to her: always thinking about her welfare, devoting himself to her every whim, managing her affairs, travelling with her wherever she went.

'Whither thou goest I will go also.'

The words floated into her mind and she smiled because for once Jon hadn't come with her but had instead gone to visit his big, domineering Mamma in Hamburg who had never ceased to be surprised that her son had actually severed the apron strings to marry a girl from a remote Scottish island.

He hadn't suggested that Rachel should accompany him to Hamburg. His monumental Mamma, with her loud, demanding voice, had never taken to Rachel – after all, wasn't she the girl who had stolen away her only son? Never mind that she was a world-famous violinist, at heart she was still as wild and as abandoned as the gypsy-like child he had fallen in love with on a fateful visit to Rhanna many years ago. She didn't have the breeding, she didn't have the poise, she only had her music and she wouldn't have made such a success of that if it hadn't been for Jon's sacrificing his own musical talents so that she could pursue fame and fortune.

Besides all that, she had been born with a terrible physical defect, and no man should have to live with such a thing: it wasn't right, it wasn't normal. Perhaps there were other abnormalities that no one knew about. Why hadn't Rachel conceived by now? She was young, she looked strong enough. It couldn't be Jon's fault: he was healthy and normal. A man needed children to keep him happy. Of course, it might have something to do with all that traipsing about from one country to the next: what sort of a life was that for any married couple? But, of course, Rachel needed the fame, the adoration – never mind her husband and the sacrifices he'd had to make . . .

Jon had heard it all many times and he never exposed Rachel to his mother's narrow reasonings if he could help it. But Rachel knew what Mamma Jodl thought of her: it was all there, in the accusing blue eyes, in the way the woman watched her and made reference to Jon's forebears.

'There has always been a son to carry on the name of Jodl,' she would say with calculating nonchalance. 'We are a family who go back a long way, and always there is the strong seed, the male line. Jon would never deliberately allow it to die out, he has always been proud of his name.'

But Mamma Jodl was very far from Rachel's mind that crisp, bright March day with Mara Òran Bay sparkling at her feet and the great dome of the sky stretching wide and infinite overhead. She had been on the island two days now but no one knew that she was here: she had wanted time to be alone, just herself and the silence, the blessed, wondrous silence she had dreamed about for so long. It was a reprieve from people. A blissful respite from hurry, noise, bustle, and – most importantly – there was no phone. At their flat in London they were besieged with requests for her presence at many and varied functions; they were inundated with mail; the door went; the phone jangled. It was an exciting but exhausting life and when it all became too much she knew she had to escape back to the peace and serenity of Rhanna, her island home, her refuge when the bigger world became intolerable.

She had come armed with enough supplies to last several days. On the boat she had worn dark glasses and had kept her coat collar muffled round her face. No one had given her a second glance. It had been a rough crossing from Oban and most of the passengers had sat in the saloon, either 'half asleep or half dead or a mixture o' both', according to Ranald who had been over on the mainland visiting one of his many cousins.

'Ay, well, if that's the case, I'd rather be dying wi' a good tot o' rum in me,' Captain Mac had returned and so saying he had staggered off in the direction of the bar, clutching an assortment of parcels, with Ranald so close on his heels that he had tripped and half fallen out of the doorway, leaving behind him a string of oaths that could only have come from a man who had spent most of his life at sea.

The expletives were like music in Rachel's ears. She had half thought of joining the two men in the bar but had quickly decided against it. Word of her arrival would spread round the island like wildfire and, until she was settled, that was the last thing she wanted.

No one had noticed her leaving the boat and she had been able to make her leisurely way to An Cala, observed only by the sheep cropping the machair and three large Highland cows, who had gazed at her benignly through untidy straggles of wheat-coloured hair.

It had been wonderful to be alone in An Cala – which was the Gaelic for The Haven or The Harbour – no one but herself, wandering through the quiet rooms, every window affording views of sea and shore, hills and fields.

Heating had been a problem. She hadn't wanted to broadcast her presence by having smoke blowing from the chimneys, so she compromised by lighting the fire only at night and by day keeping herself so busy cleaning the house she had no time to feel cold. Of course, she could have started the generator that supplied An Cala with electric heat and light, but the road was nearby, as was Croft na Ard, the home of Anton and Babbie Büttger. Anybody could have heard the rather noisy generator purring away in its shed, so she had cooked her meals on the Calor-gas stove and had eaten them curled up by the fire with the curtains pulled across the windows. Candles and oil lamps allowed her to read and light her way to bed and it had altogether been two of the most relaxing days she had spent for years.

She knew, of course, that she must soon make her presence known – the Rhanna folk didn't appreciate such secrecy and when they found out she had slipped on to the island without anyone knowing she would be the talk of the place. Behag Beag and Elspeth Morrison, in particular, would no doubt have the most to say on the subject. But for now it was enough that she went undiscovered and with an upsurge of sheer abandonment she tossed back her glossy black hair and spread wide her arms as if to embrace the ocean to her breast.

Ruth wandered slowly along the white sands of Mara Òran Bay, deep in thought, in her mind writing the final chapter of her

14

second book. The dialogue was piling in on her and, getting out her notebook, she jotted the words down before they could slip away. Ahead of her, four-and-a-half-year-old Douglas ran and played, his lint-white head bobbing about as he searched for small sea creatures in the rock pools. He was a child who craved perpetual motion and interest in his life. That afternoon he had been particularly restless and in exasperation Ruth had set out to take him for a long walk by the shore, even if it meant leaving her typewriter for a while.

But she was glad that she had come out: Lorn was always telling her that she spent far too much time in the house. Lifting her head, she took a deep breath of salt-laden sea air. Her eyes travelled upwards to An Cala, and she wondered when Rachel would come back to Rhanna. It had been some months since she had seen her friend; she loved it when Jon and Rachel came home, their lives were so exciting and there was always so much they had to tell her – the places they'd seen, the people they'd met . . .

A movement near the house attracted her attention. Shading her eyes, she stared upwards and made out a lone figure standing on the cliffs gazing out to sea. Her heart quickened. It surely couldn't be Rachel: she hadn't written to say she was coming – but who else could be wandering about outside An Cala, if not Rachel?

Calling on Douglas, she hurried with him up the steep track to the house, her violet eyes shining when she saw that it was indeed the girl who, in long-ago childhood, had shared all her little secrets.

'Rachel!' she called breathlessly, running forward as she spoke.

Rachel spun round, her heart galloping into her throat with fright. So engrossed had she been with her thoughts, with the glorious sense of being the only person inhabiting this particular spot at that particular time, she hadn't been aware of any other living soul encroaching on this private place that she considered to be hers.

She loved Ruth, she had always loved her, they had spent the early years of their lives together. She had travelled the world but never had she found anyone who could ever quite compare with Ruth: she could never be as confiding, or as trusting with anyone else, but Ruth could be possessive at times and the way she was feeling now, Rachel didn't want to be possessed by anyone, not even her childhood friend.

Her reciprocal greeting was therefore somewhat restrained and Ruth's face fell a little when her welcoming embrace was not wholeheartedly returned. With the intention of making some excuse to be on her way, she opened her mouth to call on Douglas, but he was already clinging to the hand of the lovely young woman whom he had called 'Aunt Ray' ever since he had learned to speak.

It didn't matter to him that she couldn't answer him back, he simply watched her expressive gestures, the fluent movements of her hands, and gradually he was learning the basic symbols of the sign language.

Rachel led him into the house and Ruth could do nothing but follow, though slowly, indignation growing in her at the realisation that Rachel hadn't told her she was coming to the island – when she had always declared she wouldn't feel right arriving on Rhanna with no Ruth to greet her at the harbour.

The fire was unlit and the house was cold. With a strange little smile, Rachel struck a match and held it to the twists of paper in the grate. She didn't need wood, from an early age she had been taught how to light a fire without it and she had never forgotten the art. She watched the flames curling, the smoke drifting up the chimney. It didn't matter now: she had been discovered, there was no further need to deny herself home comforts, very soon the whole of Rhanna would know that she was here. The solitude, the peace, was over.

'I'll make tea.' Ruth got up and went to the tiny kitchen, her limp pronounced as it always was when she was upset or angry. She rattled cups and saucers with energy, she found the tea caddy and poured hot water into the teapot to warm it. The tea smelled funny, sort of smoky and spicy. Just like Rachel, she thought, even her very tea has to be exotic and different. No wonder Annie, her mother, sometimes said that her daughter's head was too full of fancy ideas for her own good.

When finally she carried the tray of tea and biscuits into the living room, the fire was leaping up the lum and Douglas was ensconced in a big comfortable armchair, happily applying coloured crayons to a picture book on his lap.

Rachel kept a good supply of chalks and children's books in the house for the benefit of young visitors. She was altogether most attentive to their needs, and though each and every one of them knew that she could be as firm as she was kind-hearted, they all respected her for it and were, with few exceptions, as eager to please her as she was them.

There had been a time in her life when she hadn't wanted children but as the years had gone by her attitudes had changed till now she was more than anxious to have a much longed-for baby. It didn't matter that such an event would interrupt her career and she often thought longingly of what it would be like to have the same kind of life as other young married women. But for her it could never be like that and she knew it: her passion for music would never be stilled and always she would strive for perfection till the pinnacle was reached.

Ruth drew in a chair to the fire, smiling a little to herself when she smelled the incense that pervaded the room. Rachel said she burned it to sweeten the air and take away the mustiness from rooms that had lain empty, but the islanders had different ideas. Old Sorcha insisted on calling the strange perfume 'incest' and claimed it made her feel funny whenever she 'sniffed in the reek o' it'. And whenever Kate McKinnon visited her granddaughter she danced and swayed to Rachel's 'provocative oriental music' looking glazed about the eyes, 'as if the incest had seeped into her head and made her think about her essentials', to quote Sorcha.

Rachel had gotten over her annoyance at the intrusion, and she eagerly asked Ruth to relate all her news, her hands and fingers flying so fast they were just a blur of frantic movement. But Ruth had long ago learnt the sign language and was able to answer every question, for although her friend was dumb her hearing was perfect. Nevertheless, many assumed that speech and hearing defects went hand in hand and were quite nonplussed in Rachel's company.

Forgetting her earlier feelings of anger, Ruth explained that she was just finishing her second novel, *The Far Island*, and that the paperback of her first book, *Hebridean Dream*, was due to be released shortly.

Rachel studied her friend – she looked so happy, fair-haired, violet-eyed Ruth, so fragile-seeming with her small-boned figure and the limp that had been her legacy since birth. But Ruth was stronger than she looked: she had triumphed over a difficult childhood when she had been under the rule of her fanatically religious mother, red-haired Morag Ruadh, who hadn't so much played the kirk organ as attacked it and who had almost broken Ruth's spirit with her warped and sanctimonious outlook on life. Somehow, Ruth had emerged from those years virtually unscathed, though there were times when she could be strange and unforgiving and very unyielding. That time with Lorn, for instance, she had very nearly broken his heart by taking Lorna away with her . . . Yet who could really blame her: it had been a terrible time and she, Rachel, had been the cause of it all . . . She shuddered and turned her mind away from such dark thoughts and forced herself to talk of lighter matters. It was like old times – as the young women talked and laughed, Rachel visibly relaxed and forgot herself. She was an island girl again, carefree, abandoned, vowing to herself that as soon as the weather was warm enough she would roam her old haunts, barefoot and free, just as it had been when she was a wild, unsophisticated child with few problems to complicate her life.

Excitedly she recalled those early days, when she and Ruth, Lorn and Lewis McKenzie had wandered the island together.

'Oh, it was good, Ruth,' her fingers formed the words, 'so very, very good. I remember Lewis so well, he was so different from Lorn: he was as devilish and daring as I was myself, as strong as a young horse, while Lorn was quiet and delicate. Oh, how the years have passed – so quickly. Everything has changed: Lewis is dead, Lorn is as strong as his brother used to be. You and I were bound up with the two of them – right from the beginning . . .'

She stared into the fire, her great dark eyes burning as she remembered Lewis. How passionate they had been together in the all-consuming desire of their young love, how much they had hurt one another with their stormy, youthful arguings, how much they had hurt other people . . .

She would never love another as she had loved that wonderful young McKenzie – yet she had left him for Jon because she had always known that there could be no future for her with Lewis, and then he had died and there had been no future for him – with anyone.

Ruth looked at her friend. The firelight was glinting on her raven-black hair; her supple young body, though clad simply in a red jersey and blue jeans, still conveyed that air of erotic sensuality that drew men to her like a magnet. She looked still and composed by the fire, but Ruth knew that beneath the calm exterior she burned with thoughts of two young men, Lewis and Lorn, the twin sons of McKenzie o' the Glen, both of whom had been captivated by her in their turn . . .

Ruth lay back in her seat and she too remembered Lewis McKenzie and how the course of her life had been changed by him during those sad, terrible days when he had told her he was dying. By then, Rachel had left the island with Jon, and in his fear and loneliness Lewis had turned to Ruth for comfort. Lewis had died but his seed had lived on in his daughter, Lorna McKenzie, now nearly six years old. Lorn had married Ruth to give the child his name even though he had at first been devastated to discover that the girl he loved was carrying his brother's child.

Lorn . . . darling Lorn. Ruth had nearly lost him too but in quite a different way from Lewis. Hurtful memories came flooding back. She glanced at Rachel and resentment burned for a few moments. This black-eyed, passionate creature in whom she had always placed a rather childlike trust had had an affair with Lorn behind her back when she had been ill in hospital. It had been a dreadful time, she and Lorn had almost split up because of it . . .

Ruth gave herself a mental shake: it was all in the past, she mustn't think about it, Rachel had made a mistake, she truly loved Jon and would never do anything to hurt him again . . .

'Lorna is Lewis's child!' Rachel's hands moved swiftly, impatiently, as she made the statement.

Ruth gasped. 'How did you know that?'

'I guessed.' Rachel's hands made a succinct reply.

'But – why did you bring the subject up now? It was so long ago. Lorn accepts Lorna as his daughter, everyone, with the exception of family, thinks she's his child.'

'I was thinking of Lewis, remembering how it was with him, wondering, I suppose, what my life would be like now if I'd had his child.'

'You want a baby very much, don't you, Rachel?' Ruth spoke softly, sympathetically.

'Yes, I do. I can sense Jon's longing to have a child, and, of course, Mamma Jodl never stops hinting that it's all my fault we haven't got children. But . . .' Rachel looked straight at her friend, 'I know for a fact it isn't: I went to see a doctor, several in fact, and they all said the same thing. There is nothing wrong with me, I am fit and well and quite able to conceive.'

'Then – you think – the problem lies with Jon?' Ruth spoke slowly, unwilling to touch on such a sensitive subject, even though she sensed that Rachel needed someone to confide in. She had always been deep, had Rachel, fathomless some said. She had never spoken to her mother about things nearest her heart, Jon's mother was as close to her as the man on the moon and she obviously didn't feel able to discuss the matter with her husband, which left Ruth, to whom she had always disclosed her innermost thoughts

'I'm not absolutely sure if there really is a problem,' Rachel replied morosely. 'Our lifestyle isn't exactly a restful one, we have never been able to relax properly and give ourselves up fully to one another. We never have the time, always there are matters more pressing than our private life together. I haven't told Jon that I saw those doctors, I'll wait awhile yet.

'We have the summer ahead of us, possibly the autumn as well, we are both going to take time off and have a long, long holiday together. He'll come home to Rhanna after his visit to Mamma Jodl in Hamburg; we'll have time for one another again, all the time in the world. Who knows what will happen.'

Ruth's eyes were sparkling at the idea of having Rachel on Rhanna for a whole summer. 'Och, Rachel, that's wonderful!' she cried. 'I forgive you for not letting me know you were coming home. It's going to be a wonderful summer, I know you'll want to spend a lot o' your time with Jon, but I also know you'll spare some for me. Kate will be delighted, she aye loves it when you're home and she can show off her famous granddaughter to her cronies. Oh, look at the time! I must fly. Lorna will be home from school soon and I've still to feed the hens and get some messages from Merry Mary's, also I need some things from the Post Office.'

Rachel smiled as she followed her friend to the door. Douglas ran on ahead, eager to be off; one small adventure was over with, now he was impatient to see his sister and tell her all about the pictures he had coloured in that afternoon.

Rachel and Ruth stood for a moment at the door of An Cala. The gorse bushes were coming into flower, the sweet perfume was already invading the air, the Highland cows were browsing amongst the little sheltered hillocks, a nearby burn foamed over a tumble of stones on its way to the sea. How peaceful it was, Rachel thought happily, it was going to be lovely spending the coming months on Rhanna, everything slow-paced and tranquil, no need to hurry anywhere, no noise, no bustle.

Far below, the steamer hove into view. With mild interest both girls watched it sailing past Mara Òran Bay on its way to the harbour.

'The tourist season will be starting soon,' Rachel observed.

'Ay, it has already,' Ruth nodded.

'We'll have strangers on the island,' Rachel continued, a frown on her brow.

'Ach, don't fret,' laughed Ruth. 'They won't intrude on you or Jon. Whatever else the islanders might be, they're loyal to their own and won't tell anyone you're here. They're quite protective of their famous violinist.'

She waved and hurried down the path to catch up with her son. Rachel remained at the door, watching the steamer, and a strange sense of apprehension shivered through her, even though the sun broke warmly through a bank of cumulus that had covered it for the last hour.

Chapter Two

Doctor Megan Jenkins brought her little red Mini to a spectacular halt at the harbour, though her somewhat unreliable brakes were only partially responsible for the sudden stop. A pile of Ranald's lobster pots absorbed the rest of the momentum she had gathered on her rush down the Glen Fallan road and she tumbled out of the car, her hair in disarray, her face red with anxiety.

'You'll do yourself an injury, Doctor Megan,' observed Erchy the Post, keeping one eye on the steamer as she tied up in the harbour. 'If it's the boat you think you've missed you needny worry your head, she's just come in this very minute.'

'Thank heaven for that,' Megan said a trifle breathlessly. 'I was visiting Murdy when I looked from the window and saw the boat heading round the bay. I'm afraid I left poor Murdy half dressed with a thermometer sticking into his armpit and my stethoscope in a heap on top of his chest.'

Erchy grinned and scratched his balding head. 'Ach, he'll have a wee play wi' it while he's waiting for you to come back. Murdy was aye fascinated wi' tubes of all sorts. The inner tubes o' that old bike o' his are more often out than in and I mind once, when Auld Biddy had to give him an enema, he was that taken up wi' all the wee tubes it was all she could do to make him leave them alone so that she could do what had to be done wi' them. Now, any normal body would be fair affronted at the goings-on of enema tubes but not Murdy – oh no – they just gave him an even keener taste for them – if you'll forgive the expression, Doctor.'

He paused cryptically and slid her a sidelong glance but her attention was taken up by the passengers who were starting to come down the gangplank.

'It was a terrible thing, just, what Murdy did to himself the next time he was constipated and needin' Biddy wi' her tubes.'

Erchy spoke heavily and was gratified to see that he had aroused Megan's curiosity. 'Did to himself?' she asked with a faint smile.

'Ay, he thought he knew all about it, having watched Biddy wi' the tubes and the soapy water, so he made his cailleach wash out an old bicycle tube and bring it to the bed along wi' a great bucket o' hot water piled high wi' soap suds. Well, both him and the cailleach between them tried for hours to get things moving wi' the old inner tube. Soap suds were everywhere, on the bed, the floor, even in the cat's ears, everywhere but where they were supposed to go. In the end the pair o' them were that exhausted they fell asleep together in the wet bed. When Biddy heard tell about the affair she was over there like a shot to give them a piece o' her mind. "Is it an elephant you think you are, Murdy McKinnon?" she roared. "I've never heard the likes in all my days as a nurse and it would just have served you right if you had ruptured your bowels and we would all have had some peace without them." ' Erchy shook his head sadly. 'Ay, Biddy was never a one to stand any nonsense from anybody. Never again did Murdy try anything so drastic wi' his inner tubes but it didn't put him off his liking for them – or any tubes for that matter.'

'Quite a story, Erchy,' said Megan drily, though her eyes were twinkling. 'We can only hope he'll be safe with my stethoscope till I go back and rescue it from him.'

'Ach, poor old Murdy.' Erchy's tones were solicitous now. 'I am hoping there is nothing serious wrong wi' him, he never calls a doctor out if he can help it.'

'Just old age, Erchy, and the pains and aches that go with it.'

'Ay, indeed, it must be terrible to be getting old.' Erchy's face was perfectly straight, his words absolutely sincere, for although he was well past retiring age he vowed he would only stop working on the day he dropped dead, and since, in his own mind, such an event was 'years and years away' he went on happily with his work and was as wiry and fit as a man half his age.

'You'll be waiting for someone coming off the boat, then?' Erchy craned his neck and followed the direction of Megan's eyes. Erchy's interest in other people's affairs was legendary.

'No, not quite.' Megan kept her face composed. 'I was wondering, can you see any sign of a flying saucer? I'm expecting one to land at any minute and was told to wave my hanky as a sort of guide.'

'Ach, Doctor!' Erchy scolded huffily. 'There is no need to be sarcastic. I was only making polite conversation. It is the way o' things here, we keep ourselves to ourselves and just get on wi' our own affairs, but it would be unnatural no' to show a wee bit interest in what's going on round about.'

But Megan hadn't heard him. 'Oh, that must be him,' she murmured, her eyes on a tall, masculine figure descending from the boat.

'And who is "him"?' questioned Erchy eagerly, forgetting that he was supposed to be getting on with his own affairs.

Megan didn't answer. Leaving Erchy to observe the bustle of the harbour with avid eyes, she somewhat tentatively approached the stranger who had alighted from the boat and was standing looking around him in a questioning manner.

'You must be Herr Otto Klebb.' Megan extended a friendly hand. 'I'm Mrs James, better known as Doctor Megan – or just plain Megan if you like. My car is just over here, it's very small, I'm afraid . . .' Doubtfully she glanced at his large frame and wondered how such a big man could possibly fit into her small car.

A great stir of interest greeted the newcomer, heads bobbed, a dozen pairs of eyes followed his progress along the harbour.

Herr Klebb was not the usual sort of visitor to alight on Rhanna's shores. He was definitely foreign-looking, which fact alone was enough to rouse curiosity, but there was more to this stranger than just the stamp of a continental. He was a Presence, that was how Robbie Beag put it to Ranald McTavish, who was retrieving his scattered lobster pots with mutters of annoyance.

'A Presence wi' a capital P,' Robbie added. 'He'll be a Somebody, you can aye tell by the look they have on them, as if they owned everything and everybody and expect to get things done for them wi' just the snap o' a finger.'

'Do you suppose Doctor Megan will help me gather up my lobster pots if I snap my fingers at her?' Ranald enquired sourly.

'Ach no.' Robbie's genial face broke into grins. 'She's too busy wi' the foreign gentleman to be bothered wi' you and your pots. You shouldn't leave them lying where folks can crash into them wi' their motor cars – one o' these days someone will break a leg tripping over them and it will serve you right if you get sued for damages.'

Ranald's yelp of indignation was lost on Robbie who had gone to join an inquisitive group all stretching their necks to get a better look at 'the foreign stranger' as he had quickly been labelled.

Robbie, in his own, ingenious way, was right, Herr Otto Klebb was a Presence and a Somebody. Megan sensed these things the moment she had gazed into his piercing, deep eyes. He was at least six feet tall, well built, distinguished-looking despite a mop of dark hair that the sea breeze was blowing into disarray. His black beard was clipped to a neat point, his face was strong and ruggedly handsome but rather severe in its unsmiling repose.

It came to her that she knew very little about the man beyond his name and the fact that he had leased her old home, Tigh na Cladach, for an indefinite period. 'I need a place where I can have complete privacy. I have been working very hard and my doctor has advised me to take a long rest,' he had written in reply to her advert in an English newspaper, 'your house sounds ideal and I will require to move in as soon as possible. Please let me know when it is convenient and also please forward the timetable for steamer connections to Rhanna.'

Megan had married the Reverend Mark James on Christmas Eve just over two months ago and had moved into the Manse, which was a big, old house with enough rooms to allow the two of them to conduct their respective professions comfortably. They had both thought it a good idea to let Tigh na Cladach but hadn't expected that it would be taken quite so quickly.

For some reason Megan felt unnerved by Herr Otto Klebb and she was rather glad when Erchy strolled up to help her lift the man's cases into the boot of the car and to batten down the rusty lid with the aid of an old webbing belt. She immersed herself in the task, not daring to look to see how Herr Klebb was managing to tuck his bulky, overcoated frame into the sagging front passenger seat. But somehow he had made it and, breathing a sigh of relief, she went round to the driver's door.

'He'll be staying at the Manse, then?' Erchy hadn't offered his services for nothing, and he was most annoyed when Megan merely smiled sweetly at him before getting into the little red Mini.

At the first turn of the key, the engine burst into life so vigorously Megan was taken aback. Normally it coughed and died, choked and spluttered, before permitting itself to putter weakly into action, and she was so ridiculously pleased with it, it was all she could do not to laugh outright.

'I hope you don't mind,' hastily she covered the bubbles of laughter in small talk, 'but I have to make a quick stop in Glen Fallan to collect my tubes – er – I mean, my stethoscope. I was out on my rounds when the boat came in and had to leave my last patient in rather a rush. My husband would have collected you but Thunder – that's his car – wouldn't start when we tried it this morning . . .' She paused. She was beginning to sound like an islander and at the very thought of Thunder, with its rattles and draughts, its broken seat springs and disconcerting habit of grinding to a halt in the most awkward places, she felt the laughter rising again. For never, never, could she imagine the dignified figure of Herr Otto Klebb ensconced in Thunder's worn interior, the cracks and crevices of the leather upholstery packed with dog hairs, dusters wedged into the windows to keep out the rain and the wind, the smell of ancient pipe smoke permeating every nook and cranny . . .

'I don't in the least bit mind you going to collect your tubes.'

His voice was deep, soothing, his English perfect with only a slight but pleasing hint of foreign accent. There was no change of expression when he spoke the words but Megan got the distinct impression that he had appreciated her light-hearted chatter and was actually enjoying the experience of motoring through Glen Fallan in a cramped little Mini.

But he said nothing more. His eyes were on the hills, raking the landscape, craning his neck to get a better view of the soaring peaks rising sheer on either side. Floating wraiths of mist curled into the blue corries, the hill burns meandered amongst the hillocks, glinting in the sun as they wound their way in and out, down, down, to splash over boulders and in amongst rocks till finally you could hear the purl and music of them as they fell and tumbled into the River Fallan far below.

Fergus McKenzie of the Glen was striding over the lower slopes of Ben Machrie with Lorn, his son, running along in front, throwing out whistled instructions to a black and white Border Collie who was gathering the hill ewes, bringing them down to the fields in time for lambing.

Dodie, the island eccentric, was making his purposeful way down to the village of Portcull, a tiny white lamb tucked under each arm. Grinning from ear to ear, he was obviously extremely happy, for he normally wore a perpetually mournful expression, and only a chosen few had ever actually heard him laughing aloud, which was as well, because it was a sound that resembled a rusty hacksaw grinding through wood.

Seeing the red Mini, he scrunched to a halt in the middle of the road and, holding up the lambs, he waved them around like little white flags.

'Doctor Megan! Doctor Megan!' he yelled joyfully. 'Look and see what Croynachan is after giving me!'

The old eccentric was either losing his mind altogether or else he placed great trust in Megan's abilities as a driver. For the second time that afternoon and with a muffled curse, she rammed her foot on the brake pedal, an action which caused

28

the car to waltz round in a semi-circle before it came to rest just inches from a ditch.

Furiously she wound down her window and poked her head out.

'Dodie!' she yelled, forgetting Herr Klebb, forgetting everything in her fright and fury. 'What are you thinking of, stopping me like that! I could have killed you!'

Dodie galloped up to gaze at her in some bemusement. An elongated drip adhered to the end of his nose; the large, hairy ears that stuck out from his frayed cloth cap were purple with the cold; his big, callused hands were raw and red in the bite of the wind whistling down through the glen; the threadbare coat that covered his stooped, bony frame would have shamed a tinker and he was altogether inadequately dressed for the breezily fresh March day. The islanders regularly gave him gloves and scarves and other items of warm clothing which delighted him for a time before he mislaid them or lost them or used the coats and jackets as bedcoverings and sometimes even as blankets to tie round his beloved cow, Ealasaid, to keep her warm in her winter byre.

The older he got the more pronounced were his eccentricities, but he was sublimely happy these days, as Scott Balfour, the laird, had recently re-housed him in a sturdy croft cottage on the outskirts of Portcull. There he kept his hens and his cow, tended his flower and vegetable gardens, and was extremely contented with his lot. But the wanderlust was still in him and quite often he took it into his head to roam his old haunts, shanks's pony being the only mode of travel he had ever known and was ever likely to know, for he mistrusted anything on wheels. It was, therefore, all the more surprising that he had forced Megan to stop her car in such a dangerous fashion.

'I could have killed you, Dodie,' she repeated in subdued tones. More shaken than angry now, she was aware of the fact that Herr Otto Klebb was receiving some very peculiar impressions in his first minutes on a remote Hebridean island, even though he said nothing and appeared not to be the least surprised by his informal introduction to a Rhanna native in the somewhat misshapen shape of old Dodie.

'Ach, no, you wouldny do that, Doctor Megan.' Dodie met her words with conviction. 'Tis your place to heal people, no' to kill them.'

'Really?' Megan said faintly.

'Ay, you know that as well as me and I only stopped you because o' these.' Impatiently he indicated the newborn lambs in his arms. 'One o' Croynachan's yowes gave birth to them on the hill and she died even before they could suckle. All the Johnsons but one are in bed wi' the flu, and Archie is too busy to feed these wee lambs. He said I could keep them if they lived and I'm feart they'll die on me if they don't get warmed and fed soon.' Awkwardly he shuffled his large, wellington-clad feet. 'I was wondering, seeing as how you stopped your motor car for me, if you would maybe give me a wee run home in it.'

The enormity of the request appeared to nonplus him for a moment and two spots of red burned brightly in each ruddy, wizened cheek.

Without ado, Megan righted her car and got out to push forward her seat and bundle him into the cramped and congested space at the back. Halfway inside he remembered his manners and gazing at the front-seat passenger with his guileless green eyes he murmured courteously, '*Tha brèeah.*'

In exasperation Megan gave his rickety backside a none too gentle push and without ceremony he collapsed into the back of the car, his long, ungainly legs splayed untidily against the front seats.

'*Tha brèeah!*' he repeated, breathlessly but stubbornly.

'Yes, indeed.' Herr Klebb felt moved to make some form of reply although he had no earthly idea what the Gaelic salutation conveyed.

'It's Dodie's way of saying "a fine day", Megan explained automatically. 'Rain or shine, the day is fine to Dodie's way of thinking. You'll come across a good deal of Gaelic on Rhanna, the old folk speak it freely while the young ones pretend not to understand even though many of them can converse fluently in both Gaelic and English.'

'And you understand what they're saying?'

'Yes, I knew a bit when I came to Rhanna and I'm learning more and more as time goes by . . . Oh' – her hand flew to her mouth – 'I just remembered . . .'

'You have to call in at some house to collect your tubes.'

Megan glanced at Herr Klebb. His face had remained straight but his eyes were twinkling and she smiled in appreciation of his quick wit. Some of the tension she had felt in his company left her – but there was still that sense of being in a Presence. She was suddenly glad that Dodie was there in the back seat, where the motion of the wheels held him spellbound in a combination of silent fear and fascination, while the waves of unsavoury odours that emanated from his unwashed person let no one forget *his* presence.

'Dodie,' said Megan faintly, 'only last week I gave you a big bar of carbolic soap. Haven't you found a use for it yet?'

Dodie snuggled the lambs closer to his bony bosom, sublimely immune, as he always was, to any innuendo cast at his lack of hygiene. 'Ay, indeed, it was a fine present and just the thing I was needin' for my squeaky door hinges. I just rubbed it all over them and they have never given me any bother since.'

Megan gave up; she put her foot on the accelerator and the little red Mini fairly hurtled along to Murdy's house where she hastily collected her 'tubes' before depositing Dodie at the gate of Croft Beag inside whose portals half a dozen cockerels crowed and strutted and generally created bedlam in the once peaceful village outskirts.

A white net curtain fluttered in the window of Wullie McKinnon's croft which was situated close to that of Dodie's. A cacophony of cockerel voices blasted the air. Wullie appeared at his door, shaking his fist in the direction of Croft Beag. An oblivious Dodie disappeared into his house, intent only on tending his newborn lambs.

'The noise of these creatures drives that gentleman crazy,' observed Herr Klebb unsmilingly.

Megan did smile, but only at the idea of rough and ready Wullie McKinnon being referred to as a gentleman. With few exceptions, that particular McKinnon family were renowned for their blunt tongues and vigorous approach to life's situations, and Wullie had been endowed with his fair share of the family traits.

But Megan didn't enlarge on the subject, it would never do to divulge too many of the islanders' little foibles to a newcomer. Until she knew a little more about Herr Otto Klebb, he was very decidedly a stranger on Rhanna, and with his dour demeanour and withdrawn manner she had the feeling that he would most likely remain so throughout his stay on the island.

Chapter Three

Erchy came puffing into the Post Office with the mail, which he dumped unceremoniously behind the counter, much to Totie's annoyance for, no matter how often she told him not to, he always placed the bulky sacks where she would be most likely to trip over them.

'Erchy,' she said sternly, 'how many times do I have to tell you about these sacks? Only the other day I nearly broke my toe on them.'

He paid no heed, instead he ran his fingers through his sparse sandy hair in a characteristic gesture and intoned importantly, 'A stranger has arrived on Rhanna, he came on the boat and went away in Doctor Megan's motor car.'

'Strangers on Rhanna are nothing new,' Totie snorted sarcastically. 'They come and they go, just like the tide.'

'But this one really is a stranger,' Erchy insisted enigmatically, 'and forbye that he is foreign. You can aye tell the foreigners: they stand outside o' themselves – like ghosts.'

'Here, I saw him too.' Todd the Shod, the island blacksmith, was licking stamps with gusto and slapping them on the letters that his wife Mollie had instructed him to post. 'A big chiel wi' a beard and queer, staring eyes that fair gave a body the creeps. He threw me a look that would have withered a rose when I accidentally knocked against him as he was walking to the doctor's motor car.'

'I noticed the man as well,' volunteered Donald, the young grieve of Laigmhor. 'Fergus asked me to go down to the pier to collect some new calves and I saw this stranger coming down the plank. I noticed him because o' his coat, it had curly grey collars on it and there was money stamped all over him.'

For a few moments Totie digested the various pieces of information before saying heavily, 'Erchy, I shouldn't ask because I know fine I'll get a daft answer, but what similarity is there between ghosts and foreigners?'

'Och, Totie, surely you know that.' Erchy sounded surprised at her obtuseness. 'Tis aye the way o' it, they look as if one half o' them is all dour and disinterested while the other half is watching and observing everything that is going on.'

The doorbell jangled to admit Behag Beag, the Ex-Postmistress of Portcull, as she liked to call herself. When she introduced herself as such to tourists she made it sound like an honorary title endowed with capital letters, for that was how she saw it in her own mind. In she briskly came to dump her message bag on the counter and ask for a packet of envelopes, her quick, beady eyes darting suspiciously hither and thither before coming disdainfully to rest on the arrangement of Post Office material on the counter.

Totie was convinced that the old woman only deigned to enter the premises in order to silently criticise and as a result Totie was always on her guard where Behag was concerned.

'We have a stranger – a stranger on Rhanna,' Behag announced to no one in particular, the pendulous folds of her wizened jowls fairly quivering with each movement of her palsied head. 'I saw him, wi' my very own een, getting into the doctor's motor and driving away in the direction o' Glen Fallan.'

'Ach, that was only to collect her tubes,' Erchy put in knowingly. 'She left them wi' Murdy and God only knows what he did wi' them while she was away at the pier.'

Totie ignored this and leaned her arms comfortably on the counter, an action which incited tight-lipped disapproval in Behag, as never, never, in all her years as Postmistress of Portcull, had she ever allowed herself such levity from the business side of the establishment.

'Fancy, a stranger,' Totie said sweetly, 'getting into the doctor's car – you'll be telling us next that he threw his arms around her and kissed her in full view o' the village.'

'Mrs Donaldson!' an outraged Behag protested. 'There is no need to go that far! The man only got into her motor car and never put a finger on her – as far as I could see.'

'He's a foreigner,' Erchy emphasized cryptically. 'Thon kind o' folk are consumed wi' all sorts o' queer passions. Maybe he did kiss her for all we know – when no one was looking that is,' he quickly added at sight of Totie's somewhat fierce expression.

'Ay, and he's staying at Tigh na Cladach,' Tam McKinnon, coming in at that moment with his son, Wullie, promptly entered into the conversation with all the ease of a born-and-bred islander for whom gossip and speculation were second nature. 'I saw the smoke pouring from the chimney as I was passing and the next minute there was the doctor's motor stoppin' at the gate and this big, hairy chiel getting out.'

'Here – talking o' smoke,' Wullie exclaimed, noisily wiping his nose with the back of one large, red hand, 'last night I was going past An Cala on my bike and though it was dark I was sure I saw the smell o' peat smoke. I had a mind to go and see was there anybody in but there were no lights on, only a soft wee keek o' pale darkness at the window that was likely just the sea reflectin' on the panes. Anyway, Mairi was waitin' wi' my supper and I just went on my way.'

He had added the last part hastily, ashamed to admit that he had been too nervous to investigate the deserted-looking crofthouse sitting lonely and silent on the cliffs above Mara Òran Bay.

'You *saw* the smell o' peat smoke?' Totie repeated with a flaring of her strongly chiselled nostrils. 'Wullie, I know fine you've aye been bothered wi' your nose but surely it's time you saw a doctor about your eyes as well – if only to report that the Lord made a miracle when he made you.'

Wullie looked sheepish. 'Ach, Totie, you know what I mean, it's only my way o' speakin'. But I did smell the smoke, my nose wasny lyin', nor were my eyes – there *was* a keek o' light at the windows.'

Behag's head fairly wobbled on her scrawny shoulders and she said in a voice full of meaning, 'A foreign stranger on Rhanna and thon Rachel Jodl back on the island – sneakin' back without a word to anybody. She must meet a lot o' they continental people on her travels. Maybe the pair o' them have arranged to be on the island at the same time and each pretendin' that they don't know the other is there.'

'Och, c'mon now, Behag,' Todd said reasonably, his round, cheery face looking serious for once. 'There is no need to go that far, and it might no' be Rachel that is back, it could just as easily be Jon.'

'No, it will be Rachel,' Behag stated with conviction. 'She aye did behave in a strange sort o' way, I used to get the shivers up my spine when she looked at me wi' thon black, glittering eyes o' hers. There's gypsy blood in her and no mistake, she would put a curse on you as soon as look at you . . .'

Tam glared at her. 'I will be reminding you, Behag, that it is my granddaughter that you are speaking about: a bonny, proud lassie who just happened to be born with powers that only sensitive folks like myself can understand. Not only that, she has a talent on her the likes o' which this island has never known and is never likely to know again. Oh, ay, she might no be able to speak through her mouth but she does it wi' her violin, music that might have been composed in heaven itself, so beautiful is the voice o' it.'

It was a profound speech for good-natured, easy-going Tam; Behag had the grace to look ashamed while everyone else nodded their agreement at his words.

'As for you' – Tam spun round to glower at Wullie – ''tis ashamed I am just that a son o' mine should come into a place like this to spread gossip about his very own niece and with no more than a flimsy bit peat smoke to go on.'

Wullie grew bright red and fiercely wiped away a second drip that had gathered on the end of his nose. 'Ach, Father, I didny mean anything when I said I thought Rachel was home.' He rubbed his fingers into eyes that were somewhat red-rimmed. 'I don't rightly know what I'm thinkin' these days. These cockerels o' Dodie's are drivin' me daft altogether. He just won't shut them in at night and the whole six o' them are blastin' away at all hours o' the morning. I'm useless without my proper sleep and if something isny done soon I swear I'll go in there and shoot the whole buggering lot o' them.'

It was the cue everyone needed to turn the talk away from Rachel and the stranger, even though Totie was bristling at hearing Tam refer to her Post Office as 'a place like this', as if he was talking about a den of darkest iniquity.

With the greatest of enthusiasm everyone began sympathizing with Wullie over the subject of Dodie's cockerels whose loud, raucous crowing echoed through the village from dawn till dusk. Several of Dodie's neighbours were affected by the noise but Wullie and Mairi McKinnon, whose croft was right next to Dodie's, suffered the most. At his previous abode, buried in the hills, the old eccentric had been accustomed to doing as he pleased. Because he could never bring himself to kill anything, his hens had proliferated without bothering anyone, but things were different now that he lived in the village and a state of war existed between Dodie and his nearest neighbours which perplexed both parties a great deal, as hitherto they had enjoyed a friendly relationship.

Behag wasn't particularly interested in the chatter about Dodie's cockerels. Her attention strayed and her inquisitive eyes probed the narrow bit of window space above the fluted, flower-patterned curtain.

Flowers! In the Post Office window. Really! That Totie had no earthly idea of what was right for premises such as these. In her day, good, sensible nets had served their purpose well *and* they had lasted for years. Flowers, indeed, faded ones at that – dingy with dust, cobwebs old and new adhering to the corners – and – was that a clumsily stitched tear carelessly concealed by a glass jar of aniseed balls?

Darting forward to closer examine the window coverings her attention was abruptly diverted by the sight of Elspeth Morrison, the sharp-tongued housekeeper of Slochmhor, and Captain Isaac McIntosh, one time sea skipper, standing close together at the war memorial. It *was* them! As bold as brass the two of them, meeting at their favourite place. The scandal of it, both of them old enough to know better, behaving like two young lovers in full view of the public eye – and doing it beside a monument that deserved only humble homage from respectable citizens.

Behag vacated the Post Office with alacrity. She was most interested in the affairs of Elspeth and Captain Mac these days. For some time now, a rumour had persisted that he was thinking of moving in with Elspeth though 'just as a lodger, of course'.

Behag didn't believe that for a minute. Since the demise of his wife, Captain Mac had been casting his eye over the single women of the district. At first he had shown a keen interest in Aunt Grace, as she was known to everybody, but 'just another Jezebel', as decided by Behag, disapproval tautening her thin lips. Then Grace had surprised everyone by marrying old Joe who had now gone to 'join the mermaids in some far off shore' as Grace romantically put it. It was a well-known fact that Bob the Shepherd had had his eye on Grace for a long time and had been biding his time till the coast was clear, and Behag was shocked at the idea of twice-married Grace contemplating taking the plunge for the third time.

But first and foremost in her mind was 'the affair', as she liked to put it, between Elspeth and Captain Mac, and Behag was agog to know what exactly was going on between the pair. Pretending that she was perusing the uninspiring contents of the Post Office window, she kept her head tucked well down so that Totie wouldn't espy her there and wonder what she was doing.

Although the window was anything but clean – another black mark against Totie – it reflected enough of the village to allow Behag to observe a good deal of what was happening in the immediate vicinity. The crafty old woman often made use of available windows in this way and likened the reflections she saw to 'a night at the picture house after a good day's shopping in town'.

Not that the rigid confines of her life had ever afforded her much access to either, but on one occasion, whilst visiting a sick relative in Oban, she had surreptitiously slipped into a cinema to see *Magnificent Obsession* and to her shame had shed a few tears in the darkened hall. In no way could 'the affair' between Elspeth and Mac be termed a Magnificent Obsession, more like a Shameless Disaster in Behag's mind, and any tears she might shed over them were born of sheer frustration, since not by one word had they given away their plans to anyone. Nevertheless, Behag followed their every move with far more devoted attention than she had ever given to any romantic liaison on a silver screen, and she watched the reflected images with utmost curiosity.

Captain Mac, his white hair and beard combed to watered-down obedience, was standing very close to Elspeth's scrawny figure while they talked animatedly, and Behag fairly itched to know just what they had to say that was so interesting. She wondered if she dare take a walk past the war memorial. Elspeth had a sarcastic tongue in her head and wouldn't think twice about airing her views if she thought for one moment that she was being watched. Behag hesitated while she argued with herself. It was a free country, she had as much right as anyone to visit the memorial and pause for a moment while she remembered the young men of Rhanna who had given their lives in the wars, and – here her eyes gleamed – there was that wee wooden bench set into a niche in the stone so that folk could sit and gaze out to sea while they pondered and prayed and gave thanks for their peace-filled existence.

Also, if she went down the lane between the Post Office and the butcher's shop, she could double back to the war memorial via Todd the Shod's and in that way Elspeth needn't see her at all. She could sit on the bench and listen to her heart's content and no one need be any the wiser.

Quivering with purpose she immediately made tracks for the lane and was so deep in thought she jumped like a scalded cat when a loud, mournful voice suddenly proclaimed, 'Tis yourself, Miss Beag – a fine day, is it not? I just came outside to take a wee breath o' air to myself and feeling all the better for seeing yourself as well.'

Behag came down to earth with a thump, quite literally, twisting her ankle on a cobblestone as she turned too hastily to perceive the bedraggled form of Sandy McKnight leaning against the open side door of his butcher's shop. He was a small, miserable-looking bachelor who devoted himself to making money whilst pretending that he had no interest whatever in the material side of life.

Every Sunday without fail he was there in his place in kirk and though he had only been on the island a short time he was now a church elder, aired his many and forceful opinions at church committee meetings and led collections for the Fabric Fund with much devoted energy. He was also a keen advocate of good against evil and loudly denounced all things corrupt and sinful, including in these the evils of tobacco and spirits. But since the day that Todd the Shod had observed him smoking a pipe behind a rock on the seashore, he could have talked himself blue in the face about his piety for all anyone listened.

Thereafter he had been nicknamed Holy Smoke and whenever he aired his views to the men of the village Tam McKinnon would just smile and say, 'Himself is just fatuous, he opens that big mouth o' his and lets out enough air to fill a set o' bagpipes.'

Tam wasn't really sure what 'fatuous' meant but it sounded good and impressed his cronies who didn't know what it meant either, but they took Tam's word for it and no one else ever said it was out of keeping, not even ninety-seven-year-old Magnus of Croy who knew everything, so it must have been all right.

It was doubtful if Behag knew the meaning of the word either, although she owned a set of leather-bound dictionaries and encyclopedias that were kept well dusted and carefully placed in a prominent position on a shelf – a legacy from a distant aunt who had only ever spoken the Gaelic and who had been as wise as Behag as to their contents. But to Behag, anything that might be construed as insulting to Holy Smoke met with her full approval. Her dislike of the 'butcher man' was legendary, she shuddered every time she looked at his drooping 'bloodhound' eyes and the layers of leathery flesh gathered in folds below his chin. When Tam had remarked innocently enough that Holy Smoke's features very much resembled her own and had gone on to wonder if he was a relative of hers she had nearly had apoplexy and hadn't spoken to Tam for a month.

To make matters worse, Holy Smoke had attached himself firmly to her almost from the first day of his arrival on Rhanna, so that she had to employ every ruse she knew in order to avoid meeting him. Whenever she saw him approaching she would scuttle into a shop doorway or sprachle up a bank to hide in a clump of bushes. If none of these were available she was forced to take refuge in a nearby house and people were growing quite accustomed to having Behag suddenly shoot through their door to stand with her eye to the keyhole, or to rush to the nearest window to peep outside from the safety of the window coverings.

She was therefore all the more incensed to be caught on the hop outside the butcher's premises and it was with extreme annoyance that she glared into his mournful countenance as he rushed forward to place his narrow shoulder under her arm and say in his rather feminine voice, 'There, there, Miss Beag, just you hold on to me and we'll have you inside my shop in no time. Ice! That's what you need for that ankle and there's plenty and enough o' that in my freezer room.'

'Will you let go o' me!' panted Behag, struggling with all the might of her shrunken frame to shake him off. 'I have no need o' your shop or of your ice! Unhand me this meenit, Sandy McKnight! I will no' have the gossiping folk o' this parish bear witness to your intimate handling o' my person.'

But Holy Smoke was having none of her protests and spoke to her in a voice that was oily in its attempts to soothe.

'Ach, c'mon, now, you know well enough you like me, Miss Beag, and it's reciprocal, I assure you. Oh ay, I've seen the way you run and hide from me, it's a wee trick that women have, playing hard to get. I saw it often enough when I worked on the mainland and the island women are no exception. Now, enough o' your struggles, just you lie against me and I'll take care o' you.'

Behag was so aghast at his words that it was all she could do to breathe, let alone struggle, and in a daze of pain and shock she allowed him to half carry her into his shop where he deposited her on a chair near the counter, a bucket of sawdust on one side of her and a string of fat pork sausages dangling down from the wall on the other.

'Wait you there,' he instructed masterfully. 'I'll no' be long wi' the ice.'

'My, my, look what the wind blew in!' Kate McKinnon's loud, cheery voice bounced against Behag's eardrums like a portent of doom. 'And hangin' on to Holy Smoke as if he was the blessed St Micheal himself. Spring must be in the air right enough, Behag, wi' all these wee romances blossoming on all sides o' us. First we have Captain Mac and Elspeth, now it seems we can add our very own Behag and our dear, good butcher to the list. I never thought o' this place as being romantic but you just look the part wi' that string o' sausages draped round your lugs and that bunch o' mealy puddings sitting above your head like a chain o' wee black haloes.'

Behag uttered not a word, instead she sunk into her shrivelled frame like a frightened snail, her lips folded so tightly they were just a thin hard line in her wrinkled face. It was too much! Much too much! First that pious, insincere hypocrite pawing at her person while his ingratiating voice droned in her ears, now, Kate McKinnon of all people, with her sarcastic innuendoes and a tongue that 'ran in front o' her' as Jim Jim so aptly put it. She would waste no time in letting the whole of Rhanna know of the incident and Behag went cold as she imagined just how Kate would set about embroidering the tale. But worse than any of these was the interpretation that Sandy McKnight had put on her avoidance of him.

Her ankle throbbed but not as much as her head and she wished, oh, how she wished, that just for once she had left Captain Mac and Elspeth strictly to their own devices.

Chapter Four

Tigh na Cladach was warm and welcoming: a cheerful fire burned in the grate; the chintz furniture, the well-filled bookcases and the pictures on the walls were homely yet tasteful. A tray set with cups and saucers and a plate heaped with buttered scones sat on a small table near the fire, while the teapot, keeping warm on the hearth, emitted an occasional puff of fragrant steam.

Outside the window the great cliffs of Burg rose sheer out of the sea. Little oncoming wavelets made scallops of creamy foam on the silvery curve of the bay; a row of gulls on the garden wall were squabbling quietly amongst themselves while a group of Atlantic seals had arranged themselves decoratively on an outcrop of black reefs that stuck out from the translucent green shallows to the right of the bay.

Herr Klebb strode over to gaze from the window. He stood there for quite some time before turning back to eye the tea things set by the fire.

'Frau Megan, it is perfect.' His tones were vibrant with satisfaction. 'And I see you have been kind enough to also provide me with tea. You have done me proud and I thank you.'

'It's Tina you should really thank, she lives in the village but comes every day to the Manse to look after me and my husband. When I told her you were coming she and Eve – that's Tina's daughter – set to work on this place. I really had nothing to do with the tea but the islanders are very hospitable and to them nothing else in the world beats a good strong cuppy, especially after a long journey. But I know you drink a good deal of coffee in your country, perhaps you might have preferred . . .'

He held up his hand. 'No, tea is perfect, each time I come

to Britain I acquire more and more a taste for it and from all I have heard of Scotland I have the impression it is something of the national drink.'

Megan's hazel eyes sparkled. 'Well, I don't think the menfolk of Rhanna would agree with you there, though they would be polite about it and tell you that it was the second national drink.'

'Ah, yes, I know also about the whisky, I have heard a good many tales about the Scottish islands and the illicit whisky stills. Are there any of these left on Rhanna?'

Megan was rather taken aback, she hadn't expected this dour, reserved Austrian to display such vigorous curiosity about an island he knew nothing of, but his previously withdrawn manner had completely disappeared in the last few minutes.

'Oh, you'll have to ask Tam McKinnon about that,' she said with a faint smile. 'I believe he and his cronies unearthed an old still some years ago. It was during the time of the last war and the adventures they had with it are still talked about at the ceilidhs, though it happened well before my time on the island.'

A spark of great interest shone in his eyes. 'Tam McKinnon – tell me, Frau Megan, are there many McKinnons on Rhanna?'

At that she laughed outright.

'McKinnons, McKinnons everywhere! And if they aren't called McKinnon they're connected with them somehow: cousins, wives, aunts. Oh yes, Herr Klebb, we have McKinnons a-plenty on Rhanna.' She went to the door. 'I'll have to leave you now, but if there's anything you need we're at the Manse up there on the Hillock. Don't hesitate to ask if you want something, and Tina will be back later to make your tea. She's quite willing to cook your meals and clean for you while you're here.'

'That arrangement will suit perfectly.' He nodded. 'Oh, and while I remember, I'm expecting more luggage to arrive within the next few days.' He glanced round the room. 'I hope you don't mind if I shift some things around to accommodate it.'

'Oh – no, of course not.' Megan's mind was boggling as she tried to imagine what he meant but she didn't ask: he was preoccupied with his thoughts, the mask of aloofness had settled once more over his strong features. He was frowning as he eyed the furniture as if he was mentally re-arranging it around the room.

It was then she noticed his hands, strong yet beautifully moulded, the fingers long and supple, the nails short and carefully manicured. In Mark's study there hung a print of the famous 'Praying Hands' by Albrecht Dürer and this stranger's hands reminded her of them.

Quietly she took her leave, mystified and fascinated by the man. Getting into her car she drove quickly to the Manse to run inside and shout for her husband.

'In here.' His deep voice filtered through the door of his study. Her heart accelerated and she was enchanted afresh to be living here in this lovely old house with the Man o' God as he was fondly referred to by his older parishioners.

But the Man o' God was also very much a man of flesh and blood and he had arisen from his desk on hearing her voice and was there to sweep her into his embrace when she came through his door.

'Oh, Mark,' she kissed his nose, 'I've missed you.'

He laughed. 'We saw one another this morning.'

'That was in another life.' She ran her fingers through his dark hair. 'So much has happened since then. I had to rush down Glen Fallan to meet the boat and ruined half of Ranald's lobster pots in the process. After that I almost ran over Dodie on the way back up Glen Fallan to collect my tubes and ended up giving him and two newborn lambs a lift back to Portcull before they died. After that I almost knocked down Elspeth and Captain Mac at the War Memorial, then I passed half the population of Rhanna on my way to Tigh na Cladach. Behag gave me one of her 'Thou art a Jezebel' looks as she scurried by on her way to the Post Office, where, I suspect, the entire population of Portcull are gathered to discuss me and my activities.'

He laughed. 'I take it that, in the midst of all this hectic activity, you made time to collect our man from the boat.'

'Herr Otto Klebb, now there is a mystery man for you. He's

big and hairy and built like a great brown bear, he likes tea rather than coffee and seems to know a great deal about island ways though he claims that this is his first time on Scottish soil. He . . .'

'Come on.' Grinning he took her arm and led her to the window seat, there to clear aside two furry dog bundles that were Muff and Flops respectively. Each warm and sleepy heap groaned at the human intrusion but condescended to make room for master and mistress. 'Now,' Mark put his arm round his wife's shoulder, 'tell me all about it. Head back, chest out, deep breath, begin.'

But Megan was rushing on, a vastly changed Megan from the quiet, rather serious young woman who had come to Rhanna almost three years ago to take Doctor McLachlan's place. With an exaggerated sigh of patient resignation he allowed her to describe her meeting with Herr Klebb and when she finished up by saying, 'and he's very interested in the McKinnons, oh not just the likes of Tam and Kate but all the McKinnons that ever were born', he made a great show of surprise and said, 'Oh well, if he's here to study that particular clan we'd better sell him the house because he might just be here forever – and if Kate hears of his interest he'll never get away anyway, she would talk herself blue in the face about the McKinnons, and these just the ones in her particular family.'

Elspeth Morrison entered her cottage and made haste to put the kettle on the fire. While she waited for it to boil she stood staring into the flames, a spot of red burning high on each cheek. Her gaunt, oddly immobile face, for once burned with a welter of emotions, her eyes were dark with excitement. At last! At last! Captain Mac had decided that, come the summer, he was going to move in with her.

'Only as a lodger, you understand, Elspeth,' he had explained earnestly, burying his jolly red beacon of a nose into the depths of an enormous hanky in order to hide his embarrassment. He had thought long and hard before taking this momentous decision and he was at great pains to try and make Elspeth understand that his affection for her was purely platonic. 'It is an arrangement that will suit us both, I'm sure o' that, we are each o' us alone in the world and it will be fine for us to have one another's company in the dark nights o' winter.'

'Indeed it will, Isaac,' she had intoned primly, 'and there is no need for you to emphasize the fact that you will only be biding wi' me as a lodger. No one could ever take Hector's place in my house, dead or alive, he will aye be my man, you know that as well as I do myself.'

It had taken Captain Mac all his time not to laugh outright at this. In his lifetime, drink-sodden Hector had never known a minute's peace from Elspeth's nagging tongue. Their vigorous arguments had never been anything else but public knowledge, for Elspeth had never made any secret of her matrimonial disputes nor had Hector ever tried to hide the fact that 'the cold sea was a far better place to be than a frozen marriage bed wi' naught but the blankets to keep him warm.'

Perhaps time had softened Elspeth's memories of her empty, childless years as Hector's wife, though it was far more likely that she was doing everything in her power to ease Mac's mind about coming to live with her.

In order to hide his incredulous face Mac had pummelled his nose with alarming energy. 'Indeed, I know fine that you will aye be a one-man woman,' he assured hastily, 'otherwise I would never have suggested moving in with you. But it is an arrangement that will suit us both, you need a man to see to the heavy jobs around the house and I need a woman to darn my socks and cook my meals. You understand, of course, that I was never the sort o' man to bide in one place for any length o' time? The sea will aye be in my blood and I couldny live without my wee trips wi' the fisherlads, also, from time to time, I'll be staying wi' my sister Nellie at her croft on Hanaay.'

'Of course, I understand your life is your own to do as you like with,' Elspeth acquiesced readily. 'We will both be leading our own lives, for I have still my duties to see to at Slochmhor. Och, I know fine that Phebie imagines she can do it all herself but Lachlan needs a body like me about the place. I have had a lifetime o' seeing that he has all his wee comforts to hand and I intend to go on doing that till I drop. Besides, Phebie was never much o' a cook, she aye puts too much baking powder in the scones and too much salt in the soup, and too much salt at Lachlan's age isny a good thing. Oh, ay, you and me will lead our separate lives, Isaac, though you can be assured you will aye have a full belly and a good, dry pair o' socks on your feets. Hector had all o' these things and a bittie more forbye, but he was never the sort o' man to appreciate the kind o' comforts a good wife provided.'

'Ay, ay, good friends sometimes make better companions to one another than a wedded pair,' Mac had stated hastily, growing a bit hot under the collar at the enormity of the step he was taking. When his cronies got wind of it they would think he had taken leave of his senses altogether but he had thought the whole matter out very carefully. After a few days living at Nellie's croft she began to nag him worse than any wife and he was glad to make good his escape back to his relatives on Rhanna. But he was growing tired of all the hopping around and had decided that Elspeth was the better of two evils. She was an excellent cook, she kept a tight ship and he knew she was fond of him in her own queer way. If she too started nagging him he could always escape back to Hanaay for a few days and there was always the fishing trips with the lads to fall back on, nevertheless he was aware of a gnawing sensation of unease deep in his belly which moved him to say rather anxiously, 'You are sure you'll no' regret it, Elspeth, and maybe start being annoyed at me for getting under your feets?'

'Ach, of course not, Isaac,' she had returned coyly. 'You should know better than that.'

'And you'll no be worrying as to what folks might be saying about us? I wouldny like to be doing anything that would tarnish your reputation as the good, upright woman that you are.'

Elspeth had snorted. If only he knew! She was longing to have her reputation tarnished! For too many years she had endured the snide remarks of people like Kate McKinnon regarding her 'dried-up opinions about life'. She had been referred to as 'a spinster woman wearing the mantle of widowhood' and 'an old maid who had tripped over the marriage bed and had completely lost her way in the dark'.

She was fed up to the back teeth with Behag's continual prying and poking into her affairs and it would give her the greatest satisfaction to see the look on the old bitch's face when it became apparent that Captain Mac had moved in with her. It was therefore with the greatest conviction that she told Mac he had no need to worry on that score since 'in the eyes o' the Lord she was doing nothing wrong and to hell with gossips and scandalmongers'.

Elspeth sat back and thought of all this while she sipped her tea. For once she had no idea of any of the latest happenings in the village, so taken up was she with her own thoughts and affairs. For a long time she sat in her chair thinking about her meeting with Captain Mac at the war memorial, then, with an oddly furtive expression on her face, she made her way upstairs to her sparsely furnished bedroom. Almost on tiptoe, as if afraid that something or someone might leap out on her at any moment, she went to her dresser and from a bottom drawer she extracted an untidily wrapped brown paper parcel.

'Will you look after this for me?' Mac had asked her a few days ago on returning from a trip to Oban. 'You mind I told you that my brother's widow lives on Uist. There is a daughter, my niece, a right bonny lass who will be twenty-one in November. Joan, that's my sister-in-law, fair dotes on the girl and is planning a big party for her birthday when it comes. She is already gathering things together and bought this parcel o' stuff when I was wi' her in Oban. She doesny want Katie finding them, for she has a wee habit o' snooping into cupboards if she thinks her mother has been hiding things. They'll be safe wi' you till the time comes.'

Elspeth had agreed to keep the parcel but the moment Mac's back was turned she had decided it would do no harm to 'have a wee keek'.

The contents of the innocuous brown wrappings had taken

her breath away. Out had tumbled several luxuriant garments, including two nightdresses, one a peach satin with furls of snowy white lace trimming the low-cut neck, the other a black silk with red ribbon slotted through the black lace at the neck and tiny red bows decorating the hem.

Elspeth had never seen the likes in all her born days and she had spent some time running her hands over the wondrous material. After that she hadn't been able to stay away from her bedroom and at every opportunity she was up there, sitting on her bed, surrounded by black silk and peach satin, enchanted and mesmerized by such beauty.

It was sinful, of course, what mother in her right mind would buy such things for a young girl? It was just tempting providence, any man would go daft with lust and passion if he got just one keek of them covering a young girl's body. It wasn't decent, it wasn't right, it wasn't proper.

Even so, Elspeth's own eyes gleamed at the very thought of that lovely material touching human flesh and very daringly she had crept guiltily to her room one night, undressed and slipped the peach satin over her head. The touch of it on her body was like slipping into the cool, silken waves of the sea. Not that Elspeth had ever dipped herself in any sea, silken or otherwise, but in her heightened state of awareness she imagined that this was what it must be like. She felt pampered, delicious, almost like a girl again, and when she dared to view herself in the full-length wardrobe mirror she imagined she looked like a young girl again, virginal and untouched. Of course, the candlelight was kind, she wasn't foolish enough not to recognize that and never, never, would she dare to garb herself in such a manner in the unkindly light of day. But for just a few, short, ecstatic moments she was the young Elspeth again, before time and care had withered the flesh on her bones and robbed her face of its youthfulness . . .

A shout from outside had nearly caused her to have a heart attack, and rushing to cover the peach silk with her aged brown cardigan she had peered from her window to see Kirsteen McKenzie standing below with a message from Phebie requesting Elspeth be at Slochmhor early next day as visitors were expected for dinner.

'As if she couldny see to it herself,' Elspeth had muttered, contrarily ignoring the fact that she had, for years, tried to brainwash the McLachlans into believing that she was indispensable.

Now here she was again, surrounded by folds of exquisite nightwear that spilled over the patchwork quilt on her bed, like gleaming jewels that taunted and tormented her. It was while she was standing there that an astounding idea came into her head, one so daring that she pushed it aside with an impatient snort. But it wouldn't go away that easily, drumming at her so insistently she felt weak with the power of it, her shaking legs forcing her to sink down on the edge of the bed where she sat, staring into space, allowing the idea to gel and take shape.

Clasping her hands to her mouth, she began to laugh, a small, breathless laugh born of her own audacity. 'I'll show them,' she whispered. 'That bitch, Behag, I'll give her something to talk about, I'll give them all something to talk about . . .'

A voice from the kitchen brought her back to earth with a start. Was there never any peace on this island? At all hours of the day and night there was always someone interfering with her life. Unwillingly and reverently she put the glamorous garments back into her bottom drawer and went downstairs to find Mollie McDonald in her kitchen.

'There you are,' Mollie said with a frown. 'I was beginning to think that the fairies had spirited you away.' She omitted to add that, in her view and in that of quite a few others, Elspeth had been behaving so strangely of late she might indeed be 'away wi' the fairies', but Mollie was too respectful of the other woman's sharp tongue to risk suggesting anything of that nature.

Instead she plunged into the gossip of the moment, knowing that an interest in other folk's business was Elspeth's main pastime. But when she mentioned the 'foreign stranger' and his supposed link-up with Rachel Jodl of An Cala, she met with only luke-warm enthusiasm.

Somewhat unwillingly, Elspeth went to put the kettle on, not in the least bit concerned about a man who was just another visitor to Rhanna – even if he was a foreigner. As Mollie prattled on, Elspeth listened with only half an ear, her mind too busy with her own affairs to be bothered with those of anyone else.

Chapter Five

Tina turned a hot face from the stove as Otto appeared in the kitchen doorway. 'Och, tis yourself, Mr Klebb,' she beamed, tucking away a wilful strand of flyaway hair, 'frozen and done in by the look o' you. It is far too cold a day to go wandering down by the shore. Away you go ben the room to the fire and I'll bring your dinner through on a tray. It won't be long, I'm just waiting for the bone to go out o' the tatties.'

He looked surprised. 'Bones in the – er – tatties?' he hazarded.

'Ach, it's just our way o' saying the potatoes are still hard in the middle. Now, if you'll excuse me for speaking my mind but I don't like anybody under my feets when I'm in the kitchen, so go you through and have a nice warm to yourself by the fire.'

He seemed glad to do as he was bid and when she eventually appeared with a laden tray it was to find him sprawled in a chair with his eyes shut, a look of exhaustion on his face.

'Ach, there now, you've been taking too much out o' yourself,' Tina told him kindly. 'The island air is something you have to get used to bit by bit, the sea has a rough breath to it and tis no wonder your hands are blue wi' cold, you went out without gloves and no' even as much as a stitch to cover your head.'

As she spoke she was setting his meal down on his lap, her actions languid and unhurried, her voice lilting and calm in his ears. When she uncovered the plate a steamily delicious aroma of steak and kidney pudding assailed his nostrils and suddenly and unexpectedly he felt ravenously hungry.

'There you are now, Mr Klebb,' Tina stood back with a beaming smile and folded her hands across her ample stomach, 'just you enjoy that and I want to see every scrap eaten. Neither me nor my Matthew could ever abide waste o' any sort and don't be giving any to that cat, she has her own food in the kitchen but will try to pretend to you she's wasting away wi' hunger.'

Otto looked at the little grey tabby sitting very erect on the hearthrug staring into the fire with huge green orbs.

She had 'come wi' the house' – at least that was what Eve had told him. On his first morning on Rhanna he had gone to the door and there was the cat waiting to get in. She had stalked past his legs, straight in to the house to sit herself by the fire and look at him as if to say, 'Well, I'm home, how about some breakfast.' He had named her Vienna and in the three days he had been at Tigh na Cladach she had only budged from the house when it was strictly necessary. Now he couldn't imagine his hearth without Vienna sitting on the rug or waiting at the door to meet him when he returned from his lonely walks on the beach.

'She thinks she owns me,' he had told Tina, who had informed him, 'She will certainly never disown you as long as you pamper and fuss over her the way you do. Cats are fly craturs, they know where the monkey sleeps and this one is no exception.'

Otto was quite sure that Vienna had no earthly idea where monkeys slept but suspected that it was just another one of Tina's quaint expressions. He only knew that Vienna had found him and was here at Tigh na Cladach to stay, and the minute Tina's back was turned he slipped the little cat a piece of juicy steak which she carried off to a corner like a prized trophy.

He could hear Tina in the hall, singing in a sweet if slightly tuneless voice as she went about dusting, and he smiled to himself because he had witnessed her methods with a feather duster, flicking it about half-heartedly while she studied things that were of far more interest to her.

She had shown a great deal of enthusiasm for the books that he had brought with him and was particularly taken with a volume of Leo Tolstoy's *War and Peace*. Seeing the look on Otto's face, she had smiled indulgently. 'Ach, I know fine what you're thinking, you are wondering what can an island woman like me know about books like these. But the Scottish people have aye wanted to educate themselves, Mr Klebb. You can go into any Highland home and find similar books on the shelves, and old Magnus of Croy who lives in a thatched cottage has a bookcase filled wi' Shakespeare and Shelley, Burns and Sir Walter Scott, wi' a few volumes o' Chekhov thrown in for good measure.

'He also loves good music and on his old gramophone he plays records o' Beethoven and Schumann and that Austrian chiel, Schubert, I think he said. Magnus himself plays the fiddle and makes up wee songs and in his younger days he also played the accordion, the kettle drums, and the bagpipes.'

'Frau Tina,' Otto had said rather severely, 'you don't have to convince me, I know that the Scots have always educated themselves, they are also explorers and have travelled the world in search of fame and fortune and have sought the knowledge of other cultures, though never do they lose their pride in their Scottish roots – that I know for a fact,' he ended on a somewhat mysterious note.

'You can take *War and Peace* home with you and read it at your leisure,' he had added, and an appeased Tina had gone away clutching the book, thinking to herself that he was a generous man under that stand-offish exterior and that there was also something very odd in the way he spoke about the Scots, almost as if knew them very well or had made it a point to find out as much as he could about them.

Having finished the dusting, Tina returned to the living room to pile more peats on the fire and take Otto's tray from him. 'There now, you enjoyed that,' she said, gratified when she saw the empty plate. 'Visitors always get a good appetite when they come to Rhanna, the fresh air is just the thing many o' them need to get them back on their feets again, but you mustny think you have to go off on your own all the time. It will be nice for you to meet other lads who come from the same country as yourself. Two nice young Germans crash-landed their airyplane on Rhanna during the war and later, one o' them, Anton Büttger, who has a farm above Mara Òran Bay, came to settle here, the other, Jon Jodl, has a house near Anton's and comes to it with his wife whenever they can get away.'

Otto looked at her in some annoyance and said harshly, 'Frau Tina, because you speak English does it follow that you are from England? No, of course it doesn't and the same applies to me, I speak German but I am an Austrian and proud of it.'

Tina had coloured but she was not to be browbeaten. 'And I am a Gael, Herr Klebb, and proud to be such, the Gaelic is my native language but if I had never learned the foreign tongue I would not have been counted. German, Austrian, English, Scottish, we are all alike in the eyes o' God . . .' her dimples showed, 'just as long as we all learn English in order to understand one another!'

He looked at her, she had a nice face, open, honest and kind. Megan had told him all about Tina, how she had lost her husband when he had gone out with the lifeboat during a terrible storm only last spring. The same sea that had taken her husband had also brought with it two young men who had been the cause of a different kind of havoc on the island.

Otto didn't know all the details but he had gathered that Mark James, Megan's husband, had suffered some sort of breakdown as a result of the storm and that Tina's daughter, Eve, had been seduced by one of the young men, resulting in her becoming pregnant, and the baby was due some time this month.

Tina had had more than her share of suffering, yet a smile was never far from her face, a song always ready at her lips, and he felt ashamed for his outburst.

'We understand one another, Frau Tina,' he said gently. 'We are of the same soil, the surge of the western ocean beats as strongly in my heart as it does in yours, the voice of lonely places speaks in my soul as it has done for as long as I can remember.'

The mystery was deepening. Tina opened her mouth to speak but he put a finger to his. 'Hush, *mein Frau*, the time will come but for now I am not yet ready for it. It is enough that I am here, warming myself with spicy-smelling peat fires and finding out for myself the meaning of good, wholesome Scottish cooking, the steak pie was *köstlich* and I am feeling fit to burst. Now, if you will excuse me, I have many things to do and I am sure that you too have much bustle in your life.'

He made a neat little bow and escorted her to the door, there to lift his face appreciatively to the sky and sniff the salt-laden air.

A figure came flying along the road on a bicycle, her black hair streaming out behind her, her long legs pushing the pedals with energy.

A spark of interest showed in Otto's eyes as they followed the progress of the girl on the bike.

'Thon bonny cratur is Rachel Jodl,' Tina explained. 'She is married to Jon, the lad I was telling you about. Rachel is a famous violinist, she has travelled all over the world.'

'But, she is so young.'

'Ay, she is that, but from the start she knew where she was going. We are all very proud o' her.'

'Rachel Jodl,' he repeated thoughtfully. 'I see, and you say she is a famous violinist? Ah, yes, I've heard of her – and she is married to this German you speak of?'

'Ay, our very own Jon Jodl though, of course, she is really a McKinnon whose mother, Annie, is the daughter o' Kate and Tam McKinnon.'

She paused expectantly, Megan having told her about the stranger's interest in that particular clan, but though there was a slight lifting of his brows he said nothing and she went on, 'Jon loved Rachel from the moment he clapped eyes on her going barefoot about the island like a wee gypsy. Och, but it was such a romantic affair between the two,' Tina said dreamily. 'Just like a fairy tale, it was: he waited till she was grown up enough to marry then back he came to Rhanna to carry her off into the big, wide world.'

Otto's eyes twinkled. 'You're sure he didn't magic her away on a pure white charger?'

'Ach no, nothing like that, though mind . . .' Tina looked at him, 'Ach, Mr Klebb, you're no' the big, dour chiel you would have us think. A white charger indeed . . .'

She went off down the road chuckling, leaving Otto to go back indoors with a very pensive expression on his face.

The harbour was a-bustle with movement and noise. The steamer had disgorged its usual cargo of mail and supplies and some of the visitors were making their way to the hotel, though several straggled behind to look in the window of Ranald's craft shop and comment to one another on the price of the displayed goods.

The travelling people had also arrived on the boat and were making great play with their motley collection of dubious-looking possessions, though they weren't too busy to arrange their 'star attraction': a tattered old gnome of an Irishman bearing an accordion as big as himself, in a prominent position close to Ranald's shop. A tiny little dwarf woman with straggly black hair and a great long beanpole of a man arranged themselves on either side of the accordionist, a key was struck and a vigorous rendering of 'Danny Boy' soared aloft, causing the visitors to abandon their interest in Ranald's shop and turn it instead to the musicians.

'Ah, is it not a song to pluck the heartstrings?' inquired a young traveller with broken brown teeth, whose heartstrings were sufficiently intact to enable him to place a smoke-blackened pot at the accordion man's feet. 'And surely worth a few pennies for the honour of listening to music from the fingers of a man just risen from his deathbed. Ah yes, the good Lord Himself had a mind to take Aaron that he might join the heavenly band o' the angels but then He saw fit to spare him so that ordinary mortals like us might have the pleasure of his music.'

The dwarf woman, who went by the appropriate name of Tiny, suffered a fit of coughing at this point while Aaron himself struck two discordant notes in quick succession.

'Aaron, you say?' asked one large woman suspiciously. 'That's a very biblical name for a – er – travelling person.'

'Ah indeed, you are right in what you say, me fine lady,' the broken-toothed youth agreed while he listened with half an ear to the satisfying sound of money chinking into the pot. 'But a good upstanding man like Aaron has every right to the name that his old mother put upon him. His older brother's name was Moses and no woman could have had two finer sons. I never knew old Mo myself but it is said he was the greatest violinist this side o' heaven and played music so fine that even the very seals of the ocean would climb on to the rocks to hear him.'

'And you, young man, what is your name?'

'Nothing fancy at all, me fine missus, just plain Joe – Joe Ford Backaxle if you have a mind to hear my full title and now, if you'll be excusin' me . . .'

Rachel arrived in time to hear old Mo's name and to see the look of bemusement on the woman's face as she stood wondering if she had just had her leg well and truly pulled.

Rachel had come on the sturdy black bike she had hired from Ranald for an indefinite period. Although she had been on Rhanna less than a week, she was already a familiar figure as she flew along the island roads on her bicycle. She had suffered quite a few hints and innuendoes because of the secretive manner of her arrival, but on the whole everyone was pleased to see her back. Even Annie, her mother, who had never quite learned how to handle her beautiful daughter's fame, had greeted her warmly, and, of course, Kate had welcomed her granddaughter with open arms and had sat back to bathe in the reflected glory – 'wearing thon big head she grows whenever Rachel's name is mentioned,' old Sorcha had sniffed, turning down her deaf aid so that she wouldn't have to suffer too much of Kate's prattle.

As for Rachel, she was revelling in the freedom of being back home on Rhanna and had had a wonderful few days exploring all her old haunts and popping in to all the familiar houses to strupak and catch up on island news. She took an absolute delight in visiting Fàilte where the children fussed over her and Lorn and Ruth made time to sit with her and listen to all the exciting tales of her travels.

On hearing that the travellers had arrived, she had fairly whizzed down to the harbour to see them. Her mane of black hair had come loose from its imprisoning red band so that the wind caught it and tossed it hither and thither; her black eyes sparkled in a face that was rosy from the exhilarating ride over the moor road. Though the day was breezily fresh she wore a pair of white shorts that showed off her long shapely legs to perfection and so untamed was the quality of her gypsy-like beauty she might have belonged to the dark-skinned band of travellers themselves.

She was overjoyed to see them again. As a child, running wild and carefree over the bens and glens of Rhanna, she had often gone over to their encampment. There she had been warmly invited to 'come in about'. She had eaten and drunk with them at their smoky campfires, had played with the motley and mangy collection of cats and dogs, and had joined the dusky-skinned children in their games.

It had been her delight to lay down her curly dark head on a pillow of fragrant heather and to gaze up at the sky as she listened to some wise, sad voice recall the old days and the old ways while woody sparks exploded in the fire and a battered tin kettle sang on the hot stones.

Mention of old Mo had brought back a flood of memories. How she had loved that dear old man. He and she had played their fiddles together and it had seemed to her that the very music of heaven itself poured from his nimble fingers. To the beat and hush of the ocean, to the flight of the migrating geese, to great red balls of fire sinking into crimson seas, she and he had played their haunting melodies and she had never minded that he had 'wet his dry thrapple' with the water of life and had often become so inebriated she had had to push him home in his battered old pram and had helped to get him into bed in his tent.

At his request she had played to him when he was dying and from his deathbed he had blessed her with his last breath and had made her take his treasured violin to keep as her very own. Jon had told her it was a Cremonese, made by the great craftsmen of northern Italy, but the value of it hadn't mattered to her, more important to her was the knowledge that her lovable old rogue of an Irishman had entrusted the beautiful instrument to her care and from that day on it had rarely left her keeping.

'You have the touch of the angels in those hands, mavourneen,' the old man had said as he lay peacefully waiting for death to come to him. 'Indeed you have more gifts than you know of yourself – and many of them at your fingertips.'

Over the years his words had come true time after time for, as well as their genius for music, Rachel's hands had healing properties that had become a source of wonder, awe and fear to those who had been touched by her powers. Many mistrusted her because of her strange gifts, others accepted them, one or two who had been directly helped by them regarded her with respect and wouldn't hear a wrong word against her.

Not caring what anyone thought, she had gone off with Jon into a daunting world of music. Though young, inexperienced and often afraid, she always had Jon to turn to when the going got hard, and when he wasn't there she had old Mo's violin to see her through her lonely hours. On it she had played her finest pieces and had composed violin solos that had been hailed and recognized throughout the land. Whenever she placed it under her chin she remembered old Mo and in her heart she was certain that he was up there on the concert platform with her, guiding the bow, touching the strings along with her.

It had been a long time since she had met with any of the travellers; many of the children were new to her and stared at her with sullen eyes, while a big rough-looking man standing a little way off was watching her with brooding black brows, but the rest greeted her as if they had parted just yesterday, without fuss or embarrassment, though each and every one of them knew of her fame.

'It is yourself, mavourneen!' Tiny cried, her small Irish pixie of a face creasing into smiles of welcome. 'Bejabers and bejasus! And lookin' as fit and as bonny as the bluebells in May.'

Long ago, and to herself, Rachel had christened the dwarf woman 'Little Lady Leprechaun' because of her size and her habit of garbing herself in green, and laughing she took the tiny hands in hers and spun Lady Leprechaun round and round till they were both dizzy and breathless.

'Indeed, Miss Rachel, it is a sight you are for sore eyes!' exclaimed an odoriferous man known appropriately as Stink the Tink. 'Will you be coming in about when we have settled ourselves at the camp?'

The travellers had long ago learned to understand her sign language, but all she needed then was a nod and a smile to let them know that she would indeed be over to see them as soon as she could.

At that moment a ramshackle lorry appeared round the side of the craft shop. From it descended Ranald, who absorbed the scene in one glance, his face thunderous when he saw that the travellers were taking all the attention away from his carefully arranged window display.

'Get away from there!' he ordered The Beanpole, the idea that he might be losing trade putting a harsh note in his tone and emphasizing the 'wee bit twist to his face'. 'And don't any o' you be going round the back o' my premises to use my wall as a lavatory. If it's no' dogs and towrists it's tinks and the sooner the council do something about it the better I'll be pleased!'

Chapter Six

Behag was sitting on a kitchen chair outside her cottage, her 'spyglasses' to her eyes as she avidly watched all the activity at the harbour from the privacy of her tiny garden with its encircling wall. Her twisted ankle was swathed in bandages and she had endured a very frustrating time of it since her accident. Much to her horror, Holy Smoke had called in to see her every evening after he had shut up shop, and the agony of not being able to escape those visits had been almost too much for her to bear.

He had blamed himself for her mishap and in an attempt to pour oil on troubled waters his manner had been a combination of mournful concern and useless advice as to how best she could mobilize herself till her ankle was healed. He offered to bring in her fuel from the fuel shed, he suggested fetching her pension from the Post Office, he said he would do her shopping for her and even help her along to the kirk on the Sabbath by means of an ancient wheelchair that old Meggie of Nigg had demoted to the junk shed.

During the utterance of this last suggestion he was gazing hopefully at the ancient besom reposing in a corner, as if that too might be employed to whisk Behag around the island. A vision of her astride the broomstick, her straggly hair flying out behind her as she sailed in front of a full moon, haughtily giving that royal wave of hers, popped suddenly into his mind, and, for once, he nearly forgot to keep a straight face.

But this was Behag, a very thunderous-looking Behag, with the folds of skin at her jowls sagging further and further into her scraggy neck as she listened to him in the sort of silence that her brother Robbie had once described as 'shoutin' aloud wi' her accusations'.

So Holy Smoke wisely composed his countenance into its usual expression of doom and carried on listing all the things he felt he could do to make the old woman's life bearable. He offered her just about everything under the sun and when, eventually, he came to a halt he was breathless and bloated with his own magnanimity, but still found the strength to bow his head, clasp his hands to his perpetually downcast mouth and murmur a few words of prayer to the Almighty.

Behag sat ramrod straight, utterly disgusted by 'all the bowing and scraping' and the empty promises. But then she asked herself, were they empty? The man seemed positively to be tripping over himself to please her and – was there more than just a touch of fear in his attitude towards her?

A suspicion grew in her mind: she had seen that self-same look on another occasion, when she had been in charge of the Post Office and he had come creeping in to deeve her with a whole list of sorrows and worries that had turned out to be a preliminary to his having to part with more money than he liked.

She looked at her ankle reposing on a rafia stool in front of her. It had something to do with that, and she searched her mind, going back to the time when she had stumbled over some of the junk he had left at his side door . . .

Behag drew in her breath. So, that was it! She had injured herself because of his carelessness and he was terrified that she might think to sue him for it. She hugged herself with glee; a feeling of power possessed her, making her puff out her bony chest and smile to herself with utter satisfaction. She would make him pay all right. By the time she was done with him she would have him where she wanted him – right in the grip of her all-powerful palm.

Settling her tweed skirt demurely round her legs she cleared her throat and said, 'Well, Mr McKnight, I can see only too well how anxious you are to please me. You can just forget about all these other things, Isabel and Mollie between them have promised to see to my messages and my pension and anything else I'll be needin' while I am laid up.' She cast down her eyes. 'When Nurse Babbie was in seein' to my ankle she was just after sayin' how thin I was and how I should be buildin' myself up wi' some good cuts o' red meat. Seeing as how you're so eager to help, you will no' be mindin' if I ask you to bring a pound or two o' your best steak next time you come. By that time I will have decided what else I need to keep up my strength, at my age my bones are no' as supple as they were and as my very own mother aye said, "Old bones need good feedin' if they are to carry a body through the evenin' o' their days", and though I was too young at the time to see the sense in what she meant I know well enough now but was never able to follow her adage wi' just my pension to keep me going.'

Holy Smoke was flabbergasted, his entire countenance nosedived to his knees and he stared at her as if she had just taken leave of her senses.

'Ach, come now, Miss Beag,' he cajoled weakly, 'there is no need to go that far. If I was to hand out meat to every pensioner on Rhanna I would go out o' business. As it is I have a hard job to make ends meet and . . .'

'Best steak or nothing, Mr McKnight,' Behag intoned firmly. 'Of course, if you prefer to compensate me wi' sillar instead I will have no objections, though, of course, it would have to be done through all the proper channels.'

The butcher opened his mouth, shut it, opened it again. Like a fish out o' water, Behag thought, hugging herself at his reactions to her 'wheeling and dealing' – she had read that in a magazine and was delighted to be able to apply it to a situation of her very own.

It's blackmail! Holy Smoke decided to himself. Blatant, heartless blackmail! And to a Christian man like me who wants only to do good to my fellow men – and women!

He stuttered, he protested, he listed a whole catalogue of financial worries that kept him from his sleep at night, but Behag, firm, calm, and unflustered, was impervious to all his pleadings.

In the days that followed he appeared regularly at her

door bearing parcels of meat and poultry. Behag had never eaten so well for years and was even able to withstand Kate McKinnon's sly remarks and innuendoes concerning the butcher man's visits.

So all in all Behag was right pleased with herself and was even beginning to enjoy her invalid status. As well as all the goings-on in the village and at the harbour, she was able, with the aid of her spyglasses, to watch what went on at Elspeth's house, though she was rather annoyed that Jim Jim's gable wall restricted some of her view. Nevertheless she could see enough to satisfy her, but had been disappointed so far in that very little of interest was happening in that quarter. But it would come, she was certain of that; meanwhile there was plenty and enough to occupy her. Today it was the harbour and the tinks and 'that Rachel' cavorting amongst them as if she was one of them – though that wouldn't surprise her as God alone knew what kind of mischief the girl's mother had gotten up to in her younger days.

She panned the village, pausing again at the harbour. Wait now! Something else was happening down there. That strange foreign man had arrived and there was a lot of activity on the pier. What on earth was that swinging on the end of the ship's crane? A crate of some sort! Now, what was in it and who was it for . . . ?

There was indeed a great stir of excitement at the pier. First Otto Klebb had arrived in the minister's motor car. Mark drew Thunder to a squealing halt and felt quite gratified that the engine kept ticking over after he had removed his foot from the accelerator.

'Are you sure you don't want me to stay and help?' he enquired of his passenger, but Otto shook his head and gave a wry little smile.

'You are very kind to ask but the village stalwarts were very keen to offer their services when they heard that I was expecting an important shipment to come off the boat. It was good of you to bring me down in your car, I could easily have walked.'

Mark threw back his dark head and laughed. 'You're too

polite, Otto. After a run in poor old Thunder most people tell me they wished to God they had walked! It is an experience that takes a bit o' getting used to but never mind, you're here, and I will bid you good day and good luck getting Tam and the others back up to your house.'

'But, it is they who are taking me back to the house to help me unload the lorry.'

Mark grinned. 'It is well seeing you're new here, Otto, but you'll learn, you'll have to if you're to survive living on Rhanna.'

With a cheery wave he revved up and rattled away, leaving Otto to make his way down to the crowd that had gathered on the pier to watch proceedings. On the way Otto passed Rachel. Briefly their eyes met and held; awareness sprang between them. It was her first encounter with the man whose name had touched many pairs of lips since his arrival. Those black, intense eyes of his were compelling in their power. Her heart beat a little faster. So, this was 'The Stranger', this big bear of a man with his distinguished demeanour that suggested great strength of character and a magnetic personality. He gave the distinct impression of one who was used to having his commands obeyed and from all she had heard of him he had already gained a reputation on that score by sending everyone scurrying to obey his will 'wi' just the snap o' a finger'.

Executing a polite little bow he dismissed himself and she watched him walk away, something telling her that her stay on Rhanna was to be one that she wouldn't forget in a hurry. The thought brought that strange little shiver to her spine again and she couldn't tell if it was one of apprehension – or anticipation.

The sight of the enormous crate swinging on the end of the crane had brought forth much speculation from the onlookers.

'It could be a bed,' hazarded Graeme Donald, who had abandoned his net-mending in favour of the latest diversion. 'Folk can be very queer about beds and like to sleep on their own instead o' one that dozens o' people might have used.'

Fingal McLeod agreed thoughtfully. 'Ay, people do some terrible things in bed. I wouldny like to sleep on one that wasny my own in case somebody else had done worse things on it than I had done myself.'

'A bed that size!' Todd the Shod expostulated. 'No, no, it canny be a bed – unless Mr Klebb is planning to ship over an elephant to sleep on it.'

'Here, maybe he is Count Dracula in disguise,' suggested Ranald, who, as well as being a keen reader of mystery and adventure stories was also a devotee of horror films and went to see as many as he could when he had reason to visit the mainland. 'I saw a picture once where Dracula shipped himself over the sea in a coffin which was stored in the hold. His henchman kept a tight watch on him and made sure his master was always back in his coffin before sun-up.'

Ranald's eyes gleamed. 'It was terrible just, by the time the boat touched dry land he had drunk gallons o' blood. Half the folk were dead or dyin' and a whole new batch o' vampires were busy sharpening their fangs ready to do business the minute they went ashore.'

'Ach, you and your horror stories!' Captain Mac said scathingly. 'How can Mr Klebb be a vampire when he walks the daytime hours the same as the rest o' us . . . ?'

The arrival of Otto on the scene effectively quelled further comment. Tam too arrived, looking puffed and important, for had not the 'stranger mannie' more or less implied that he was to direct proceedings that day? Tam was full of himself, though he was also rather peeved that he hadn't been told just what it was that was arriving on the boat.

'All in good time, Herr Tam,' was all Otto would say, and Tam would have argued further if he hadn't been so tickled at being referred to as 'Herr Tam', which to his ears sounded very much like an honorary title.

Aaron was leaning against Ranald's boatshed while he watched proceedings from a safe distance. Aaron had always watched anything of an energetic nature from a safe distance ever since he had been called to help with a flitting which he claimed had racked his back so badly it was a wonder he hadn't landed up an invalid for the rest of his days. Not that that would have worried him greatly. Mo, his brother, had spent his latter years being pushed around in a huge baby carriage, his excuse being that his legs were incapable of carrying him, and there might have been some truth in that since he was 'legless wi' the drink' half the time and the other half he passed sleeping off his excesses.

It was a blue, blue afternoon; the sea was aquamarine, the sky azure, and the two met and married in a tranquil celebration of coming spring. Thus thought Aaron in his rather poetic way. He liked poetry, did Aaron, he liked to read it and listen to it and sometimes he enjoyed making up little verses when he felt the inclination to do so.

He liked Rhanna; it was good to be back on the island with all the long days of summer ahead.

His glance fell on Rachel who was on the fringe of the crowd looking on, an onlooker like himself, never quite belonging but seeing more and hearing more because of it. Creative people like him and her were like that, they had to stand back in order to see everything from a wider angle than mere ordinary mortals. He was glad that Mo had given her his violin, Aaron had never grudged her that though he knew for a fact that a few of the others had, in particular, Paddy, whose resentment over the affair had been simmering for years.

Aaron's languid gaze shifted to Paddy who was sitting on a rock idly playing with pebbles. Aaron sighed, he hoped there wouldn't be any trouble with Paddy that summer. Paddy somehow always managed to make trouble and the other travellers were kept on their mettle whenever it looked as if something was brewing in his mind.

Ranald was backing the lorry as far down to the landing pier as he dared. There was much loud shouting and instructions. The big foreign-looking man was in the midst of it all, giving out orders which everyone seemed only too eager to obey.

Feeling safe amidst all the diversions, with everyone's attention centred on loading the crate on to the lorry, Aaron slunk to the back of Ranald's boatshed to relieve himself against the wall.

'My, my, would you look at that now,' observed Hector the Boat who was diligently if messily slapping tar on the upturned bottom of a big clinker dinghy. 'That shed will be floatin' away if he's no careful and one o' they days its founds will be that rotten it will come crashin' down about Ranald's ears. I'm surprised it's lasted so long, for if it's no' dogs peein' against it, it's some dirty old bugger who hasny the decency to use the bushes like every other body.'

'Ay, ay, terrible just,' agreed Jim Jim, who was bothered with a weak bladder and who had, on countless occasions, been one of the 'dirty old buggers' as well as watering just about every bush and tree this side of the island.

Aaron was barely halfway through his ablutions when he was joined by two small boys who, without preliminary, solemnly undid their trousers to add their contributions to the wall.

The large visitor lady, not in the least interested in the arrival of the crate but totally fascinated by the tinkers despite having been taken in by them, had, after a minute or two of indecision, made up her mind to follow Aaron to see what he was about.

When she saw the trio of masculine figures rowed against the wall, letting off steam as it were, her face was a picture of shocked surprise.

'Really!' she exclaimed forcibly. 'How utterly disgusting! There are places for that sort of thing, but then I expect people like you must be used to behaving like animals!'

Aaron, his back bristling with embarrassment, remained rigidly facing the wall, but his young confederates had no such reservations. With mischievous grins splitting their merry faces they turned round to vigorously shake their small appendages at the aghast lady.

Her face crimson with outrage, she made a hasty exit from the scene much to the boys' disappointment as they had been hoping to squeeze some more fun from the incident.

Jim Jim and Hector roared with laughter. 'Tis a miracle she

saw them at all for all the stoor and the steam,' Hector said in delight.

'Ay,' Jim Jim agreed, 'and if the poor wifie but knew it, she herself might be forced to behave like the animals when she realizes there is no proper water hole at the pier or anywhere else for that matter. The council lads on the mainland are in no hurry to build a wee hoosie and it might be years before they make up their minds.'

Hector grinned. 'And by that time, Ranald's shed and all who sail in her might just break from her moorings and slip into the sea leaving no survivors.'

Chapter Seven

Otto was beginning to realize what Mark had meant when he wished him luck getting home. Just when it seemed the lorry was at last about to move off, Ranald glanced in his wing mirror and what he saw there made him jump yelling from the cab to chase after Aaron who, disliking trouble as much as he disliked work, took to his heels and went pelting energetically in the direction of Glen Fallan.

'Come back!' Ranald roared, standing in the middle of the road and shaking his fist at the disappearing Aaron. 'I know what you were up to! You were fouling my premises again. If I catch you at it once more I'll have the law on you, that I will!'

Since the law was safely ensconced several miles over the ocean in Stornoway, Aaron knew well enough that it was an empty threat, even so he had had experience of Ranald McTavish's temper and he kept on running till he had put a good half-mile between himself and the village. Feeling very hard done by he sunk himself on to a heathery knoll, there to regain his breath and wait for the rest of his band to catch up with him.

'My good man, you have my sympathies,' the large lady visitor threw at Ranald as she passed by. 'Why these people can't use the public conveniences like everyone else is beyond me but as I have already said, they have no shame or any sense of self-respect at all.'

'Public conveniences?' Ranald stared at her in surprise then glanced behind him as if to ascertain for himself that a public toilet hadn't miraculously sprung up on the pier. 'Towrists – mad

– the lot o' them,' he muttered, before going back to the lorry to vigorously kick it into life once more.

Four men were perched on the back of the lorry, one more was in the cab beside Ranald and Otto. Tigh na Cladach was reached without further interruption; at the gate two more of the village men were waiting to help with the unloading and Otto breathed a sigh of relief when at last the crate was sitting at the gate ready to be unpacked.

Armed with jemmies and hammers, the men set to with a will, for it could be safely said that each and every one of them was agog to see what would finally be revealed. The metal bands that held the wood fell away, then the wooden slats themselves were removed and finally, with many warnings from Otto ringing in their ears, the men peeled away layers of packing and padding.

At last, at last, it stood there in all its naked glory, a Bechstein baby grand piano, its rich dark wood gleaming in the sun.

'My, my, she is beautiful just.' Reverently Tam removed his cap, as if he was in the presence of some grand lady.

'Ay, a fine piece o' workmanship indeed,' added Ranald, who had, all of his days, loved working with wood and enjoyed the challenge of restoring battered sea vessels to something of their former glory.

Wullie looked at the piano then at the house. 'She'll no' go in there,' he stated with conviction. 'Yon doors are narrow and there's that funny wee bit turn as you go from the lobby ben the room.'

'She will go in.' Otto was already, and quite unconsciously, adopting the islanders' habit of bestowing male and female genders on all sorts of inanimate objects. 'Myself, I have measured and made certain before sending for my piano. It is a big enough house, the doors are good and wide: up on her end in a very undignified fashion, my Becky will go in. One inch, two inches at a time, you will carry her and I will be here guiding you every footstep of the journey. Wullie, will you be so good as to hold her here and you, *Herr* Tam, be so kind as to come to this end. Gently, gently now, Becky is very precious to me and I will not like it if there is one single scratch on her when finally she is settled.'

'*Herr* Tam', beaming from ear to ear at being singled out as the leader, went willingly to do as he was bid but the smiles soon left him during the marathon task of getting the piano through the narrow gate and up the path to the house.

Vienna came out to sit on the step and daintily wash her white bib before settling back to view proceedings in a very statuesque manner.

Bit by bit, little by little, the procession made its slow and painful way up to the house. The men sweated and puffed, they cursed and they groaned and all the while Otto hovered, making sure that not one single mark broke the perfect skin of his beloved baby.

At one point he even took out his hanky to flick away a speck of dust and accidentally gave 'Herr Tam's' nose a wipe in the process.

After the door had been negotiated with great difficulty and the men had paused to gulp in air, Wullie was rash enough to lean his arms on 'Becky' and brought upon himself a sharp rebuke from her owner.

Otto had already enlisted the services of Mark and Megan to help him clear a space over by the back window of the sitting room which looked out to the sea and the sands and the great bastion of Burg rising sheer out of the ocean, a view which never ceased to enchant the new resident of Tigh na Cladach.

On this spot Becky at last came to rest and with one accord the men gave vent to rasping gasps of relief now that the ordeal was over.

Vienna, her tail waving in the air, came over to sniff and examine the latest addition to the household. Otto threw her an indulgent smile, his dark eyes snapping as if at some private joke.

'The little cat, she is thirsty,' he told the men, 'and you, you must also be ready for something to drink.'

Again Tam removed his cap, this time to scratch the sweaty red band it had left on his forehead. 'That is indeed kind o' you, Mr Klebb,' he intoned with admirable restraint since, at that moment, he could have drunk a bucket of beer to himself and still have come back for more.

'Very well, here you wait; Vienna shall have her milk and you, gentlemen, I have the very thing to quench your thirst.'

He went out of the room with his cat at his heels. Todd looked at the red faces of his cronies with gleaming eyes. 'Ach now, is he no' learning fast, our stranger mannie? Wait you! He might have brought a crate o' thon strong spirits they drink in his country. You mind Anton had some sent over from Germany last New Year and everyone that had a taste o' it were falling about the island for days afterwards. Saps I think was the name he put upon it and, by jingo!, it fairly sapped the good out o' my liver. For a whole week I couldny touch the meat Mollie put on the table before me and she was that angry she near brained me wi' my plate and called me an ungrateful bodach but I was so ill I wouldny have cared if I never saw food again.'

'Schnapps that would be,' Graeme Donald corrected Todd. 'I mind o' it fine because wee Lorna McKenzie said her father was over playing a game at Anton's house and it sounded like the one she played with cards at her granny's.'

At that moment Otto came back, bearing in one hand a kettle full of hot water, in the other a tray set with eight mugs, which he placed on the coffee table near the fire. 'Now, gentlemen, if you will just come over here and make yourselves comfortable.'

Mystified, the men went to array themselves round the table, as they did so eyeing one another with raised brows and some discomfiture.

From his pocket Otto extracted four Oxo cubes. Solemnly, and with more than a little ceremony, he split them with a sharp knife and then placed half of a cube into each of the surrounding mugs. Making great play with the kettle, he held it high so that the water gushed into the cups to produce a weak brown concoction topped by frothy foam. Picking up a spoon, he proceeded to stir the beverage vigorously so that little circles of bubbles swirled around merrily.

The men swallowed hard, the expression on each face was one of misery and disappointment.

'Ay, ay now, that is indeed kind o' you,' Tam, electing himself as spokesman, muttered the words faintly while he licked his dry lips, not daring to look at the others for fear of what he would see on their faces. 'An Oxo cube is just the job on a thirsty day like this.'

'Ay, and half an Oxo cube is even better,' Ranald mouthed sarcastically, a wonder in him that anybody else could surpass himself for the meanness that he preferred to call thrift.

'Ach well, I'll get away home for a drink o' plain water.' Todd shuffled to the door. 'It will slake my thirst better than the salty stuff you have there in the cups.'

Todd must certainly have been upset as never, never had he been known to drink water which he said gave him the belly-ache. The others followed him, their footsteps as heavy as lead, the conviction growing in their hearts that 'furriners' were indeed difficult to understand with all their strange habits and customs.

An Oxo cube might be fine in Austria but on Rhanna it was unthinkable – nay, unheard of – for anyone to offer the likes to thirsty, hardworking men.

Otto looked downhearted though a smile quirked one corner of his generous mouth. 'So, you go, you do not wait for my next trick – and I had truly believed that I could persuade you to stay and drink some of this.'

With a magician-like flourish he whipped a tea-towel from an innocent-looking cardboard carton which was reposing beside the brass coal box.

At least half a dozen bottles of best malt whisky gleamed golden in the firelight, nestling beside them were a dozen bottles of beer, and, towering over everything, was an enormous flagon of schnapps with a picture of a fire-throwing dragon painted on its glazed surface.

'The *Uisge Beatha*,' Todd whispered in awe, ' enough to sink a battleship.'

'The *Uisge Beatha*?' Otto repeated questioningly.

'Tis the Gaelic for the water o' life,' Graeme explained willingly, 'and, by God!, we'll be doing the Highland Fling from Portcull to Portree once we have had some o' that golden glory safely inside us.'

'Ay, and it's no' a battleship I'll be sinking,' Tam said happily, 'it is myself who will be drowning in it and never wasting a drop in the process.'

For the next two hours they had a wonderful time. Otto played the piano for them while they got well and truly drunk, so much so that not one of them thought to question the fact that it was mainly Scottish music which flowed out from his nimble fingers.

They danced and they jigged, they hooched and they yooched while they birled one another round, faster and faster, their tackity boots thumping the floorboards and rattling the cups in the dresser.

Vienna, disturbed out of a quiet nap on Otto's bed, padded downstairs to see what all the noise was about, took one look at the wildly cavorting figures and fled.

Erchy, on his way over to Nigg with 'the mails' came up the path to deliver a letter and was soon absorbed into the happy scene. The whisky, the beer, the schnapps flowed as swiftly and as easily as the music. Todd forgot what 'the saps' had done to his liver and went about with a large glass of it in his hand shouting, '*Prost! Prost!* Drink up your saps and get lost! lost!', while everyone else cried '*Slàinte!*', which was the Gaelic for good health, to Otto, to each other, and even to the cat when at last she dared to put her little pink nose round the door.

When eventually they reeled merrily from the house there was a unanimous vote to the effect that it had been a great ceilidh and that Otto was 'the best bloody stranger ever to have set foot on Rhanna's shores,' though, when the various spouses beheld the state of their menfolk, they weren't so sure and said he must be mad or bad, or a mixture of both to encourage such goings-on in the doctor's house and all because of some ancient old piano.

It took Erchy some time to resume his rounds, mainly because he had to sit in his van for fully twenty minutes whilst he tried to ascertain the difference between the gearstick and the handbrake. When at last he was satisfied, the vehicle lurched away to an interlude of adventure. On the high cliff road to Nigg it scattered the sheep who were partial to parking themselves in the passing places. Before Erchy knew it, twenty or so sheep were stampeding along in front of him, gathering more flocks on the way so that before long there were at least fifty ewes and several lambs thundering in a terrified mass along the treacherous road.

At his first port of call, Erchy delivered old Meggie's mail to young Maisie Brown whose three children gaped at him as he tried to insert a competition leaflet into a surprised collie dog's left ear.

At the next croft he posted a letter in Aggie McKinnon's astonished mouth, informed her that that would keep her quiet for a while and also that she made a fine letter box, and went merrily on his way, feeling right pleased with himself.

Before the turn-off to Nigg, the post van veered on to the moors to take a nose-dive into a waterlogged peat bog where it settled with a soggy groan and one or two slurping wheezes. And that was where, some time later, half a dozen angry crofters, one highly indignant Aggie McKinnon and eight yapping sheepdogs found him.

As one, with the exception of Aggie who suddenly remembered she had forgotten her 'teeths' and went rushing away in embarrassment, they set about asking him 'what the hell he was playing at scattering their flocks far and wide.' They ranted and raved, the dogs barked and fought with one another and bedlam broke out on that normally deserted stretch of moorland.

Erchy heard not a thing. With his head on his mail sack, his feet on the dashboard, he was dreaming happy dreams, a most beatific smile of joy stamped firmly on his ruddy features. For some reason that would only ever be known to himself, he had, at some point, removed his socks and had affixed them to the windows, one on either side of the post van. The wind had filled them and there they blew, looking like two elongated woolly balloons, the bits of sticking plaster that covered the holes in the heels standing out like two dirty pink crosses for all the world to see.

Rachel wandered slowly along Burg Bay, lost in thought, her hands buried deep in the pockets of her green wool jacket. It was cold for early April, the wind soughed low over the Sound of Rhanna, churning up the white horses, tossing them contemptuously against the rocky outcrops which abounded in these dangerous waters. In the leaden grey of the squally sky the gulls were screaming as they fought the blustery breezes that tossed them about like bits of paper and often forced them to land on the grass-covered crags where they niggled and squabbled, or threatened one another with gaping, vicious beaks.

It was wild and windswept and wonderful. Rachel's ears tingled; her face felt the way it did on rising when she splashed it with cold water from the ewer on her dresser, fresh, alive and glowing; her hair was a mass of wind-tossed curls but she made no attempt to restrain it. The scarf that she had tied round her head before leaving the house had blown off soon afterwards and she had stood watching it as it went flapping away like a flimsy bird, soon to be lost in the marram grasses above the beach.

She wondered why she had worn it: she had always hated anything that restricted nature, but living for so long on the mainland had robbed her of many things. Jon said it had tamed her; she had laughed at that and said it had maimed her, but deep down she was still the unfettered Rachel who had wandered the wild, free lands of her beloved Rhanna and whenever she came home she gradually rid herself of the chains of convention and reverted gladly to the island ways.

Ruth had asked her to go over to Fàilte that morning but for some reason she had wanted to be alone just to think, and had promised to go over later.

She paused for a moment to gaze at the awesome spectacle of Burg rising dramatically out of the sea. Black and forbidding it was pitted with dank caverns, criss-crossed with bare ledges where seabirds nested and screamed and drifted like snowflakes in the wind that eternally battered the exposed outcrop.

Some of the basalt columns had become separated from the mother rock to form structures that looked like gigantic stepping stones and all around were the sharp, glistening fangs of the reefs piercing up out of the restless waves.

Rachel caught her lip and gave a little laugh of sheer joy. She loved it, she adored its splendour and its solitude, its grandeur and its turbulence, and at times like these she wished that she wasn't human but some drifting being who had the power to wander the wind and the storm, the oceans and the skies, for ever and ever and never feel the mortal need for human companionship and comfort.

To be human was to want, to desire, to feel loneliness and to pine after things and people that you had thought you could do without just as long as you were free to roam the wilderness and to climb the high bens where it seemed that no other footsteps but yours had trod . . .

She was missing Jon, it was as simple as that. She had needed to be alone, it had become imperative to her just to be by herself so that there was only the demands of her own body to be met and catered for; the freedom, the peace, had been wonderful, no rush, no hurry to obey the hands of the clock – there was only one clock at An Cala and she often forgot to wind it, the dawn, the day, the sun, the moon had been all the indications she had required to let her know that time was passing.

But the moments, the hours, the days of solitude had served their purpose; the silence of An Cala that had soothed her so much in the beginning was now becoming oppressive and though Jon had written to say that Mamma was on the mend and he would soon be joining her on Rhanna, it wasn't soon enough for her. Hour by hour she was becoming more and more possessed by the old restlessness and she hated herself for being mercurial and foolish but could do nothing to stop the craving for excitement that was mounting within her.

It was freezing standing there at the edge of the waves and

with an impatient sigh she began to walk up the beach towards the shelter of the dunes.

Burg Bay was vast, even with the tide coming in as it was now there was at least a quarter of a mile of shell sand and pebbly shore between the dunes and the sea. Pausing for breath, she closed her eyes for a moment. All around her was the moan of the wind and the surge of the ocean, now near, now far, pulsing, pounding, the heartbeat of the sea, mingling and merging with her own vibrantly beating heart – then she became aware of another sound, that of music, throbbing through air, time, space, powerful, passionate, compelling.

Opening her eyes, she looked up and saw the chimneys of Tigh na Cladach. She saw the blue haze of wood smoke tossing about, she smelled its piquancy and knew its delight and quickly she walked up the beach till she could see the little garden ablaze with yellow trumpets blowing in the strong breezes – the daffodils that Megan had optimistically planted and which somehow survived the spring gales.

From this house the music poured, swelling upwards in great crescendos of sound like the storm-lashed waves washing the winter shores. It was magnificent, breathtaking; Rachel stood entranced, her clenched fists held to her mouth.

Down below, a stooped, black-coated figure passed by, leading a sturdy lamb on the end of a rope. Despite all Dodie's efforts the frailest twin had died and though he had been heartbroken he had set about ensuring the health and strength of the survivor and now took it everywhere with him. It soon learned to follow him around like a faithful dog, even trotting to the wee hoosie with him when he had to obey the calls of nature.

Rachel prayed he wouldn't take it into his head to come and talk to her, this was her moment, her time, her personal private enjoyment of an experience so profound she felt the hot tears pricking her lids.

But she needn't have worried, Dodie had never been able to make much sense of her sign language – combined with his own speech difficulties it was all just too much for him. If by chance they did meet he was wont to shuffle his feet awkwardly or simply stand and stare at her as if he expected some miracle might restore her speech at any moment.

He glanced up and saw her and the familiar '*Tha brèeah!*' filtered to her thinly on the wind before he went on his way, his long coat flapping behind him like one of Ranald's vampires.

She let go her breath, then, as if drawn by a magnet, she followed the music to its source, opening the little gate set into the sturdy dyke that took so many batterings from the high, winter seas it had to be repaired every year. Tiptoeing to the window, she stood with her back to the wall and let the waves of glorious sound soak into her.

So enthralled was she, she wasn't aware that the music had stopped till the door in the solid stone porch was wrenched open and Herr Otto Klebb stood framed in the aperture, his head thrust forward to avoid banging it, having learned to his cost that he was too tall to go through the opening in the normal way.

But to her it was a sign of aggression and she stared at him, her heart beating swiftly in her breast, all the sophistication and poise that had been hers for so long falling away in one short burst of apprehension so that she was left feeling like a small child who had been caught in the act of doing something that was naughty and forbidden.

Chapter Eight

Otto said nothing, instead, and without ado, he reached for her hand and pulled her inside, straight to the sitting room where he spun her round to face him, his expression dark and forbidding.

Rachel held her breath; she didn't want to feel like this, embarrassed, silly, utterly devoid of the pride that had always made her hold her head high, no matter the circumstances. She had felt more confidence on the concert platform, facing an audience of hundreds, than she did standing before this man who, in just a few short minutes, had robbed her of everything that had taken her years to master.

Yet fierce as he appeared to her now, he had already endeared himself in the hearts of those islanders who had crossed his path. Tam and his cronies were full of him and they had forced everyone else to be full of him too. The tale of the ceilidh, his generosity and the wonderful Scottish music that had flowed effortlessly from his clever fingers had spread far and wide. He had become Mr Mystery Man Number One, and those who had walked on Burg Bay had been enchanted by the music pouring from the shorehouse, for, as well as the piano, Otto was accompanied by a full orchestral backing, using the tapes that he had brought with him to Rhanna.

'It is like having a symphony concert on our very own doorstep,' Barra McLean had enthused, even while something about Otto tugged at her memory. But for the moment she couldn't quite think what that something was, and as she was a connoisseur of good music, she was quite content to enjoy Otto's playing while she could. Later she might remember where she had seen him before, if indeed she had seen him at all.

As far as everyone else was concerned he was just a man who happened to have an excellent talent for the piano, and though the kind of music he played wasn't everyone's cup of tea, the passion and the power of it enthralled them anyway and fitted in well with the wild, romantic setting of lonely Burg Bay.

And now Rachel had heard that music for herself and had been even more appreciative than anyone, but she hadn't bargained for an outcome of this nature and wished she hadn't been so foolish as to venture near the house.

She wanted to turn her head away in order to avoid the questions in his penetrating gaze, but no, she wasn't going to let him see how much he had startled her! So she met his eyes with her own and as she looked at him fully for the first time awareness accelerated her already fast-beating heart. This man was no ordinary stranger! She knew who he was – he wasn't Otto Klebb, he was Karl Gustav Langer, world-renowned concert pianist and composer, who had played in all the great concert halls of the world.

He had composed modern classical music, for orchestra, films, and the stage and he had made recordings of all his own works as well as the great classical works of Mozart, Beethoven, Brahms and many others. Rachel had attended one of his concerts some years ago; she had been very young but she had never forgotten the experience, it was imprinted in her memory, both the music and the man.

One of her greatest ambitions had been to play with him on the concert platform. She had played solo parts with many great symphony orchestras throughout the world but she had never achieved her ambition to play with Karl Langer, perhaps because he hadn't been heard of so much in recent years. It had been rumoured that he had retired because of ill health; other sources said he had been weighed down by private and personal worries and had bowed out of the limelight only temporarily. Whatever the cause he had disappeared from the world stage – and now here he was, the great maestro and teacher, standing before her as large as life and twice as forbidding, his eyes raking her face as if he was trying to read her mind.

And he did, quite brutally, as if he blamed her personally for having found out his identity. 'You know who I am,' he growled, a look of thunder darkening his brow. 'I expected this moment of truth but I didn't wish it to happen so soon and particularly when I was just beginning to enjoy my anonymity. When I encountered you at the harbour and saw the look on your face I knew that it would only be a matter of time before you recognized me. Tina told me who you were and I cursed the fates that put us on this island at the same time. Rachel Jodl, the beautiful, young violinist, already attaining dizzy heights on the international concert stage. Unable to speak but saying it all through music. You see, I know all about you, I have heard your name spoken amongst the stars; little did I think I would bump into you on a remote Hebridean island.'

She wanted to ask him so many things – why he had chosen Rhanna as his hideaway, where he had gleaned his knowledge about Scotland, why he was so interested in the McKinnons. She also wanted to shout at him, to tell him that she belonged here on this island, that her heart and spirit were rooted in the very soil from which she had sprung, but nothing, of course, would come out, only a very faint sobbing sound that was her soul trying to be heard.

He studied her and he wondered if she knew how beautiful she looked with her wind-tossed black curls framing her face. The bracing air had made the roses bloom in her satin-smooth cheeks, her tall young body was graceful and sweet yet there was such an air of sensuality about her that it tantalized and teased and seemed to beckon, and all without any effort on her part. And those eyes – black and hectic with the life forces that he knew were churning inside her – at that moment they also flashed with anger, frustration and a hundred questions waiting to be answered.

Again he seemed to read her mind and a wry smile twisted his mouth. 'You and I, *mein Frau*, have come to this island for the same reasons: to rest, to recharge the batteries, to be the free spirits we can never be in public with a thousand eyes watching us. My time here will be short – six months – a year if I am lucky. I have much to do before my stay is up, I have come on a journey of discovery, a pilgrimage if you like. It will be a summer of sadness and of joy – but I go too quickly. All in the course of time, as I keep telling my good friend, Herr Tam. I only ask you not to give my little secret away. Karl Langer belongs to the world; Otto Klebb belongs on this island, everyone knows me as such.'

Then he bent and kissed her, so suddenly she had no chance to take evasive action. His mouth was firm and warm and passionate, she didn't struggle or move away, she was too mesmerized by the events of the morning to be surprised at any further happenings, and – something else – she was stunned and thrilled at being kissed by this man, the charismatic stranger who had turned out to be the maestro, the admired and adored Karl Gustav Langer. Famous as she herself was, it wasn't every day that she found herself being kissed by someone of his calibre and she allowed him to kiss her, deeper and deeper till he let her go as abruptly as he had claimed her.

He smiled at the look on her face. 'Your mouth needed that kiss as much as mine did. Don't worry, it will not happen too often, only when you tempt me beyond endurance. I am aware of your married status, Frau Rachel, and I am not the sort to come between a man and his wife.'

For the first time in his presence she smiled, the radiance of it lighting her face.

He nodded. 'I will tell you what you must have heard a hundred, no – a thousand times, your smile, it is enchanting, a delight to behold, your face in repose haunts the heart, and as I have no desire to be haunted by you or anyone else, I wish for you to keep on your face, the smile. Ah, little Rachel, if only you could speak to me, this conversation is very one-sided. Show me something, some gesture, some word, that will let me know what you are feeling, thinking.'

She reddened, communication with those who didn't understand the signals of her hands always seemed so hopeless and she stood there, nonplussed, feeling more helpless than she had ever done in her life before. She shivered. It was cold in the room, the smoke that she had noticed coming from the chimney had promised warmth, but was in fact only arising from a large lump of damp driftwood that smouldered unproductively in the dismal grate

'The house, it is cold.' He spread his hands and shook his head. 'I am a poor housekeeper, I play the piano yes, but the fire to light, no. Tina does it for me when she comes to make lunch but today I thought to surprise her by doing it myself. Since the arrival of Eve's baby, Tina has much to do and I have no wish to become a nuisance to her.'

It was Rachel's turn to take over. Throwing him a mischievous glance, she took his hand, led him to a chair and made him sit in it before she went out of the room. In the back porch she found kindling, coal, a shovel and a zinc bucket. On a shelf in the kitchen cupboard she discovered a hoard of old newspapers and one of Tina's aprons hanging behind the door. Piling everything into the bucket, she returned to the sitting room where he still remained seated, an expression of amusement on his face.

Removing her jacket, she donned the apron, signalled for him to observe what she was doing, then knelt before the grate to gingerly lift out the smouldering log, which she placed on the hearth. Next she riddled out choked cinders and ash which she shovelled into the bucket. Very carefully she piled paper, sticks and small pieces of coal on top of one another, applied a match and in minutes a cheerful blaze was leaping up the lum.

'*Voilà!*' he cried in delight, his strong face sparkling. 'You have many talents, *mein Frau*. Would your admiring fans ever guess, seeing you in your jewels and your finery, that the dazzling young violinist can change herself back into a Cinderella with just the flick of a match?'

She threw him a glance of reproach and he had the grace to look ashamed. 'But of course, I forgot, you are an island girl, you knew these things from the cradle. How fortunate, to be great and yet to be humble, you would survive where I would perish. Now look at us, Vienna sits by the flames warming her pretty little toes, I, too, sit but I have learned how to light fires, and you, you have black hands and soot on your nose.'

He stood up and took one of her dirty hands. 'Come, you will wash, I will make us a hot drink – no, not the famous Oxo of Herr Tam's stories, I make better cocoa. When we have cleaned and warmed ourselves and drunk my lovely cocoa I shall play for you, anything you want to hear, and I promise you won't have to stand outside of my window like the little match girl: you will be inside, warm, and dry and fed – just like my Vienna.'

They laughed, they had a wonderful time. When Tina came puffing in to attend to her belated duties she found the pair of them ensconced together on the couch, heads bent over pages of music scores, which also littered the table and spilled on to the floor and on top of the cat, who, blissfully asleep by the fire, was oblivious to everything.

Tina stared at the cosy hearth. 'Och, Mr Klebb, you've lit the fire!' Her pink pleasant face was dismayed. 'Surely to goodness that is no job for a gentleman!'

'Frau Tina, don't fash yourself,' he grinned, delighted at having the opportunity to air one of Tina's own expressions, 'a gentleman didn't light it, a lady did, this young lady. She got down on her hands and knees and in minutes the blaze was leaping. I observe, I know now how to do it, the burdens of looking after me will be one less.'

'Ach, you have never been any bother to me, Mr Klebb, but wi' Eve just having the baby I canny have her doing too much in the house, so you'll have to excuse me if I am sometimes a wee bittie late in coming over here.'

She couldn't keep the the pride from her voice. Little Matthew John's arrival into the world had caused a great stir of excitement. Tina had never been so rushed as she attended to her daughter, saw to the baby and 'did' for Otto. But she didn't mind. Her life had meaning again, the house was no longer the quiet place it had been since the death of her husband Matthew, and she hummed a lilting, tuneless little tune as she went through to the kitchen to see to Otto's lunch.

'Stay and have some with me,' Otto said to Rachel. 'Tina

always makes too much for me and Vienna is growing fat with all the scraps I give her.'

Rachel barely hesitated before she accepted. She forgot all about her promise to have lunch with Ruth and Lorn at Fàilte, not till the afternoon was halfway through did she remember and by then it was too late.

When Rachel finally appeared after tea, full of apologies and of her time spent with Otto, Ruth looked at Lorn but held her tongue. She had seen that look on Rachel's face before and remembered it only too well. Lorn remembered, too, and turned his head away in shame, not wishing to be reminded of that turbulent affair he had had with Rachel behind Ruth's back.

But Ruth wasn't going to let go so easily. That night, when the children were in bed and it was just herself and Lorn in the house, there was a strange expression in her violet eyes when she faced him. 'It's happening again, Lorn,' she said slowly. 'Rachel has that special glow about her when she's getting up to something she shouldn't – usually wi' a man,' she ended bitterly.

Lorn wriggled uncomfortably. 'Och, come on, Ruthie, how can you say that? She and Otto have a lot in common, that's all, she's missing Jon and has grown tired o' her own company.'

'Ay,' Ruth spoke slowly, thoughtfully, 'just like you and she had a lot in common when I was away and poor Jon had to leave her to her own devices for a while. She tires o' her own company quickly, does Rachel. I wonder if she and Jon had a row and she's not saying anything. Look at the strange way she behaved when she came home, no' saying a word to anyone, just creeping on to the island like a thief in the night.'

'That's it, isn't it, Ruthie?' Lorn's face was flushed, he hadn't liked being reminded of his affair with Rachel and privately he thought that whenever she appeared she always seemed to cause trouble of one sort or another. 'You're still mad at her for no' telling you that she was coming. And another thing,' he hid his discomfort in anger, 'you're beginning to sound like old Behag! Surmising things that might never have happened or are ever likely to happen. Just because Rachel is attractive to men doesny mean that she wants to pounce on everything in trousers, she has too much sense in her head for that.'

He had said all the wrong things. Ruth's face was like thunder. Shaking back her fair hair from her face she said through tight lips, 'Ay, Lorn, you of all people should know how attractive she is to men, and the pair o' you had no sense at all in your heads when you tumbled in the heather for all the world to see! As for trousers! Rachel prefers men in the kilt, they're more available – in every way.' Her face red with temper, she went on, 'When we used to play together as children it was a favourite game o' Rachel's to try and look up men's kilts to see what was going on up there. Not even the old men were safe from Rachel's prying eyes and to this day, whenever she's around, old Colin of Rumhor gives her a wide berth. Maybe he's feart she'll try to find out how he managed to father six children wearing his threadbare kilt when Jon in his perfectly presentable trousers can give her none!'

Normally Lorn would have thrown back his head and laughed uproariously at that, but tonight neither he nor she were in a laughing mood and the pair of them retired to bed in the highest dudgeon to lie back to back, as far from one another as possible.

After that day Rachel was a regular visitor at Tigh na Cladach. In order to get there she had to go through the village of Portcull, on foot or on Ranald's bicycle, or she walked there via the beach. Either way she soon had the curtains twitching and the tongues wagging, but, being Rachel, she held her head high and went on her way regardless.

'Arrogant, aye was, as brazen as her mother and a bit more besides,' sniffed Behag, who, fully recovered from her accident, was very definitely making up for lost time. She might have chosen to prolong her convalescence had it been to her advantage, but on the day that Holy Smoke brought an enormous bunch of daffodils instead of the usual parcel of meat she knew it was time to let go of a good thing.

'As long as he gets them for nothing he'll bring you flowers till the house looks and smells like a funeral parlour,' Kate had said with a smirk.

'It was kind of Mr McKnight to pick the flowers from his own garden,' Behag had said huffily, more in defence of herself than the butcher. 'At least he paid me some attention while I was laid up wi' my ankle – more than I can say for some.'

'Attention!' Kate had hooted derisively. 'The daft bugger was feart you would sue him for your ankle and fine you know it. Don't forget, I was in his shop the day you hobbled in wi' your arms that tight round his neck I thought you would choke the life out o' him. At first I thought maybe you were lettin' your passions run away wi' you and had given in to him at last, but no, we'll have to wait a whilie yet for that to happen. In the meantime you got your money's worth from the poor bodach, and now instead o' steak it's flowers, which I saw him takin' out the kirk, wi' my very own eyes. He'll be robbin' the kirkyard next, just to keep you going, for nothing but weeds grow in that neglected garden o' his.'

Seeing Behag's downcast face, she relented. 'Ach, you were quite right to get as much as you could out the mean sod but don't be too clever if you know what's good for you. Give him an inch and he'll take a mile and if he goes on bringin' you bunches o' second-hand daffodils there might just be a marriage proposal at the end o' it. Holy Smoke aye has his eye on chance and this is a nice wee house you have here, Behag. If he thought he could save a bob or two he would marry you, just to move in here and let his own crofthouse out to the towrists.'

Behag was aghast; in next to no time she was scuttling about as if nothing had ever happened to her ankle. When Holy Smoke appeared next day behind an even larger bunch of flowers, she snatched them from him, and told him that her ankle had 'knitted nicely' and that she would be putting the flowers in kirk in time for the Sabbath as someone had been stealing the floral arrangements from the altar – 'and may the Lord have mercy on his soul,' she had added as a wicked afterthought.

His face on hearing that was a picture and she had wallowed

in the satisfaction of seeing him sprachle away down the brae as fast as his legs would carry him.

Breathing a sigh of relief and feeling that she had escaped his clutches in the nick of time, she returned to the firing line of everyday affairs, and only just in time too. Things were happening on the island, so much so that the activities of Elspeth and Captain Mac, which so far had been disappointingly sluggish, could keep for a while. The 'stranger mannie' and 'that Rachel Jodl' were a much more intriguing pair and so Behag returned to the fray, fully restored to health and her tongue in 'fine fettle' as old Sorcha so aptly put it.

In the midst of all the talk, Otto and Rachel, locked in their own little world of music and magic, were hardly aware of the stir their relationship had engendered, until Tina, who loved them both, decided that it was high time they did.

So one day, 'Mr Otto' as he had become to those who felt that to address him solely by his Christian name was taking too much of a liberty, found himself confronted by a very embarrassed Tina, pink in the face but nevertheless determined to have her say.

'Mr Otto,' she began, keeping her lovely languid eyes firmly fixed on the view of Sgurr nan Ruadh outside the front window, 'I know it is really none o' my business, and if it was just me I wouldny say anything that might hurt you, but I think it is only right you should know that folks are talking about you and Rachel behind your backs.'

'Talking about us, Tina?' he repeated, his brow furrowed in puzzlement.

'Ay, talking about you, Mr Otto.' Nervously she caught a strand of flyaway hair and tucked it into the elastic band that was holding together an untidy ponytail. 'Rhanna is just a tiny wee island and some o' the nosier folk make it their business to take an interest in what other folks are doing. Rachel is a bonny lass and you, Mr Otto, if you don't mind me saying so, are a very striking-looking man and wi' her being married it just doesny seem right for the pair o' you to be seen spending so much time together. I don't know what your wife would have to say if she found out about it but I know what Jon would think if he saw you laughing and enjoying yourselves together the way you do.'

'Tina,' taking her hands he shook his head as he looked down at her from his considerable height, 'my wife I don't have anymore, and even if I did, myself and Frau Rachel have done nothing to be ashamed of. If Herr Jon came here tomorrow he would have no cause for jealousy, I assure you. I am aware of his wife's beauty, what man wouldn't be? But we have much in common, Frau Rachel and I, we laugh because we enjoy the same things, we make good music together but that doesn't mean that we also make love behind the scenes. If people want to talk about the things they make up in their heads then so be it. I will not forbid my little Rachel to come here because to do so would make nasty feelings between us and I will not spoil a young woman's happiness for the sake of the idle tongues. So you see, little Tina, you must not worry anymore about us, there is nothing to worry about.'

Tina, red with shame and discomfiture, was saved further embarrassment by the arrival of both Rachel and Eve. Up the path they came together, fair-haired Eve fully recovered from the birth of her son, raven-haired Rachel, breathless and laughing, having run to catch up with Eve on the road.

Otto was entranced by Eve's baby and as soon as she came over the threshold he took the little boy from her and began to croon to him.

'Look, he listens, he enjoys my terrible singing!' laughed the big man in delight. 'Everyone should have babies, I wanted dozens but, alas, it was not to be . . .'

He caught the warning look on Eve's face but it was too late. Quickly he glanced at Rachel and saw there the stark longings of a young woman who ached to have children but whose arms remained empty.

Later, when it was just he and she alone in the house, he took her face in his gentle hands and gazed deep into her eyes. 'My little one,' he said, his soothing voice low and tender, 'forgive me, I did not know of your yearnings to have children. But you are young, there is plenty of time, before you know it there will be one, two, even three babies in your life. Believe me, it will be so.'

She looked at him for a long time; there was pain in her heart but there was hope as well. This dear wonderful man, with his fierce manner and generous heart, had become her mentor, her friend, and her trusted companion. If he said she would have babies then she believed him.

His hands were warm against her face, she felt the power and the passion that was strong within him. 'Her beloved stranger': in her heart that was how she thought of him, how she would always think of him now. Something so poignant seized her she was shaken by the tug it had on her emotions and she turned her face away from him so that he wouldn't see the sadness staring stark and painful from her eyes.

Part Two

EARLY SUMMER 1967

Chapter Nine

It had been cold and wet during the early part of spring but now, as the days lengthened, they became warm and golden, filled with the promise of new life and hope. Slowly the fresh young grasses and heather shoots emerged from the tangle of winter browns and reds on the hills; roe deer and rabbits feasted on the tender new shoots; lambs gambolled and played in the fields; the skylarks spiralled upwards to hover in the blue yonder, spilling out their trembling notes of ecstatic song.

Green mattresses of machair became covered in thousands of yellow buttercups that danced in the breezes and seemed to drape the earth in sunshine, while acres of tiny white daisies were like patches of snow spread over the landscape. The scent of flowering gorse hung sweetly in the air, drowning the senses like heady wine; the great blue ribbon that was the Sound of Rhanna sparkled and shimmered in the sun, and in the calm shallows, the children on their Easter holidays splashed and danced, grew brown and healthy, and wished that some disaster might overtake the school so that its portals would remain closed for many moons to come.

Dodie's cockerels crowed loudly from dawn till dusk, driving Wullie and Mairi McKinnon so crazy they spent the greater part of each day thinking out ways to rid themselves of the nuisance. Something would have to be done, they told one another, but for the moment they couldn't think what form that something would take, short of braining Dodie and shooting his blasted birds into hell!

Rachel and Otto, oblivious to all but the wonders of a

Hebridean spring, greeted each new day with delight and made the most of every minute.

Jon hadn't arrived as promised. Mamma, he wrote, was feeling weak and shaky after an unexpected bout of flu, but as soon as she was well enough he would be on his way as speedily as was possible.

> I miss you, my darling gypsy. It seems such a very long time since I held you and laughed with you. The days go by very slowly here and the only way I know how to get through them is to keep thinking of you and what it will be like when at last I join you on our beloved island.

Rachel could hear the voice of longing in the writings of her dear, gentle Jon, and when a letter like that came from him, she would sit very still by her window and imagine that he was on the steamer as it sailed into view on an ethereal sea, coming closer and closer to Mara Òran Bay and the harbour.

But the pull of life pulsed strongly in her veins and always, always, her footsteps took her to lonely, enchanting Burg Bay and the beloved stranger who waited for her as eagerly and as impatiently as she waited till it was time to go to him.

She knew she ought to visit her mother more, though Annie never made any particular effort to look pleased when she did go. Rachel wanted to feel close to her mother but always there had been a barrier between them. Annie had never had the ability to communicate easily with her beautiful, gifted daughter. When she was younger, Rachel had been frustrated and hurt by this attitude, but as she grew older her highly developed senses told her that it wasn't an intentional slight but one born of many things that had puzzled and frightened her mother.

It had taken years for her to accept the fact that she had given birth to a defective child. The way to understanding had been slow and painful for her and the death of her husband, Dokie Joe, hadn't helped matters. Rachel had adored her father and had resented Annie's second marriage to big, strapping Torquil Andrew. Then had come Rachel's fame, and Annie faced a further struggle as she tried to cope with a young woman who might have sprung from an alien womb, so divorced was she from the reality of Hebridean life.

Only gradually did Annie come to realize that success and fame had never really gone to her daughter's head, rather she had clung more fiercely to her beginnings than ever and was always proud to tell everyone of her birthplace, no matter how elevated they might think themselves to be.

Even so, in Annie's book, Rachel was Somebody with a capital S and, no matter how hard she tried, she often felt awkward and clumsy when her daughter came to visit and she could never stop comparing her untidy little cottage with the opulent surroundings Rachel must be used to.

She had been horrified when both Jon and Rachel had tried to persuade her to let them build a bigger house for her. 'What would the nosy cailleachs think o' that?' had been her reaction. So Rachel had to content herself with sending her mother enough money to keep her comfortable and this Annie did not object to since she was careful never to 'display her wealth in public' but invested it instead in 'bits and bobs that anyone might possess', putting the biggest portion into the bank for a rainy day.

But there were some lighthearted times to be had in Annie's company. In her younger days she had often been the talk of the island with her 'fleering after men o' all sorts'. She had been merry and quick-tongued, full of laughter and fun and, even now, some of the best ceilidhs were held in her house, especially when Kate was there to add her zestful talk to that of her daughter.

Rachel thought the world of her grandmother and enjoyed the informal atmosphere of her cottage. 'Orderly chaos' was how Kate described it. She never put on airs for anyone: 'take me as you find me' was her motto and that could mean anything, from catching her with a headful of formidable curlers, to finding her up to her elbows in the sink sloshing soapsuds around with gusto.

Quite often too, Tam might be 'having his head sheared' with a pair of ancient sheep scissors, or he might simply be sprawled in his favourite chair, snoring his head off and not liking it one bit if Kate poked him in the ribs to don his jacket for 'the visitors coming to the door'.

'But, Kate,' he would protest, 'you're wearing your curlers – surely that's worse than me no' having on my jacket.'

To which she would ably and unreasonably reply, 'At least I'm wearing something that hasny got holes in them. Look at your socks, Tam McKinnon, holes in them as big as your head, put your shoes on this minute, I won't have folks saying that I'm neglecting you by no' darning your socks.'

'But, Kate, you don't darn my socks. The last time you put a bit mending to them was when old Joe was biding here, you were just showing off when you darned his socks *and* his drawers. I knew fine you would never keep it up when the poor auld bodach left home.'

'Tam McKinnon! I don't darn your socks because I'm too busy *knitting* the damt things. Now, no' another peep out o' you or I'll keep you indoors for a week to do all the mending you aye manage to shirk.'

Rachel never minded these altercations between her grandparents, she knew well enough that Kate's bark was worse than her bite. Rachel always got a warm welcome from the pair of them and, in their house more than anywhere else, she felt as if she had never been away from home and loved it when Kate smothered her in an apron, dumped a bag of flour on the table and told her to make pancakes. As a child, making pancakes and scones in Kate's gloriously cluttered kitchen had been one of the highlights of her life and she remembered vividly the large table-top littered with bowls of eggs, luggies of milk, pats of butter and most of all, flour, flour, everywhere – on Rachel's hands, her face, her apron; clouds of it dancing in the sunbeams spilling through the window; particles of it making the cat sneeze and fall off her chair; dustings of it covering Tam's cap as he sat reading his paper, perfectly oblivious to everything but yesterday's second-hand news. Then the delicious delight of tearing apart piping hot pancakes to sniff their steamy aroma and eat them running with butter and bramble jam. Neither of them had minded the mess she'd made, not like Annie who lived in a jumble but couldn't be bothered showing her daughter how to bake because it would just make more mess.

Rachel had good reason to love her grandparents, but lately she had neglected everyone in favour of her beloved stranger. Ruth, who had looked forward to a long summer spent in the company of her childhood companion, couldn't hide her displeasure at being given the go-by, and the looks she cast at Rachel whenever they encountered one another in the village were anything but friendly.

But Rachel could no more resist the pull of Tigh na Cladach than she could help breathing. She and Otto had spent some wonderful musical evenings together. She had taken along her treasured Cremonese violin and they had played piano and violin concertos and solo pieces, each of them in their turn sitting back by the fire to listen to the other.

One evening they invited Lorn and Ruth to supper at the shorehouse and after an initial spell of awkwardness Ruth had soon bloomed under the soothing influence of music and song. Lorn was a fine musician in his own right, he could play any tune on his fiddle and it wasn't long before feet were tapping as Scottish reels and strathspeys filled the room. Otto was a perfect host, mannerly and considerate, his strong personality and ability to converse on most subjects putting everyone at ease. When it was time to go home Ruth felt ashamed for thinking the things she had about Otto and Rachel and she didn't even make comment when Lorn's expression said 'I told you so.'

Otto had heard a lot about McKenzie o' the Glen and, wishing to get to know him, had sent an invitation to Laigmhor. Fergus, feeling that he would come under the microscope, wasn't so keen to accept but Kirsteen was curious to meet the man whose name was on everyone's lips and coaxed and persuaded till he agreed to go, if only for the sake of peace. They were accompanied by Phebie and Lachlan and Mark and Megan, who were regular visitors at Tigh na Cladach. It wasn't long before a full-blown ceilidh was in full swing in the shorehouse.

It seemed music and rhythm were inherent in Scottish blood, and Otto was enchanted by the Gaelic songs from Lachlan and the amusing Glasgow ditties that Phebie and Mark sang, their heads close together as they gave it 'laldy', to quote Mark.

Only Fergus refused to take part, his natural reserve making him seem dour and unyielding in the laughing company. He sat by the fire, fiddling with his pipe, wishing it was time to go home but knowing there was little hope of that when Kirsteen was so obviously enjoying herself.

'You're getting to be a bodach before your time,' she hissed at him at one point. He glowered at her and dug a twist of wire deeper into the stem of his pipe, his mind more on the spring lambing than anything else.

Rachel played a medley of tunes on her violin, followed by a haunting and evocative selection of Scottish ballads which seemed to bring the wind sighing into the room and evoked the wild beauty of lonely wide spaces. Her young face was pensive in the lamplight as she became lost in the music. She was wearing a simple white dress that enhanced the tanned skin of her smooth limbs and made her look more than ever a child of light and air and beauty.

Otto watched her entranced, fascinated by her talent, by her dazzling appearance, but most of all by the impression she gave of a being as one with the earth and of the heavens at the same time. She was transcendent yet so vibrantly tangible it was taking all of his willpower to go on treating her as he sensed she wanted to be treated, as someone with the same interests, the same loves as himself, things to be enjoyed without emotional complications getting in the way. She was such a child in many ways but the woman in her couldn't deny her outstanding desirability. Jon was a lucky man; he shouldn't leave her alone for so long . . .

The playing ended. He came back to reality with an effort and, remembering that he was host of the evening, he sat himself down at the piano and performed a solo recital of some of the best-loved composers. It was breathtaking, magnificent; the waves of glorious sound filled the room, effortless and compelling. It was as if he was on stage, giving of his best, his fingers flying over the keyboard without hesitation, his strong face set into lines of concentration as he immersed himself in his playing.

The last notes echoed into an enchanted silence. Everyone was stunned with the magnificence of the performance. It seemed too trite to clap or make any of the usual sounds of appreciation.

Lachlan shook his head as if to reluctantly clear it of the magic that had filled it for the last half-hour. 'Herr Otto Klebb,' he said softly, 'who are you, man? You're no ordinary pianist, that's for certain. You belong on the concert platform – and don't try to tell us otherwise . . .'

Otto jumped up abruptly from his seat. 'Doctor Lachlan, your estimation of me is too high, I have performed on stage, it is true, but not for a long time, no one remembers me now, it was all so long ago. Now, let us drink and be merry – the night, she is young. I have many stories to hear about the islands and I have all the ears for listening.'

Kirsteen laughed. 'You need the old ones for that: the seanachaidhs, Bob the Shepherd, Magnus of Croy, for instance. They're becoming a dying breed but there are still a few of them left on Rhanna, thank goodness.'

'Then we shall have them, we shall have everything that is Scottish and wonderful – but this night is for us and I wish not to waste another minute of it.'

His exuberant personality was very catching and he seemed to fill the whole room with his tremendous vitality. He was attentive and kind and treated the womenfolk with the greatest respect and courtesy. Kirsteen, Megan and Phebie had had their hands kissed on arrival and they blossomed under his charm and his manners.

Fergus had looked surprised when his wife's hand had been seized and kissed. To himself he had thought the action foreign and showy but had to admit that the man was certainly as everyone said, a Presence with a capital P, and more of a mystery man than ever with his musical talents and his appreciation of all things Scottish. Fergus, never a man to feel at ease in social gatherings, applied a match to his pipe and wondered if Donald had checked the lambing fields before going home . . .

'McKenzie of the Glen!' Otto was standing there, two huge glasses of schnapps in his hand. 'I have heard much said of you, many good things,' he grinned, ' others not so good, but we can, none of us, be perfect. It seems, however, there is one field in which you excel. Strong men like Herr Tam McKinnon and Herr Shod the Todd have the envy in their eyes when they speak of it: it seems, according to them, that you can drink every man on this island under the table and never be the worse for it yourself. With that in mind I make a challenge to you, drink with me the schnapps, let me discover for myself this wonderful constitution of an ox I have heard so much about.'

'Havers, man,' Fergus returned succinctly, 'Tam and Todd aye did exaggerate. I am no better and no worse than them and fine they know it.'

Otto's eyes gleamed. He proffered one of the glasses. 'Prove it.'

Fergus caught Lachlan's laughing eyes, he also saw the sympathy in Mark's. Mark didn't dare touch strong liquor – the events of last year had ensured that everyone had discovered the reasons for that – even so he knew how to enjoy himself, and all at once Fergus felt boorish and mean because he could take a good dram knowing that he would waken up next day without the ache of addiction gnawing at his innards.

He looked at Otto. The man was laughing, his keen dark eyes were alive with challenge. Fergus took the offered drink. 'Slàinte!' he muttered and drank the liquid down in one gulp, never so much as one flicker of an eyelash showing that he thought the stuff terrible and nowhere near as good as a good whisky.

Half an hour and two drams of schnapps later he was glowing from head to foot. His dark, handsome face was just a little flushed and he knew he was in perfect control of every one of his senses, therefore it came as a great shock to him to suddenly find himself singing, the notes soaring out clean and clear, as if from the throat of another being over which he had no control.

The chatter in the room ceased, everyone stared, McKenzie o' the Glen singing! Ay, and singing in a voice that was unexpectedly pure and tuneful, a soft, lilting tenor with a beauty of tone that was a delight to hear. The song he sang was 'Vienna, City of my Dreams', and every word, every intonation was perfect.

A pin could have been heard to drop when he came to the last word, but no one was going to let go so easily: everyone took it up, and the haunting melody filled every space in the room:

> Farewell Vienna mine,
> I'm in the spell of your charms divine,
> Dressed like a queen with lights so gay,
> You are the love of my heart today . . .

Rachel had never heard anything so moving. She hardly dared glance at Otto but couldn't help herself. He sat in his chair, his head thrown back, his eyes black and stark with emotion, she caught her breath, something so poignant twisting in her heart she didn't know she was crying till she tasted the salt tears on her lips . . .

> Farewell Vienna mine,
> Laughter and music and stars that shine,
> Wonderful city where I belong,
> To you I sing my song.

The room was suddenly as silent as it had been when Fergus started to sing. A moist-eyed Otto threw his arm round Fergus's shoulder. 'My friend,' he said huskily, 'I take off to you my hat. That was wonderful, superb . . .'

'Och, c'mon, man,' Fergus was overcome with embarrassment at the other man's flamboyancy, 'there's no need to go that far . . .'

'But there is, there is need to go even further. You and I, McKenzie of the Glen, will have another little glass of schnapps, and then we will sing together the songs of Vienna made so famous by the unforgettable Richard Tauber, yes?'

'No,' Fergus said, but he did. He and Otto stood before the fire and they sang the remainder of the night away, much to the delight and amusement of the rest of the company who joined in when they knew the tunes and kept respectfully quiet when they didn't.

When everyone eventually piled out of the shorehouse into a clear, stark, starry night, Otto was singing 'I Belong to Glasgow' in his cultured Austrian accent while Fergus, whose voice had noticeably degenerated in the last half-hour, was attempting a German drinking song.

'My friend,' Otto gave Fergus an affectionate hug, 'we are both equally drunk and therefore we are both equally master drinkers. Next time I will drink with you the Scottish whisky but first, we must get you home in one piece. I have a feeling your legs won't obey the commands of your head.'

'Problem solved.' Mark, who was the only entirely sober member of the company, took a hold of Fergus and propped him against the wall, where, with Kirsteen on one side of him and Otto on the other, he managed to remain standing while Mark's long legs took him swiftly up the brae to the Manse. Ten minutes later he was back at the shorehouse with Thunder, into whose shabby, draughty interior Fergus was stuffed without ceremony to be driven home in anything but style.

It was a laughing group who helped to extricate his rubbery limbed body from the car and then to carry him into Laigmhor. Once inside the door he threw everyone off and said with great dignity and in an unnaturally high-pitched voice, 'I am per – per – perfectly capable of sheeing myshelf to bed, thank you and goodnight,' only to collapse on the bottom step of the stairs with a loud hiccup.

Kirsteen collapsed down beside him, giggling. 'I have never, never seen him like this and he'll certainly never live it down.' She looked at him. His dark head was lolling on to his chest, one big, strong brown hand was hanging down limply at his side. With another hiccup he began to sing 'Simple Little Melody', and he was still singing when the others somehow got him upstairs between them and into bed where they took off his tie and his shoes before pulling the quilt over him.

'He'll have a beauty of a head come morning,' Lachlan predicted with a grin. 'One thing's for certain, he'll no' forget the night that our Austrian friend challenged him to a schnapps-drinking contest.'

'Ach, I doubt if he'll remember anything about it.' Kirsteen's fair face was sparkling with mischief. 'Only, I'll make sure he does, down to every last little detail.' With love in her blue eyes she stroked the hair from his brow. 'My darling Fergie, he's a man of surprises. I knew he loved Richard Tauber, he always listens to him on the wireless, what I didn't know was how beautifully he could sing, I've never heard the likes from him until tonight.'

'Ay, he was always good at keeping things up his sleeve,' Phebie observed, her plump, pleasant face rosily pink from both her exertions and a good drop of the *Uisge Beatha*, 'and he looks so snug and comfortable lying there I'll be joining him if I don't get to my own bed soon.'

'I could drop you off if you like,' Mark offered, but Lachlan, whose own old car had been laid up for weeks, hastily shook his head.

'It's a fine night, the walk will do us good. I've got a hole in my back where Thunder's springs were digging into it on the road up here. I think I'll revert back to the old ways and get a horse, saddle sores are infinitely preferable to rusty springs and cramp.'

'*You* get a horse, Lachy McLachlan!' Phebie said firmly. 'I'm saving up to get us a decent car, and even if I never learn to drive the damt thing I can aye get somebody who does and we'll wave to you as you ride by on your smelly old steed.'

Laughing they bade goodbye to Kirsteen and went their separate ways at the gate. Megan settled herself beside Mark in Thunder and as they drove back up to the Manse she said thoughtfully, 'You know, Lachlan was right about our mystery man, he does belong on the concert platform, I have a feeling that there is a great deal about him we have still to find out.'

Mark nodded, concentrating hard on manoeuvring Thunder, whose lights left a lot to be desired, along the glen road. 'Ay, he is quite a man, is our Otto, his manners are impeccable and his charm rubs off on everybody. Fergus isn't exactly renowned as a chatterbox but he blossomed tonight under Otto's influence. I've been to quite a few gatherings with McKenzie but it's the first time I've heard him singing with such abandon, he has a fine voice too. He must have practised a lot in the bath, or up on the hill with only the sheep as an audience.'

'There was something about his eyes, something strange,' Megan said slowly, speaking as if to herself, her own gaze staring unseeingly into the velvet black of the night. 'But I can't quite put my finger on it.'

'We are talking about Fergus, aren't we?'

'No, Otto.'

'Well, he consumed a fair amount of hard spirits, anybody's eyes would be glazed and queer after a session like that.'

'No-o, it wasn't that – something else . . . Oh well,' she shrugged herself out of her reverie, 'it doesn't matter, it was a great night, and to think I thought that Otto would remain as unapproachable and as remote as he was when first he came to Rhanna. It just goes to show that first impressions don't count.'

'He was being wary,' Mark decided, turning in thankfully at the Manse gates. 'He likely wanted to size us up before deciding that none of us would be able to fathom who he was and why he came here, both factors which still remain something of an enigma.'

'Rachel, of course, had a lot to do with bringing him out of his shell. She and he are real buddies, I don't suppose . . .'

'No, Megsie, you mustny suppose,' he told her firmly, putting his arm round her and giving her nose an affectionate peck. 'This little nose is a doctor's nose and must on no account be poked in where it doesn't belong – leave that to people like Behag and Elspeth, you can be certain they are already making merry with their gossip and I can't have my new and innocent little wife adding fuel to the flames.'

'You're right, of course, you usually are. I *am* getting to be a bit of a cailleach, I suppose that's what comes of living in a close-knit island community.'

He took her arm and led her indoors where they were immediately surrounded by a bevy of canine and feline bodies. When they had laughingly extricated themselves from wet tongues and hairy paws, Mark took his wife into his arms and nuzzled her lips with his.

'You'll never be a cailleach,' he murmured tenderly, 'not until you're at least one hundred and ten years old. And I'm not always right, in fact, I'm often wrong, but on the subject of Otto and Rachel I prefer to give them the benefit of the doubt. Now, how about a nice hot cup of cocoa before bed, my treat?'

'Mmm, sounds good – but bed sounds even better, you could be my hot water bottle, my feet are like ice after just fifteen minutes in poor old Thunder.'

His dark eyes glinted. 'Bed it is, Mrs Mark James, I might just make an excellent hot bottle, but I'm in a wicked mood tonight and somehow I think I'm not going to be very interested in your feet, though they, of course, will warm up with the rest of you, I promise you that.'

His mouth fondled her ear, she shivered and forgot all about Rachel in the pleasure of being the wife of this tall, wonderful man who took his job as minister of Rhanna very seriously but who was first and foremost a husband par excellence.

After seeing the visitors off, Otto came back into the room, his face alight as he strode over to Rachel and took her hands. '*Liebling*,' the endearment caressed her ears, 'it has been a perfect evening, such music, such charming people, so natural and entertaining. The ladies I adore, the men I feel I have known all my life. McKenzie of the Glen has, on the outside, all the rough edges of an uncut diamond – but inside,' he put his hands on his chest, ' he has the heart of gold and the character of steel. He and I, we click. Tomorrow we go fishing in the Fallan river but somehow, I think, he will not remember that in the morning time.'

He sighed as he studied her. Only one lamp burned in the room, she looked shadowy and mysterious, her great dark eyes were luminous in the quiet, secret planes of her face. She was regarding him in that quizzical way he had come to know very well and he sighed for many things, but most of all for the absence of a voice from the throat of such an exquisite creature.

'*Ah, mein Mädchen*,' he whispered, 'only to hear one word from your lips would be, for me, paradise. We speak to one another with our hearts, our eyes, and our music, but I am greedy: I have need to know more of you, your thoughts, your fears, your dreams, and so, tomorrow I begin to learn the language of your hands. Tonight I am too tired to want even to listen to my own voice . . .'

He paused and looked above her head to the window, and without another word he led her over to look outside. A feeling of pure magic stole over them; she put her head on his shoulder and together they watched a huge silver moon rising above the sea, spinning a pathway of crystal light over the sparkling waters, etching the great cliffs of Burg into stark black silhouettes against the star-spangled sky.

'Come, *liebling*,' he said at last, though the softness of his voice did not break the spell. 'Together we will walk through that enchantment. I will pluck moonbeams for your hair and steal a star for us to wish upon.' He laughed. 'Forgive my little fantasies but moontime always makes me feel romantic and weaves the poems in my head. We will go to bed with the wonder of this night held in our hearts, you in your small corner, and I in mine.'

She wanted the night to last forever, she didn't want to go back to the emptiness of An Cala when here, with Otto in the shorehouse, there would be warmth and comfort, love and passion, all the things that were missing from her life just then. She was never more happy, more relaxed than when she was with him and she had to concentrate her thoughts on Jon, how much he meant to her, how she had promised never to betray him again for another man . . .

She moved away from the window. Otto went out to the hall and came back with one of his own warm jackets which he tucked round her shoulders. Hand in hand they wandered through the moonlit perfection of a Hebridean night to An Cala, waiting lonely and bare up there on the cliffs above Mara Òran Bay.

Chapter Ten

The minute Rachel stepped over the threshold of An Cala she sensed that the house was no longer empty and unwelcoming, the feeling of life was in the atmosphere, and though it was dark in the little hallway it was a friendly darkness and she wasn't afraid to go further inside to investigate.

It was very quiet. The house wore that cloak of soundless peace that seemed to enclose it after gloaming had departed and night had settled over the countryside. Even so, her heart beat a little faster as she stood there in the deep stillness, and she just about jumped out of her skin when, on the wall beside her, the ornate clock she had brought back from a trip to Germany chimed out the hour of one o'clock.

She stayed very still outside the parlour door while her racing pulse galloped on, bringing in its pounding beat the first small niggle of unease. Then, with an impatient shrug, she put her hand very gently on the doorknob and slowly, slowly, began to turn it. The hinges creaked slightly. She held her breath as bit by bit she pushed open the door.

Not even she was prepared for the sight that met her eyes, for there, sprawled by the dying embers of the fire, was her husband, dead to the world.

Jon! Her heart cried out his name; a few swift steps took her across the room, straight into his arms. He awoke with a start but she gave him no chance to say anything, instead she smothered him with kisses until he broke away, breathless and laughing.

'Let me look at you!' he cried, quickly lighting the oil lamp and retrieving his glasses from the fireside table. Putting them on he held her at arms length. 'More beautiful than ever,' he said, the light of love shining in his eyes. 'Your holiday on Rhanna has done you much good, you are brown and healthy and perfect. Ah, *liebling*.' He sighed, folding her in his arms. 'How I've missed you and counted the days till I could be with you. It has been forever, but we will make up for it, the summer is ours to pass as we will. The decision to come home to Rhanna was arrived at in haste and I had no time to write and let you know when I would be coming.'

She had a thousand questions to ask, and her hands flew so swiftly he laughed and shook his head in some bewilderment. 'You go too quickly for me, or perhaps I am just out of practice. Firstly, I came on this evening's boat, you weren't here so I lit myself the fire and settled down to wait – and wait – and wait.' Tenderly he kissed her nose. 'I think to myself, she is at Ruth's house and will be home soon, then when soon passed I have the idea that there is a ceilidh somewhere and she won't be home till late. But my little wife, she still doesn't come at twelve of the clock and I am tired from the journey – and so, I sleep, and now I wonder, what has kept her out till the little hours of the morning.'

She found it hard to meet his eyes, such honest eyes, brown and gentle and trusting, sometimes she laughingly told him that he looked like a big puppy dog, but she didn't convey that to him tonight, not when she had just come fresh from the arms of another man whose kisses still tingled on her lips. For Otto had indeed walked her home, but he hadn't been able to resist crushing her to his chest and covering her mouth with such bruising kisses she had at first been dismayed before she had responded to him with a passion that equalled his.

'Forgive me, *liebling*,' had been his parting words, 'I told you I would only kiss you when I was tempted beyond endurance: tonight I very much needed to kiss you, and now go home before I lose my control altogether.'

He had walked away quickly, leaving her to stare after him, every fibre in her so thoroughly awakened she had been trembling with emotion. Her legs had felt so shaky, her heart had beaten so quickly, she had had to allow some time to elapse

113

before attempting the climb up the cliff path to An Cala – and now, here was Jon, tugging at heartstrings that were already weak with feelings.

Dear, darling Jon. She was glad, so glad to see him, she felt that somehow he had saved her from herself and she was so genuinely pleased to see him her face was aglow with the relief she felt at having him home at last. But his questions awaited an answer and as quickly as she could she told him that she had indeed been to a ceilidh though she omitted to say where it had taken place. Somehow she wasn't yet ready to tell him about Otto but his next words made that kind of evasiveness very difficult indeed.

'Has it been all fun, *liebling*?' he asked lightly. 'Or have you kept up some violin practice? I know you want to forget the world for a while but you have a very large following out there, I have to be a hard taskmaster and we must work out some sort of schedule in order that you do not allow yourself to become rusty.'

'There is a man – he has come to live at Doctor Megan's old house,' unwillingly her fingers spelled out the words. She paused, wondering if she should tell him the truth about Otto. She had given her word not to say anything to anyone, but Jon was her husband: if anyone could be trusted to hold their tongue he could. She gazed at him; he was waiting, a quizzical half-smile lifting the corners of his mouth. Making a swift decision, she told him everything, ending, 'With him I have had the most wonderful time, he plays his piano, I my violin. So you see, darling Jon, I don't need a schedule to make me work, Otto is my encouragement, he makes everything so happy and pleasurable, it is a joy to be with him.'

Whilst talking about Otto, her face had become more alive, more glowing than ever. Jon saw the light in her eyes and slowly he nodded. 'I see you have everything you need here on Rhanna, all the freedom in the world, friends, family, above all a man who is in tune with your spirit and who makes his music with you.' He gave a rueful shrug. 'Perhaps I make a mistake when I think you must be missing me as I missed you, you – light up when you talk of this man.'

'No, Jon, no!' Frantically she tried to make him understand how lonely she'd been without him but still he seemed unconvinced and in desperation she threw herself at him to kiss him with such eagerness he was soon lost in the sweetness and insistence of her mouth.

When at last he spoke he sounded shaky. 'Oh, *mein* Rachel. Always, always, I melt in your arms. I tell myself one day I will be strong and not give in to you so easily but . . .' he spread his hands, 'I can never resist you and you know it.'

For a long time after that they sat on the rug in front of the fire, holding one another, but she sensed a restlessness in him, his mind wasn't fully on her, he kept glancing towards the door, a strange expression on his thin, aesthetic face.

All at once he got abruptly to his feet and began pacing the room in a worried fashion, then, with his back to her, not meeting the questions in her eyes, he said in a low voice, 'Rachel, I don't know how to tell you this, it will come as a shock and perhaps I should have mentioned it right away, but seeing your happiness I couldn't bring myself to ruin our reunion.'

Scrambling up from the rug she went to him and put her hand on his arm but still he wouldn't look at her and she became angry because the only way she could communicate with him was through her hands, and how could she speak to him in that fashion if he couldn't see what she was doing?

He passed a hand over his eyes in a characteristic gesture. 'I'm sorry, *liebling*, I'm not behaving very well, perhaps, after all, I shouldn't have come . . .'

'Jon!' Pulling on his arm she made him turn to face her. 'What is it?'

'It's – it's – Mamma.' Somehow he got the words to come out. 'She's here, Rachel, upstairs asleep in the little guest room. She insisted on coming with me, she wanted, she said, to see for herself the island that we love so much, she said it was time she saw my wife's birthplace. Also – she felt the change might do her some good as she's been very low since her illness and taking the flu didn't help matters . . .'

He couldn't go on. Rachel gave him no chance anyway, her eyes were like black burning coals in the deathly pallor of her face. At first she had stared in disbelief as he had talked, now she balled her hands into fists and began to beat them against his chest.

NO! NO! NO! The screams of protest filled every space in her pounding skull but only the barest of sobs made themselves heard. To have his mother here, on Rhanna, spoiling everything with her hints and innuendoes, her accusations and her black, glowering glances, was just too much to bear.

No! No! No! Her face crumpled. She subsided against him, shaking her dark head. She couldn't, she wouldn't live under the same roof as that formidable woman who had never accepted her as a daughter-in-law and never would.

'Rachel – oh, my *liebling*,' gently he took her hands and clasped them to his mouth, 'please, don't be so unhappy, it will only be for a little while. Mamma is used to the city, she doesn't like the country and will hate an island even more. A week, ten days at the most.'

It was eternity! Rachel saw the days stretching ahead, filled with Mamma, her demands, her likes, her wants, her needs. Limp as a doll, Rachel pulled her hands out of Jon's grasp and moved away from him.

She went to the door. 'Rachel,' he began, but she was already out of the room. He could hear her going upstairs, and not being very quiet about it – she would waken Mamma and that was the last thing he needed just then.

A great sigh gusted out of his chest. The start of his holiday looked very bleak indeed, with the two women in his life hating the sight of each other and making no effort to hide their feelings, be it in private or from the rest of the world.

By the time he got upstairs the room was in darkness and Rachel was in bed. Very quietly he got undressed and slipped in beside her. It was very peaceful, the sky outside the window was littered with stars and even as he watched, the edge of the full moon came into view, peeping through the muslin curtains as it climbed higher. Gradually the room became filled with its silver light and in a moment of contentment he gazed round at all the familiar things that were so evocative of his times spent at An Cala.

The furnishings were simple. Both he and Rachel had agreed that the house, with only a few exceptions, should look as it might have looked fifty – a hundred years ago. Here in their bedroom there were no exceptions: the bride's kist under the window, the sturdy mahogany wardrobe and dresser, the pewter basin and jug, the enormous brass bed with its wonderfully soft feather mattress, even the very rag rugs on the wooden floor, were as they must have been when An Cala was a working croft and its rooms had rung with children's voices and the sound of tackity boots taking their work-weary owner upstairs to well-earned rest.

Jon loved it all; he knew every nook and cranny, every creak and sigh of the old timbers, even the very smells of plaster and wood and cobwebby cupboards filled with household necessities. There was no fighting the spiders on Rhanna, the minute their webs were intentionally or accidentally wrecked, they immediately set to work, spinning bigger and better ones, so that you soon came to realize how pointless it was to keep brushing their nebulous threads away.

The bright face of the moon stared at him calmly as he lay there watching it. Slowly he turned his head on the pillow to look at Rachel. Moonbeams were spilling on to her tumble of black hair; he could see plainly the glossy sheen on the little curls at the nape of her neck and – his heart accelerated – her naked shoulders were like alabaster against the dullness of the patchwork quilt.

She moved slightly; he felt the heat of her flesh burning through the flimsy satin of her nightdress. Oh God! How he ached to touch her. He had waited so long for this moment of nearness and now this: her back hunched sullenly against him – no sign to let him know if she was awake or asleep, only that brief touch of her thigh letting him know that she was there, in the bed beside him . . .

All at once a mighty snore reverberated through the wall, followed by another and then another. Each one was louder than the one before, shattering the silence of the house. Jon couldn't believe his ears. It was the first time that he had slept in such close proximity to his mother, and as he lay on his back, counting each explosive sound, a horrible conviction grew that, between one thing and another, there would be no sleep for him that night.

Beside him Rachel tossed, then she sat up, her whole attitude tense and listening. Mamma had settled down to a steady rhythm of snores. Rachel could picture her lying there on her back, like a mountain, her lips sucking inwards, outwards, in, out, in, out . . . and wasn't there now a whistling accompaniment at the end of each rumble? In, out, whistle, in, out, whistle . . .

Rachel glanced at Jon, he gazed at her, a spurt of laughter escaped him. Two seconds later they had collapsed into one another's arms, Jon helpless with mirth, she so filled with it her stomach ached and she could only find release in little gasps and grunts and funny half-sobs that made her throat ache too. Tears poured unheeded down their faces while they clutched one another in agony. Such laughter generated a lot of warmth and Rachel threw off the quilt, eager to feel the deliciously cold, moonlit air washing over her body.

She was very desirable lying there in the silver-blue light. Her nightdress shimmered, her supple limbs moulded themselves into the feathers. Jon forgot about Mamma, forgot about everything except the beautiful creature lying beside him, half woman, half child. Always he had thought about her in that way: compared to him she was so young, a mere girl of nineteen on their wedding day almost seven years ago.

But tonight she was all woman, all desirable, all tempting in that heavenly light spilling over the bed. She melted into his arms. At first her skin was cool under his hands but soon it burned with heat, the satin material of her nightclothes seemed to merge with her flesh, a combination that drove him so crazy with desire he forgot to be careful and tore away the thin restraining garment. Her breasts sprang out, full and ripe and so deliciously tantalizing he wanted to feel them under his teeth. It was always like this, she could bring out the animal in him with just a mere stirring of her lovely limbs, but tonight she too was awash with an untamed passion, the arms that urged him ever closer were fierce and insistent and with a helpless groan he succumbed.

They bruised one another with their kisses, kisses that went deeper and deeper till their tongues played and fought and brought them both to peaks of greater longings. He nibbled her lobes, she squirmed and pushed his head down to her breasts and made no protest when he gently bit her soft flesh and caressed her nipples with just the tips of his teeth.

'*Liebling*,' he murmured huskily, 'you will always be mine, always.'

Rachel closed her eyes. She had imagined that she would feel oppressed having Mamma in the next room but instead the idea excited her. Here she was, with the old lady's adored son in her arms, doing things to her that were for her alone. Jon loved her no matter what Mamma said or did, and nothing could take that away.

He was trembling with his need for her. His mouth moved down from her breasts to caress the soft flesh of her belly. She writhed beneath him till he gave a little cry of helplessness and pushed her legs apart with a mastery that thrilled every fibre of her being. Once upon a time he had been gentle and rather ineffectual during their lovemaking till he found out that that kind of treatment did nothing at all for someone with her kind of wild passions. Now he allowed himself to be completely free with her, which resulted in a relationship that was pleasurable beyond belief.

Roughly he drove himself into her; his sinewy body rippled under her hands. She bit her lip and allowed herself to climb to the crests with him till he cried out and fell back exhausted, bathed in a dew of sweat. A fiery warmth swept through her body; she felt totally relaxed and wonderfully fulfilled.

Twice more in the course of the night he took possession of her body, and each time they both reached peaks of ecstasy that pulsed in their loins till it seemed that nothing could quench the fires burning within them, and all of it was achieved to the tempo of Mamma's snores in the room next door.

Rachel awoke late next morning. By the time she had washed and dressed it was later still, and when she finally made her way down to the kitchen she was horrified to see that Mamma Jodl had made breakfast and was cosily ensconced beside Jon at the table.

He raised his head to look rather sheepishly at his wife but neither she nor he had any chance to say anything, for Mamma got in there first.

'Ah, Rachel, at last you have decided to join us. Jon could not wait for you to attend to his needs – a man must eat a good breakfast, and so I have the search in the cupboards – but . . .' she spread her plump hands and shrugged, 'no food there for a man like Jon. Where is the cold ham? I ask myself. And the cheese, it is fit only for *kinder*, too mild, too without taste; the bread it is too soft; the coffee, it is not in existence – and so, I have to go against my will and make the tea with the funny smell and the eggs with the shells that have still the hen's *schmutz* upon. Yaa!' she lifted her broad shoulders in an expressive shrug and glowered scornfully at her boiled egg.

Mamma didn't have good English; she used her hands and her eyebrows to get over her many points – and in any case, most of the time she was displeased about something and only needed to grimace or utter 'yaa!', which was her favourite expression of disgust, to put over her opinions.

As she rose from her seat to fetch the bowl of eggs, Rachel was struck afresh by her size. Every bone in her body was heavy and big, her discontented face was large-jawed but handsome nonetheless. She had enormous feet, and legs like tree trunks; her well-corseted hips and stomach produced a trimness which only served to emphasize the magnificence of her bosom which swelled out in front of her like a great feather bolster. It was quite a daunting experience to see those vast proportions sailing towards one and Rachel never could make up her mind whether to duck or hastily dodge out of the way.

She seemed to fill every space in the kitchen, and Rachel's resentment at having her here at An Cala boiled in her breast. The kitchen was Jon and Rachel's favourite room, they had painted and papered it in sunshiny shades of lemon and white. The farmhouse dresser, the wooden chairs, the well-scrubbed table, the worn but wonderfully comfortable armchairs, even the brass fender and coal box, had all come from an old crofthouse in Nigg and blended well with the general decor. When Rachel and Jon were at An Cala together they lit the fire in the homely hearth and used the kitchen as a place to eat and relax in.

To Rachel, Mamma's presence in this room was a violation of everything that was private and precious in her life and she had to force herself to go to the table and watch as Mamma's big hand scooped an egg from the bowl to place on Jon's plate, after which she turned to her daughter-in-law.

'The *schmutz* eggs – you want?' she asked in a flat voice.

Rachel shook her head and reached for one of the delicious oatcakes that Tina had recently given her.

Mamma scrutinized the girl's face. 'Like a bird, you eat – no wonder you are thin and pale of the skin. The eyes, they are black underlining, your mouth, it has the swelling lips. They are the only part of you with the fat that should not be.'

Rachel met Jon's eyes, they flashed their secrets to one another. Mamma intercepted the look but chose to ignore it, instead she went on, 'The sleep good you escaped, I too did not sleep well, all night I turn and toss about, and mostly I lie with my eyes open, hearing the noisiness of a strange house.'

Jon choked, Rachel rushed round to thump his back, her lips brushed his ear, he looked up at her and again their eyes sent out their messages.

As soon as the meal was over Mamma began immediately to gather up the dishes and pile them up on the draining board. She was already taking over, Rachel thought bitterly, before we know it she'll be telling us when to go to bed, when to get up . . .

'There is no hot water in the tap,' Mamma complained loudly.

'This morning I look also for the bathroom, there is none to find, so I take my wash in cold water from a jug in my room. Last night there were no lights to find, only an oil lamp and candle.' She emitted a noisy sigh. 'It is so different from Hamburg: there I have all the things I am used to having.'

'Of course it's different from Hamburg, Mamma,' Jon explained patiently. 'It is an island, many of the houses here don't have electricity, we are lucky, we have a generator which hadn't been cranked last night but I will see to it this morning.'

'You have plenty of money,' Mamma pointed out stubbornly. 'You could have the electricians put in.'

A faint smile touched Jon's mouth. 'Piped all the way under the Atlantic ocean? No, Mamma, I think Rachel and I are not that rich. As for hot water, there is a back-boiler behind the fire here, when I have had a chance to light it you shall have all the hot water you need.'

'That is all very well, Jon,' Mamma was growing a bit red, 'but what good is hot water without the bath, the washstand? I am a woman who is used to having the clean person.'

Jon remained calm; Rachel had always found his courteous manner towards his mother extraordinary. She had asked him once how he managed it and he had replied, 'It is the only way to live with her. Look at how you and she war with one another, she believes the young should respect her at all times – and of course – she *is* my mother,' he had added, as if that explained everything.

'We fully intend to build a bathroom, Mamma,' he told her soothingly. 'Our trouble is we are never here long enough to see to such things. Not only that, Rachel and I like to be as natural as possible when we're here and don't mind the odd little inconveniences.'

'Little inconveniences! Pah! And is it natural to go to a *hütte* in a field to perform there the needs of the body. This morning I go there, I sit, I jump off my sit when a large hairy *kuh* bellows at my elbow and when I step outside I stand in *kuh dung*!'

Rachel hid a smile, Jon too had difficulty keeping a straight face. 'We call it the wee hoosie here, Mamma, and if you shut the little gate in the fence the cows won't come in.'

'The comedy I do not find!' Mamma snapped. 'You were never like this when you live with me in Hamburg, Jon.' She looked meaningfully at Rachel who stared back and would have stuck out her tongue if it had been anyone else but Mamma. 'You have there all the cultures, all the good tastes, it is not civilized to stand in *kuh dung* and wash from a cold water basin. Myself, I will not go to a *hütte* in the fields again!'

Then you'd better stock up on syrup of figs, Rachel thought gleefully. As my mother used to say, 'you'll get constipation and cramp if you keep it in.'

'And what about the bath?' Mamma wailed. 'How am I going to give myself the wash, tell me that, Jon?'

Jon looked embarrassed. 'We, Rachel and I, use a zinc tub, Mamma. We set it here in front of the fire, fill it with hot water and lock the door.'

There was a pregnant silence as each of them became immersed in their individual thoughts.

Vivid pictures flitted through Rachel's head. A whale, she decided, lowering itself into a fish kettle.

Jon's face grew as red as his mother's as he imagined her getting stuck in the tub, leaving in her wake a great tidal wave that filled the kitchen, with himself and Rachel wading through the flood to go to her assistance . . . an appalling vision.

'The humility, the indignity,' Mamma whispered with uncharacteristic lack of fire. 'I will not do it – I cannot.'

Rachel felt sorry for her – but not sorry enough. She knew Otto had a bathroom at Tigh na Cladach but she certainly didn't want her mother-in-law poking her nose in there.

Jon was kinder, however. 'My friend Anton, he has a nice bathroom at Croft na Ard; I am sure he and Babbie will not mind letting you have the use of it.' He was growing tired of the subject and wanted to ask his mother outright why she had come to Rhanna when she must have known how different it would be to anything she had been used to, but, conditioned to a lifetime of subservience, he held his tongue. He was greatly relieved to see that his suggestion met with her approval, though he worried about how the Büttgers would react to his request.

'I will go over there later today and ask them about it.' His words came out rather woodenly but Mamma didn't notice. Mollified, she filled a kettle and put it to heat on the stove for the dishes. Meanwhile Rachel, who was determined to let the other woman see that it was still her kitchen, made tracks to the table to clear it, leaving Jon to gather together kindling and coal in order to get the fire going and thus provide Mamma with her desired hot water.

The dishes done and the sink thoroughly cleaned, Mamma peeled off her apron. 'I go now into town,' she declared with determination. 'Proper food you must get, Jon, if you are to keep up your strength to live the way of the heathens. First, the *Bäckerei*, pastries, yes, good solid bread; then the *Fleischerei*, red meat with blood running. You always needed blood running in your meat, Jon; from boytime I give you it to make you strong.'

Jon sighed. Here we go again, he thought, explanations! For her, on Rhanna, always there will be the explanations that will not be allowed to sink in.

'Mamma,' he began a trifle wearily, 'there is a butcher on the island but there is no bakery – and it isn't a town. Portcull is a small village with only a few shops; the women do a lot of their own baking, though Merry Mary does get in things like bread and rolls and a few stodgy cakes.'

'Stodge! I will not have the stodge, no, I will tell this happy Mary to serve to me the apfelstrudel, and if that she has not got I go from there to here till I find.'

Jon gave up. Once Mamma set her mind on something it was useless to try and make her change it. She went to don her hat and coat, each of which was trimmed with grey fur, right down to the hem of the long coat.

Jon gave her directions to the village and off she swept, a string message bag clutched in one hand, a large leather handbag in the other. At the gate she turned and executed a regal wave and then marched down the road as if she had been doing it all her life.

124

'She has certainly recovered from her attack of flu,' Rachel observed rather sarcastically.

'Perhaps it is the island air,' Jon hazarded, not relishing further discussions about his mother.

But Rachel wasn't in a mood for argument, she was thinking of Otto: he would be wondering what had happened to her when she didn't turn up at Tigh na Cladach. She looked at Jon, dare she suggest that they both go over there so that she could introduce them to one another? But Jon had other ideas: she had forgotten his promise to Mamma over the question of a bath.

'Come, *liebling*.' He took her in his arms and kissed her hair. 'It is a lovely morning, a walk on the shore will do us good and then we will pay a visit to Anton. If Mamma doesn't have somewhere to go and bathe we will never hear the end of it.'

She went to get her jacket. Mamma! Mamma! Mamma! Was that all she was going to hear for the next week or two? What Mamma wanted, the kind of things she needed to make her happy: because keeping Mamma happy was of paramount importance to both Jon and herself, otherwise they could forget any ideas of domestic harmony at An Cala. An Cala! The Gaelic for a safe and peaceful harbour! Rachel had to smile; she wondered how her mother-in-law would get on at Portcull – the villagers ought to have had some sort of warning of her impending arrival . . .

'I wonder how she will get on with the islanders.' Jon voiced his wife's thoughts. 'She'll never make herself understood, not only that, she is only familiar with German currency and won't be able to tell the difference between a mark and a shilling. She'll argue, she'll get red in the face – and she will start shouting.'

'And she'll make enemies,' Rachel predicted. She hoped to herself that Mamma would meet Grannie Kate: Kate could sort anyone out, no matter their nationality. If the man in the moon himself came down to Rhanna, Kate would be able to deal with him and not take too long about it either. Rachel felt better; she hoped Behag and Elspeth might bump into Mamma as well. Behag would shrivel her with just one glower and Elspeth would beat her into the ground with a few painful lashings of her razor-sharp tongue.

Rachel grinned. She went to take Jon's arm, smiles begat smiles, and by the time they reached Mara Òran Bay they were in such high spirits they raced one another along the silver-white sands and into little coves that were private and sheltered and just made to be lingered in when it became imperative to steal a few laughing kisses.

Chapter Eleven

As it happened, Mamma took Rhanna by storm, completely disconcerting everyone she met, and as that included some of the less staid inhabitants, she was destined to make her mark in a way that would always be uniquely hers and hers alone.

In the first instance she bumped into Dodie, literally. With his head down because he was crying and didn't want anyone to see, he came loping swiftly along the road, the tails of his greasy old raincoat flying behind him, his fists screwed into his eyes, so blinded by tears he couldn't see where he was going and cared less. Full tilt into Mamma he careered, and the impact stopped him so thoroughly in his tracks he staggered backwards, shaking his head as if to clear it, all the wind knocked out of his sails.

Dodie was not in the best of moods: he had just had a terrible argument with Wullie McKinnon over the subject of his cockerels. At first it had been an amicable enough encounter, Wullie had strolled into Croft Beag, going over in his mind what to say to the old man that wouldn't offend him too much because it was an easy enough matter to bring him to a state of tears. So Wullie had been lost in thought when he encountered Dodie, and Dodie, taking his neighbour's mild manner as an indication that the rift between them had healed, had been very courteous and attentive, showing Wullie his vegetable and flower plots and the patch of richly manured ground where he grew the juicy sticks of rhubarb that were his pride and joy.

He had also hastened to make Wullie a strupak and it was while they were ensconced in the kitchen, drinking tea and eating the pancakes that soft-hearted Mairi had handed in earlier, that the visitor had gradually brought the talk round to poultry.

'Your hens will be laying well the now, Dodie,' Wullie had begun obliquely, maintaining an unnatural politeness in view of his reasons for being there.

'Oh ay, indeed they are,' Dodie agreed eagerly, dunking his pancake into his tea and quickly stuffing the soggy particle into his mouth before it disintegrated into his cup. 'Every morning I go to the hen hoosie to see how many eggs my hens have had.'

'Ach, hens don't have eggs,' Wullie said scornfully, 'they *lay* them.'

'They have eggs,' Dodie persisted, 'and then the eggs have chickens – tis the natural way o' things.'

'But eggs don't have chickens, chickens just come out o' the eggs, Dodie,' an exasperated Wullie cried.

'Ay,' Dodie said patiently, feeling that his visitor needed to be humoured, 'the same way as a calf comes out o' Ealasaid.'

Wullie tried another tactic. 'Cockerels don't lay eggs, do they, Dodie? They just strut about all day, treading the hens and yelling their heads off. They're no' really much good to anyone, all they do is make a God-awful racket and eat up all the food.'

Dodie sighed. 'Ach, but, Wullie, you were brought up on a croft, surely you know the only way that hens can have chickens is to be treaded by the cockerels.'

He spoke to Wullie as if to a child who needed the facts of life explained to him carefully and gently.

'*One* cockerel, Dodie.' Wullie was losing some of his cool; he brushed away a drip from the end of his nose with an agitated hand. '*One* cockerel is all it takes to father hundreds o' chickens.' He paused – he was beginning to sound like the old eccentric. 'To fertilize hundreds o' *eggs*,' he amended hastily. 'Six is just a waste o' time and a buggering nuisance into the bargain.' His temper was rising and he stood up, unable to sit still for a moment longer. 'I'll get rid o' them for you in no time, just a wee twist and it will all be over, you don't even have to watch.'

Dodie was horrified; he had never been able to bring himself to kill anything, far less his beloved chickens, who had proliferated unchecked when he had lived in his lonely cottage up on the hill.

Holy Smoke had already offered to thraw the cockerels' necks and string them up in his shop, affably saying he would share the proceeds with Dodie. He had been rubbing his hands together at the time, an action peculiar to him when talking about money.

Dodie had simply turned tail and run from the scene to tell the story to the first person he met. 'He calls himself a man o' God,' he had sobbed, 'when he is nothing but a heathen goin' round killing poor, defenceless animals.' And now, here was Wullie McKinnon, uttering the self-same murderous words as the butcher man. In panic Dodie had risen to his feet to order Wullie out of his house and never to darken his door again.

'I'll be back!' Wullie had yelled. 'And next time it will be wi' a shotgun! I'll do more than scare the shit out o' these bloody birds o' yours! I'll blast the lot to kingdom come and think o' the deed wi' pleasure when I'm lying sleeping in my bed for the first time in months.'

Dodie had been really scared then, and in his fright he had taken to his heels, straight to the village to tell his woes to someone. That the first person he bumped into should be Mamma was, to his simple mind, just a continuation of his experiences with Wullie, and he backed away from this large, strange woman, the tears coursing in dirty rivulets down his sunken cheeks.

She was so taken aback she began to rant at him in German while he babbled back in Gaelic. To make matters worse, Dodie's pet lamb had followed him into the village and, being a ram lamb, it was only too ready for a bit of fun and games. It charged straight for Mamma and playfully butted her in her stiffly corseted rear. She shrieked, Dodie's nose frothed with fear and for the second time that day he took to his heels and galloped away, the lamb gambolling behind him.

Mamma stared after them. In no time at all they had disappeared from view and she blinked, feeling that she might have imagined the whole episode – had not her stinging backside given her a grim reminder that it had all really happened. But Mamma was made of stern stuff: in next to no time she had girded her loins and was able to take stock of her surroundings. Jon had certainly been correct in telling her that only a few shops serviced the village, but some was better than none and, fully recovered from her experiences with Dodie, she made purposeful tracks for the nearest shop.

Into Merry Mary's she charged, going straight to the head of the little queue and completely ignoring Kate McKinnon who had been first in line and who was rendered speechless for at least thirty seconds.

'You have for me the pastries?' Mamma demanded of Merry Mary. 'I am liking fresh my apfelstrudel; for me the stodge I do not want, it chokes up the system.'

Mamma used a very peremptory tone – after her encounter with Dodie she was taking no chances with anyone else, her idea being that if you got in there first you would show them who was the boss. In Mamma's book anyone who stood at the business side of a counter must be made to understand that the customer was always right and they existed to serve and no questions about it.

Merry Mary was completely taken aback: one minute she had been having a nice cosy blether with her customers, the next she was suddenly faced with this huge monument of a woman with a face on her that would have floored Goliath himself. The little English woman could only stare open-mouthed but Kate, who had recovered her powers of speech, had enough to say for the two of them. Tapping Mamma on one formidable shoulder, she said ominously, 'And just who do you think you are, madam? Barging in here in front o' everybody without as much as a by-your-leave?'

Mamma chose to deal with the first part of the question and ignore the rest. 'I am Frau Helga Jodl,' she intoned proudly, pulling herself up to her full, impressive height and thrusting out her considerable bosom, much to the enjoyment of Robbie Beag who admired well-upholstered women. 'I am *mutter* of Jon Jodl who is married to Rachel Jodl, the famous violinist.'

It was typical of Mamma: very seldom had she praised Rachel to her face, but if she could capitalize on her name she never hesitated to do so. In this instance she hoped that it would intimidate this rather fierce-looking woman whose own generous bosom had further blossomed in the last few minutes.

'Oh, is that so,' Kate nodded conversationally, 'our very own Rachel, eh? I hope she will teach you some of our manners while you are here, for though I say it myself, Rachel aye did have good manners and her being famous hasny altered matters in that respect.'

'Rachel! Manners!' Mamma spat. 'Pah! I have yet to see these manners you speak about, she is not showing them to me since her marriage to my son. She cannot speak, no, but her eyes, they send the rude messages. She has not the respect for her elders, she has the solkiness, she . . .'

'She is my granddaughter,' Kate finished Mamma's sentence in her own words, her sparking eyes sending out dangerous signals of anger yet controlled.

In the face of such righteous ire Mamma hadn't a leg to stand on. She backed off, wishing with all her mighty might that she was back home in Hamburg where the shopkeepers scurried to her bidding, which meant that she was always served and on her way home before anyone else. Taking a deep breath, she turned her back on Kate and was about to address Merry Mary once more when a voice, even more forbidding than Kate's, spoke at her elbow.

'Just a minute, just a minute! Who said you could go first, Mrs Whatever? I was here before you and I am no' waiting a damt minute longer to get served, so just you get out o' the way at once and let me in there before I am forced to take action.'

Mamma turned to see the round face of Aggie McKinnon, who was related to Kate through marriage, glaring at her. If there had been a contest on physical proportions between the two, Aggie would have won hands down, not only was she as rotund as an elephant, she towered above the other woman to such a degree that Mamma was dwarfed by her.

Aggie was normally a sweet-natured, placid soul who liked to agree with everyone for the sake of peace. In common with most of the islanders she enjoyed a good chin-wag and usually never minded if she was last out of whatever shop she happened to be in, but this morning she was in a hurry. She had already wasted a lot of precious time picking Barra McLean's brains for a recipe concerning spicy buns, the island bus would be coming along any minute and she was anxious to catch it so that she could get home and listen to *Morning Story* on the new-fangled radio her Merchant Navy husband had just brought back from America. So, all in all, she considered that she had every right to contest her place in the queue and it was now her turn to draw herself up to her alarming height and thrust out her vast bosom till it was almost touching that of Mamma's.

The two battle-axes faced one another, nostrils flared, guns at the ready; the rest of the shop settled back to watch with the greatest of interest, eager to see who would fire off first. But the promising battle never got off the ground for at that crucial moment the bus arrived at the harbour, the squealing of its brakes being the only indication it needed to let everyone know it was there.

Aggie, her message bag only half filled, shot Mamma a look that promised a revival of the argument at a later date and out of the shop she stomped in high dudgeon.

'It's no' often Aggie is in such a hurry,' Merry Mary observed.

'Ach, she wanted to catch the bus,' Barra explained. 'She likes to listen to *Morning Story* on the wireless and Colin Mor has brought her a fine new one from America.'

Mamma pricked up her ears at mention of the bus: she was beginning to believe that she had landed in a place that might have been Mars, so lacking did it appear to be in modern amenities.

'There is a bus on this island?' she enquired excitedly, visualizing herself being transported to the nearest town, where she could get down to her shopping in earnest.

'Ay, you could call it a bus – at least –' Kate purported a great show of doubt and, addressing herself to her contemporaries, she went on in some puzzlement, 'I've often wondered – is it a bus?'

'It *might* be a bus!' came the chorus.

'Or it might be the Loch Ness monster in person,' Jim Jim said with a grin, 'the way it lumbers along on dry land wi' its bones sticking into every one o' *my* bones.'

'If Erchy would wash the damt thing we could maybe see if it says "bus" on it,' Robbie hazarded, putting on a great display of helpfulness.

'Pah! The comedy I do not find!' Mamma spat. 'I would like to know please' – it was the first time she had used the word 'please' – 'if it goes to a town where I can buy the better food.'

It was Mamma's bad luck that the only sobering influence present in Merry Mary's shop that day wasn't in a mood to be helpful. Barra normally tried to keep the peace, but Mamma Jodl's belligerent attitude had seriously affected her reasoning nature and she was the first to speak.

'A town, you say?' She nodded thoughtfully. 'Well, there is the Clachan of Croy – though I wouldny call that a town . . .'

'No,' Kate chimed in, her face perfectly composed, 'it is more in the nature o' a small city – a very noisy place, I never go there myself unless I can help it.'

'A – city.' Lovingly, Mamma rolled the word round her tongue and without ado she gathered up her bags and went bustling away outside to the waiting bus.

Everyone looked after her, round-eyed.

'You shouldny have done that, Kate,' Barra reproved. 'I admit I was going to have a wee bit fun wi' her but I wouldny have went that far.'

Robbie supported his wife's words, 'No, it wasny very nice to do that to a stranger – and a furriner into the bargain.'

But Kate was unrepentant. 'Ach, it serves the bossy besom right – and just think – she'll get to see the island in style and will experience firsthand the delights o' our island bus.'

Very determinedly, Mamma walked the short distance to the harbour, boarded the bus, and settled herself behind the driver's seat. To supplement his income, Erchy had purchased the vehicle some years ago, and, with the aid of a local-government subsidy, he managed to make a fair profit, especially in the tourist season when trips round the island were in reasonably high demand. Visitors' cars weren't allowed on the island because of the narrow and often dangerous roads and also because of the difficulty of shipping them over on the steamer.

So people like Erchy had quite a monopoly over the question of transport, though he was apt to bemoan his lot and make out that running the bus didn't pay and that he was presented with considerable difficulties when it came to maintaining the vehicle. Any servicing it got was carried out by himself at the side of his cottage. Tam said he didn't know the difference between a spark plug and a bolt, and there might have been some truth in that, for Erchy was anything but mechanically minded, but he cheerfully upheld the view that any sort of bus was better than none and no one needed to use it if they didn't want to.

He knew fine, of course, that people *would* use it whether they liked it or no as few of them owned a car, which presented a great deal of problems when it came to getting from A to B. All things considered, Erchy and his ramshackle bus were in near-constant demand, except, of course, for when he had to exchange his bus driver's role for that of the island postman, or even occasionally for a 'funeral assistant', when he was called on to drive a dearly departed to the kirkyard in the elegant Rolls Royce that Todd the Shod had won in a competition some years ago and which he hired out to wedding and funeral parties. Over the years people had become used to Erchy in all his various guises and the topic of how he kept his bus tacked together had grown stale with the passing of time.

Thus Mamma found herself on a lumpy, hard bench, surrounded by faces she didn't know and which didn't interest her anyway. The well near the driver's seat was a jumble of parcels and boxes as Erchy hated cramming up his post van with the more bulky items, since it meant he had to waste time searching through them every time he came to a stop. It was far easier to carry them on the bus, and it didn't matter if they were accompanied by the odd creel of fish or a sack or two of rabbits. The bus had become quite a favourite rendezvous for those interested in the barter system and many a fresh salmon, poached from Burnbreddie's river, had been furtively exchanged for some other ill-gotten gain. Erchy himself had often accepted a few rainbow trout in lieu of a fare and he was quite happy to add the tag of bootlegger to his various other titles.

There was always a distinct odour of fish in the bus. It hung in the air to mingle disagreeably with other smells of mothballs, mints, tobacco, whisky, sweat and stale beer. Mamma wrinkled her nose in disgust and sat fretting for the driver to appear so that she would catch the shops in Croy before they shut.

But Erchy was in no hurry, he was too busy discussing football with some local lads who had been to the mainland to see some of the last matches of the season and who were only too anxious to tell him about their experiences, both in and out of the football grounds. When he finally appeared, to take his place behind the wheel, he was whistling cheerily and was so carried away with good humour he peered into his mirror and shouted, 'Ride a pink pig on the highway to Nigg!' followed by, 'Bums ahoy on the road to Croy!'

The menfolk merely grinned at his nonsense but one or two of the womenfolk expressed their disapproval in loud snorts while Aggie, who had not yet forgiven Erchy for mistaking her mouth for a post box, glared at his reflection in the mirror and hunched herself dourly into her seat.

Mamma tapped Erchy on the shoulder with a none too gentle finger and requested that he drop her off at Croy, to which he grinned and sang, 'Croy, Croy! The next best thing – to Troy.'

The bus started up. They were moving off when a flying figure waved them down and in came a stringy-looking, garrulous visitor, wearing baggy shorts under a cracked and roomy waterproof. She plumped herself down beside Mamma and immediately began to talk, too taken up with describing some adventure she'd had to notice Mamma's lack of response.

'Just one moment.' Erchy was up again, tying the door with a piece of dirty string. 'Canny be too careful.' He smirked and settled himself once more behind the wheel. The vehicle emitted a series of groans, wheezes and two alarming bangs before it condescended to heave itself out of a pothole, whereafter it

135

proceeded sedately along the front, leaving in its wake a hideous-smelling cloud of diesel fumes.

Erchy was a somewhat erratic driver. On perfectly good stretches of road he would bowl along at a gentle pace suited to his vehicle's temperamental mechanism, but once out on the open road, which for most of his route consisted of narrow little winding ribbons, a change would come over him, and today was no exception.

Through the village of Portcull, past the Schoolhouse, the Manse and the Kirkyard, he was the Erchy that everyone knew – placid, smiling, easy-going to a fault – but as soon as he hit the narrow cliff road to Nigg a grimness settled over his countenance, his mouth became a tight line and his eyes calculating slits in his screwed-up face.

It was as if he saw the road as a challenge to his driving abilities, for no sooner had he come to the first warning sign than he was hanging over the wheel, his foot rammed hard on the accelerator. Round hairpin bends he screeched, scattering the sheep, turf and loose stones flying from under the wheels to go bouncing and whizzing down to the rocky shores far below.

The garrulous visitor was exclaiming in the loudest of voices about the scenery. She had introduced herself to the bus as, 'Viv, botany, geology, history, Creag an Ban cottage, second on the right, B&B, Nigg,' and thenceforth had appointed herself unofficial tour guide. She obviously knew the island well; every passing-place, every patch of heather, every boulder had a story to tell. Ring marks, cup marks, glacial features, duns, forts, ruins of every sort, alpine plants, rare flowers – she rhymed them all off with expertise, her voice wobbling in her throat with every bump. She gave not a blink, nary a pause as Erchy not so much guided the bus along the road as pointed it and hoped for the best.

The islanders were used to such roads: they had lived with them all of their lives. The days of horse-drawn traffic had been far more alarming than the deceptive safety of Erchy's bus, so they listened with half an ear to 'Viv, Creag an Ban, B&B, Nigg,' as they dozed, sucked mints or sent odoriferous clouds of pipe smoke into the already choked atmosphere.

But Mamma was new to it all and Mamma was scared. Viv was in raptures over the scenery. 'Oh, look, just look down there!' she cried, pointing to the sea foaming into rocky coves far below. 'The water! Have you ever seen such colour? So vivid! So ultramarine!'

Mamma was beyond making any sort of response; her heart had long ago leapt into her throat and there it stayed as they plummeted down the braes, spun round tortuous twists and curves and climbed up impossibly steep hills, with sometimes a hairpin bend at the top to complicate matters further.

It seemed a miracle that the vehicle ever made it to the top of those daunting slopes but somehow it sobbed and panted its way to victory.

At one point they met Rab McKinnon ambling along in his tractor. Erchy emitted an explosive curse and just about rammed his brakes through the floor in his efforts to slow down. The vehicle shuddered, every joint took the strain, but miraculously it lumbered to a halt in time to allow Rab to potter unhurriedly into the nearest passing-place.

Erchy drew alongside and for fully five minutes he and Rab blethered about subjects ranging from farming and fishing to the weather, and more football.

Mamma could barely contain herself; wildly she glanced round at her fellow passengers. The only muscles that moved were those necessary to the masticating of mints, the sucking in and blowing out of pipe smoke; there were no signs of agitation on any of the faces with the exception of Aggie's as she wondered if she was going to make *Morning Story* or not.

Aggie caught sight of Mamma's bewildered countenance and moved uncomfortably. She was sorry now for her outburst in the shop – after all, the woman was new to the island, her English wasn't very good and everything must be very strange to her. No one had really given her a chance to explain herself, though it was just a pity she had got off to such a bad start. She wondered why Jon's mother had come on the bus: she had said something to Erchy about Croy but why on earth would she want to go to such an isolated spot? There was nothing at Croy except a few houses and the ruins of the old Abbey, but perhaps she was like the Viv creature – interested in historic buildings – though she didn't give the impression of being anything else but a rather impatient visitor who didn't like to be kept waiting for anything.

Oh well, it takes all types, thought Aggie before opening her mouth to give her lungs full throttle, 'Are you two plannin' on exercising your jaws all day? Some o' us would like to get home, Erchy McKay, and if you don't get goin' this minute I'll report you to the authorities!'

Aggie had no earthly idea what sort of senior body was involved with the running of Erchy's bus but it sounded good and had the effect of making him withdraw his head immediately and slam the vehicle into gear.

Rab took his pipe from his mouth to give everyone a languorous wave and seemed completely unconcerned when he was enveloped in a cloud of exhaust fumes.

A few minutes later Aggie alighted from the bus and off she went towards a little white crofthouse sitting atop a grassy knoll, her fat, rolling gait carrying her to her door in an apparently effortless fashion. She was no more than thirty, fighting fit despite her girth, and ever since her marriage to Colin Mor it had been a joke among the menfolk that he had been the only man brave enough ever to have taken her on and survived.

Several more passengers were decanted at various spots along the way, together with a few parcels. The creel of fish was deposited at Annack Gow's cottage; one sack of rabbits went to an old crofter who would later skin them and sell them to his neighbours, much to the annoyance of Holy Smoke who felt that he and he alone should be the sole purveyor of fresh meat in the district.

Old Johnny Sron Mor, named so because of his enormous nose, met the bus at the turn-off to Croy and into his hands Erchy delivered the second sack of rabbits destined for the population of hungry cats that Johnny had gathered around him over the years. Money changed hands, another exchange of news took place, Johnny 'aying' and 'oching' while Erchy delivered some titbits of gossip.

Mamma boiled over. She was the only one left on the bus now and as she sat there listening to the two men gabbling away in the Gaelic, she was more than ever convinced that she had not only landed on foreign shores, she had also unwittingly involved herself in a situation that was like nothing she had ever experienced in her life before, and was never going to experience again if she could help it.

'I wait to go to Croy!' she boomed. 'I wish to get to this place before one of the clock and I command that you take me – NOW!'

Up until then there were few people in Mamma's life who had ever failed to obey her demands. But then she had never had to reckon with Hebridean islanders whose idea of speed was to think about it first before deciding if it was worth all the effort.

Most of all, she had never had to reckon with Erchy, who, renowned for taking life easy, had been known to read the papers and have a nap in his post van, and all in the busy round of his working day. Erchy enjoyed guessing the contents of folk's mail and he thrived on gossip. He was thriving now on Johnny Sron Mor's account of a fight between two neighbours, and the face he turned back into the bus to look at Mamma was pained in the extreme. It was with the greatest reluctance that he bade Johnny good day and set his bus rather grudgingly on the bumpy road to Croy.

Chapter Twelve

Kate was in her garden, half-heartedly tackling a flourishing patch of dandelions which Tam had promised to annihilate two weeks ago. Kate wasn't in the least bit interested in weeding but had chosen this spot near her gate so that she could watch for the return of Erchy's bus. Ever since she had sent Mamma on her wild-goose chase, her conscience had been bothering her, and on returning home from Merry Mary's she had partaken of a hasty lunch before going out to the garden armed with her hoe. It was a rusty apology for a garden implement – Tam had said he would make her a fine new one 'whenever he had a spare moment' but, as yet, the spare moment had not presented itself – so in between bobbing up to look over the wall, she was kept busy battering the head of the hoe back on to its pole, with the result that the dandelions were given a further reprieve while she alternately cursed Tam, the weeds, the midgies, and the advent of Mamma Jodl on to the island.

But Kate never stayed in a bad mood for long. Despite the midgies it was a fine day, calm and warm; the Sound of Rhanna was blue and serene; the slopes of Sgurr nan Ruadh wore a furring of fresh new green; little trails of mist floated in and out of the corries; Sgurr na Gill was blue in the distance and wore a fluffy cloud cap on its highest peak. The skylarks were trilling in the fields behind her house; a curlew bubbled out its haunting song from the shore; the sparrows were perched on her washing line, looking for all the world like a row of fancy little pegs as they preened themselves and twittered to one another.

A figure was coming along the road from the direction of Port Rum Point, an unfamiliar figure to Kate, and she watched its approach with interest while pretending to examine an exuberant waterfall of purple aubretia growing on her wall. The figure came nearer and soon proved to be none other than Herr Otto Klebb whom Kate, much to her chagrin, had never had any opportunity to speak to as he was apt to keep strictly within the boundaries of Tigh na Cladach and Burg Bay.

'Tis yourself, Mr Klegg,' she greeted cheerily. 'A fine day, is it not?'

To that he made no reply, instead he said rather sourly, '*Mein Frau*, the name is Klebb, K–L–E–B–B, Klebb. A cleg, I believe, is the Scottish name for a large biting insect, known elsewhere as a horsefly.'

'Och well,' Kate replied without hesitation, 'if the cap fits – wear it.'

Otto wasn't used to Kate's ready tongue and he was not amused. 'I assure you, good lady, I neither bite nor suck blood, so the cap, it will not fit.'

Looking at his large, strong teeth, Kate wasn't too sure. She wasn't taken with his surly manner either and, stepping back a pace, she surveyed him for a few moments before throwing down her hoe and stomping away up her path, tossing back, 'If you'll be excusin' me, Mr – er – Otto, I have left Tam's dinner on the stove.'

'Stop, Frau McKinnon!' he roared. Kate stopped dead in her tracks.

'It is Frau McKinnon, is it not? Frau Kate McKinnon?'

Kate retraced her hasty steps, more out of curiosity than of a desire to commune further with this big bear of a man with his dour face and bad manners.

'Ay,' she nodded warily, 'it is Kate McKinnon, no other, and if you don't mind me saying so, I am used to gentlemen treating me with respect. No' even my Tam, in all the years we've been wed, has ever shouted at me the way you shouted, and if you wereny a stranger on Rhanna, and if my very own mother hadny taught me the manners I have on me now, I wouldny have thought twice about just walkin' away and leavin' you in the lurch. You furriners are all the same when it comes to bad manners: we had one in the shop earlier, a German like yourself, a battering ram she was, just charged in and . . .'

'Frau McKinnon,' Otto's voice was clipped, 'I tell this to Frau Tina, I tell it to you: I am an Austrian, not a German, I . . .'

'Same difference,' Kate returned smartly, 'at least, where rudeness is concerned.'

Otto had the grace to look ashamed. 'The apology I give; I am not myself since my head swells to twice its size in the night and greets me with much pain when I wake.'

Kate nodded knowingly. 'Oh ay, Tam has that same problem after a night on the tiles. We were all after hearing the ceilidh at the shorehouse last night. Todd said he couldny sleep for it and my Angus thought he heard McKenzie o' the Glen bawling and singing outside your house at some God-forsaken hour. Of course,' her eyes twinkled, 'I told Angus it couldny be, Fergus McKenzie only ever sings when he thinks he's alone on the hill, nothing on earth could make him raise his voice in the company o' other human beings.'

An appreciative grin banished Otto's dourness. 'The schnapps, Frau Kate, yes, the schnapps could do it . . .' he hesitated and looked towards the house, 'I wonder, if perhaps you are not too busy . . .'

Kate frowned then her face cleared. 'Ach, of course, Mr Otto, you would like a good strong cuppy to clear your head.' She knew there was more to it than that but being Kate she was wily enough not to enlarge on the subject there at the gate, 'in full view o' the world,' as her daughter Nancy would have said.

She made to go indoors with her unexpected visitor then remembered Mamma Jodl. 'Away you go ben the room,' she said to Otto. 'Up the lobby and second on your left – I'll no' be a minute.'

Going back to the gate, she made a hasty assessment of the scene. There was no sign of the bus but her son, Wullie, was coming along, a gloomy expression on his face. Like his mother he was always a mite too ready with his tongue; also, like her, he had a conscience and he was now regretting his indelicate handling of Dodie over the affair of the cockerels.

'Have you seen Dodie?' was his greeting as he came up to the gate. 'I told him I would shoot his bloody cockerels and I've no' seen him since. He'll likely be hidin' somewhere, greetin' his eyes out. I was comin' to look for him anyway but Mairi says I'll no' get any tea the night if I don't find the old bugger and bring him back.'

'Ach, Mairi!' snorted Kate, who often found it hard to be patient with her ineffectual daughter-in-law. 'Surely you'll no' let a simple sowel like her boss you about. As for Dodie, he'll come home when his belly starts rumbling and no' before. Meanwhile, my lad, you can make yourself useful by biding here at my gate and keeping a look-out for the bus coming back: I am busy entertaining a special guest but want a word wi' Erchy when he comes.'

'But, Mother,' Wullie protested, 'I have more to do wi' my time than stand here like a haddie watching for the damt bus.'

His words were spoken into thin air: Kate had already disappeared into the house to 'entertain her special guest'. Her son was left to fume and fret and furiously wipe away the drips from his nose, the idea never entering his head to disobey his mother, for even though he was a grown man, if she took it into her head to chase him with a broom or swipe him over the face with a dish cloth, she wouldn't think twice about it – as he had learned to his cost over the years.

And right well did Kate treat her visitor. Hospitality was only one of the many social graces she didn't stint on, in fact, despite her blunt tongue and often intimidating ways, she was renowned for her kindness and was always one of the first to provide home baking for any local function, be it in aid of church funds, the lifeboat sale of work, or any other of the numerous events that took place on the island.

She plied Herr Otto Klebb with tea till it was almost coming out his ears; she piled his plate high with tattie scones, buttered oatcakes, girdle scones and anything else she could lay her hands on. Altogether she lavished him with loving care and attention, not because she had wholly forgiven him for his earlier brusqueness – she would smart over that for a good while to come and might even cast it up to him if she felt it was warranted – but simply because to her keen gaze he looked pale and drawn and in need of her administrations.

Also – and this was the big one – her instincts told her that he hadn't just sought her out to sit in her kitchen drinking tea – oh no – he had come to tell her something or ask her something or even confide something to her, though she hoped fervently that the last was not the case. With her open, honest nature she found it very difficult to hold on to a confidence, as she herself would have been the first to admit.

While he was enjoying his strupak, she filled a large mug with more scalding tea from the seemingly ever-productive teapot, threw some scones on to a plate and rushed outside to thrust them into Wullie's surprised hands. 'Here, take this,' she ordered, 'and don't let anyone see you supping tea outside my gate like a tink. Inside the wall wi' you, my lad – and remember – wave Erchy down and don't let him get away till I have had a word wi' him.'

'But, Mother . . .' Wullie began, but she had disappeared once more and with a sigh of resignation, keeping one furtive eye open, Wullie ate his strupak to the echoing blasts of Dodie's cockerels from further along the village.

When Kate returned, her visitor was sitting back, wiping his mouth with a large, snowy white hanky, 'Frau Kate, that was *wunderbar*. I congratulate you on your culinary prowess. May I now ask that you sit down and have with me the chat. It will not take long but the things I have to say are of great importance to me. You are the one I seek as I have heard of the greatness of your knowledge pertaining to the history of the people on this island.'

Kate's bosom swelled. Like her husband and his cronies before her she fell under the spell of Herr Otto Klebb; she forgot about his previous rudeness – the manners he presented to her now were impeccable, his magnetic eyes were upon her, mesmerising, captivating.

She thought to herself, this is it. She sat down opposite him and waited.

For quite a few moments there was silence. He had closed his eyes; he was so quiet and faraway she thought he had forgotten her and was therefore all the more startled when his eyes suddenly flew open and without hesitation he said, 'Frau Kate, what would you say if I told you I am a McKinnon, the same as yourself?'

Kate was stunned, so much so she couldn't say anything at first, far less comment on the question he had just delivered with the force of a sledgehammer. She sat back in her chair and took several deep breaths, then, true to form, she nodded and said cheerily, 'Ach well, Mr Otto, you wouldny be the first to come into my house and tell me that. Only last year I was able to give all sorts of information about the McKinnons to a fine wee English woman whose ancestors came from the island of Mull. She went away from Rhanna wi' stars in her eyes and though I say it myself I made her time here so happy I wouldny be surprised if she comes back to visit me one o' these days.'

'Frau Kate,' Otto spoke sternly, 'I am not here for the fairy tales! My roots are here on this island of Rhanna.' Leaning forward, he looked her straight in the eye. 'My grandmother was born and bred here; she lived in Croy on the north eastern shores. Her house, it was thatched; her parents made their living on land and on sea. When she was seventeen she became pregnant by a young man from the same village. Her parents, they were scandalised – they sent her away to live with relatives in Canada. There my mother was born. My grandmother never came back to her native lands, she never married: she couldn't forget her "dear young McKinnon" as she called him. Fortunately she was an adventurer, she loved to travel, and she took her daughter to many places in the world. My mother grew up, she too enjoyed to travel: she met my father in Germany. He took her back to his native Austria and there they married . . .'

He had forgotten Kate; he was lost in the story as it unfolded from his memory. His voice was soft, husky, as he went on, 'I was born in Vienna. My grandmother, she lived with us. All through the years of my boytime she tells me about this island and of the young years she spent here. She never forgot, she described it all so clearly: the ocean, the hills, the purple of heather in autumn, the miles and miles of golden beaches. She spoke of the summer shielings when she and the other young people of the island went up into the hills to mind the cattle. She sings to me the songs they sang, the stories they tell to one another when the gloaming steals over the hills and the sea is growing dark; she tells me how boys and girls sleep together, the bedclothes swaddled in such a way that they could not make contact with one another – they were trusted by their elders to behave in the proper way and few of them broke that trust. My grandmother was one of the few: when I am older she tells me of her love for a McKinnon boy. In here . . .' he placed a hand over his heart, 'she aches for this boy and he for her, but they are too young, they know their parents will not consent to their marriage – and so . . .' he spread his hands, 'you know the rest. My mother is begun, the young girl who was my grandmother is sent far away over the sea but she never forgets her beginnings. When she is old and her eyes are growing blind I see the tears in them as she remembers, and there am I, the young man now, my own heart yearning for an island I have never seen but vow to visit one day. She also said I got my gift for music from my grandfather, the young Magnus McKinnon. He writes songs for her, he plays an old fiddle, he sits by the sea and he serenades the girl he wishes to marry, and then one day she goes away and he and she never see one another again – and then she dies and leaves with me a legacy of music and memories that are as much an ache in my heart as they were in hers when she was alive and telling to me her wonderful tales.'

He had brought a breath of pure romance into the homely cluttered room. Kate, her own eyes blinded by tears, buried her face into her apron and gave herself up to a 'good greet'.

'Ach, Mr Otto, that was beautiful just,' was her shaky verdict when she had recovered sufficiently to trust herself to speak. 'Never in all my days have I heard the likes . . .' She raised a tear-stained face. 'It will be Magnus of Croy that the lassie left behind. Och, it is sad, sad, to think o' the heartache he and she suffered over the years, for he never wed either. Many's the time I've listened to him talk o' his bonny Sheena; he said he never could love anyone the way he loved her. Even yet I've seen his eyes grow misty and faraway when he talks o' the old days. I'm no' a body that is easily taken in by daft talk, Mr Otto, but when Magnus gets going wi' his tales o' the summer shielings and how himself and Sheena used to walk hand in hand over the heather braes, talking and singing, I just want to listen to him all day, for he is one o' the finest seanachaidhs on the island. After Sheena went away he buried himself in his stories and music, and if you go over to Croy you'll hear his music long before you come to his cottage . . .'

She paused to stare at Otto in wonder as the full import of his revelations began to sink in. 'He is your maternal grandfather, your very own flesh and blood – tis no wonder you love music for he is full o' it . . .' She shook her head and looked at him, her eyes sparkling suddenly. 'I wouldny be surprised if I myself sprung from that particular McKinnon line for is not my very own granddaughter Rachel brimful o' musical gifts . . .'

She was completely carried away, so much so she forgot that she was a Uist McKinnon and that it was more likely Tam, Rhanna born and bred, who might have passed on any talents. But a notion like that would never have occurred to Kate, for when it came to music she maintained that Tam had bricks in his head, so untuned was he to melody and song.

'Ah, Rachel,' Otto said with a smile, 'when I heard she was a McKinnon, I think of my grandmother telling me of all my Rhanna kinsfolk and it pleases me to know that this beautiful young woman is one of those I have waited so long to meet.'

Kate frowned. 'You seem always to think o' your grandmother in connection wi' Rhanna. What about your mother? Did she never hanker to know more about her Scottish connections?'

Otto sighed. 'There a generation was skipped. My mother was a society beauty. She flitted from one bright light to the next; it was beyond her to sit still for any length of time: my grandmother's breath would have been wasted on her. No, I was the beneficiary of those memories, I was hungry all the time to know more, on every word I hung. My mother had not the time for me, she was a creature of gaiety and laughter; it was my father and my grandmother between them who encouraged my passion for music. I was still a boy when my mother died; my lovely, special grandmother led me into manhood, she guided and counselled me – without her I would be nothing. I still hear her voice, as soft as the Scottish mists I see here on the hills. She was the last of my family to die; my wife lives but she is no more in my heart. We part amicably, we were never in love but tolerated one another for as long as we could. There were no children – and so— '

A wistful smile touched his face. 'I retrace my grandmother's journey, back over the sea. I wish first to know her beloved soil and so I follow her footsteps, I tread the earth she has trod. I rise up very early one morning when no one is about and I make the long tramp to Croy, there I sit on the heather and I gaze out to sea, feeling in my heart that I am looking at it through my grandmother's eyes. Tina has already told me of one Magnus McKinnon of Croy and has described to me where he lives, I find his house, I look and I wonder, "have I at last come to my grandfather's house?" It is early, there is no music, there is no life, and so next I seek the house of my great-grandparents, but there is only a ruin. The dry, grey ribs of the roof stick into the sky, the thatch hangs in tatters into rooms that once rang with the joy and the laughter of a young girl who used to live there. But it is not dead: for me, she is everywhere. Inside the ruin I find the fireplace where the family once sat; in the rubble there are some rusty pots and pans; on a small broken table there is an old bible, the pages are damp and stuck together but on the flyleaf there is an inscription, very faded but still discernible. It is in the language of the Gael . . . I have it here for you to decipher . . .'

Reaching into an inside pocket, he withdrew the ancient book. It was falling apart but the gold tooling was still there on the threadbare spine. Kate took it, her hands trembling in case she should further damage the treasure. The brown leather casing was cracked and barely held together by the binding and she held her breath as she turned it over and looked at the inscription on the parchment-like flyleaf.

'My specs, Mr Otto,' she whispered, almost as if the very breath from her voice might turn the fragile pages into dust. 'On the wee table by the fire.'

He handed them to her, she perched them on the end of her nose and stared at the spidery writing. 'It is very old Gaelic, Mr Otto, but I can still make it out. It says, "to Sheena, on her twelfth birthday, blessings be with you all the days of your life, from your mother and father, 14th June 1882." '

'Sheena,' Otto spoke the name with reverence, 'it was her bible. I'll cherish it always: she held it, she must have read it by the flickering light of a crusie. She told me about crusies, the fuel that was used was fish oil, they were crude and primitive but they served their purpose.'

'Ay, indeed they did, Mr Otto. Some o' the old folk still use them to this day only they don't burn fish oil anymore. Old Magnus has several hanging from his fireplace – och, but you'll have to go and visit him! I can just see his face, the pair o' you will have that much to talk about, so many years to catch up on. It will be a bonny day for him when his very own grandson walks through his door, and himself thinking all these years that there was no kin left in the world to call his own.'

She jumped to her feet. 'This calls for a dram! I canny remember when last I felt so wobbly and queer inside. Fancy! Old Magnus wi' a real flesh-and-blood grandson. He never even knew that he was a father, for Sheena's parents never spoke o' it. No' till their dying day did they mention their lassie's name again, but it was her who was in their hearts and on their lips when they drew breath for the very last time.'

She poured two generous drams, gulping hers down without as much as a grimace. When Otto hesitated over his she tilted the glass to his lips, laughingly telling him he needed a hair of the dog and to get it down like a man.

But several things were puzzling her, and the questions came tumbling out. Why, for instance had he left it so long to unveil his secret? And why did he choose her to tell it to when the island teemed with all sorts of McKinnons.

'I canny understand why you didny tell Rachel first. You and she have been seeing a lot o' one another.'

'The answer to that is simple, *mein Frau*: you are the senior member of her family, it was your place to be told first. Naturally I wanted to tell you and Herr Tam together but he wasn't here and I couldn't waste any more time – also . . .' he cleared his throat and went on tactfully, 'you have lived more years than our little Rachel, the memories in your head go back a long time. You would hear things from your parents about the folk they knew in the old days.'

'Oh, ay, right enough,' she nodded, 'they often spoke o' Neil and Ishbel and the heartache they brought on themselves by sending their own lassie away but never telling anyone why she had gone, just that they thought she would have a better life wi' relatives o' theirs abroad. They never mentioned Canada; Magnus kept asking but they would never say and in the end he just buried himself in his croft and his music.'

She gave Otto a mischievous look. 'They were dark horses – like yourself, hoarding all their wee secrets, for you have still to tell me why you didny say right away that you were a McKinnon. Were you sizing us up, Mr Otto, checking first to make sure we were a worthy clan to belong to?'

He gave a wry smile. 'You have a devious mind, Frau Kate, but this time you do not guess the truth. I waited because I wanted to make sure I would be accepted. My grandmother tells me many times about the islanders' mistrust of strangers who bulldoze their way in when they have only newly set foot on the land. So, I wait, I get to know Herr Tam, I meet others and have with them the ceilidhs and the drams. I make my music with Rachel, people become aware of me, they wish to get to know me better, gradually I become accepted and then I know it is time to show to everyone my true colours.'

Kate grinned. 'Ay, and bonny colours they are too.' She extended one large, capable hand. 'Welcome to Rhanna, Mr Otto, and a bloody great genuine welcome to a bloody great family . . .' Refilling their glasses, she raised hers to the ceiling and shouted, 'To the McKinnons! *Slàinte Mhath!*'

Following her example with exuberance, he repeated the toast, adding, 'And here's to the clan gathering of all the McKinnons, here on Rhanna! It will be the finest, the biggest, in all of the Hebrides!'

'A clan gathering?' Kate's eyebrows shot up, her face sparkled with interest.

'A clan gathering, Frau Kate, but please leave the arranging to me – though of course I will need your help in spreading the news of it around the island.'

Kate, who always made full use of 'Highland Telegraph', looked suitably modest. 'Ach, you can rely on me for that, Mr Otto, just you say the word and I'll . . .'

At that moment Wullie came rushing in to convey to his mother that Erchy's bus had just come into view. She stayed long enough to tell Otto to make himself at home and to be sure and put the cork back in the whisky bottle before he left, then she made haste to follow Wullie outside in time to flag Erchy down as he approached her gate.

'What have you done wi' the big German wifie?' she demanded as soon as he had swung the door open on its one rusty hinge.

Erchy scratched his head. 'Done wi' her? None o' the things I would have liked to do wi' her, that's for sure. She nearly brained me wi' her handbag when I suggested she wouldny find much to suit her in Croy, so I just left the besom to it. The last time I saw her she was sprachlin' along the track towards Croy Beag.'

'You'll have to go back.' Kate was clambering on to the bus as she spoke. 'The daft cailleach thinks there's a city out there on the moors and if we don't find her she might drown herself in a peat bog.'

'A city?' The look Erchy gave Kate suggested she was altogether mad. 'What way would she be thinkin' there's a city at Croy?'

'Because I told her.' Kate's reply was succinct. 'Just get goin' and ask no questions for once in your life. Wullie, you come wi' me, you might be needed in case o' an emergency.'

'There will be an emergency if I don't find Dodie,' Wullie grumbled, 'and wi' the luck I'm havin' these days the emergency could easily be me.'

Nevertheless he got in beside his mother, consoling himself that anything was better than tramping for miles in search of Dodie when he might just come upon him from the comparative comfort of Erchy's bus.

But Erchy wasn't for giving in to Kate so easily. 'I'm no' going back to Croy,' he stated stubbornly. 'The Portvoynachan lot are waitin' for me at the harbour and I'm no' changin' my route just for the sake o' thon bossy big wifie. Everybody knows I'm a stickler for timetables and I'll no' have my reputation ruined for anybody.'

'Reputation!' Kate snorted. 'The only reputation you have is for scaring the shat out your passengers, and if you're no' doin' that you're either snoozin' or readin' in your post van! You can pick up the Portvoynachan folk later; just tell them there's an emergency in Glen Fallan for that's the way we'll be going. It's the quickest route back to Croy and the road goes right to the clachan once you get past Croft na Beinn.'

Erchy gave in. When Kate made up her mind about something she usually got her way – and he didn't dare say that this mad notion of hers would cost her. Unbeknown to her he had recently borrowed ten pounds from Tam and had no intention of paying it back for some time to come. So if he did this favour for Kate, and she somehow found out about the loan, she couldn't very well hold it up to him in the face of his undoubted magnanimity.

Feeling very martyred and extremely hard done by, he tied up his door, vented his feelings by revving up with unnecessary vigour thus causing an extra large emission of diesel fumes and trundled along to the harbour to inform his would-be passengers that he had been 'commissioned' to do an extra run to Croy, which would only take ten minutes at the most and that he would be back 'in two flicks o' a lamb's tail.'

'The way he drives I wouldny be surprised at that!' Malky of Rumhor commented, venting his disgust by spitting energetically on to the cobbles and rubbing it in with the toe of one stoutly booted foot.

Chapter Thirteen

In between outcrops of rock and great clumps of flowering gorse, Mamma glimpsed Erchy's bus dipping and diving, climbing and clawing its hazardous way back over the cliff road to Glen Riach and Burnbreddie.

The journey from Nigg to Croy Beag had been a hair-raising one for Mamma, who had imagined that there was not another road on earth that could possibly be worse than the one they had traversed from Portcull to Nigg. But there she had been wrong. The way through Glen Riach and the lands of Burnbreddie had been gentle and pleasurable. In those rolling silvan pastures Mamma had felt a deep appreciation for nature's bounteous glories, which, for her, was unusual, as the countryside had hitherto never stirred a response in her heart beyond wishing that she could get out of it as speedily as possible since 'all that space' made her feel insecure. But she had had to admit to herself that there was something about the serenity of the purple-blue hills of Glen Riach that caught her imagination.

The great undulating green and amber mattress that was the Muir of Rhanna also brought a sense of peace to her soul. Here the shaggy blonde Highland cows browsed peaceably amongst the heathery knolls, and in the distance, glimpsed between gaps in the rocky coastline, was the sea, unbelievably blue and beautiful, stretching on and forever into hazy infinity.

Despite the bumps and rattles of Erchy's bus she had been lulled into a sense of deep tranquillity that made the shock of the last part of the journey all the more terrifying. Quite suddenly it seemed, they left the moors behind as the vehicle plunged down a near-perpendicular pass between the hills and the sea. Just as suddenly they came to a sharply rising slope up which they crawled at a snail's pace, enveloped by diesel fumes and the stench of red-hot metal.

Up, down! Up, down! The lie of the land became predictable but never monotonous. One minute Mamma's heart was in her throat, the next it had plummeted to her stomach. Looming ahead was a great lump of jagged rock and Mamma's feet were rammed down hard on an imaginary brake – not for one minute did she think anything could get through the impossibly narrow gap, far less a bus. But without hesitation Erchy plunged through the crack, known locally as The Wedge for obvious reasons. After that the road became ever narrower till it was little more than a track winding above the cliffs. Down below, the sea boomed into subterranean caverns, great sprays of white foam burst over reefs and rocks and washed the black, slippery feet of basalt crags sticking up out of the waves.

At this point the roar of the ocean filled Mamma's ears. It echoed and reverberated in every cranny of the bus. Erchy, who had recovered his good humour soon after leaving Johnny Sron Mor at Nigg and who had, incredibly it seemed to his one and only passenger, cheerfully whistled the rest of the treacherous miles away, informed Mamma that the road at this point was built on top of a vast underground sea-cave which was reckoned to have eroded the rock for at least two miles inland at a conservative estimate, for nobody had ever dared explore further.

'There was no air, you see,' he went on chattily, dodging a lamb that had leapt into his path in search of its sure-footed mother, who was browsing amongst the rocks above the cliffs. 'It was a long time ago and they were using these paraffin torches. Two miles in and the lads were pantin' and gaspin' for air, the torches went out, the tide was comin' in, and they would never have made it back if they hadny left a piper at the entrance. To the skirl and blast o' the bagpipes they at last came tumbling out and no one has gone in since, though some say the caves at Dunuaigh, where the monks hid from the Vikings, join up wi' this one, which in recent years has come to be known as

Big Ben because o' the boom it makes at high tide. If you look over there to your right you'll see one o' the blow holes where the water comes spoutin' out from the force o' the waves.'

Sure enough, some distance away, a great spray of water was jetting into the air. It was an exciting, magnificent place to be, and if Mamma had witnessed it in different circumstances, she might have been more appreciative. As it was she was too busy 'gaspin' and pantin'' for air herself to pay much heed to Erchy and his tales. She was tired of the whole episode and was wishing with all her shaky heart that she hadn't made this perilous journey, shops or no shops, city or no city.

As they left Big Ben behind, the way became gentler, and Mamma was just getting her breath back when ahead loomed another gigantic rock with only a tiny arched aperture leading to the other side.

'Gregor's Gap,' Erchy threw over his shoulder, enjoying enormously his impromptu role as tour guide. 'Poor old Gregor lost his life here one dark winter's night. He had been having a wee bit o' a ceilidh wi' one o' his neighbours and might have had one too many. Whatever the way o' it, he missed the road and drove his tractor right into the rock and both himself and the machine went rolling down to the sea far below. It was sad, right enough, because he was normally a canny sort o' man and had been riding this road ever since the days o' horses and carts but, of course, an engine is no match for a good horse that would take a body home blindfolded over any sort o' road.'

Mamma made no reply; she cared nothing for the unknown Gregor who, in her opinion, had diced with death and had only gotten what he deserved. She was sick and tired of Erchy and his gory tales and when he at last brought his bus to a halt outside a five-barred gate, she could hardly wait to be rid of him and his dreadful contraption.

'Tell me, where is this place of Croy?' she demanded over the roar of the red-hot engine.

Erchy scratched his head and treated her to a puzzled grimace. 'Over there.' He pointed vaguely. 'You can just see the tops o' the houses from here. You have to go through that gate –

and don't forget to shut it or Johnson o' Croynachan will have something to say if his cattle get out – and follow the track which takes you right to the clachan.'

Mamma made to squeeze past him but he stayed her by blocking her path. 'If you don't mind me sayin' so, you'll no' find much o' anything over yonder – unless, of course, you have relatives who'll let you bide wi' them till . . .'

'Let me through at once.' Mamma brandished her handbag, swinging it in such a way that it caught Erchy on the side of the head, so that the only things he saw for quite a few moments were stars.

When he recovered his equilibrium Mamma was already off the bus and making her determined way through the gate.

'How will you get back?' he yelled. 'The folk hereabouts only have tractors and pony carts and I'll no' be back this way for another three days!'

To his amazement he imagined that she shouted something about getting a taxi, but he was in no mood to pursue the matter further. Let the old bitch discover for herself the problems of getting about in this part of the island. It was bad enough for people who were born and bred here but a townie like herself simply had no idea of the difficulties involved, and bloody well serve her right if she got her arse soaked in a peat bog in the course of her travels!

With the feeling that he had done his duty as a good honest citizen of the island he revved up and drove away, his ruffled feathers gradually settling at the thought of the dram he would most certainly receive if he called in at old Meggie's on the way back to Portcull.

Mamma was fuming as she stomped along the track to the village. She could hardly believe that any road, in any part of the world, could stop at a five-barred gate leading on to the moors. But then, she had never experienced any of the roads in Scotland, never mind those on a Hebridean island. The roads on Rhanna had certainly been up-graded – if one could call the re-surfacing of the existing narrow tracks an improvement.

Funds had not stretched to the more remote hamlets, with the result that Croy, which was divided into Croy Beag (little Croy) and Croy Mor (big Croy), had been left to its own devices, though the road did go as far as Croy Mor from the Glen Fallan side.

Unfortunately for Mamma, she was on the Croy Beag side and her dismay on reaching the small handful of houses perched on a cliff overlooking the ocean was considerable.

Here there was a sense of timelessness. Some of the houses still had thatched roofs; peat smoke hung lazily above the chimney pots; chickens poked and pried around the houses and spilled over into the heather; great shaggy Highland cows browsed and ambled about, so that wherever you looked you saw huge horns sticking out of gorse bushes or the feathery rear ends of hens lancing up out of the wild flowers growing in the ditches.

Acres of buttercups and daisies smothered the green of the machair, blazing yellow and white all the way to the edge of the cliffs where they merged with the azure of the sky and the dark, deep blue of the sea.

It was a small world of perfection, yet it was vast. The ocean rolled off into horizons unlimited, misty islands floated on the edge of the world, gulls, puffins, kittiwakes, and terns tumbled and dived in the great bowl of the sky and out on the distant waves white-winged yachts drifted on the dream-like reaches.

Mamma, however, was in no mood to appreciate the scenery. The suspicions that had beset her on reaching the five-barred gate were now a near-certain reality. There was no city of Croy, nothing even resembling a town existed on this island, she was stuck here in the middle of nowhere with no shops, no transport, very little in the way of creature comforts, and it was hot, hotter than she had imagined a Scottish island could be. She had long ago peeled off her fur-trimmed coat and hat but even so she sweated – and her stomach was starting to rumble. She had a delicate constitution, she wasn't yet fully recovered from the virus that had struck her down in Germany, she needed to take food regularly or she could get dizzy, or faint, or do any of the dozen and one things she usually did to get attention – especially to get Jon's attention. But Jon wasn't here, nobody was here who could possibly understand how delicate she was, how much she needed unrestricted care and comfort – how much she needed to make herself understood in a land that was so far removed from her beloved Hamburg.

A bent old bodach was coming along the track. In one hand he carried a milk pail and a three-legged stool, in the other was a Harry Lauder walking stick, as full of curves and twists as the roads that the bodach had trod all his life. He leaned on it heavily, his gnarled old fingers clutching it so tightly they looked as if they might have been moulded into the wood. He had a thatch of white hair, nut-brown skin, a wonderfully wise face, blue, blue eyes and, when he opened his mouth to smile politely at Mamma, one tooth set in the middle of his otherwise toothless mouth.

This was ninety-seven-year-old Magnus of Croy – respected, well-loved, a highly regarded member of the island community, storyteller, bard, musician, teacher, friend, a comfort to children and adults alike, a sympathetic ear to those in need of guidance, a font of wisdom to anyone who wanted advice on any subject, because his grasp on world affairs and general knowledge was legendary. All of his life he had studied music and books and newspapers, none of which had ever had the chance to gather dust in his house as even now, in his remarkable old age, he sought learning and retained what he had learned as easily as any man half his age.

Mamma did not return his smile; she had not yet learned her lesson. If she had played her cards right she would undoubtedly have been invited in to the old man's homely, comfortable cottage, to rest and partake of a strupak of tea and scones; as it was she saw him as just another eccentric 'foreigner' and showed scant gratitude when, after a very mannerly salutation, he enquired if he could help her at all.

'Help! There is no help on this island!' she snarled impatiently. 'I come to look for the city of Croy, I find there is none, my feet, they are on fire! My head, it is spinning. I need to find someone of intelligence who can understand what I am saying.

On this island there are only those who make the comedies and frighten me to my grave! I must have a car to take me to the house of An Cala but that is an order too tall for a backward place like this!'

Magnus drew himself up, he had never been able to suffer fools gladly and this large woman, with her handsome, scowling face, gave every indication of being one of the most ignorant persons he had ever yet encountered in all the years of his long life. Nevertheless he was Scottish, hospitality was inherent in him. Only a slight coldness in his keen blue eyes indicated his contempt for her attitude, and he was big enough and tolerant enough to be able to say kindly, 'If you would care to rest in my house for a wee whilie I will get one o' my neighbours to take you home. He doesny have a motor car but he has a fine fast tractor which would get you over to Glen Fallan in no time . . .'

'A tractor! Pah!' Mamma, her face red, interrupted him most rudely and in her excitement she began to speak rapidly in German. Magnus looked at her, he was buggered if he was going to help her now, and to even things up he lapsed into Gaelic and, flapping his fingers, he indicated a track which snaked its way over the moors towards the Glen Fallan hills.

Mamma stared horrified. She was wishing that she hadn't been so hasty in her condemnation of the neighbour's tractor, but it was too late to change her mind: Magnus had gathered up his stool and his milk pail and was off to milk his cow, never deigning to give her so much as a backward glance.

With a great self-pitying sigh, Mamma heaved herself up from the boulder on which she had been sitting and began trudging along the mossy path that Magnus had indicated. Peaty brown burns burbled at her feet, bumblebees and heath moths flitted and droned in amongst the tiny wild flowers that starred the carpets of lichens and mosses growing over the stones; the sweet scents of warm grasses and heather hung agreeably in the sun-filled hollows.

Mamma took a deep breath – these smells, they were good, she decided, and, just for a moment she found herself comparing them with the fumes of traffic she had become so used to in cities.

The water of the little streams also had a clean, fresh smell; the sound of it purling over the stones had a special kind of music to it, as if it had gathered on its way the secrets of hidden places and was whispering them to the low, caressing breezes as they passed each other by.

Mamma gave herself a mental shake. Such nonsense! She must be losing her senses. This great, lonely, wild place was her enemy. Her legs were itchy and sore where horseflies and midgies had bitten them. She hadn't known such pests as midgies existed till she had come to this God-forsaken island and the sooner she could leave all of such horrors behind the better it would be for her.

Still, the water looked tempting and her feet were hot and aching. She could do worse than stop for a minute to cool her burning flesh. A few minutes later she was sitting on a rock, her outer layers laid carefully over the bare branches of a dead bush, her shoes and stockings beside her, her feet planted firmly in a little moorland burn. The water slid over her ankles, ice cold, deliciously soothing. The sun had broken through a layer of cloud and beat down warmly on her back. It was a completely new experience for Frau Helga Jodl: she who had always been surrounded by people was now sitting alone in a great expanse of amber moors, divested of garments she had only ever before removed in the privacy of her own home; the curlews were bubbling out their golden song in the heather; the skylarks were spilling out their trembling notes above; and a corncrake sent out its sharp, imperative call from some hidden secret place.

But Mamma was not going to give in so easily to such pure and simple pleasures: every fierce, city-fied fibre in her resisted the delights of this vast, perfumed wilderness. She wanted only to wallow in self-pity. She told herself that she was abandoned and alone in an empty, lifeless desert – birds were just birds, they didn't count, flowers she could buy anywhere in any shop in any city or town, water was only natural when it came out of a tap – and only gypsies and the simple-minded took off their shoes and stockings to dip their feet in a wandering stream.

The last thought made her hastily withdraw her own feet from the water, dry them as best she could in the grass and quickly don her stockings and shoes. A movement behind made her turn round to find herself looking up the wet and gleaming nostrils of a cream-coloured Highland cow whose enormous curved horns were outlined against the sky. Beside the cow stood a sturdy calf, front legs spread, head lowered as he stared with unblinking curiosity at the human object that was so obviously fascinating his mother.

For the umpteenth time that day Mamma's heart leapt into her throat. She shrieked and, scrambling upright, she stopped only long enough to gather up her precious hat and coat before backing off from both cow and calf and walking rapidly away. But as fast as she walked so too did the mischievous cow and her frisky offspring, who, every so often, took it into his head to butt playfully at the air and kick up his heels.

'I say to you, go!' Mamma commanded at one point, standing her ground and frantically waving her arms about. The cow also stood her ground, and, lowering her head, she emitted a series of grumbling bellows while her calf watched, his wet nose dripping health, his fur-fringed lips also dripping, in this case the slobbering residue of his mother's milk quickly snatched from her teat while she was communing with Mamma in her own particular language.

For the second time that day, Mamma wielded her handbag, this time in the direction of the cow, who stepped back a pace but who was not for relinquishing this unexpected game which had intruded into an otherwise perfectly ordinary day.

Desperately Mamma's gaze panned the landscape. Nothing! Just miles and miles of heather moor and then more of the same – but wait! There was something else! Smoke, drifting, billowing, perhaps a chimney – and where there were chimneys there had to be a house, and any house with chimneys that smoked had to contain human life of some sort. In those fraught moments she didn't care what sort of humans might live there. People were people when all was said and done and what did it matter if they spoke in that queer singing language that had beset her ears since leaving Portcull. She would find comfort, shelter, perhaps even food. She would be pleasant, she would be grateful, she would get there as quickly as she could, even though her feet were once more giving her hell.

She set off, the cow and her calf following along at her back, like two large dogs who expected a bone at the end of their travels. They mooed, they drooled, they skipped, and gambolled and played. They urinated in great steaming waterfalls, and they released alarmingly huge portions of manure, whose porridge-like consistency created semi-liquid platters that were immediately pounced on by armies of dung-flies that seemed to appear from nowhere.

Mamma was heartily sick of her unwanted followers, yet, strangely, by the time she topped a rise and saw distinct signs of habitation in the distance, she was no longer afraid of the animals, seeing them instead as nothing more than a nuisance who had taken a fancy to her and who had, for the last half mile . . . she had to admit it . . . made her smile against her will with their sly good humour, their natural curiosity, and their unstinting passion for following faithfully in her footsteps.

When finally she arrived at the tink encampment it was hard to know who was the most surprised. She had imagined she was making for some sort of village. From a distance the tink tents had looked like little houses and, as she drew nearer, her mouth had fairly watered at the savoury smells drifting towards her on the breezes. Her face as she stood on the edge of the camp was a picture: shock, horror, dismay all registered on her countenance at one and the same time. She couldn't decide whether to stay and make the most of the situation, or to turn tail and run, cows or no cows. But thirst, fatigue and hunger were powerful persuaders; here there was sustenance, here there was rest – and if she was lucky she might just satisfy all of her needs without being robbed or having her throat cut or a combination of the two. For to her uneducated city eyes the travellers looked a rough and ready bunch with not one jot of civilized veneer on their suspicious country faces to suggest that they were possessed of any social graces in their make-up.

So she stood and stared and openly displayed her hostility, her disgust – and – let it be said – her contempt. She looked just what she was, a big, domineering, city-bred, well-dressed woman who gave the impression of having lived in a land of plenty all of her days and who was used to getting her own way how and when she wanted it. If she felt apprehension or fear she kept it well buried, for in reality Mamma was an exceedingly tough lady who had seldom suffered anything worse than occasional and convenient bouts of severe hypochondria.

It wasn't every day that the tink camp was visited by a lady of Mamma's physical grandeur and all too obvious opulence. The rings on her fingers gleamed, the necklace at her throat glinted fire, she most certainly had not purchased her dress at a jumble sale and her handmade shoes, though dusty and rimmed with cow dung, were made of the finest leather decorated with fancy buttons and silver buckles.

It was not surprising, therefore, that the travellers gaped and stared and eyed one another in questioning doubt, but they appeared harmless enough and big, bold Mamma felt it safe to delve further into the interior, where she got the biggest surprise of all. At the heart of the camp was the fire and seated beside it was Stink the Tink fixing his rabbit snares – and beside him was Dodie, calm and quiet now that he had a large mug of broth clutched in his hands, made by Stink's wife Alana in a great black pot over the embers at the edge of the fire.

Dodie, who had never received anything other than kindness from the tinks, had reached the camp long before the bus had made it to Croy Beag. All of his life he had travelled the highways and byways, and he was familiar with every shortcut on Rhanna. Those on the Muir of Rhanna he knew like the back of his hand, and in his fear of Wullie, his terror of Mamma, he had simply headed for a place where he knew he would receive a welcome and something to fill his stomach.

In his wildest dreams he had never thought to encounter the 'wild furrin wifie' in this least likely of places, and when she came striding over to the fire to stare at him with as much surprise on her face as was registered on his, he rose clumsily to his feet, spilling his soup all over himself in his fright. His lamb, curled up cosily beside the fire, didn't give the intruder a second glance but Dodie was all too conscious of what it had already done to Mamma and he stared at her in abject dread, adrenaline pumping as he prepared himself for take-off.

But Stink was his usual unruffled self. Having listened with half an ear to Dodie's babbled account of his morning encounters, he guessed that the unexpected visitor was the 'wild furrin wifie', but with her red sweating face and her look of exhaustion, she didn't seem all that intimidating to him.

'Will you be sitting yourselves down,' he directed, looking up from his snares to include Mamma in the invitation. Patting the smoke-blackened upholstery of a broken-down car seat, he went on, 'Here ye are, missus, this is for you,' and, raising his voice he roared, 'Alana, be putting out some more soup for the lady! My hands are dirty and not fit to be serving food.'

Mamma accepted the invitation gratefully. If she had been asked to park herself on a chamber pot she might have done so, so much did her tired legs quake and her empty stomach rumble. Pausing only long enough to flick her hanky half-heartedly over the sooty car seat, she sank down into it with the look of one who was sampling the most luxurious armchair in the land.

A red-haired, merry-faced woman emerged from one of the tents to ladle steaming-hot soup into two mugs, one of which she passed to Dodie, the other to Mamma, with hands that looked filthier than those of her husband. She had just spent a morning feeding her children, feeding her husband, tending the fire, airing the bedding, gathering fuel, which included dead heather shoots and ancient cow's dung, and had just gone into her tent to wash when Stink's orders had reached her ears. But Mamma didn't even notice her hands: she was too intent on getting food into her mouth to care very much about anything else.

Alana, whose arm was round Dodie's bent back, soothing away his fears as if he was one of her children, nodded sympathetically and observed, 'Tis hungry you are indeed, missus. We don't see many fine ladies like yourself in this part o' the island – but then, it's a nice day for a walk over the moors – as long as you know where you are going.'

Fortified and rested, Mamma was recovering some of her mettle. 'The walk I did not take willingly – I try to find the city, the city of Croy. I come on the bus, I suffer much pain, and when I arrive I look and look for this city but it is not there . . .'

'The city o' Croy?' Stink blinked and glanced meaningfully at his wife. He looked worried. Perhaps Dodie was right after all: they could be dealing with a mad woman here. He wondered which was the best course of action, to humour her or to see her out of the vicinity as quickly as possible . . .

The matter was taken out of his hands, however, when several of the womenfolk, curiosity getting the better of their reserve, came over to arrange themselves round the fire, and some of the men did likewise, Aaron parking himself on a boulder right next to Mamma's car seat.

When Little Lady Leprechaun came leaping into the scene, Mamma simply gaped. Despite having made a good recovery from her experiences she was still at the stage where her stunned mind was unable to take any more surprises and she could be forgiven at this point for wondering if a sense of normality would ever return to her life again.

Lady Leprechaun was used to people staring at her and she didn't bat one eye at the look of wonder on the visitor's face, instead she poured tea and handed it to Mamma along with a huge doorstep of bread spread with margarine and treacle. The offerings were gratefully received. If Jon had been present, he too would have stared at the sight of his big, fastidious Mamma tucking into bread and treacle and downing great volumes of black tea from a smoke-begrimed tin mug.

The womenfolk plied her with questions. In her halting English she told of her encounter with Kate in 'Happy Mary's', her subsequent 'ride into hell' in a 'mad bus with an equally mad driver', her search for the city of Croy, and her meeting with a senile old man with a 'curly walking stick' who had pointed the way into the wilderness where, footsore and weary, she had been chased by two mad cows for 'so many miles I lose count.'

As one, the tinks turned to gaze at the 'two mad cows' who were peacefully grazing their way back to more familiar territory.

'It would be a joke,' Aaron decided. 'Kate McKinnon is full o' mischief and never means half of what she says. The old man would be Magnus o' Croy, one o' the wisest folk o' these parts . . .'

'Bejabers and bejasus!' Paddy burst out rudely. 'The whole business is nothing but a bloody farce and we're just wastin' our time listening to the like o' such nonsense. Magnus would have helped ye if ye'd let him, missus, and just who do ye think ye are, comin' in about our camp and belittling a man whose boots ye should have kissed!'

Mamma was not intimidated, glowering long and hard at the rough-looking Irishman she thrust out her bosom and intoned, 'I am Frau Helga Jodl, *mutter* of Jon Jodl and mother-in-law of Rachel, the world famous violinist.'

Paddy's eyes narrowed, a gleam of interest shone in their black depths. Her words had reminded him afresh of Rachel and her precious violin and his voice was smooth when he said, 'Indeed, is that right, now? Tis no wonder that the stamp o' a fine lady is upon you and if you'll allow me the honour o' seeing you home I'll just go and hitch up old Shamrock and give the trap a bit o' a clean. We can't have a lady like yourself mucking up her skirts, can we now?'

Mamma watched Paddy's retreating back and felt slightly uneasy but not as uneasy as Aaron, who knew that Paddy's conciliatory gesture was only a means of using Jon's mother for his own shady ends.

Mamma, safely settled in the trap, was quite upset when she saw Paddy heading her way with Dodie in tow. It had been bad enough sitting next to the aptly named Stink at the fire but at least he was well enough kippered in smoke for his smells not to make themselves too apparent. Dodie was a different matter entirely: one didn't have to be rubbing shoulders with him to notice his lack of personal hygiene and when it became obvious that he was also to get a lift home in the trap she squeezed herself as far as possible against the side of the seat and surreptitiously retrieved her hanky in order to prepare herself for what was to come.

But Dodie's objections to having her as a travelling companion were even stronger than hers. When he realized what was happening he simply could not stop a tide of terror rising within him. 'Ach no,' he babbled to Paddy, 'I dinna want to go in the trap. I'll just walk home wi' Curly, he's no' used to horses and will maybe shat himself wi' fright if he's made to go against his will . . .'

'Just you be gettin' in, Dodie.' Paddy gave the old man a none too gentle push. 'It's no' Curly you're thinkin' of, it's yourself, because I know fine you're feart o' the wifie.' Raising his voice for Mamma's benefit he went on, 'She's a lady and ladies don't bite – except . . .' He made a horrible grimace accompanied by a few ape-like postures. '. . . when they turn into gorillas and tear you from limb to limb.'

Paddy was the only one of the travellers that Dodie neither liked nor trusted as, whenever he got the opportunity, he took great pleasure in trying to frighten the old man. Temporarily forgetting Mamma, and in his hurry to get away from Paddy, Dodie fell into the trap, sprawling against a loudly protesting Mamma who hastily applied her hanky to her nose and let blast a stream of vitriolic German into one of Dodie's large, hairy lugs.

Without ceremony Paddy seized hold of Curly and threw him in to join the rest of the passengers. The terrified lamb bleated loudly and lifting his tail he sprayed his master's legs with a good dollop of little round droppings.

Paddy took the reins, Shamrock flexed his sturdy hocks, rolled his eyes, and with an effort began to trundle the trap along the mossy, rutted track that led past the Monk's tombs of Dunuaigh towards Croynachan and Glen Fallan.

Squashed in her seat, Mamma endeavoured to avoid the

wild-eyed Curly and to keep her distance from Dodie. He, meanwhile, not daring to speak or look at her, made every effort to keep *his* distance from *her*, all the time wishing to himself – wickedly – that she would be the next recipient of his adored lamb's frequent and plentiful offerings of little round, hard balls of dung.

Chapter Fourteen

Glen Fallan undoubtedly boasted the best stretch of road on the island and Erchy took full advantage of the fact. He bowled along at a steady pace and was somewhat annoyed to see Elspeth in the distance, waving her hanky in such an imperious manner it was obviously a signal for him to stop. He screeched to a halt beside her and in she climbed. When she instructed him to drop her off at Slochmhor, there was nothing in her manner to suggest that she was quite delighted at having this opportunity to 'save her legs' as she hadn't expected to see the bus today.

'This isny an official run and I'm in a hurry,' Erchy grumbled. 'The Portvoynachan lot are waitin' for me at the harbour and I have no time to spare.'

Elspeth glanced meaningfully at Kate and Wullie. 'I see,' she said stonily. 'Those and such as those, eh, Erchy McKay? Things are indeed changing on this island. There was a time when nobody thought twice o' giving a helping hand to their neighbours but of course,' she sniffed and stuck her sharp nose in the air, 'sillar is all that counts wi' some people and it's a true enough saying that money is the root o' all evil. I have seen— '

'Ach, let her in!' Kate intervened impatiently. 'We're just wasting time gabbling away about nothing. You sit by Wullie and me, Elspeth, and take no more heed o' the man, he's in no mood to see reason and would waste an hour just arguing for the sake o' it.'

Rather haughtily Elspeth took a seat behind Kate and Wullie, assuming an attitude that suggested she had no wish to communicate with anybody in her present ruffled state.

But Kate had never been one to let opportunity slip through her fingers, she took a positive delight in other folk's affairs and had been itching for a long time to know more of Elspeth's. The sour-faced housekeeper of Slochmhor had been keeping a very low profile of late and nobody had been able to find out very much about her affair with Captain Mac, not even Behag whose devotion to Elspeth's every move, via the medium of her 'spyglass', had become quite a talking point among her neighbours.

Kate's interest wasn't quite as intense as that, nevertheless she saw no harm in trying to pierce Elspeth's armour of secrecy.

'You'll no' have so much time to spare these days, Elspeth,' she began chattily, poking Wullie in the ribs when he dared to snigger. 'Only the other day Phebie was saying she doesny see near so much o' you now that you and Captain Mac are busy plannin' to set up home together.'

Elspeth treated the back of Kate's head to a positively poisonous glare. 'Phebie never said the words! She knows better! Herself and Lachlan have never indulged in common chit-chat, especially when members o' the household are under threat from idle gossips. As for Captain Mac, he has been dividing his time between his sister on Hanaay and his cousin Gus here on Rhanna and, of course, he is away wi' the trawlers whenever he has the chance. I myself have seen very little o' him, we have our own lives to lead and are too busy to be bothered wi' very much else.'

'Ach, my, and here was me thinkin' the passions were just leapin' in your veins, Elspeth,' said the incorrigible Kate while at her elbow Wullie snottered profusely in his efforts to choke back the laughter. 'It just goes to show you are what you aye said you were, a one-man woman who can never forget Hector marching home from the sea to crush you in his arms and smother your lips wi' red hot kisses. I mind o' those days fine, he was a man o' few words – but they say that the silent ones are the worst and long spells at sea breeds fantasies and longings that have to be spent on somebody. Ay, Hector might no' have been much to look at but he was a man and these wee, thin ones are the worst when it comes to lust in the marriage bed.'

She had hit a sensitive nerve, the only thrilling times in Elspeth's austere marriage to Hector had been when, sodden with drink and past all human reasoning, he had forcibly taken possession of her gaunt body. In spite of herself she had loved every rough, exciting minute of those brutish experiences whose aftermath had seen her praying half-heartedly to the Lord to forgive her for such sinful enjoyments.

But she didn't need the likes of Kate McKinnon to remind her of things that were best forgotten. Inwardly she fumed and vowed afresh to turn the tables on the Kates and the Behags of this world and to show them a thing or two that would 'shock the breeks off them.'

Oh ay, her turn would come, indeed it would. The future held some purpose for her, meantime she felt better in the knowing that she hadn't risen to the bait dangled by Kate McKinnon. She had not succumbed to her usual rigid denials and above all, and most importantly to her at this time, she had conducted herself with dignity and had not given this awful McKinnon woman one jot of satisfaction over the question of herself and Captain Mac. Let them pant and drool and watch her through their spyglasses, let idle old Behag break her ankles – and maybe her neck as well – in her endeavours to find out what was going on in the lives of other people. When Elspeth's turn came, and indeed it was coming very soon, the old bitch would maybe lose her eyesight into the bargain when at last all was revealed . . . something – at this point she squeezed her fists together and closed her eyes – something not one of them would ever have bargained for in all the years of their gossiping existence . . .

Slochmhor hove into view. A spot of red burning high on each taut cheek, Elspeth stood up and removed herself from the bus, every muscle, every bone, bristling with pride and self-respect.

'Here, you forgot the fare!' Erchy yelled after her.

'My good man,' she intoned haughtily, 'this is not your day for the Glen Fallan run. Officially neither you nor your bus are here, therefore, officially, neither am I. I dislike people who say one thing and conveniently forget it when the question o' sillar arises, so take yourself and your disgraceful bus out o' my sight, you each spoil the landscape and do no good at all for the environment.'

With that she was off, scuttling towards Slochmhor's gate, her head high, her bony shoulders thrown back, paying no heed at all to Erchy's yelled insults concerning her state of meanness.

'Ach God!' Kate threw herself against Wullie and the pair of them erupted into guffaws of unrestrained mirth.

'Elspeth was aye a match for you any day, Erchy,' Kate gasped, wiping her streaming eyes and paying no heed to Erchy's oaths, which, in any case, were drowned out by the echoing roar of the engine as the bus zoomed through the narrow opening of Downie's Pass.

It was just past this point that they saw a pony and cart looming in the distance. As it drew closer, it soon proved to be Shamrock with Paddy at the reins and Dodie and Mamma ensconced in the back.

'Would you look at the old bugger!' Wullie cried, craning his neck to get a better view of the cart. 'Being driven home in style, no doubt wi' food in his belly and plenty o' sympathy inside his head.'

'And there's that bossy, big German wifie!' Kate added. 'A bit green about the gills but hale and hearty just the same. After me worrying about the old witch and goin' to all this bother to fetch her.'

Erchy exploded. '*You* went to all the bother! I'll have you know I have upset my whole afternoon's routine just to please you, Kate McKinnon! I have tholed cheek and insults and went hundreds o' miles out o' my way and I haveny even had my dinner yet!'

'Ach, stop havering,' Kate said calmly. 'I know fine you aye stop at old Meggie's or Aggie's on the way back from Croy. Meggie is aye good for a dram and a plate o' mince and tatties and Aggie's broth pot is never off the stove. And seeing you have come this far you may as well go on to Croft na Beinn. I've no' seen Nancy for a long time and I have some news to tell her that will bring the sparkle back to her eyes, for she's no' been too well this wee whilie back.'

Up until that point Erchy had had every intention of turning the bus and heading back the way he had come but the chance of a tea and pancake strupak at Nancy's homely table was too good an opportunity to miss – and if it was accompanied by some juicy piece of news so much the better. The Portvoynachan lot would have grown tired of waiting anyway and would have managed to make their way home without him.

With a fresh surge of vigour he blithely drove on to Croft na Beinn where Wullie and his mother quickly disembarked.

'You'll be in a hurry to get back to the harbour, Erchy,' Kate imparted with a sprite in her eye, 'so we'll no' keep you a minute longer. You've done your good deed for the day but then, I aye knew your heart was bigger than your head – though only just.'

Erchy's face fell, but he had his pride and would never for one moment push himself in where he wasn't wanted. Nevertheless, he was determined to salvage something from the wreckage of his day, but when he broached the subject of fares to Kate, adding something about the cost of fuel, she merely grinned broadly and told him smartly he could deduct it from the interest due on Tam's loan.

Erchy's face grew red, he gaped, Kate's eyes danced. 'Ay, my bonny man, there's no' much that goes past me – as you yourself have said often enough. I'm much the same as you in that respect – surely we've known one another long enough for you to realize that. But dinna fash yourself, Erchy, what I have to tell my Nancy will be common knowledge this time tomorrow. All you'll need is a wee bit patience and a good big pair o' willing lugs, and, as everybody knows, neither your nose nor your lugs have ever let you down yet, and for that, may the good Lord be thank-et.'

So saying, she took Wullie's arm and, chuckling, the pair of them went off to regale Nancy with the latest exciting news concerning the Clan McKinnon, leaving Erchy to make his dejected way back to Portcull and the empty harbour.

*   *   *

Croft Beag was Paddy's first port of call and Dodie gave a sigh of relief at being home. He had almost forgotten Wullie in the trauma of being stuck beside big, overpowering Mamma Jodl, who had made her disapproval of him quite plain by her scowls and her hanky held frequently to her nose. In his innocence Dodie had imagined that it was Curly's smells she objected to and as he saw his little croft coming into view he decided that Wullie was definitely the lesser of two evils. He climbed down gladly from the cart, away from Mamma, away from the rough Irishman with his leering smiles and sly eyes, and led away his precious lamb who had left his mark all over the cart, on the seat, on the floor, even on Mamma's shoes – though she had been so taken up with keeping her distance from the old eccentric she hadn't yet noticed the state of her footwear.

As Dodie reached his gate Paddy half rose up in his seat to flap his arms like wings and make hideous cackling noises, both of which actions were meant to represent Dodie's infamous cockerels.

Safely inside his gate, Dodie waited till the cart was moving away, then, with a great show of bravado, he yelled Paddy's name and when the Irishman twisted round to look, he held his fingers to his nose and waved them about, before fleeing as fast as his great, clumsy feet would allow up the path to his house, Curly gambolling and skipping behind him.

It was Mamma's turn next and she never imagined she could be so glad to see An Cala sitting so quiet and peaceful in its field overlooking the sea. Paddy brought the cart to a halt, Shamrock snickered and when Mamma got down he looked as if he was smiling as he felt the weight on his shafts lightening.

'I'll bid you good day, then, Missus.' Paddy nodded pleasantly. 'Unless of course you would care to invite me in for a cup.'

Mamma had to force herself to appear grateful for the lift but she couldn't bring herself to extend her gratitude any further than a rather gruff '*danke*', after which she made to take herself off.

'Wait, Missus!' Paddy's command was imperative; unwillingly

she turned round to meet his hostile eyes. 'Tis manners in these parts to be pleasant to your neighbours, ay, neighbours! We're as good as your like any day and if it hadny been for us saving your bacon you would still be wandering about like a tink on these damt moors!' He made a great attempt to control his temper and went on in quieter tones, 'It's no' much to ask, a cup o' tea in return for a favour granted. I'm your friend, Missus, and I'd never see you stuck. Rachel likes us tinks, she wouldny turn any one o' us away from her door, so what do you say, mavourneen? Just a minute to slake my thirst and then I'll be off.'

With poor grace Mamma acceded to his request, and while she was making the tea Paddy roamed restlessly around the kitchen, finally taking himself off to the parlour the minute her back was turned. It was in this room that he found what he was looking for and his eyes fairly gleamed at the sight. Rachel had three violins to her name, but it was her cherished Cremonese that she had brought with her to Rhanna. It reposed inside a very old but extremely beautiful leather case, given to her years ago by a man who had restored her violin to its former glory and who had been horrified to see such a precious instrument housed inside a cheap and ordinary case. It was at the beginning of Rachel's career and she hadn't been able to afford anything better. She had been overwhelmed by the gift and had treasured it ever since. Paddy ran his rough hands over the soft leather grain. He couldn't open it, and he hadn't the time to try and discover the whereabouts of the key, but it didn't matter, the time wasn't yet ripe – and old Mo's violin wasn't going anywhere – yet . . .

An odd little smile quirked the corners of Paddy's cruel mouth. 'I'll be back for ye,' he muttered, patting the case with calculated tenderness. 'By rights ye belong to me: the old man wasny in his right mind when he gave ye away to that conniving little gypsy, but we'll soon fix that. Ay, indeed we will.'

Mamma appeared in the doorway, suspicion on her face, but Paddy was immediately all smiles and charm and grateful for the tea which he drank down in one gulp before taking himself off with all haste.

As soon as he was out of sight Mamma sank down into a chair, kicked off her shoes and gave vent to an enormous yawn. Never, never, in the whole of her life, had she walked so far or been so humiliated; never had she met such strange people, eaten such peasant food, ridden home in such primitive style.

She ached, she burned, she stank – almost as badly as that dreadful old man who had accompanied her in the cart. She needed to wash herself, to change her clothes, to eliminate all signs of the most terrible hours she had ever spent – but first she had to have rest. It had all been too much for her, especially in the delicate state of health she was in.

With a weary sigh she rose out of her chair and dragged herself upstairs to creep between the sheets and give herself up to bliss, too exhausted to care that Jon wasn't there to worry and fuss over her and listen with all of his ears to her tales of woe and deprivation.

Rachel and Jon had had a very enjoyable time at Croft na Ard; Anton had been delighted to see his old friend again. The three of them had gone off to work in the fields till Babbie came home at dinnertime when they had laughed and talked and reminisced over a good Scottish meal of mince and tatties followed by apple pie and cream.

Jon broached the subject of the lack of a bathroom at An Cala, following it up rather tentatively with a request for his mother to use the facilities at Croft na Ard. Babbie and Anton had willingly agreed to the proposal though Babbie had laughingly added, 'Don't forget, I'm out all day and Anton is usually in the fields: sometimes the kitchen fire isn't lit till evening to heat the water, especially in the summer when quite often we just boil kettles on the stove and bathe in the zinc tub here in the kitchen.'

'Ah no,' smiled Jon, 'Mamma will never use the tub, that is the main reason we make our request to you to use your bathroom. My mother . . .' he searched for the right words, 'she is a woman of generous build. She would, perhaps, have difficulty climbing in and out of something she calls a big basin.'

Rachel grinned at this and she and Jon went home in the best of moods only to be greeted by an empty house and the sight of Mamma's equally empty shopping bag lying on a chair.

'She didn't get her apfelstrudel,' Rachel observed with a few quick gestures. 'In fact, she didn't get anything, her bag is completely empty – except' – she stared – 'for a few little hard balls of sheep's sharn.'

'Where *has* she been and what has she been up to?' Jon said with a frown. 'She isn't here, yet she must be, unless her bags and her coat and hat came home under their own steam.'

A quick search upstairs provided the answers. Jon came downstairs smiling. 'She is fast asleep like a baby. I think today my mother has had some adventures,' he sighed, 'and no doubt we'll hear all about it till we are deaf with her tales of woe.'

Rachel went to put on her apron. 'I'll make her an apple tart,' she decided in an odd burst of affection for her mother-in-law. 'It won't be the same as apfelstrudel but it's the next best thing. Babbie's apple pie has put me in the mood for baking, but don't expect too much, it's a long time since I guddled with pastry and I might have forgotten the art.'

She spent a busy afternoon baking tarts and scones and cooking a delicious evening meal. Her apple tarts were perfection, light and tangy with just a hint of nutmeg and cinnamon to add to the flavour, but when Mamma came stomping downstairs early in the evening she was in no mood for anything except to talk about her day's misfortunes.

Jon listened, he sympathized, he soothed, but when Rachel served Mamma with a tempting savoury tea and it was rejected after only a few mouthfuls, he frowned. When she pushed away the apple tart without tasting it at all he burst out, 'Mamma, Rachel has spent many hours making this meal for you, she made the apple tart specially, she . . .'

'It is not the apfelstrudel,' Mamma spoke heavily. 'The pastry, it looks heavy and I will not ruin my stomach with the stodge.'

She pushed back her chair, she got up and without another word she went to the stand in the hall to take down her coat and hat and don them before going back to the kitchen to announce,

'I go to your friend's house for the bath, I smell myself badly, the hot soak I need to have.'

Jon's face reddened. 'Mamma,' he said sternly, 'you can't go to Croft na Ard at this hour, Babbie and Anton will be at their evening meal, they work hard all day, they . . .'

But she was off, the door closing behind her firmly and loudly. 'I'm damned if I'll see her up the road!' Jon cried, for once in his life really angry at his mother's inconsideration.

Rachel set about clearing the table. Let the old witch stay away all night if she wanted! There was nothing at An Cala to occupy her anyway, she would only talk and talk, and rant and rave, and all about herself as usual. Rachel felt sorry for Anton and Babbie but glad that she and Jon would have the house to themselves, free to pursue their own pastimes and pleasures.

Mamma was only gone a short time. The house of Croft na Ard had been empty and deserted, there was no one in: she wouldn't get her bath after all, she would have to wash here in the kitchen, but not in the tub, never in the tub, she was a lady, she would not be humiliated, she would sponge herself down, she would be clean somehow!

Rachel disappeared into the parlour, glad to get away from Mamma and her ceaseless chatter. Even though it was just Jon and his mother left in the kitchen it was soon a hive of activity, with son running to do mother's bidding, stoking the fire, filling kettles, setting them to boil and laying out towels and soap and face flannels.

'And now, go,' Mamma ordered when everything was to her satisfaction and the curtains and blinds had been tightly drawn, the doors firmly locked.

Jon escaped gladly. In the softly lit parlour Rachel was burning incense, the room reeked with the sweet, evocative odour of jasmine, and she was playing oriental music on her little battery operated tape recorder. When he came through the door she went straight into his arms and they both swayed round the room in a dreamy silence. That afternoon Babbie had given Rachel red roses from her garden and she had woven them into her hair; the perfume of them filled Jon's nostrils. She was wearing a flimsy blouse with nothing underneath, her breasts were warm and soft against his chest. He forgot his mother, desire flooded his loins, he pressed himself hard against her and she responded by winding her arms round his neck and drawing his head down till his lips met with hers.

'Rachel,' he whispered against her hair, 'you are a temptress. I want you very badly, tonight you are lovelier than ever.'

Her kisses melted on his mouth. With a groan he buried his face in the creamy skin of her neck and took the ripe fullness of her breasts in his hands. She swayed and moved against him, his breath came quicker, they stopped dancing and gave themselves up to one another. His hand slid down to her thighs, he heard the soft intake of her breath, their limbs quickened and merged, their kisses became deeper, more demanding, more bruising than the one before, and then he opened her blouse and his lips found the hard, burning tips of her nipples.

Lost in passion, helpless with desire, they sank down on to the rug in front of the fire, forgetting everything and everybody in their heart-racing excitement. Her long, lithe legs captured his hips. He pushed up her skirt, undid his trouser zip . . . and at that precise moment Mamma appeared in the doorway, her head swaddled in towels, her body wrapped in a voluminous purple silk dressing gown with dragons luxuriantly embroidered on the back.

She stood there dumbfounded for a few brief moments, but soon found her tongue. 'Jon!' she cried, her voice hard with shock, deliberately using the admonishing tone she had used to him when, as a small boy, she had caught him out in some naughty act. 'I bathe, I turn my back only a short time but enough for my son to change himself into an animal of the field. Since your boytime I teach you the manners, the breeding, the respect, all these you have lost since your meeting up with this – this untamed, disrespectful child! I will not have it, Jon! She has turned you into a heathen!'

While she was ranting, Jon and Rachel were fixing their clothing, scrambling to their feet. Jon was breathing heavily in a mixture of frustration, receding passion and rage.

'Mamma!' he said furiously. 'Rachel and I are not committing a sin: we are married – remember? And it is our house; we love one another, I have been away from her for a long time and we haven't had much chance to be alone since I came home. We – I – thought you would take a long time to wash. You told me at least an hour . . .'

'So, I was too quick for you, eh, Jon?' Mamma said heavily. 'How could you do these things while I am in the next room! Was last night not enough for you? You have the noisy bed, all night long I hear the bedsprings creaking. I lie awake listening – creak! creak! creak! – and always there are the sighs and the moans and all the other sounds it is not nice for a woman of my age to hear!'

Rachel was livid. Her eyes were black, burning coals in the pallor of her face. Her hands curling into fists, she stared at the older woman and she wondered, had all that loud and raucous snoring of last night been a front? Had the old bitch deliberately pretended to be asleep when all the while she had been listening through the wall as hard as she could . . . ? Another thought struck Rachel: had this dreadful woman intentionally rushed through her toilet in order to creep and snoop through the house hoping to spring humiliation on Jon and herself?

Rachel's nostrils dilated, she could control herself no longer, her fingers were a blur of movement as she told Mamma just what she thought of her.

But it was all lost on Mamma Jodl: she hardly understood one single symbol of her daughter-in-law's sign language and merely snorted when at last Rachel's nimble fingers grew still.

'Pah!' Mamma snorted. 'All this flapping about with the hands, it is very undignified and also extremely tiring to watch. Why didn't you marry a girl who could speak with her mouth, Jon? Life would have been much simpler for us all.'

At that Rachel couldn't contain herself, how dare the old battle-axe speak about her as if she wasn't there? She looked as if she could easily kill her mother-in-law there and then. Every muscle in her body became tightly coiled, her black eyes were wild and dangerous, she looked like a leopard ready to spring and Jon, knowing that his wife was perfectly capable of striking out when thus enraged, made haste to intervene. But she shook him off, nothing or nobody was going to stop her now. The large, fat, ignorant old bugger she had inherited when she married Jon might not understand the deaf and dumb language but there was one sign that was universally recognized and, by God, she was going to let her have it! Rushing up to the other woman, she stuck her two fingers so forcibly into her face that Mamma had to move back a pace in order to avoid them being rammed up her nose.

The old lady could pretend obtuseness when it suited her but on this occasion, with the V-sign almost touching her eyeballs, she could do nothing but recognize it for what it was. Her mouth dropped open in utter dismay while Rachel, breathless and beside herself with fury, just kept on poking her two fingers in the air while she glared threateningly into the older woman's eyes.

Jon's rancour against his mother, for causing yet another scene, was in no way diminishing, but when he looked from Rachel's ferocious young face to Mamma's flabbergasted expression he suddenly saw the funny side of the situation and fell back in his seat in a fit of laughing, quite unable to stem the flow of mirth once it had started. It was more a nervous reaction than anything else. Jon wanted only harmony in his life, and he especially wanted to enjoy this precious holiday on Rhanna with his wife, but his mother's disruptive presence was making the possibilty of any sort of pleasure more remote by the minute, and his laughter was tinged with an odd sort of hysterical desperation.

For Rachel, the sound of her husband's merriment was the last straw. She had to get away, get out from under the feet of both mother and son, anywhere, everywhere, just as long as she could flee this house that had, in the space of just a night and a day, become a hell instead of the haven she had always considered it to be.

With an odd little half-sob she ran to the hall and wrenched her coat from the stand. Jon was at her back, pleading with her to either stay or let him go with her but again she shook him off and ran from the house, struggling into her coat as she went.

She had no clear notion of where she was going, her feet carried her along swiftly, pounding the short turf of the clifftop, slithering and sliding on the loose, sandy soil of one of the many sheep tracks that led down to the shore.

A fresh, cool breeze blew up from the sea, the clouds were scudding across the sky so that the moon sailed in and out of purple-grey cumulus and fitfully cast its silver-white light over the great grey-bellied reaches of the Sound of Rhanna.

Bitterness boiled in Rachel's breast as she hurried along. She hated Mamma, she hated Jon: he had laughed when he should have been supportive and helpful, he had never stood up to that monstrous old bitch he called mother. All along she had smothered rather than mothered him and he had gone along with it till now it had come to this, an open rivalry between the two women in his life for his love and attention. Well, he could have Mamma if that was what he wanted, she'd had enough, she wouldn't stay in that house another day. Tonight she would pack her bags, tomorrow she would go and stay with Ruth till the steamer came on Friday. There was nothing to keep her here now, nothing . . .

The wind tugged her hair, pulled at her coat; the sigh of wide and lonely places surged in her ears; the beat and roar of the ocean filled her senses.

Dazedly she paused in her flight and gazed around her. She was on windswept Burg Bay, to her left the cliffs rose up, black and sheer against the glowering night sky. The towering fangs of the reefs, those grey, forbidding old men of the sea, hunched themselves into eerie shapes and seemed to gaze moodily down at the water restlessly swirling round their feet. Moonshadows wavered on the sand, flitting in and out of the rocks according to the whim of the wind-tossed clouds until the moon was obliterated completely by banks of blackness and it was dark, dark, lonely, desolate, but complete and magnificent in its wild, hushed, secretive whisperings with only a seabird's lone cry to intrude into the solitude.

But not so dark – up there – on the cliffs – a light shone like a beacon through the velvet night gloom, beckoning, signalling, guiding . . .

Then she knew why she mustn't leave Rhanna: someone up there needed her, for his sake she had to stay. She sensed loneliness, sadness, fear, all mingling with strength and power and love of life. She had to go to him: he was calling, calling. In her heart she could hear his voice; in her soul she could hear his music.

Again her feet took wing . . . and this time they weren't running away.

Chapter Fifteen

Rachel entered Tigh na Cladach via the back porch and without hesitation went straight to the softly lit sitting room. There she found Otto sprawled in a chair by the fire, deathly pale, his pain-filled eyes black and dazed so that at first he wasn't aware that she had entered the room.

'Otto!' Her heart cried his name. A few quick strides took her to his side and as she stooped to gaze into his face she knew why she had experienced these moments of pain and poignancy whenever they had been quiet and alone together. He was a very sick man: this big, wonderful Austrian, with his marvellous physique, his vigour, his delight of life, was dying.

All along she had sensed it – the shadow of death had been there in his eyes even while he had talked and laughed and played his spellbinding music. She had known, but even so, now that the moment of truth was here, the knowledge hit her like a sledgehammer.

'Rachel.' His mouth struggled to form her name. He seemed to come back from a very long way and his hand came up to enclose hers. 'Pills – in the bedroom – get them – quickly please.'

She didn't remember running upstairs but quite suddenly it seemed she was standing in the bedroom with its rose-sprigged walls and camped ceilings, its rose-coloured bed light shining down on the big, soft feather bed.

Frantically she gazed around, blinded at first by anxiety and fear, then her eye fell on the bedside cabinet – nothing there except a volume of Burns' poems, another of Robert Louis Stevenson's *Kidnapped*. But wrenching open the little drawer she saw them, a motley collection of brown pill bottles, full, half-full and some empty.

Her hands shook slightly as she picked them up and looked at the labels. He had asked for pills but which ones? Wildly she wondered if she should take them all down to him but then she remembered his pain and seizing the one containing morphine she raced down to the kitchen where she filled a glass with water and went back into the sitting room.

Taking the bottle from her trembling grasp he gulped down two of the pills and sat back to look at her. 'In a little while I will be better,' he told her breathlessly. She sat there with him, quiet and still by the fire, her mind strangely calm, her hands, those slender, delicate, soothing hands, wherein lay a power that could not be denied, placed cool and tender upon his clammy brow.

Gradually he relaxed, pain departed, he took several deep breaths and taking her face in his hands he turned it towards him till he could look deep and straight into her eyes.

'You know, don't you, *liebling*?'

She nodded; he gave a funny little half-smile. 'From the beginning I felt you were different from anyone I had ever known. You have the sixth sense, the eyes that see deep and clear beyond the soul. I have been ill for a long time, Rachel. I have the treatment, the spells in hospital till I am sick and tired of it all and want only to die in peace – but first – I must come home to my grandmother's island, the beloved lands whose memories take her sweetly and serenely through all the years of her exile.'

He told her then what he had told Kate that morning – of his connections with the Clan McKinnon, of Magnus his maternal grandfather, his plans for a clan gathering – and of things he hadn't told Kate – his determination to visit the island where it had all began for him and where, in a spiritual way, it would end for him.

'I will go back to Vienna to pass my final days. But here,' he placed a clenched hand over his heart, 'this part of me will remain behind on Rhanna. In my boytime I hear the ocean, I walk the hills, I smell the perfume of the moors, all through my grandmother's voice, I wasn't to know that coming here would capture my heart for all time and never let go of it, no matter how far I might travel when the time comes for me to go away.'

She made no gesture, her heart was too full for her even to attempt to let him know how she felt. A time like this needed words and those she could never utter. She filled the minutes with practical actions, piling the fire high with peats, placing his slippers on the fender to warm, going through to the kitchen to pour milk for Vienna, rolling newspapers into twists for the morning fire, finally making cocoa, which he and she drank in an oddly tranquil silence.

At one point she knelt by him and placed his slippers on his feet. His hand came out to touch the top of her dark head. '*Liebling*,' he said huskily, 'something brought you here tonight – when I needed you, you came. Today I learn that your husband has come home to you – but – would it be selfish of me to ask . . . would you stay with me for a little while?'

For answer she curled herself at his feet and clasped her hands round her knees. The eyes that gazed into the fire were big and dark with the pain that burned in her heart. Her beloved stranger had touched her life only briefly but she knew that the strange sweet power he had over her spirit transcended the bonds of flesh, the passage of time. He would remain with her forever, long after he was dead and gone and only the voice of his living soul spoke to her in the eternal winds blowing over the land.

For Otto Klebb was life, a life that would flourish beyond the grave. His magic, his music, his memory, would remain behind for always and at the thought of that a wonderful sense of peace flooded her being. And the peace remained with her for the rest of that evening spent with him. They felt no need to communicate, each was content in the knowing that the other was there, a harmony of everything that was the essence of understanding and love in the human consciousness.

The hands of the clock on the mantelpiece were at two a.m. when she finally rose to take her leave. She wanted to help him upstairs to bed but some of the old vigour was there in his voice when he held her close in his arms and said into her hair, 'My *liebling*, there are some things I must do on my own, going to bed is one of them, dying is still a good way off for me and to have you there in the intimacy of the bedroom might prove to be a temptation I could not resist.' He held her away from him to look into her eyes. 'We could not live with ourselves if we betrayed what we feel for one another with the weakness of the flesh. I make a vow to you, when my dying time is here, when I pass over to the valleys of the unknown, I will carry with me cherished memories of a young girl who is more to me than flesh. You are of my soul, Rachel *liebling*, and, no matter how hard it is for me to touch you without possessing you, I will not tarnish what we have found together on this earth by giving in to the needs of my body.'

Her eyes were dark and shiny with unshed tears, her heart knew the beauty and pureness of his words. Helplessly she nodded and kissed him gently on his brow.

He smiled. 'We have many things to do, you and I. I have some months left to me and I want to fill them with the knowledge of your world. You will teach me your sign language so that I can understand all the things you want to say to me, I see many expressions in your eyes but not enough to let me know what is in your heart. And now . . .' his mouth nuzzled hers, 'you must return to your husband, I will not be the cause of enmity between you – so go quickly, before all my good resolutions crumble into the ashes of meaningless talk.'

Unwillingly she let go of his hands. Every fibre in her, every cell in her body, begged her to stay and surrender her love to him. She knew her weaknesses only too well, one encouraging gesture from him would be her undoing, and so she went away quickly as he had bid, into the loneliness of wind-washed night where the sad murmurs of empty places found an echo in a heart that was full to bursting with emotion.

She was cold by the time she reached An Cala. Jon had left a lamp burning in the hall, the soft halo of light only served to emphasize the surrounding darkness and she made her way upstairs swiftly and silently.

The coolness of the sheets embraced the coldness of her flesh but there was no comfort to be had from Jon. This time it was he who kept his back turned on her. His quiet breathing told her nothing: he could have been asleep, or half-asleep, or wide awake, listening for her coming home, whichever way, she knew he would make no move towards her that night and the silence of the room enshrouded her, with not even a grunt or a snore from Mamma's room to break the stillness.

For a long time she lay thinking about Otto, her feverish thoughts taking her round and round in endless circles. Then she remembered his strength, his stoic acceptance of what was to be, the beautiful words he had used to describe his feelings for her, now and hereafter. The tension left her limbs, leaving her weak; peace once again flooded her being, making her strong. She sighed and pressed herself into Jon's warmth. He half turned and put his arms around her and in the comforting reassurance of that familiar embrace her fears melted like snowflakes and she was soon asleep.

The news concerning Otto's connection with the McKinnons flashed round the island. In a very short time every corner buzzed with the juiciest piece of gossip to have hit Rhanna for ages. In cottage, croft, barn, biggin, shop, shieling, anywhere people could meet, tongues wagged, heads nodded and a most enjoyable time was had by all.

'Hmph! The McKinnons again!' Old Sorcha expostulated when the news seeped through to her head via her deaf aid. 'Why is it they get all the attention? And that Kate! There will be no living wi' her. She'll steep herself in airs and graces and go about behaving as if she was the only body wi' a clan to her name.' In her excitement she turned up her hearing aid so that everybody in the vicinity was just about deafened by the high-pitched wailing noise it emitted. Face red with ire, Sorcha continued, 'Do you mind that time, last year, when that nice wee English wifie looked to Kate for information about her McKinnon connections? And Kate, the sly besom, telling her all those lies about being a Mull McKinnon when all the time she belongs to that bunch o' cut-throats over on Uist?

'She's just no' worthy o' all the attention paid to her when here is me, old enough and able enough to mind o' things that happened in the last century! It's no' fair! It's just no' fair!'

'Here, I'll thank you to keep a hold on your tongue,' Todd the Shod interposed with an aggrieved air. 'My mother was a Uist McKinnon and a finer branch o' the line I have yet to meet. They never cut anybody's throats, maybe just punched each other's noses now and again at a ceilidh, but nothing worse than that. Here,' his ruddy face brightened, 'I've just reminded myself, seeing as how my mother was a McKinnon it means I'll be legally entitled to go to this grand Clan Gathering that Mr Otto is planning on. I must get Mollie to mend that wee hole in the back o' my kilt for it will be a Highland dress affair, and even though mine's a McDonald tartan I canny let the side down wi' holey pleats.'

Todd wasn't the only one on the island to rake up a convenient McKinnon connection that would enable attendance at Otto's Ceilidh, as it was quickly becoming known. Everyone, it seemed, had a McKinnon relative buried in the family closet, and even though bringing them out for an airing might risk the uncovering of some unsavoury skeletons, it was a risk that was considered worthwhile in the event.

'Otto doesny know what he's letting himself in for,' Fergus predicted dourly. 'Every bugger wi' a bit McKinnon tartan to his name will lay claim to clan rights – the hall hasny yet been built to accommodate them all.'

'What about you?' Kirsteen said mischievously. 'Have you got any McKinnons lurking in your cupboards?'

He glowered at her and she burst out laughing. 'Och, c'mon, Fergie, just think, if you could pull a long-lost Uncle McKinnon out o' your hat you might just get to attend Otto's Ceilidh and would be free to drink schnapps till it was coming out your ears!'

Fergus still had a sinking feeling every time he thought about 'the night of the schnapps'. His pride had been badly bruised at the very idea of being 'drunk and incapable', as Behag would have put it, and the realization that he had been put to bed by Lachlan, Mark James, and their womenfolk, was enough to bring him out in a cold sweat whenever he pictured it in his mind. He was therefore not at all amused by Kirsteen's teasing remarks and inwardly vowed to get his own back on Otto 'one o' these days' by making him drink whisky till it was coming out *his* ears.

When all the fuss and talk reached the hairy lugs of old Magnus of Croy he was inclined to the belief that it was all 'just a lot o' exaggeration', but when Kate and Tam came to see him with the news that he was 'the grandfather o' a very fine foreign gentleman', and hastily filled him in with the facts, he turned very pale and collapsed into the nearest chair.

'Be getting me a dram from the sideboard' he instructed with great dignity. With alacrity Tam went to carry out his instructions, pouring a generous amount of whisky for everyone 'by way o' a wee celebration'.

Kate hugged herself at the look on the old man's face when little by little the news sunk in and he sat back to say huskily, 'I never kent that my Sheena went away from Rhanna carrying my bairn – and now this – our grandson, after all these years, I canny rightly take it all in and it will be a wee whilie before I can really believe it's true.'

'You'll believe it when you see him,' Kate assured him happily. 'He is a big, fine, bonny chiel wi' a good McKinnon face on him and a talent for music that was surely passed on to him by his very own grandfather. Ach, just you wait, Magnus, when you meet him you'll know he's your flesh and blood, for the bond has aye been there between you. He was very close to his Grannie Sheena, ever since he could understand what she was talking about she told him about you and about this island. Such bonny stories, I had a wee greet to myself they were so sad, and you and he will just talk and talk till you are blue in the face and fair gaspin' for breath the pair o' you.'

* * *

And she was right. The day that Mark drove Otto to Croy Beag in Thunder was one that would forever live in the minds of both grandfather and grandson.

It was a warm, balmy day, the sea was blue beyond the cliffs, the little bays sparkled with sun diamonds. Tiny inshore islets were alive with basking seals; a school of dolphins arched through the water, their glistening bodies riding the waves with grace and delight; gannets plummeted and soared; rows of cormorants stood on the reefs, drying their wings in the crystal cool breezes blowing over the ocean.

Nearer to hand, cows grazed the machair; chickens clucked and poked; lapwings rose up from the heather uttering their unmistakable musical alarm calls; burns tinkled down from the hills; a tabby kitten pranced and danced after the heath moths that flitted about from one tiny wildflower to the next – and from a thatched white cottage whose windows and doors were painted a cheerful bright red, peat smoke rose up into the sky and strains of fiddle music floated out to join the rest of the music of a perfect summer's day.

The two men stood listening, Mark in appreciation, Otto in wonder, his strong, handsome face rather pale in a mixture of anticipation and apprehension.

'My friend,' he said after a while, 'would you come in with me? The occasion, it is of great moment, I am not sure I can handle it on my own.'

But Mark shook his dark head and placed an encouraging hand on the other's shoulder. 'No, Otto, I'll bide out here for a while. You've waited a long time for this moment and it's only right that it should belong to you and old Magnus. I guarantee you'll only be in the house a few minutes and you'll think you've aye belonged – and think o' this – your grandmother used to come here – her feet have trod the path you see before you. Go along it and look at it all as if you're seeing it through her eyes, and when you see the old man for the first time, remember how he and your grandmother loved one another, how they were parted with love binding them over the miles and the years. If you think you feel strange, just remember how it must be for him, believing that he had no family left in the world till you came to the island. Everybody loves Magnus, you will too, and he'll welcome you with open arms.'

He was right: no sooner had Otto stepped over the threshold than Magnus was up on his feet, his wonderful blue eyes misty with emotion as he beheld his grandson for the first time – a tall, handsome man, darkly bearded, broad shouldered, standing in a ray of sunlight spilling in through the door.

'Son,' he murmured and going stiffly forward he clasped the big man to his bosom with such a strength of love that Otto found himself returning the gesture, his heart full to bursting in the knowledge that, at last, he had come into the heart and the home of 'Grannie Sheena's man'.

'Son,' Magnus said again, standing back to gaze at the powerful face, the magnetic eyes of his grandson, his beguiling, one-toothed smile coming readily to his nut-brown face. 'Come you in and sit you down. First we will have a strupak and then we will talk – ay – by God and we will.'

Otto remembered Mark and looked beyond the small-paned window, but Mark had taken himself off on a walk over the moors and was already just a speck in the heat-hazed distance.

An hour passed on timeless wings. The old man's house was a wonderland of knowledge and learning. Dusty shelves were filled to overflowing with books; reams of poetry, music, songs, all written and composed by Magnus himself, spilled from every conceivable space. A tiny enclosure, which Magnus proudly referred to as his 'music room', housed an ancient piano, an accordion, two fiddles, a set of kettle drums and another of bagpipes. 'Though I havny the breath to play them much these days,' he explained regretfully, 'only sometimes, on a summer's night when the moor has that strange sort o' bewitchment about it, I canny resist taking a wee walk over to Baldy's Burn where I can sit and play my pipes in peace.'

Otto was enchanted by everything he saw, touched and heard, and the hour was too short for the pair to say all that they wanted to say to one another.

Mark returned from his walk and gratefully gulped down two

cups of tea, and then it was time to go with many promises from Otto to come back at every available opportunity.

Otto was tired by the time he and Mark reached the five-barred gate, and when he climbed into Thunder he sat back in the ancient leather seat and closed his eyes.

Mark glanced at him. Was it his imagination, or had the big Austrian grown a bit thinner since coming to Rhanna? He certainly seemed fit enough and his zest for life was gaining strength the more he familiarized himself with the people of the island, but there was something about his face, some slight change, that Mark found rather disquieting.

But he made no comment till they were at the gate of the shorehouse when he turned to Otto and said lightly, 'I'm about to let poor old Thunder have her summer siesta. I'm a bicycle man during the longer days,' he smiled, 'much to the disapproval of old Behag who thinks it's undignified for a minister to go fleeing about the place on a bike. The point I'm trying to make is this, it does my old motor no good at all to be laid up for too long and you would be doing me a favour if you would take her off my hands and keep her on the road for me. She's had a complete overhaul by one o' the more mechanically minded village lads and shouldn't let you down too badly. It would mean you could go and visit Magnus whenever you have a mind so all in all, everybody would be happy.'

Otto looked gratefully at Mark. He didn't fancy Erchy's infamous bus and had been wondering how he would make the difficult journey to Croy Beag without transport. He knew that this 'man o' God' had deliberately made the acceptance of Thunder easy for him and he said quietly, 'I would be honoured to have the use of your car and I'll take good care of her, I promise you that.'

Mark grinned. 'She has a mind o' her own – she'll take care o' you in her own particular way, it might no' always be what you have in mind for she can be gey unpredictable but at least you'll have some fun – and frustrations – getting to know her.'

And so it was settled. Otto, who had hitherto kept rather a low profile, never venturing very far from Burg Bay, soon became ubiquitous. Wherever he went he was invited to partake of strupaks and his company was eagerly sought at ceilidhs and other such social gatherings. He soon felt himself to be an accepted member of the island community and became a familiar sight driving along the roads in Thunder.

One or two of the islanders thought that they had seen him somewhere before but couldn't be sure where and when, if indeed they had seen him at all, but Barra McLean, who all along had puzzled over Otto's identity, went home one day to look through the collection of records that she had brought with her from Glasgow. She hadn't played them for a long time, simply because there was no electricity supply in her house to work her record player, which meant that it had lain at the back of a cupboard gathering dust. She had soon found what she was looking for and she sat back on her heels, staring at the face of 'the foreign stranger' on one of the record sleeves – younger looking to be sure, but the black hair and beard, the riveting eyes, were unmistakable just the same.

'Karl Gustav Langer,' she whispered, 'at last, I know who you are.'

She felt awed, honoured to think that such a great man had come to Rhanna to live among its people – and more – that the very same man was a McKinnon with Hebridean blood running proud and strong in his veins. She realized that, for all the obvious reasons, he wanted to remain anonymous, and she vowed to herself there and then that, as far as she was concerned, his secret was safe for as long as he wanted it to be.

So Otto went on his way undiscovered, delighting in his freedom, meeting people who had only been names to him before. One of these was Shona McLachlan, only daughter of McKenzie o' the Glen, who helped her husband run his veterinary practice at Mo Dhachaidh, the old house which had once belonged to Biddy McMillan, a fondly remembered character who had nursed the island population for most of her life.

The surgery was quiet when Otto went there with Vienna, who

had worried him with some rather strange behaviour of late. At the sound of the bell, Shona came out into the hall, tall, slender, attractive, her mane of auburn hair tied back with a black velvet ribbon, her amazingly blue eyes shining with interest in her fine-featured face. She knew Otto at once, having seen him many times passing Mo Dhachaidh in Thunder, but this was the first face to face meeting and, holding out her hand, she introduced herself.

He couldn't keep the admiration out of his eyes, this was unmistakably Fergus McKenzie's daughter – that proud tilt of her head, the same fearless eyes, the way she had of carrying herself, the same quizzical half-smile at the corners of her mouth, the dimpled cleft in the middle of her firm little chin.

As they stood there, a mini tornado in the shape of five-year-old Ellie Dawn McLachlan, burst out of one door in the hall and in through another, a few seconds later popping her head out to say 'hallo' to Otto before disappearing once more.

Shona smiled. 'My daughter, the eldest, the other is only two but already she bosses her brother about something terrible.'

Otto nodded. 'Children, they are a joy. Myself . . .' he held up the basket he was carrying, 'I only have a cat, she adopted me when I first arrived and now she will not leave my side. But she is unwell, her behaviour is very peculiar, she mopes in the house, she hides in cupboards, she scratches up the cushion in her bed, she makes hideous wailing noises, she eats like a horse and now she will not eat at all. I thought perhaps your husband could have the examination of her.'

Shona lifted the cat out of the basket. Gently she pressed the soft belly and laughed. 'You can save yourself the bother and the expense of seeing Niall: your cat is having kittens, that's all. Her time is very near and that is why she is looking for a quiet place to give birth.'

Otto stared. 'But she never leaves the house, she is a home cat, she only goes out when it is strictly necessary!'

Shona's eyes twinkled. 'Indeed, that is why she is pregnant, it must have been a necessity for her to sneak out on the tiles for a clandestine meeting with her suitor – probably Murdy

McKinnon's big tom, he's very charming and persuasive and has fathered umpteen generations of cats.'

Otto threw back his head and gave vent to his deep, booming laugh. Niall came out of his surgery at the sounds of merriment and the three of them stood chatting till Otto decided it was time to go home on a matter of great urgency, namely the birth of Vienna's kittens.

'You must come to the McKinnon Clan Gathering,' was his parting shot. 'Everyone else seems to be pulling McKinnons willy nilly out of their hats so you must do the same. It doesn't matter if they have been dead and buried for hundreds of years, your claim will still be valid. I have decided to hold my gathering at the end of July, so that gives you ample time to produce something reasonably suitable. Bring your parents too – I know Fergus will want to pay me back for all that schnapps I made him drink and Lachlan must be there to keep order.'

When the door had closed on him, Shona and Niall looked at one another. 'I can see now why the island is fascinated by him,' was Niall's verdict. 'The magnetism of the man is unmistakable and he is also very persuasive.' He took her arm and kissed the tip of her nose. 'Let us repair to the kitchen for a good hot cuppy and over it we can rake up our dead relatives – figuratively speaking, of course. We'll see what we can come up with in the shape o' some poor old ghost who is just hanging around waiting for us to discover his McKinnon connections!'

Bit by bit, Otto became well known to everyone and it wasn't long before he was being hailed as *Mac nan Èilean*, which in Gaelic means Son of the Island and was one of the greatest accolades he could ever receive since it was normally only born and bred islanders who were bestowed with Gaelic titles of such a fond nature.

At every opportunity he visited his grandfather till it seemed the two had known one another all of their lives. Together they composed songs and sat in the music room playing the treasured collection of musical instruments – Otto the ancient piano, Magnus the fiddle, and sometimes the bagpipes out there in the open moors, much to Otto's enchantment.

He also took his grandfather to Tigh na Cladach where a ceilidh had been arranged. It proved to be a memorable musical evening. Rachel, Jon and Lorn played together on their fiddles, and were soon joined by old Magnus on his, his silvery white head a startling contrast to the three dark young heads close by.

Mark James sang 'Song of Rhanna' in his rich baritone voice. The words, composed by him, had been set to a poignantly beautiful tune of Rachel's making. Three years ago it had been something of a hit in the music world and every time an island wireless was turned on the strains of the song had soared forth till very soon it was on everybody's lips.

And now Mark James stood in Otto's sitting room, looking not in the least 'minister-ish' in an open-necked blue shirt and cord slacks, his ruggedly handsome face serious and just a little sad as the words soared forth:

> Take me back where I belong,
> Where the skylark sings his song,
> And the peace of island life is all around.
> Where the people raise a hand,
> And there's a welcome in the land,
> And honest, friendly faces can be found . . .
> Take me home, oh, take me home,
> For I no longer want to roam,
> My heart is yearning for the hills, the glens,
> For the sea's tumultuous roar,
> For the spume upon the shore,
> For the mist that veils the corries on the bens . . .

'*Wunderbar!*' Otto applauded in delight and went immediately to the piano to pick up the tune. The others took up their fiddles, everyone began to sing, and very soon 'Song of Rhanna' became a symphony of words and music that just went on and on because no one wanted the uplifting experience ever to end.

But then came a pause in proceedings when the merrymakers sat back to rest and partake of a well-earned drink.

From a corner of the room Jon watched Rachel and Otto. There was something between the two that he couldn't quite fathom, it was as if they shared some secret that no one else knew of. She was very attentive to him, he equally of her, yet not once did they touch or even communicate very often, but each glance, every quiet smile, held more meaning than any physical contact ever could.

Suspicion and jealousy smote Jon to the quick. He had been married to Rachel for almost seven years yet he was still besotted by her. He was only too aware of the power she wielded over men, wherever she went they surrounded her in admiring droves and little wonder, hers was a dark and fiery beauty with her tumbling mass of jet black hair, her flashing dark eyes, her superb body and her long, shapely legs. All that, together with her intensely passionate nature, was a combination of physical and mental attraction that few men could resist, and Jon often felt that he was perhaps too tame and quiet for a young girl of such vitality. He was in his forties, old enough to be her father, but Rachel had never minded that – in fact – now that he came to think of it, she always got on well with older men and Herr Otto Klebb must be nearer fifty than forty.

Jon thought back to that night she had run from the house after the row with his mother. She hadn't returned till the early hours of morning and next day when he had challenged her she had admitted quite frankly that she had gone to visit Otto. After that he had noticed a distinct change in her: she was withdrawn and distant, she went off on long, lone walks, she didn't play her violin as often as she used to and when he spoke to her about it she just looked at him with smouldering fathomless eyes and turned away from him without explanation of any sort.

Not even Mamma's continued presence, her interference in the running of the home, and her loud and frequent complaints seemed to affect Rachel any more, and Jon's thoughts would turn to the vague hints and innuendoes concerning his wife and Otto, that he had only half listened to on his return to Rhanna.

Not that Rachel was any less loving towards him, in fact their love-making was more sensuous, more wonderful than it had ever been, but always there was Otto. She went to visit him as frequently as she dared and quite often accompanied him to Croy Beag to visit his grandfather.

She had been instrumental in organizing this ceilidh, gathering together the best musical talent in the village to entertain both Otto and Magnus. She had been adamant about not inviting Mamma. 'She will just want to talk about herself in that loud voice of hers,' she had indicated quite plainly to Jon, 'and that is the last thing I want at this ceilidh. She hasn't met Otto yet and will only monopolize him all night, and I'm also afraid that she might recognize him as Karl Langer and let the whole world know.'

To say that Mamma wasn't pleased at this decision would be putting it too mildly. She had told Rachel she was mean, petty, selfish; she thought only of herself, her needs, her desires; she cared nothing for a sick old woman who was a virtual outsider in this small-minded community with its gossip, its sly sneers, its unfriendliness.

Rachel merely listened to all this without so much as a bat of an eye before calmly turning on her heel and walking out of the room, leaving Jon to console his mother as best he could. He finally hit on the only solution he could think of, that of suggesting she could go over to Anton and Babbie's for the evening, and rushed to Croft na Ard next morning to guiltily tell them the news.

They had received his rather garbled explanation with admirable poise and so Mamma had been delivered to their doorstep late that afternoon, complete with a pack of cards, which she loved to play and could never get Rachel interested in, a quantity of cold ham for her tea because she was afraid of the 'stodgy' Scottish food, and her soap bag and talcum powder, since she might as well avail herself of 'the soak' while the opportunity presented itself.

In truth, Jon was glad that his mother wasn't at the ceilidh – he knew she would have talked too long and too loudly about herself, as Rachel had said. As it was, it had been an exceptional evening and he had enjoyed it, but now, seeing his wife and Otto so attuned to one another in every way, he was wishing that he hadn't come either and he turned away from the sight of them, his sensitive face pensive, his brown eyes bewildered and hurt.

He wasn't the only one to see that there was something going on between Otto and Rachel, Ruth too watched and wondered, and as the evening wore on all her former suspicions returned with renewed force. She hadn't seen nearly so much of her old friend as she had hoped, when Rachel came to Fàilte it was almost as if she did so more from a sense of duty than from a real desire to visit, but her pleasure in seeing the children was as genuine as ever. She brought them small gifts, she played with them and entertained them in her own inimitable way, but somehow she didn't have nearly so much to say to Ruth as she used to and after a while she would make some excuse and rush away as if someone or something far more exciting awaited her.

'She's frightened you might start asking awkward questions,' Lorn said when Ruth broached the subject. 'She knows you only too well and doesn't want to be forced into a corner.'

'And just what do you mean by that, Lorn McKenzie?' Ruth flashed at him, tossing her fair hair back from her angry little face. 'What awkward questions would I ask? And why would I force her into a corner?'

'Ruthie,' Lorn said with a sigh. 'You know full well what I mean. Rachel and you are like sisters, you can almost read one another's minds. She knows that you were suspicious about her and Otto, she's aware that there has been talk and she just doesn't want to hear you lowering yourself to the ranks of the island gossips, that's all.'

'Oh, that's all, is it?' Ruth returned tearfully. 'Well, she doesny know me as well as she thinks she does, I would never stoop as low as Behag or Elspeth, or any o' the other scandalmongers o' this place! I'll admit I thought she was growing a bit too fond of Otto but Jon's home now and all that's over and done with!'

But now Ruth wasn't so sure – she saw what Jon saw, she

thought what Jon thought – she glanced at him and noticed the flush of humiliation staining his thin face and her heart went out to him. She and he had been through all this once before; Lorn had come back to her, more loving, more devoted than he had ever been, but would Rachel ever be truly Jon's? Could that exciting, beautiful, restless creature ever truly be any man's one and only love?

A sudden burst of gypsy music filled the room, Rachel had seized her violin and she was playing in a fever of wild abandon, her black hair falling over her face, her dark eyes shining in passionate acknowledgment of music, and love and life.

Her roving, mischievous glance fell on Ruth. She smiled; Ruth didn't return the smile, instead she pretended not to see it and turned away from it as if it was a wicked thing unworthy of response.

Rachel didn't notice, her smiles didn't reach her heart, she only played her violin to cover up for Otto who had gone upstairs to take the pills that would ease the spasms of pain that had suddenly seized him.

The minutes passed. All the attention was focused on her, her flying fingers, the evocative, carefree tunes spilling effortlessly out. When Otto came back, her bursting lungs let go of the air she had held in while she waited for him. He threw her a glance of reassurance together with a slight nod, signifying there was nothing to be afraid of.

She smiled at him, she wanted to take him in her arms and soothe away his hurt and his fears. Two people in the room saw the meaningful glances and they each felt sick at heart and terribly alone in their doubts and worries about the future.

Chapter Sixteen

It was official! Captain Mac was moving in with Elspeth! Bob the Shepherd, who owned a fine new van that he had bought from a win on the football pools, was there at the gate of Elspeth's cottage, helping Captain Mac move in his few bits and pieces of possessions.

The old shepherd was wearing a grim expression on his weatherbeaten countenance because never, never, had he imagined that any man, far less one of Mac's intelligence, could sign away his freedom in such a rash manner and to that sour-faced cailleach into the bargain.

Bob had never allowed himself to 'fall into a woman's clutches', as he put it. When his win on the pools had become common knowledge, half the spinsters on the island had tried to ingratiate themselves into his favours but he was having none of that and had soon sent them packing with a few choice words.

The prospect of marriage had never entered his head until the advent of 'Aunt Grace' Donaldson on to the island, but she had gone and wed herself to Old Joe whose death last autumn had left the way clear for Bob. But out of respect for Joe they had decided to wait 'a whilie' and now the old shepherd was impatiently waiting for her to say the word. He had never met a woman like Grace: she was an excellent cook, she kept her home spick and span, yet she liked to see a man smoking his pipe and enjoying a dram. Her sense of humour was frank and down to earth, she never put on airs and graces for anybody, and more importantly, she was a warm-hearted, kindly little soul with a way about her of making a man feel he was the most wonderful being that the world had ever produced, yet she never cloyed or clung or did any of the things that other women of Bob's experience were inclined to and he could hardly wait to leave his lonely biggin on the slopes of Ben Machrie and move with her to the fine house he had bought for her some time ago.

Ay, Grace was a woman any man would want in his home, but that Elspeth was a different kettle of fish altogether with her vinegary nature, her razor-sharp tongue and an inclination to cleck and gossip about everybody's business except her own.

Bob was not the only one to hold these views. In general, the men of the island were flabbergasted to think that any man in his right mind could willingly lay himself bare to the dangers of such an arrangement – and 'wi' that greetin' faced cailleach too.'

'She'll chew him up and spit him out in wee pieces,' said Tam in disgust. 'Thon poor man o' hers led a dog's life and was aye glad to get back to sea just to get away from her endless nagging.'

'Ay, I mind o' the poor bugger drinkin' himself senseless just so's he could sleep away the hours on dry land,' nodded Jim Jim solicitously, even though he'd had plenty of altercations with the deceased Hector in his lifetime.

'It wasny all Elspeth's fault,' Robbie dared to say uncomfortably. 'Hector aye had a drouth on him for strong drink, long before he ever wed himself to the cailleach. I mind when he was just a lad, drinkin' himself sober at the ceilidhs, pickin' a fight wi' anybody he could and tryin' to get the lassies into a corner wi' just one thing on his mind.'

Tam grinned appreciatively. 'Oh ay, Hector was aye good at gettin' his hands up the lassies' skirts. How he ever came to pick Elspeth for his wife beats me for I doubt he would get his fingers bitten off him if he tried that on wi' her.'

'I heard tell she was hot stuff in her time,' Jim Jim murmured cryptically.

'Ach, you're blethering!' hooted the men. 'The only thing that was ever hot about Elspeth was her tongue!'

'Na, na,' Jim Jim insisted. 'One time, when she was just a bit girl, she near went mad wi' lust one night at a village dance. She had been having a wee fly tipple to herself and the whisky must have done things to her blood, for it was said she got this poor innocent lad into a hayshed and just about tore the breeks off him in her hurry to get at his equipment. In no time at all she had overpowered him and, by jingo!, she let him have it – the lot – everything was hangin' out! She was plumper then, wi' good rounded hips on her and breasts as fine and rosy as any man could wish for. She went at that poor lad till he was raw and done in and pleadin' for mercy but she wouldny let him go till all her fire was spent and she lay back, laughin' and gaspin' like a hoor wi' the croup.'

Jim Jim's eyes were gleaming; the men looked at him. Tam's big happy smile beamed out. 'You fly old bugger!' he said delightedly. 'The innocent young lad wi' the unwilling equipment! By God! Now I've heard everything! I thought I knew all there was to know on this island but it just goes to show, there's aye some juicy wee titbit lurking about in the haysheds!'

Jim Jim had turned bright scarlet, he tried hard to plead innocence but to no avail. His cronies forgot the fate of Captain Mac and turned instead to 'teasing the breeks' off poor old Jim Jim who squirmed as his weak bladder filled up, and prayed that none of this would reach the ears of his wife Isabel who fondly believed that she had hooked 'a virgin mannie' when she had taken Jim Jim to be her lawfully wedded husband.

The womenfolk were generally more tolerant than the men and told one another that the pair 'couldny do much harm at their age.'

'Good luck to the sowels – Captain Mac needs somebody to look after him and Elspeth is just a poor lonely cratur' who needs a good man about the place,' Kate intoned magnanimously, even though she was hugging herself at the idea of being able to 'torment the shat out the cailleach' now that she had 'a man biding wi' her in sin.'

Behag was not one of those to wish Elspeth luck. She was beside herself with self-righteous disapproval of such an immoral arrangement, while inwardly a glow of excitement smouldered:

205

she had waited a long time for this day and she went scuttling indoors to polish her spyglasses in readiness.

As for Captain Mac, he didn't give a fig for all the speculation about his decision to live with Elspeth. He was heartily sick of his unsettled way of life and was actually looking forward to 'putting his feets up in comfort' and to sitting down at a table where the food was that good you were 'feart to eat it in case it would disappear.'

His cousin, Gus, who was eighty and a worse cook than Mac himself, had not been an easy man to live with. At night his snores resounded through the house. He dropped food into his beard and ate the particles as and when he found them, hours or days later. He did terrible things with his nose: sometimes he pummelled it till it squeaked wetly, other times he picked it and wasn't too fussy where he wiped his fingers afterwards, but mostly he drew it over the already glazed surface of his sleeve, and with that same sleeve he often took it into his head to polish the beer glasses.

He wheezed, grunted and cackled when he was listening to a wireless set that was as ancient as himself. It was powered by an accumulator and it crackled and groaned in unison with the old man. To make matters worse, Gus was half deaf, and kept the volume of the wireless turned up at full blast so that it was difficult to make out anything for all the noise.

He broke wind at the table – from both ends of his anatomy, great gusting burps, loud generous belches, combining so boisterously with the other sounds that Mac was frequently moved to wonder how anybody could produce such rip-roaring eruptions and still remain intact.

Gus kept three ferrets in his wee hoosie at the bottom of his overgrown garden. All his life he had kept ferrets to catch the rabbits which formed a greater part of his diet. But now he wasn't as active as he used to be in that respect and the little creatures had become restless due to lack of employment. In their desire for action they rattled the spars of their cages and altogether combined to make such a din that Mac was loath to visit the place after dark, with the result that half of the time he was constipated and the other half he was running to the wee hoosie, several times in a day, owing to the laxatives he was forced to take to keep his bowels from 'going out o' business altogether'.

On one memorable occasion one of the ferrets had escaped and had bitten Mac on his well-rounded bottom just as he had dropped his trousers on one of his 'cascara runs'. His yells had brought Gus running, a sight which in itself was well worth seeing as one leg was 'laid up wi' the rheumatics' and the other was 'seized up' owing to a war wound from his Merchant Navy days. The resulting stilted gait had once been described by an observer as 'a hirpling hen wi' the gout', which was an apt, if picturesque, summary of the old man's condition.

He had been totally unsympathetic about poor Mac's wounds, being more concerned about the safety of his ferret than anything else, and had yelled on his cousin to do something about catching 'the buggering thing'. But all Mac could do was hop about from one foot to the other in a mixture of pain from his bites and frustration in knowing that his calls of nature were receding further and further into the distance till soon they would be lost beyond recall.

Gus had caught his buggering ferret, but Mac's bite marks had festered and he had been forced to call out Megan and had had to suffer the untold humiliation of 'baring his bum to the leddy doctor'.

The same lady doctor had only just managed to keep a straight face in the course of her administrations to Mac's private parts, but the minute she stepped outside the house she had erupted into helpless laughter and had had to run to her car with her hanky stuffed tightly against her face just in case anybody should be looking from the window.

It had taken Mac a long time to forgive his cousin for that painful episode in his life. He hadn't been able to sit down comfortably for days and was so afraid of going to the wee hoosie he had again become badly constipated and this time he'd had to visit Megan in her surgery on an embarrassing quest for 'something to ease his blocked tubes', which was the only way he could think of to describe his problem without too much damage to his pride. Megan, completely misunderstanding, had produced her stethoscope to solemnly listen to his chest, and he had left her surgery with a bottle of cough medicine, his 'tubes' becoming more blocked by the minute. Next day, in complete desperation he had gone back to her, and almost dying of shame he had blurted out the exact nature of his trouble, the red stain on his normally happy countenance concerning her so much she had taken his blood pressure and sounded his heart for good measure.

After that, Mac hadn't spoken to Gus for a week but that didn't worry the old man, he had a number of cronies the same age as himself who came to play cards till all hours and who drank rum the likes of which Mac would only have used to rinse out his chamber pot.

So all in all Mac was mighty glad to escape his cousin for a while, though the old man assured him his bed was 'aye ready', adding with a wicked chuckle, 'fleas and all'.

Gus had never married, and little wonder was Mac's opinion, no self-respecting woman would have put up with him for one minute – though, of course – and at this juncture in his musings Mac's jolly bulbous nose turned a shade paler – he must have been young at one time and possibly quite eligible, which just went to show how dangerous it was for anybody to marry anybody.

Mac's thoughts were rather garbled at this point and in his dismay he vowed afresh to keep Elspeth at a safe distance and never to let her think for one moment that theirs was anything more than a purely business arrangement.

Though Elspeth was absolutely overjoyed at having Mac in her home at last, not one muscle of her stern face gave away the fact. She was determined to show him that theirs was a purely platonic friendship – for the moment – and she allowed him to settle in at his leisure, giving him ample time to arrange his room the way he wanted, never saying a word when the smell of tobacco smoke filtered hazily downstairs and all through the house.

In fact, she stood at the sink and positively revelled in the manly odour. It had been many years since a pipe was smoked in her home and it was good, oh so good, to have a man about the place again and one that she was truly fond of into the bargain.

She spent the afternoon concocting a mouthwatering evening meal, a strange little drone issuing from her throat, which was the nearest she ever got to singing as she worked. Phebie had said she could have the day off, after they had come to an agreement that Elspeth should now only work part-time at Slochmhor, except when Mac went off on one of his frequent fishing trips or to his sister Nellie's house on the island of Hanaay.

Phebie was secretly delighted that at last she would have her house to herself more often. When the children had been at home and when she herself had been kept constantly busy helping Lachlan run his practice, Elspeth's help had been more than welcome, but though he was now retired and Fiona and Niall married with homes of their own, Elspeth still clung to the belief that she was indispensable and that no one knew how to look after Lachlan the way she did. There had been times when Phebie could have screamed with the frustration of being bossed about in her own kitchen but both she and Lachlan put up with it because Elspeth had been such a longstanding and faithful housekeeper and a staunch devotee of the entire McLachlan family.

To have turned her away in her lonely old age was simply unthinkable to the kindly McLachlans but now Mac had afforded them a way out and Phebie could have personally pinned a medal on his chest so relieved was she that he had provided a solution to her problems.

So quite a few lightened hearts went about their business that fateful day of Mac's move. He himself began to feel more at ease as the day wore on and nothing very terrible happened to make him feel threatened in any way. Indeed, it was a pleasure to be in Elspeth's home, which was clean without being clinical and tidy without being too orderly. Here there was no loud blaring wireless to contend with, just the nice rhythmic tick of the 'waggit the wa'' clock, the singing of peats in the cosy hearth'— and no Gus picking food from his beard or picking his nose behind a crumpled edition of the *Oban Times*, which would later be torn into untidy squares for use in the wee hoosie.

Elspeth's wee hoosie was a pleasure to visit, discreetly situated as it was behind a flourishing floribunda rose where bees buzzed and the perfume of the flowers invaded the air. The wee hoosie itself was a small, private world with a good big snib on the door. Real toilet paper hung on a properly placed holder, a lavender-smelling air freshener dangled from the low roof and the floor was cosily covered in flower-sprigged carpeting. On a tiny shelf sat a basin and a jugful of water with a bar of white toilet soap nearby; behind the lavatory pan stood a bucket of water to flush toilet waste down into a pipe and from there to a crude septic tank that Hector had built in his more sober and visionary days. It was a unique arrangement, much envied by those neighbours who only had dry lavatories, which had to be laboriously emptied at least three times a week.

Mac was much taken by it and spent some time examining its structure before his eye took to roving once more. It was surprisingly bright in the small enclosure – white painted walls reflected light from a tiny muslin covered window. A picture of a kneeling, virginal-looking woman dressed in white, with tightly clasped hands held to her lips, hung in a strategic position. Mac gulped when he saw it. A small stab of anxiety pierced his contentment: he knew that Elspeth was a fairly religious woman but wasn't this taking matters just a bit too far?

Then he chuckled, maybe she was like him, praying for a good deliverance as she sat in the wee hoosie, staring at the picture. Perhaps she found inspiration and hope in those praying hands – for all he knew, maybe she emulated the action and sang a hymn or two as well – anything was possible in a wee hoosie of any sort and the old sea dog thoroughly enjoyed his first visit to this tiny sanctum. He even remembered to wash his hands and place the towel carefully back on its hook, and when he emptied the pail down the pan he went dutifully to fill it again from the old well near the house.

At teatime Elspeth served up a delicious and filling meal, she was attentive to his needs without fussing and when it was over he sat back replete, telling her that it was the best food he had tasted for a long time and that she was 'a grand cook'.

'Ach well, tis a long time since I had a man in the house to cook for,' she said primly, her eyes turned down so that he wouldn't see how much his compliments pleased her. 'I'm used to doing for Lachlan and Phebie but somehow it is just that wee bittie better when I'm working at my own stove.'

He rose to his feet, offering to help with the dishes but she pushed him back, saying that he wasn't to do woman's work, and directed him instead to sit down and smoke his pipe as she 'fair enjoyed the reek o' it.'

Mac's cup was full to overflowing when evening came round and it was just him and Elspeth, seated at opposite sides of the fire, she quietly darning, he smoking his pipe, his stockinged feet firmly planted on the hearth, his tot of rum at his side, his large hairy-backed hands holding firm on the poker as he waited for it to grow red hot in the glowing heart of the fire.

'It's nice this, Elspeth,' he said contentedly, his big, happy nose glowing redder by the minute from the fire's heat.

'Ay, it is that, Isaac,' she returned. 'It makes a change to have a bit o' company in the evenings.'

Picking up his rum he held it against the lamplight so that he could enjoy what he called the 'ruby lights dancing in the glass'. He always did this before downing the liquid, it was a prelude to anticipated enjoyment, a moment to reflect the quiet, good things of life and the simple pleasures yet to come.

The poker was almost ready. Mac made to withdraw it from the embers but Elspeth's hand came out to enclose his. 'Let me do that for you, Isaac,' she said and without hesitation she plunged the red-hot tip of the poker into the glass of rum. As the sizzle and scent of burnt rum filled the air, Mac's nostrils twitched, for no smell on earth was sweeter to him than that, it brought back memories of seafaring days when hot rum had chased the cold from his bones and heated the blood in his veins.

'Ay, tis a grand smell,' Elspeth said, much to Mac's surprise. 'It minds me o' my father, sitting warm by the fire after a day half frozen tending his sheep on the hill. He wasny what you would call a drinking man but he liked his tot rum and my mother never minded, for she knew well enough how hard he worked his bit croft. There he would sit, his feet on the hearth, she rubbing the chill from his hands and when the time was ripe, taking the poker from the fire to thrust it into the glass. I used to sit back and watch and never to this night have I seen and smelt the likes. Tonight you minded me o' those times, they were hard but happy and I often think how it used to be when Mother and Father were alive.'

Her eyes had grown moist. It was a side of Elspeth that Mac had never dreamed could exist. He moved uncomfortably in his chair and placed one big purpled hand over hers, he made a few soothing noises and told her that when he stayed with his sister Nellie on Hanaay they often sat at the fire talking over the old days when their parents had been alive.

'Ay, lass,' he said softly, 'they were the best times o' our lives, when we were young and all the world was busy and full and our mother and father aye to hand to listen to our ails and worries.'

Elspeth sniffed, impatiently she drew a hand over her eyes. 'Ach, I'm just a silly old woman,' she said gruffly, 'but if you don't mind, Isaac, I'd like a spot o' your rum – just to keep you company, of course,' she added hastily and with a touch of her old asperity.

Mac stared, he chuckled, he poured her a small quantity of spirits and for the rest of the evening the two of them sat, companionably sipping burnt rum and reminiscing about their individual upbringings. The hours slipped easily by and he didn't even mind when she demanded one of his socks so that she could mend the hole in it while her darning box was out.

There was something very comforting about a woman with

busy hands. Mac hadn't enjoyed himself so much for a long time. He discovered that Elspeth wasn't nearly as strait-laced as she would have everyone believe: she laughed at some of Mac's cleaner jokes and made one or two quite rude ones of her own, she was also a fairly good mimic and at one point had him holding on to his stomach as she imitated Behag's mournful tones and made an astonishingly accurate portrayal of Holy Smoke's actions in his butcher's shop, and another of Canty Tam's leering grin and predictions of gloom and doom.

But as bedtime drew nearer Elspeth reverted to her old self. Her tones became brisk as she informed Mac that there were certain rules in her home that must be adhered to, no smoking in bed was one, breakfast at eight sharp was another, 'and of course,' she went on firmly, 'we like to steep ourselves in the tub twice weekly, Monday nights and again on Saturday to make ourselves decent for the Sabbath.'

'We?' Mac hazarded faintly, and when she said it was only a figure of speech she sometimes used he thought to himself she was just emulating a certain queen of Victorian times who had first coined the expression.

'I'll no' expect you to accompany me to the kirk, Isaac,' she continued. 'Only if you have a mind to do so and only if you want to be seen wi' me; I'll no' force you to do anything you don't want, so you need have no fears on that score.'

Mac was mighty glad of that: he was still reeling from the shock of having to 'steep' twice weekly, for, even though he was very fussy about his appearance and kept his white beard and hair squeaky clean, he was otherwise wont to have a quick sponge-down in front of the fire when it suited him, and not before, since it was his belief that too much water was a bad thing for the skin. But on the whole he thought that her requests were reasonable enough and told her so, adding that he hoped she didn't mind but he would be going off fishing with the lads early on Monday morning.

She didn't mind, in fact she was positively anxious for him to pursue his usual wanderings, adding, 'They will be needing me at Slochmhor. Phebie tries but will never admit she's no use at all when it comes to running a home and, of course, Lachlan must have proper food and has aye relied on me for that.'

After that the pair retired to bed on the best of terms, each going their sedate and separate ways. But the second Elspeth's door closed on her she stood with her back to it, pressing her clasped hands to her mouth, a spot of crimson burning high on each gaunt cheekbone. He would be off on Monday! She could hardly wait for it to come! At last! At last! She would have the moment she had been waiting for all these weeks and a strange little strangulated gurgle of excitement broke from her throat as she thought about Monday with shining eyes.

Late on Monday morning Behag looked from her window and saw a row of flimsy garments hanging on Elspeth's washing line, completely unlike the usual assortment of sensible vests, flannel nighties, and long-legged knickers. There had been a time when Behag was shocked to see pink silk bloomers on the line but this – this was beyond belief and rushing for her spyglasses she focused them on Elspeth's drying green. What she saw nearly gave her apoplexy for there, flapping gaily about for all the world to see, was a row of satin lingerie and nightwear, the like of which Behag had only ever seen in a brochure full of sex aids and sensual garments that had been sent to her from some firm with a London address.

Behag never knew how such a publication had found its way into her home. She had been shocked to the core, she had thrown it in the bucket, she had vowed never to set eyes on it again – but it had haunted her. In her head she kept seeing things she had never dreamed existed; she had fought a terrible battle with her conscience and after much anguish and soul-searching she had guiltily retrieved the glossy leaflet from her bin and had avidly devoured every page. Praying that nothing and no one would disturb her, she had studied each illustration from every angle. With popping eyes she had stared at weird contrivances designed to be attached to the human body to induce 'the ultimate in sexual pleasure'.

She had been appalled, amazed, intrigued, for in her innocence she had imagined that human beings only needed their own natural accoutrements to get through life and even then, the good Lord had only meant them to be used for the means of procreation. At this point she had blushed profusely as even to dwell on such matters was to her mind the ultimate sign of degradation.

She then turned her attention to the garment section, which bore the heading, 'Things to Please the Man in Your Life'. Luscious silk pants and peep-hole bras; furry knickers – here Behag gulped and wondered if they tickled – see-through black nighties; things that were described as G-strings which seemed to cover nothing at all and must have been extremely uncomfortable to wear; sheer black stockings; frilly garters . . .

Eagerly she flipped over the pages until she got the biggest shock of all: a whole section devoted to 'our exciting selection of the latest in rubber wear' – figure-hugging trouser suits; black masks with evil-looking eye slits; others with what looked like mini-elephant trunks where the nose should be. Behag paused – it couldn't be . . . it was! Her eyes nearly fell out her head. Why would they want to put a thing like that on a mask when men had been created with perfectly efficient ones in their trousers . . . ?

She couldn't go on, violently she hurled the offending literature into the fire then scuttled as fast as her legs would carry her to the sideboard wherein was kept the 'medicinal whisky'. On this occasion Behag felt fully justified in helping herself to a good tipple and she sat back, her glass held tight in her shaky hand, her palsied head nodding to and fro as she watched the flames licking the elephant trunks and the peep-hole bras. Never, she vowed, would she look at such degenerate trash again – and now here was Elspeth, brazenly displaying the fact that she was a fallen woman who had succumbed to wicked temptation and vice. True, the things on her line were more glamorous than shocking but even so, Elspeth and Captain Mac must be having a fine time to themselves, the evidence was there for everyone to see, flagrantly displayed without subtlety or shame . . . the . . . the hussy!

And wait! Wasn't that Elspeth herself coming out to survey

her washing with a decided air of satisfaction? She had turned, something in her hand glinted, she was holding it to her eyes and – Behag's heart jumped, her face grew hot – the saucy besom! *She was standing there with a pair of spyglasses, watching to see if Behag was watching her!*

Behag quickly turned her own spyglasses away from Elspeth's domain and pretended to pan them over the rugged slopes of Sgurr nan Ruadh, trying hard as she did so to compose her bloodhound features into lines of complete and perfect innocence.

Elspeth lowered what she called her 'peepscope' and laughed till the tears ran down her face. No one who knew her would have believed she could have been capable of such abandoned mirth but then, never before in her life had she done anything so daring, and she scuttled into the house to hurl herself into a chair where she hugged herself in a gluttony of self-satisfied glee and wondered who would be the next to notice the contents of her washing line.

Chapter Seventeen

As expected, Behag was not the only one to notice the contents of Elspeth's washing line: everyone who had to pass her house to get to the village couldn't help but see the display of silks and satins dancing gaily in the breezes. It was a provocative sight and in the main the reactions ranged from downright shock to disbelief, and – in some cases – amusement.

If it had been Rachel's washing it would possibly have merited a few dry comments but would have been allowed to pass since she was 'a young woman o' the world wi' a lot o' fancy ideas inside her head'. The same might have applied to many of the younger island girls who shopped a lot by mail order catalogue, and even if they couldn't be described as women of the world they were certainly prone to much temptation as they perused glossy pages containing the latest in feminine fashions.

The older women also made use of mail order catalogues but their interests lay mainly in good sensible garments, both for their menfolk and themselves, and if they considered undergarments at all it was with practicalities in mind and they were apt to settle for things that would help them combat the rigours of long, cold winter days and nights.

It was therefore not surprising that they could hardly believe the evidence of their own eyes when they surveyed the array of frilly knickers, seductive nighties and lacy petticoats pegged in such a way on the line as to show the plunging necklines, the frothy edgings . . . and . . . when rays of sunshine slanted from behind, the transparent quality of the material.

It wasn't long before a small group of housewives were huddled together in the village street, talking about Elspeth in hushed tones – except for beings like Old Sorcha whose deafness led her to the assumption that, in common with herself, everyone had to be shouted at; and folk like Kate McKinnon who very seldom whispered about anything and who certainly had no intention of discussing Slochmhor's housekeeper in a subtle manner.

'The cailleach has been acting gey strange this whilie back,' she stated with conviction. 'In my opinion she is going off her head altogether and Mac had better watch that she doesny murder him in his bed one o' these fine nights.'

'Ach, come on now, Kate,' said Isabel nervously. 'There is no need to go that far, she is just having a wee bit fling to herself before it's too late. She will settle down when she comes to her senses and if I know Elspeth that will be sooner rather than later.'

Kate exploded: 'A fling! Surely you are no' trying to tell us she's sowing her wild oats at her age! She scattered those long ago if she scattered them at all . . . though, mind you' – she eyed Isabel contemplatively as Tam's tale about Jim Jim's youthful experiences with Elspeth in the hayshed leapt suddenly into her lively mind – 'from what I've been hearing about her she's no' aye been as prudish as she makes out. Seemingly she robbed at least one mannie o' his virginity way back in the year dot and for all we know, there could have been others.'

Isabel looked at her askance and the others clamoured to know more, but Kate, feeling rather ashamed at divulging what had been a confidence, declined to enlarge on the subject, much to the chagrin of her cronies.

'Ach, it is just a lot o' fuss about nothing,' Aggie McKinnon suggested in her fat, gentle voice. 'Elspeth has as much right as anyone to wear nice things if she wants to and surely it is nobody's business but her own if she hangs them out to dry in her own green, I would do the same if they were mine and be proud o' it.'

Secretly, Aggie longed to be able to wear the kind of things that were the talk of the moment, but with her physical proportions it was out of the question, though that didn't stop her from dreaming or from poring over the enticing displays of feminine garments in her own mail order catalogue.

Kate glanced sympathetically at Aggie's generous rolls of flesh. 'Och well, you are a young woman and would have every right to wear such things if you wanted,' she said kindly and the others nodded for, despite their talk about Elspeth, it would be apt to say that more than just one of them had, at some time in their lives, hankered to be glamorous and to look as seductive as the film stars they gazed at on the silver screen on their shopping trips to the mainland.

At this point they were joined by one or two of the menfolk who had been 'fair tickled' at the sight of Elspeth's smalls, even though they wondered at Captain Mac's rashness in allowing himself to be taken in by 'a few wisps o' lace' that wouldn't decently have covered a 'clockin' hen's arse'.

None of them could picture Elspeth in frills and froth, and Robbie, grinning from ear to ear, echoed Aggie's words when he told the women, 'It is just a flash in the pan and will blow over in no time at all. It is none o' our business what other folks do wi' theirs and it might be better if we don't say a word to either Captain Mac or Elspeth.'

'Ay,' agreed Tam, whose embarrassment for the old seafarer was as acute as if it had been Kate displaying 'her goods' on the washline, 'he wouldny like it if he thought we had been washin' his dirty linen in public . . .'

He paused, surprised at himself for the paradoxical turn of phrase. Robbie grinned dryly, the women giggled, making Tam feel that he had said something really quite amusing.

At this juncture Sorcha looked over Kate's head and in her excitement at what she saw turned her deaf aid down and exclaimed in her loudest tones, 'Well, some folk have no shame and that's a fact! Fancy, the cheek o' it!'

As one, every head swivelled round and there was 'the hussy' herself, calmly making for Merry Mary's shop, swinging her shopping bag in an oddly carefree manner, her head held proud and high, not one single muscle betraying anything but the utmost confidence as she paused for a moment to haughtily survey the tight little gathering in the street before she marched firmly into Merry Mary's.

'I'll say this for her,' said Tam, 'she aye did handle herself well and you can bet your boots she'll no' stand anything from you lot if you as much as breathe one word about her frilly knickers.'

'The thought never entered my mind, Tam McKinnon!' Kate said indignantly, hoisting her own shopping bag into a prominent position. 'Her knickers, and what she does wi' them, is no concern o' mine and I'll thank you no' to keep me back a minute longer. I have my messages to get and Mary said she would keep me a fresh loaf and a bag o' rolls which I said I would collect before ten o' the clock – so, if you'll be excusin' me . . .'

Along the pavement she marched with alacrity, followed by her cronies anxious not to miss any of the fun that would surely develop in Merry Mary's premises. Kate might not come right out with anything that could be construed as straightforward cheek but, mischievous devil that she was, she would hint and tease and torment Elspeth unmercifully, and it was always interesting to see how a situation like that would develop.

Only Aggie hung back. She was a kindly, soft-hearted soul and she had no great desire to hear the formidable Kate tearing poor old Elspeth to pieces, she would visit the Post Office first and by the time she got back to Merry Mary's it might be quieter and she could shop at her leisure while she waited for the bus.

Mamma had had enough of the house, so, squaring her shoulders, she set off briskly in the direction of Portcull. It was a beautiful day: Mara Òran Bay sparkled in the sun, the translucent green water was calm and peaceful though a lively breeze rippled the blue surface of the Sound so that it sparkled and shone in a myriad of breathtaking colours.

The lapwing chicks had grown into downy speckled balls with long legs that carried them swiftly through the grass, but the parent birds were never far away and the minute they sent out their alarm calls down the chicks cooried till danger was past. Skylarks sang in the blue vault of the sky, a glorious tumble of sound that seemed never-ending, for as soon as one bird swooped to the ground another would rise up, warbling out a joyous melody that peaked to a crescendo high above the earth. The scents of summer perfumed the air – Anton was cutting his hayfields – the rich, sweet smell drenched Mamma's senses as she walked along, wearing only a print dress and a cotton cardigan.

Something about the wide, clean beauty of the Hebridean landscape touched Mamma's awareness. She paused to gaze over the heat-hazed moors rolling away to the velvet green slopes of Ben Machrie; she looked with appreciation at the great cliffs of Burg in the distance, misty and blue, plunging down to meet the deeper blue of the ocean. The journey over those same cliffs in Erchy's bus had paled a little in her memory; she hadn't been back to the village since that day but had decided that morning it was now or never to take the bull by the horns and face once again those dreadful island women.

Mamma was badly in need of some stimulating company. Jon was very quiet these days and was withdrawn and pensive; Rachel was also preoccupied with her thoughts and took herself off on long walks so that she was hardly ever in the house, and when she was she spent her time moping in her room and seldom played her violin, much to Jon's bafflement. Relations between the two were somewhat strained, but for once Mamma didn't dare say anything in case she got her head chewed off. She hadn't yet forgiven Rachel for her rudeness – the girl was positively bad mannered, she had scant respect for her elders and seemed unable to tell the difference between right and wrong – but of course, what else could one expect, springing as she had from a background in which no one had much grasp of life's little niceties.

The dazzling white houses of Portcull were drawing closer; Mamma's steps slowed, she stopped swinging her string shopping bag and clutched at it instead. Passing Ranald's craft shop she received pleasant nods from one or two people she didn't know and had no wish to know. The harbour was quiet with only some fishermen spreading their nets and a row of pipe-smoking old men sitting on the wall. From them she received curious glances together with a few friendly grins. The amount of teeth those smiles revealed depended on the age of the worthies: toothless gaps were much in evidence and some had no teeth at all. Mamma thought it disgraceful that anybody should appear in public without teeth – especially in this day and age when a good set of dentures were easily come by. She didn't stop to consider that 'a good set of dentures' were rather difficult to procure on an island where 'the dentist mannie' only visited twice a year. This meant that for the rest of the time the islanders had to visit a mainland dentist, or, in the case of the old and infirm, keep their ill-fitting 'teeths' steeping in a cup, except for the purpose of masticating food, or for Sabbath vigils in kirk when they were given an airing for cosmetic purposes.

'Sour-faced cailleach,' muttered Hector the Boat as Mamma went on her unsmiling way, heading first for the butcher's shop because she had heard that he kept very good home-grown meat.

Holy Smoke's eyes gleamed when he peered between a row of black puddings hanging in his window and saw her approaching. Quite unconsciously he rubbed his hands together: he hadn't yet encountered Jon's mother and saw only a 'towrist', a foreigner at that, no doubt with plenty of money to spend and only a hazy idea of the value of British currency. No one else was in the shop, they were too busy gossiping about some silly petticoats old Elspeth had hung on her wash-line, and for once the butcher was pleased to have empty premises, since the presence of Kate or Barra would only undermine his influence over this promisingly ignorant customer.

But Mamma had had ample time to do her homework and she made mincemeat of Holy Smoke. With magnificent aplomb she sailed majestically into the shop, grimacing as flakes of sawdust worked their way into her open-toed sandals to irritate her feet. Wasting no time she demanded to be served with frankfurter sausages, when these weren't forthcoming she flared her nostrils impatiently and turned her attention to the neat lines of black and white puddings dangling from hooks behind the counter.

Holy Smoke's confidence returned and he spent several minutes praising the merits of his home-made mealy puddings, but when he stopped to get his breath it was to the realisation that he might as well not have spoken at all, because his customer had completely lost interest in any of his puddings, be they black or white.

In the end she settled for a large, juicy-looking haggis, three lamb chops, a pound of stew, two kidneys, a small string of plump beef sausages and a quantity of steak mince 'for the cat'.

Mamma didn't have a cat, in fact she wasn't keen on them at all but she wasn't going to tell that to Holy Smoke. When he had deftly wrapped her meat into a bulky package and was toting up the price, Mamma stopped him when he mentioned how much it would be for the mince.

'In my country, cat meat is cheap,' she said haughtily. 'The same applies here, does it not? I give you sixpence, no more, no less.'

Holy Smoke's face turned purple, Kate would have revelled in his discomfiture and would have patted Mamma on the back for turning the tables on him.

'Sixpence!' he cried. 'My dear lady, I'll have you know, I gave you the best mince in the shop! I'm no' a rich man by any means and if . . .'

'I am not your dear lady,' Mamma said firmly, 'and I take myself out of your shop with nothing if you persist in cheating me just because you see before you a woman who is not of this place. Cheap cat meat – or nothing.'

It took the butcher all his time not to argue back but he had his reputation to think of and, muttering darkly under his straggly limp moustache, he marked up sixpence against the mince even though it went against his grain.

Mamma, however, had not finished with him. When it came to counting the money into his hand she made him so thoroughly confused with her loud, verbal conversions of German and British currencies, he ended up cheating himself of ten shillings and was never so glad to see the back of a customer in all his life.

She left him standing at the counter, shaking his head, his brow furrowed in puzzlement as he went through his list all over again, tapping his head with his pencil, counting with his fingers, growing more and more confused as he mumbled on about German marks and schillings.

Mamma was feeling light-headed with triumph as she left the butcher's shop. No one was going to get the better of her on this island, she had put the boot on the other foot, she had shown that dreadful little meat man who was the boss . . . She straightened her back and puffed out her vast bosoms. She, Frau Helga Jodl, was ready now for anything . . .

Agnes McKinnon was coming along the street, all sixteen stone of her, marching stolidly towards the Post Office, which was situated on Mamma's route. Mamma hadn't forgotten her confrontation with Aggie in Merry Mary's, she had no wish for another, and she shrank back a little as the young woman came thundering along. There was certainly no avoiding this magnificent McKinnon and Mamma girded her loins as she prepared herself for battle.

'It is yourself Mistress Jodl,' greeted Aggie, her round pink face the very essence of good nature, no sign of ill-will in her attitude or in her plumply cosy, lilting voice.

Mamma was completely taken aback and more than a little relieved to be hailed in such a fashion, though she wasn't too sure about the 'mistress' part of it. She had still to learn that in Scotland it was a form of address that frequently took the place of 'Mrs' and was considered a sign of respect in the homes of the gentry where it would have been impolite to refer to the lady of the house as anything else but 'mistress'.

Mamma, however, knew nothing of this but in view of Aggie's friendliness she was prepared to let it pass this once.

'I have been looking out for you,' Aggie went on, 'and I'm right glad we have met, for I have been wanting to say sorry to you for shouting at you in Merry Mary's shop.'

'Say sorry – to me?' Mamma repeated the words in disbelief, no one had apologized to her for anything since her arrival on Rhanna.

'Ay, you see, I was in a hurry, but that was no excuse to talk to you the way I did and you a stranger on the island,' Aggie stated, beaming at the older woman in the most cordial fashion.

Mamma was completely flummoxed. She drew a deep breath. 'Myself, I was rude,' she found herself saying, 'I go first when first is not my place.'

'Och well,' Aggie continued to weave her spell, 'we all make mistakes, and wi' you being new here it must all seem a bittie strange.'

Mamma shook her head sadly. 'It is the same wherever I go: I am rude, I push in my way, I speak too much the mind. People, they tell me I am domineering and unkind.'

It was like uncorking a bottle that had been jammed tightly for a long time but once unstuck it all seemed to pour out. The flow of self-loathing continued, she appeared only too anxious to lay the blame for everything at her own door. Aggie nodded and clucked sympathetically and wondered if she should get envelopes as well as stamps when eventually she got to the Post Office.

Mamma paused for breath, her face crumpled. 'No one likes me, Jon is the only one who has any time for me. My husband, he was the little man, he give in to me whatever I say – it was not good – I never did anything he wanted and now I find it very hard to listen to anything anybody has to say.'

Aggie's soft heart melted, she laid a plump hand on the other's arm. 'Och, there now,' she soothed. 'You mustny worry, it is never too late to mend your ways.'

But Mamma would not be consoled, dismally she shook her head. 'I am not wanted here, Rachel dislikes me more than anyone, I have given her good reason to behave to me as she does. I think, perhaps, I will go back to Hamburg.'

'Oh no, you mustny do that.' Aggie was beginning to feel she had bitten off more than she could handle. 'Give yourself

225

a chance, I'm sure you are a very nice lady underneath your – er – skin.'

Mamma drew a shuddering breath. 'It is no use, no one wants to know me. Jon has Rachel, I am shut out. The feeling in here' – she placed her hands over her massive chest – 'it is of loneliness. They have their music and the secret glances and the funny swaying they call dancing; they have no time for me and will not even play with me the penuckle. I learn it from the Americans after the war but Rachel has no liking for it.'

'*Penuckle!*' Aggie's face lit up, she fairly shouted out the word. 'Oh, I just love penuckle – poker too! Colin my husband is in the Merchant Navy and learned a lot o' card games when he was in America.' She gazed at Mamma with dancing eyes. 'You must come to our house for a wee night wi' the cards, some o' the neighbours come in too and we have a dram while we're playing. No' for money, you understand, well, maybe just a bob or two for the sake o' a bittie excitement. I'll get Rab McKinnon to come over for you tonight in his tractor, you'll fair enjoy yourself.'

During this discourse Mamma's handsome face had been alight with interest but it fell at Aggie's last words, she was remembering that the young woman lived halfway along the cliff road to Nigg. The journey there had been bad enough in Erchy's bus and she had vowed never to attempt it again in any sort of vehicle, far less one of those noisy monsters she had seen lumbering about the island.

'A tractor?' she repeated faintly, the appeal of a cosy evening with the cards diminishing suddenly.

'Och, you need have no fear of that,' Aggie assured her cheerfully. 'It is a very comfortable tractor and Rab is a good careful driver who never touches a drop till he is home safe and dry. The journey won't take long and the summer nights are good and light, and just think, you'll get to play penuckle till it's coming out your ears.'

Mamma was weakening, and in a sudden burst of decision she relented and said she would be happy to come.

Aggie nodded. 'That's settled then. If you care to wait till I come out the Post Office, I'll see you along the road, for I have still to get some things in Merry Mary's before the bus comes.'

'Ah, yes, the bus,' said Mamma, sympathy in her tones for anyone who had to travel that dangerous road in a vehicle that was, to her, equally dangerous.

'Och, I'm used to it.' Aggie laughed and made tracks for the Post Office, in that establishment avoiding a few curious questions as to her conversation with Mamma and making good her escape as soon as her purchases were made.

The two women walked companionably along, heads close together as they chatted.

'They have become bosom pals all of a sudden – in every way that I can see,' said Fingal McLeod, who, in common with a lot of the island men, liked to see a 'well-filled' woman.

'Ay,' agreed Ranald, his gleaming eyes roving appreciatively over Aggie's rear end as she passed by. 'Our Aggie is lookin' well these days – she is cheekier than ever.' He snorted with laughter at his own joke and went on, 'Colin Mor is taking a big risk leaving her as often as he does, there's many a man on Rhanna would jump at the chance of a night o' fun in her bed.'

'Who is the other one?' enquired Rab McKinnon, trying to keep his tone as disinterested as possible. He was sixty, a widower with a strong, weatherbeaten face that seldom gave anything away. His blue eyes looked out calmly on the world but there was a hint of steel in them and though he was mainly a silent man he was a tough advocate if he thought anyone was getting an undeservedly raw deal.

'Jon Jodl's mother,' supplied Murdy readily. 'She's a real tartar from all I hear and played havoc in Merry Mary's shop when she had only newly set foot on the island.'

Rab nodded. 'I heard o' that. They say Kate McKinnon sent her on a wild-goose chase to the other end o' the island where she lost herself on the moor and ended up supping broth at the tinks' camp over by Dunuaigh.' He frowned. 'It wasny nice o' Kate to do that to a stranger, she'll be thinkin' we're all tarred wi' the same brush.'

'Ach, she deserved it,' said Fingal heartlessly. 'She near

227

frightened the shat out o' poor old Dodie when she rode home wi' him in the tink's cart. He said he would rather meet a spook than cross paths wi' her again and hardly goes outside his croft these days in case he might meet her again.'

'Here, talkin' o' Dodie, is Wullie McKinnon doing anything about the cockerels?' asked Ranald. 'I hear tell he canny sleep at night for the noise and is willing to pay someone to do something about it.'

Ranald's eyes were shining, if anything he was even more of a money grubber than Holy Smoke and was always first on the scene when opportunity presented itself.

Rab left the men to their talk and went off to the harbour to wait for the bus, little dreaming that he had been earmarked to chauffeur 'the tartar' to Aggie's croft that very evening, whether he liked it or not.

Merry Mary, remembering her last encounter with Mamma, looked rather worried when that same lady came stomping into the shop with Aggie at her elbow. The little Englishwoman had spent most of her life on Rhanna and was so attuned to island ways, both in speech and manner, that only the very discerning observer could tell she wasn't a born and bred Hebridean.

She thought the same as any islander, her reactions to certain situations were the same, she felt and behaved like an island woman and even looked and sounded like one with her open, honest face, her whimsical speech and her big, cheerful smile that was never far from her mouth.

But she didn't smile when she saw Mamma entering her premises. The shop, which only minutes before had been full of blethering woman, had emptied itself as one by one the customers dispersed about their business, so Merry Mary had no one to back her up should the big bossy German woman start any of her nonsense.

But she needn't have worried, something had happened to Mamma in the last half-hour, she had opened up, she had blossomed, she actually stuck out her hand to seize a hold of Mary's and pump it up and down till the little lady felt sure her arm was about to drop off at any minute with muscle fatigue.

Aggie made her purchases and the three women stood chatting. Mary began to feel so relaxed she was soon leaning her arms on the counter in a characteristic gesture, beaming and nodding so much her limp ginger hair fell over her eyes, giving her the appearance of a rather scruffy tabby who had just spent a harrowing night on the tiles.

She even dared to ask Mamma about her adventures in Erchy's bus, even though Aggie was making warning signs that told her to hold her tongue.

But the change in Mamma, whilst anything but complete, was making rapid progress. She gave such a vivid and funny account of the episode, her broken English only adding spice to the telling, that she soon had the other two laughing and wiping their eyes and, thus encouraged, Mamma then plunged into a vivid description of the scene with Holy Smoke in the butcher's shop.

'You never!' Aggie cried admiringly. 'Oh, wait till I tell Kate, she's aye taking the rise out o' him herself but never has she managed to get one over him as good as that.' She glanced at her watch and gave a little yelp. 'Where has the time gone? The bus will be here soon so I'll just go and wait wi' Rab at the harbour and tell him about tonight.'

Mamma got up from the sack of potatoes on which she had been sitting. 'And I too must go, the dinner will be late in making but the cat, she will enjoy her meat all the more for waiting.'

The sly humour of the remark wasn't lost on Mary or Aggie, they stared at her appreciatively and as she departed the latter called, 'We will be seeing you tonight then, Mistress Jodl.'

'Please to call me Helga,' Mamma requested with dignity and walked away, a spring in her step and a new look of happiness on her hitherto dour and unsmiling countenance.

The change in Mamma became apparent the minute she stepped over the threshold of An Cala. She was humming a catchy little German tune under her breath as she unpacked her shopping bag and placed the things in the meat safe in the cool pantry by the back door. Without a single grumble she went out to the wee hoosie which had been the bane of her life since her arrival on Rhanna. For the first few days she hadn't used it at all for 'certain important functions' with the result that she had 'shat bricks for a week', according to Rachel, and had eventually been forced to take the syrup of figs offered to her by her daughter-in-law who simply couldn't keep the smiles from her face during the administration of the laxative.

After that she used the wee hoosie under great sufferance, but use it she did, complaining all the while about the flies, the midgies, the earwigs, 'the cows who look in the window and lick the panes', the spiders, the cobwebs, in fact everything and anything she could think of to make life uncomfortable for those who had to live with her.

Now, however, she said not a word regarding 'the inconvenience', as she had labelled the outside lavatory, instead, over the midday meal that Rachel had prepared, she regaled the young folk with her morning's adventures, her eyes glinting when she told them about her encounter with Holy Smoke, her face lighting when she recalled her meeting with Aggie.

'Tonight I go to play penuckle in her house, I meet the neighbours, I have the dram and the buttered bannocks that Aggie makes to soak up the whisky. I will not play for real money, only a bob or two to make the game exciting.'

She was really only repeating the things that Aggie had said and she didn't understand half of it but it sounded so funny to hear her talking about 'drams' and 'bobs' in her broken English that both her listeners thoroughly enjoyed her chatter.

So taken was she with the unexpected turn of events she ate every scrap of her meal, even though it was an Italian dish which normally she purported to despise. She even thanked her daughter-in-law for making it before scraping back her chair to tackle the dishes with haste in order that she could go upstairs to look through her wardrobe for something to wear that night.

* * *

When Rab duly arrived that evening in his tractor her enthusiasm paled a little, but he wasn't a man to stand any nonsense from anybody and succinctly told her to 'hop in' since the engine was apt to cut out if it idled too long.

Mamma, looking very spruce in her summer finery, climbed into the machine with some difficulty, but a helping pull from one of Rab's brawny arms soon saw her settled beside him and away they went, bumping and lurching on the road to Portcull, she wordless for once, he naturally so since he was a man of few words who 'couldny abide senseless chit-chat.'

Rachel and Jon stood at the door of An Cala watching them go. Such a strong sense of relief invaded them both that they held one another's hands till the tractor was out of sight, before wandering away down to the beach to walk by the sea, revelling in the freedom, delighting in the fact that, at long last, Mamma had found somewhere to go, something to do that she would enjoy, leaving them to pursue the simple joys that had always meant so much to them in leisure hours that were precious and necessary to them in the busy course of their lives.

Part Three

LATE SUMMER 1967

Chapter Eighteen

As the summer progressed the thing uppermost in most people's minds was the imminence of the McKinnon Clan Gathering. A great feeling of anticipation was in the air as people began to make their preparations. The question of what to wear was no problem for the menfolk: Sunday best suits were always to hand, hanging in the wardrobe, carefully preserved in mothballs, ready just to be taken out, brushed down and perhaps given an airing on the wash line if the weather was dry. But for this occasion something rather more special was called for and all over the island, kilts of every conceivable tartan were brought out of wraps to be carefully inspected for wear and tear before being cleaned, mended, and generally made spick and span for the big day.

It wasn't so simple for the womenfolk, however. A bit of appropriate tartan was certainly called for, be it a ribbon, a sash or a brooch, but trimmings like these had to be fixed on to something decent – it wouldn't do to don any old blouse or dress that had been worn dozens of times before – and soon the age-old cry went up, 'I haveny anything to wear! I'm sick o' looking at this old thing! I'll have to get something new!'

The bairns too had to be a credit to their parents at 'Otto's Ceilidh' and so trips to Glasgow or Oban were much to the fore and parcels from mail order catalogues began arriving every other day.

Erchy had seldom been so busy, he grumbled long and hard at all the extra work and for a time was forced to cut his bus schedule to just twice a week, which caused his regular passengers to grumble long and hard also.

Old Magnus of Croy, normally calm and collected, became quite upset when he discovered that the moths had made merry with his kilt, which had been carefully wrapped in tissue and placed in a bride's kist together with camphor-saturated wads and at least a dozen mothballs. But the old man had had little reason to wear Highland dress for at least ten years and somehow the moths and the grubs had invaded the kist. When he at last beheld the damage he shook his head sorrowfully and declared that he 'couldny go to his grandson's gathering looking like a second-hand tink!'

News of his plight soon reached Otto's ears and over to Croy he drove post-haste in Thunder to put his arm round his grandfather's shoulders and say softly, 'I am the only male McKinnon on this island with nothing appropriate to wear at my own clan gathering – and so – I make the trip to Glasgow to buy my first Highland dress. But I have no experience of such things, the help and advice I badly need, so how would it be if grandson and grandfather made the journey together? We will stay in the best hotel, we will paint the town red or purple or whatever colour you like, and while we are there you too can take the opportunity to buy the new kilt.'

'Ach, it will just be a waste at my age,' said Magnus gruffly, but his blue eyes were brilliant with excitement. He hadn't been off the island for many years and had never expected to see bright city lights again. Secretly he was delighted and thought it would 'make a wee change', out loud he announced with great restraint, 'You're right, son, they'll see you comin' a mile away and try to take advantage o' you. It might be wise for me to be there, just to make sure you get the right tartan and all the other bits and pieces to go wi' it. But there is no need to bide in one o' they posh hotels, they're a bunch o' robbers who are aye lookin' for you to cross they're palms wi' sillar for doing jobs they're paid to do. I have an old friend in Glasgow, he'll put us up no bother, his wife's a great cook and doesny talk too much, they'll no' be lookin' for a penny piece between them, just a good bit dram and a blether in return for bed and board.'

It was settled. Some days later Otto and his grandfather left the island, the old man resplendent in his best Sunday suit, trembling a little with excitement but conducting himself with great dignity and bearing.

Otto had only been on Rhanna a few months but already he considered it home and felt strange to be leaving, if only for a short spell. He stood at the rails, a handsome figure in tweed jacket and light trousers, black hair and beard perfectly groomed, his magnetic dark eyes alight as he surveyed the hills and the glens he had come to love dearly.

But he had lost weight in the last month, his face was thinner, his clothes loose where once they had fitted, perhaps a little too neatly, but as yet only Rachel knew how ill he was, no one else seemed to notice the change in him. On the face of it he had kept up a good show of vitality and strength, and had become such a well-kent figure at functions of any sort that the islanders had come to expect *Mac nan Èilean* to be there amongst them.

Only recently there had been a summer fête in the grounds of Burnbreddie in aid of the church fabric fund. Scott Balfour, the laird, had asked Otto to open it and this he had done willingly, even going to the lengths of requesting the use of Burnbreddie's piano so that he and The Portcull Fiddlers could give a concert on the platform that had been erected inside the marquee.

The people of Rhanna had come to love and respect him and many a hand was raised in farewell as he and Magnus sailed away from the island on the steamer.

High on the cliffs above Mara Òran Bay, Rachel also watched the boat heading out towards the Sound, and a pain like a knife twisted in her heart. She didn't know how much longer she could hold Otto's tragic secret to herself. She had lost count of the times she had been on the point of sharing the burden with Jon but each time she had held herself back and taken herself off on one of her solitary walks, so many emotions boiling in her breast she thought she would explode with the hurt of them.

She wished things were as they had been at the start of spring when all the world seemed light and bright and she had looked forward so eagerly to a long, carefree summer on Rhanna. She had been relaxed and happy then, there had been no worries, just herself and the days: the dawns and the gloamings, filled with peace and gladness. She alone had known the seas and the skies, clean and clear, wide and bright, created for her pleasure as she wandered free and at will over empty places that demanded nothing but instilled quiet joy and deep appreciation for everything that was good in life.

Jon's coming had brought a mixture of feelings: she wanted so much to enjoy the island with him but Mamma's presence had overshadowed their happiness till now there was a barrier between them that somehow couldn't be surmounted. Yet she was wise enough to know that it wasn't all Mamma's fault. The knowledge of Otto's illness had been a traumatic blow for her, the world seemed to have ended that night he had taken her into his confidence. He had become very special to her, there existed between them an attraction that was more than just physical, a unique perception of one another's feelings that went far beyond anything that she had ever experienced before. She was aware of Jon's jealousy and she understood it even while it was beyond her to stay away from Otto. He needed her so badly in his lonely fight against an illness that was sapping his strength more and more as the days went by – and she needed him, she couldn't deny it, he was like a magnet, drawing her to him, making everything and everyone else seem mundane and dull in comparison.

As she stood there she remembered the shared joys they had experienced that summer: there had been some wonderful times in old Magnus's cottage with the three of them enjoying their own impromptu little concerts; once they had walked over to the tinks' camp at Dunuaigh where they were invited to sing round the camp fire in the gloaming – to drink smoke-flavoured tea and eat farls of oatcake straight off the girdle, piping hot and dripping with butter.

But best of all was the day she had spent at Burg Bay with both Jon and Otto. She had taken each of them by the hand and they had run barefoot into the sea where they had paddled in the shallows, splashing one another, laughing and playing like children, never wanting any of it to end. Later, with their shoes strung round their necks, they had walked along the beach before collapsing in the sand to rest. Jon had lain on his back, watching the fluffy clouds floating by; she and Otto had glanced at one another, their eyes meeting and holding, dark with the knowledge that moments like these were very precious to them and would get fewer and fewer as time went by. He had quickly learned the sign language so that now they could commune easily with one another and convey the things that were in their hearts.

They didn't know that Jon saw the way they looked at each other or that the jealousy in his heart was growing blacker and stronger with every passing day.

The boat had all but disappeared on the horizon, she sighed and she was glad, glad that she too was leaving the island for a time: too much had happened in just a few short months, she had to stand back from it, get it all into perspective. It wasn't just Otto and Jon, it was herself, she needed time to think, to look into her heart and her mind. She had to belong to herself again, for something so earthshattering was happening to her she couldn't really believe it herself yet. She had lain at night thinking about it, wondering if it could really be true: it seemed so impossible yet there was every reason for her to hope and pray and dream. But then came sleep and the dawn and the start of another day with people and emotions claiming too much of her attention.

For some time now, Jon had been growing anxious about the amount of time she was spending out of the public eye: at this stage in her career she needed to stay in the limelight, he told her, and it would be a good idea for her to take advantage of her time in Scotland. He had lined up a concert in the Usher Hall in Edinburgh, recordings at the BBC studios in Glasgow, and, if she agreed, he could arrange for her to appear in other cities throughout the country and still be back on Rhanna at the end of a fortnight.

At first she had fiercely resisted the suggestions. Jon had kindly but firmly tried to persuade her into accepting but she hadn't listened, she hadn't wanted to listen, instead she had stayed away from the house as much as possible and had refused to even look at her violin. But as time wore on she knew she was wrong and he was right and for the past week she had been practising morning, noon, and night and was now ready to leave.

She would be back in time for Otto's Ceilidh – nothing or no one was going to make her miss that – and with a resolute toss of her head she went indoors and began to look out the things she would need for her trip.

Mamma wouldn't be accompanying them, she seemed more than willing to stay at An Cala on her own: she had made friends on the island, she had had some wonderful times at Aggie's house and Rab McKinnon was going to show her the island – not in his tractor, she only suffered that if it was completely necessary – no, definitely not the tractor. Rab was going to borrow his uncle's car, true it had lain rusting at the back of the byre for 'a good wee whilie', Rab had explained tongue in cheek, but with a bit of luck, some second-hand tyres, a squirt or two of oil, a bit of elbow grease, it would be as good as new in no time.

Mamma didn't question any of that, perhaps she didn't want to, Rab's word was good enough for her: he was to be trusted, he always meant what he said, he was dependable, strong, and reliable – and even if the car wasn't, it was a much safer bet than the tractor, and it was bound to look better than any tractor any day.

Wullie McKinnon awoke from a deep sleep, the morning was bright and early – too bright and early, the hands of the clock were at four a.m. Outside the window the pearly sky was rosily flushed; the hill peaks wore lacy caps of mist; on the green lower slopes the sheep and cows still lay in sleepy repose; not a wisp of smoke came from the scattering of little white cottages; shades covered the windows like secretive eyelids; not a soul was about, it was that special time of day when the land breathed quietly and gently and gave off an air of belonging only to nature.

At least it would have been quiet and gentle if it hadn't been for Dodie's cockerels, trumpeting away as loud as they could, so effectively drowning out a melodic dawn chorus that even the very birds gave up the effort and huddled themselves sulkily into their feathers.

Wullie sat up in bed and nearly wept. He had bags under his eyes from lack of sleep, his face was haggard and drawn. 'That's it!' he exploded, his nose frothing with rage. 'I'm going to do something about these bloody cockerels – this very day!'

Mairi stirred and grunted and opened one sleepy eye. Since childhood she had been deaf in one ear and though it was certainly a great inconvenience there were times when it was a blessing in disguise and especially so since Dodie and his cockerels had come to live in the adjoining croft. All she had to do was bury her good ear into the pillow and she became oblivious to all unwanted noise, she was therefore not as sympathetic as she might have been to her husband's woes, except in the daytime when the cockerels' continual vying for supremacy got on her own nerves and she might gladly have brained Dodie if she had been that sort of person.

But she was a gentle, tolerant soul in the extreme and had always concerned herself with the old eccentric's welfare. The summer days had passed, Wullie had fretted and fumed but had never carried out his grim threats against the nuisances; this morning, however, there was something in his tone that warned her he meant business and she too sat up, her hair standing in spikes, her newly wakened eyes slowly emerging from sleep and dreams till gradually the rather vacant brown depths betrayed a vapid sort of anxiety.

'Ach, Wullie,' she clucked, in a voice to suit the occasion, 'you'll no' go and do anything foolish, I hope. These birds mean a lot to auld Dodie and you know what he's like if he gets upset.'

But her husband was beyond all reasoning. 'Upset! After I've killed his chickens I'll thraw his bloody neck while I'm about it! I've tholed him and his pests till I canny take any more and you can talk yourself blue in the face about him and his worries for all the good it will do any o' you.'

For answer Mairi threw back the covers and hopped out of

bed. 'Och, calm yourself,' she said soothingly. 'I'll make us both a nice cuppy and we can drink it in bed while we talk this over like two sensible people.'

Mairi's answer to all seemingly insuperable problems was 'a nice cuppy', but it didn't work on this particular morning. As soon as the world was up and doing Wullie was up and doing also, seeking out Robbie Beag who, as one-time gamekeeper of Burnbreddie, must surely know all there was to know about fowl of any sort.

Robbie took off his cap and scratched his head whilst listening to Wullie's outpourings of troubles. He knew for a fact that Ranald and some of the other men had put forward one or two useless suggestions for dealing with the cockerels and Robbie was slightly annoyed that Wullie hadn't come to him sooner since he was obviously the man for the job. But Barra had warned him to bide his time and as he had never been one to push himself forward, he had waited patiently for his font of knowledge to be tapped.

And now here was Wullie, almost foaming at the mouth as he described his feelings, ending in a breathless rush, 'I'll make it worth your while, Robbie, it won't be much but enough to buy you a good dram or two.'

Robbie affected to think the matter over carefully. He hummed and he hawed and generally delayed his answer, then, when Wullie was almost at bursting point, he said with a nonchalant air, 'I'll no' deny you have a problem there, Wullie, and though I say it myself I'm the man you're lookin' for. But there are one or two wee risks attached and I'll be lookin' for more than just a couple o' drams – a bottle o' best malt would go down much better and would make it worth my while.'

Wullie pondered for only a moment before nodding so eagerly the latest drip flew off the end of his nose. 'Right, a bottle it is, where, when, and how?'

'Well, when I worked to Burnbreddie and we wanted to catch the young pheasants we used to put a wee drop o' whisky in a peck or two o' meal; before we knew it they were as meek as lambs and just askin' for us to pick them up and do what we liked wi' them.'

To Wullie this was a terrible waste of good whisky but he was ready to try anything and nodded his agreement.

'We canny do it during the day when Dodie is about,' Robbie went on, his genial face growing pink at the thought of the adventure ahead, 'and it's no use at night when the birds have gone to roost and wouldny come down even to eat their grannie.'

Wullie couldn't see the relevance of that but made no comment as the plan unfolded.

'Morning is the best time,' Robbie decided. 'Before anybody is up and about, including the chickens, we have to be there to make sure the cockerels get to the meal first, and as it's light so early we'd best just spend the night in the hen hoosie, it's a good big shed and we'll be comfortable enough wi' just a couple o' blankets and a tot or two out o' my bottle.'

'But I had thought to give you that when it was all over,' objected Wullie.

'Na, na, taste and try before you buy, my father aye told us that and I have never forgotten the sense o' his words.'

Wullie agreed grudgingly, final arrangements were made and both men went home to tell their respective wives of their plans. Mairi thought of 'poor auld Dodie' and called on the Lord 'to spare him'; Barra told Robbie he was going soft in the head in his dotage but went to the linen kist to look out some blankets and then to the dresser to seek out a pair of his thickest winter socks.

Early next morning the sun rose on a sleeping land. All was as it had been at the same time on the previous day, with one difference – there was no raucous crowing from Croft Beag to break the golden silence. Only the sounds of the summer countryside could be heard: the burns tumbled down from the hills; corncrakes rustled the grasses; a curlew bubbled out its liquid song on the shore; the sea lapped the silvered sands; peesies ran with their chicks; gulls rode the silken air currents;

small birds spilled out their tiny hearts in triumphant praise of the new day. It was perfection, it was bliss.

If Wullie had been safely tucked up in his snug bed he might have been more able to appreciate all of these things, as it was both he and Robbie had spent an extremely uncomfortable and smelly night. The odour of hen's droppings was anything but conducive to sweet dreams and the wooden floor seemed to produce ever more splinters as the night wore on. Despite the blankets, it was cold, draughty and hard, and at two of the clock Robbie had suggested that a swig from the whisky bottle might serve to make the situation more bearable, though 'only a wee one', since he had to be awake to make sure the cockerels availed themselves of the doctored meal.

On first entering the shed, Wullie had been keen to simply grab the cocks and throttle them there and then but, as Robbie had pointed out, there was the pecking order to consider. The biggest and most royal of the birds was right at the top, as befitted a king of his size and status, the other five were on different rungs of the ladder, so to speak, and to try and catch them all at the one time would have created a hell's own din and would undoubtedly have brought Dodie running helter-skelter to see what all the fuss was about.

'You would just waken the whole neighbourhood,' Robbie insisted. 'Far better to do it my way, I know what I'm talkin' about. If you're so smart why did you no' just do the job yourself and save me havin' to bide in this shitty shed when I could be home in my own bed wi' my feets on Barra's nice warm bum.'

Wullie was mad at himself for upsetting Robbie's placid temperament. He gave in, and producing the bottle of best malt he passed it to Robbie for the first swig and waited politely for his turn.

That had been more than three hours ago. Now the first faint fingers of sunlight probed gently but insistently through the cobwebby window pane. They found the spiders and sent them running into their corners, they caressed a heap of crumpled blankets on the floor and slowly crept up to touch two faces, one round, smiling and absolutely dead to the world, the other thinner, younger but equally serene, as its owner wallowed in the best sleep he had enjoyed for weeks.

The relentless light explored further; it found an empty whisky bottle clasped lovingly to Robbie's quietly heaving bosom, the glass winking and gleaming with every tranquil breath he took.

Otherwise the shed was empty of life: the cockerels and their harems had risen at first light, delighted to find breakfast served so early in the day. The tempting bowls of meal didn't last long, the potion was gobbled up in no time at all and out into the morning tripped the hens.

Now they were staggering about in the yard in varying stages of inebriation: some so drunk they had fallen on to their backs and there they lay, bellies to the wind, their funny big chicken feet stiffly saluting the heavens; others were just wandering about aimlessly, tripping themselves up, so that every so often one would take a nose dive into a grassy mound where it remained, impaled on its own beak.

As for the cockerels, they were a sorry sight: no more did their bright red combs waggle proudly, instead they flopped miserably, along with everything else that they normally carried upright. True, King Cock did make an attempt to find his voice, he arched his throat, stuck his beak in the air and opened his lungs, but only a strangulated hiccupping sound emerged. Thus discouraged, he settled himself moodily into his feathers, lifted one leg and promptly fell over.

Luckily for Wullie and Robbie there weren't many people abroad at that time of the day, only Canty Tam stood at the gate, staring with all his lop-sided might at the hilarious scene, his vacant eyes wide and wondering but unable to relay any message to his brain that made sense.

He leered, of course – Canty Tam always leered, no matter the occasion – then with a sense of importance almost choking him he ran to knock up Dodie. While he waited for signs of life he stood back from the door, looked up at the window and yelled on the old man to hurry up as all his hens were dead or dying.

His loud, excitable voice filtered into the hen hoosie. Robbie was the first to stir, grudgingly he emerged from what had been a very satisfying dream in which he had been chasing Aggie McKinnon through the heather, brandishing a hat made out of King Cock's tail feathers. Aggie had been stark naked, her girth had slowed her down, and it had been an easy enough matter for Robbie to catch her and present her with the hat. Smiling at him coyly, she had placed the hat on her head and had stood there, looking at him invitingly, wearing nothing but the hat and her birthday suit. Robbie had been on the point of collecting his reward when he was rudely roused, and he had to sit very still for a moment while he gathered his senses together.

Wullie's sleep had been deep and dreamless, all he wanted was to remain in that state forever but some bugger was kicking up a terrible racket outside his window . . . those bloody cockerels were still at it . . . He awoke with a start, his heart thumping, surprised to find that he wasn't in his own bed with Mairi warm and sleepy beside him.

In some alarm he gazed dazedly around him. Awareness hit him like a blow, he looked at Robbie, Robbie looked at him, as one they scrambled to their feet and went racing outside, just in time to see Dodie and Canty Tam bearing down on them, their clumsy feet carrying them swiftly to the scene of drunken debauchery.

'My hens! My bonny bairnies!' The tears immediately coursed down Dodie's wizened cheeks as he beheld the scene before him. 'What have you done wi' them, Wullie McKinnon?' he cried, dropping on to his knees to take King Cock to his breast and rock him back and forward as if he was a baby.

'Ach, come on now, man.' Robbie tried to sound reassuring even though he was as surprised as Dodie by the sight of the inebriated poultry. 'We haveny done them any harm, they're no' dead – just – er – a wee bittie drunk.'

'Drunk!' Dodie's nose frothed as profusely as Wullie's who, standing in the full glare of morning light was a sorry sight to behold with his hair standing on end and 'the snotters blinding him', according to the nature of his affliction.

'Drunk!' Dodie repeated. 'How can my bonny hens be drunk,

they have never touched a drop o' the de'il's brew in the whole o' their lives?'

Robbie tried to pour oil on troubled waters, but it was no use, Dodie was so enraged he threatened to call in the police and both Wullie and Robbie gulped.

In the old days the law had been 'Big Gregor' who had spent his visits ceilidhing at relatives' houses and generally catching up on island news; now there was Clodhopper, named so because of his enormous size fourteen shoes and his peculiar habit of standing first on one foot and then on the other.

But there was more to Clodhopper than just big feet. His visits always held an element of surprise because there was never any warning as to when he might appear, he positively revelled in his position of power and thoroughly enjoyed snooping about at all hours of the day and night.

He took a special delight in hiding behind rocks and bushes and pouncing on people if he suspected them of wrongdoing. But his *pièce de résistance* was to lurk on the shore near the hotel, waiting for closing time and the revellers to emerge and drive off in their various modes of transport. Once he had booked Donald Ban for speeding through Portcull in his tractor, though Donald swore blind he had been going so slow he would have been faster getting out and walking.

Rhanna had been shocked to the core, for Donald hadn't even been drunk at the time, and folk told one another that things were getting so bad with Clodhopper he would be accusing them next of speeding on their bicycles.

Fortunately he only ever showed up about twice a year. Nevertheless, Dodie's threats were rather worrying for Robbie and Wullie, each of whom had given Clodhopper reason for suspicion on more than one occasion: Robbie for poaching, Wullie for driving his father's builder's van without a licence.

'Och, Dodie, you'll no' do that,' said Wullie, who was looking quite pale. 'You and me have been friends for a long time, you wouldny go and betray a man who has never grudged you a helping hand in the whole o' his life.'

'You're no' my friend anymore,' Dodie said with a watery

sniff. 'All you ever do is shout and swear at me and I'm that feart o' you I wish I was back in my own house up on the hill. I could do what I liked there and no one was any the wiser.'

'Ach, the Hellish Hags o' the Hill would have got you in the end,' Canty Tam said with conviction. 'I've seen them up there, black spooks wi' bat's wings and awful evil faces on them. They have hideous voices too, screechin' and cacklin' and flappin' about, just waitin' to pounce on anyone who goes near their lair. My mither warned me never to go on that hill on my own for fear one would catch me and carry me away forever.'

His predictions of doom and gloom had an immediate effect on Dodie, he forgot all about the police and burst into tears instead, which gave the two mischief-makers the chance they needed. Each putting an arm around Dodie's shuddering shoulders they led him away into the house to ply him with tea and sympathy, leaving Canty Tam to rush away and tell his tale, suitably embroidered, to anyone who would listen.

In days to come neither Robbie nor Wullie would be allowed to forget the episode of the drunken chickens, though for the moment that was the least of their worries. More immediate were their efforts to console Dodie and try to dissuade him from drastic action, which was rather difficult under the circumstances. The hens went off laying for a week and the cockerels didn't crow for at least two days, though on the afternoon of the third the familiar cacophony once more blasted forth.

Wullie's troubles had begun all over again, but help came to him from a most unexpected quarter.

One morning, on answering an abrupt knock at his door, he stared with surprise at a young man standing on the threshold. He was tall and lanky, his smooth skin sported a stubbly growth that was at least a week old, dangling from one ear was an ornament that resembled a curtain ring, and his greasy fair hair was tied back and held in place with an elastic band.

He introduced himself as Andy from Ayrshire, told Wullie he knew all about his problems with the cockerels and that he could have them crated and ready to leave on the afternoon boat.

'I'll tell the old man that my pal's a cockerel fancier,' he explained, rubbing his nose with a nicotine-stained finger. 'I'll gie him the patter, butter up his birds, offer him a price and before you can say cock-a-doodle-doo, they'll be mine. Of course,' he went on glibly, 'it will cost ye. I'll have to pay the old geezer and I'll need something for my trouble. Thirty pounds and the job's done, half for me, the rest for him.'

Wullie nearly had a fit. Thirty pounds! It was too much! First a bottle of best malt for that useless gowk Robbie, now this queer-looking young fart with his hawk-like face and his earring.

Wullie withdrew into the house for a quick confab with Mairi who had been watching proceedings from the window.

'He'll be one o' they flower people they have over on the mainland,' she hazarded. 'They go about looking like that.'

'Either that or a hippie,' said Wullie, who wasn't too sure of what was in vogue at the moment and didn't much care. He was only too eager to see the back of the cockerels, but the thought of parting with all that money made him hesitate.

'Ach, it's worth it.' Mairi made up his mind for him. 'I have a wee bit money put by and everyone wants their hair done for Otto's Ceilidh so I'll soon make up the loss. You're my man after all and I canny have you going off your head for the sake o' a few pounds.'

To her surprise, Wullie kissed her soundly on the nose before rushing outside to tell Andy from Ayrshire he had a deal and the sooner the job was done the better.

True to his word, that very afternoon, the young man presented himself at Wullie's door complete with the birds that were confined in two ancient peat creels. 'I let the old man keep one,' Andy explained, 'he insisted on that.'

'One is better than six, Wullie,' said Mairi soothingly. 'And you'll hardly ever know it's there since they only crow if there are others to compete with.'

Wullie saw the reasoning in that. He handed over the thirty pounds, the young man thanked him politely, shouldered the creels and went on his way. Wullie watched till he was out of sight before letting out a great whoop of joy, then, before Mairi knew what was happening, he had swung her into his arms to carry her up to the bedroom for 'a bit o' a cuddle by way o' celebration'.

Ranald looked fondly at the five pound note nestling in the palm of his hand. 'Everything went according to plan then,' he stated glibly. 'I told you it would work, son.' He grinned, gazing fondly into Andy from Ayrshire's grubby face, delighted to think that he was the instigator of such a successful ruse. 'Fifteen pounds wasny much to ask for peace o' mind. And Dodie would be pleased to get a fiver for his cockerels, especially if he thought they were going somewhere they would be admired and cared for.'

'Oh ay, by the time I had filled his lugs wi' praise he would have given me the bloody birds for nothing and I would have got away wi' it.'

And that was exactly what had happened. No one ever knew what really transpired between Dodie and Andy from Ayrshire, but, on the strength of a promise from the young stranger, Dodie had gladly parted with his cockerels, receiving not a penny piece in return.

Andy had piled on the compliments. 'These birds are a credit to you. They'll have to prove their worth, of course, that's why I canny give you more than my word at the moment, but I know my pal will be that pleased wi' them he'll want more o' the same, so you keep the big one to carry on the line and I'll be back next year wi' cash in my hand.'

Dodie, beaming from ear to ear, felt that it had been an honour to do business with Andy from Ayrshire – and King Cock was staying, he would do his work well, he was forever treading the hens and was father to more clutches of chickens than Dodie could count.

Andy from Ayrshire hoisted his rucksack on to his shoulders and stuck out his hand. 'Thanks for the bed, Ranald, I've fair enjoyed my few days on Rhanna. I'll look you up next time I'm on the island' – he winked – 'by that time Dodie's cockerel will have got to work and Wullie will be only too pleased to stump up peace money.'

Ranald, feeling right pleased with himself, pumped the young man's hand and told him there was always a bed waiting for him. 'Though mind,' he added pleasantly, 'prices are aye going up and it might cost you a wee bit more to bide in my house next time.'

Andy merely grinned and walked away down to the harbour to check that the cockerels were all right before sitting himself down on a bollard to count his money. Twenty-five pounds, not bad for a day's work, the arrangement had been fifteen pounds to be split three ways – that poor bugger, Wullie, would be too embarrassed ever to admit to anyone that he had parted with thirty pounds to get rid of the cockerels, and the poor old boy with the funny smell had promised never to tell a soul of the deal he'd struck with a summer visitor.

Slapping his knee, he gave a chuckle of pure triumph. Ranald thought he was crafty, he didn't know the half of it – Andy from Ayrshire nearly choked with mirth as he wondered what the opportunist would have said if he had discovered that his holiday lodger was something of an expert on poultry and that he really did have a pal who was a cockerel fancier, and one, furthermore, who would pay a handsome price for Dodie's five prize birds.

Chapter Nineteen

One of the first things Rachel did when she arrived back on Rhanna was to go and see Lachlan. He was working in his garden, tending his herbaceous bed, which somehow managed to survive and thrive despite the fierce winter winds that could sweep through the glen with vicious intensity. It was now a riot of colour and at first Rachel didn't see him, so high grew the hollyhocks, so exuberantly bloomed the lupins, the delphiniums and the marguerite daisies.

But he saw her and he emerged from behind a clump of love-in-the-mist, to wipe the sweat from his brow with an earth-begrimed hand. He greeted her warmly, his brown eyes crinkling. 'Rachel, you're back – I heard you on the wireless only yesterday and thought you would be away for a good whilie yet.'

She hesitated, unsure of how to go about explaining her reasons for being there, wishing with all her heart that she could communicate in the normal way. It wasn't everyone who understood her sign language, though Lachlan had always taken a special interest in her and was able to some extent to know what she conveyed with her gestures.

He saw her face and took the matter out of her hands. 'Come on, let's go in. Phebie aye has a cuppy about now and I'm that thirsty I could drink a potful all to myself. I was always more used to tending humans than gardens, but I'm learning, and in many ways plants are like people, a bit o' loving care and patience works miracles.'

When Phebie saw the visitor coming indoors with her husband she went to get an extra cup, but after she had drunk hers she didn't stay long in the room. Years of being a doctor's wife had taught her diplomacy, she saw that Rachel had something of great importance on her mind and Phebie, who was first and foremost a woman of great insight as well as instinct, had a very good idea what that something was, and with a murmured excuse she made her exit, leaving Lachlan to look questioningly at Rachel who, in a high state of tension, was sitting on the edge of the chintz-covered couch.

With a few swift movements she indicated exactly why she had come. Lachlan didn't need to understand the sign language to know what she meant. He sat back and studied her, remembering the day he had delivered her and Annie's shock when she had discovered that her beautiful baby had been born dumb. No one could have known that that same child would grow up to be so talented and successful, least of all Annie, who had never held out much hope of her daughter making anything special of her life.

But in recent years, the one thing that Rachel had wanted more than anything was a baby of her own. The passing of time had pushed that desire more and more into the realms of impossibility, now here she was, telling him very plainly that she thought she was pregnant and wanting him to verify it for her.

Going over to her he sat down and took her hand in his reassuring clasp.

'Rachel,' he began gently, 'much as I would love to, you know fine well that I'm not in the position to examine you and tell you what you want to know. Megan is the one you want, I canny just go behind her back and start diagnosing her patients. When I first retired, one or two of my old patients came to me wi' their ails but I was having none o' that and I'm sure a sensible lass like you can understand why.'

Rachel looked at him, she smiled and nodded, she seized a pad and pen from a nearby table and began to write furiously.

When he saw what she had written his smile was one of acquiescence. 'Facts and figures, eh? Dates and times. Right,' he looked her straight in the eye, 'everything points to you being about four months pregnant though I'm not going to be trapped into saying that you *are* pregnant . . .'

He got no further; she threw herself at him and hugged him so hard he emerged laughing and breathless and in time to see her disappearing out of the door. In minutes she was a blur on the glen road as she pedalled with energy to the Manse, where everything was quiet as morning surgery had finished fifteen minutes ago.

But Megan saw her just the same and told her what she already knew. In a hectic state of delight she took Megan's hand and shook it but that wasn't expressive enough for her passionate nature, a surprised Megan found herself being danced round the room then outside to her car where Rachel stood, pointing back towards Glen Fallan.

'Right.' Megan laughed, caught up in the girl's euphoria. 'You want me to take you to see Lachlan, I know fine you have a soft spot for him and I was going to see him this morning anyway before starting on my rounds. Just let me get my bag and I'll be right with you.'

Thus Lachlan found himself seated once more with Rachel in the parlour while Megan talked with Phebie in the kitchen.

Rachel had a lot of questions to ask and in her impatience her hands flew so fast he found it impossible to understand anything, so, with a great gusting sigh, she had to start all over again till he got the gist of her questioning, mainly why such a thing had happened after all this time.

'Och, it's not so long, lass, plenty of women have been wed longer than you before they conceived. You lead a very busy life, when you came to Rhanna you left pressures and commitments behind you for the first time in years, you shook off the fetters and relaxed, it's as simple as that. Go home now and tell Jon, he'll be over the moon, you've shared your joy wi' me, now it's his turn.'

But she shook her head and put her fingers to her lips, trying desperately to tell him, no, she needed time to adjust to this momentous happening, she wasn't yet ready for Jon to know. She saw Lachlan's face, surprised, puzzled. She smiled at him reassuringly and was on her way out when Megan stopped her in the hall to ask if she would like a run home, but she declined: it was a beautiful day, she would have to collect her bike from The Manse, she wanted just to walk and think and try to assimilate the wonderful thing that had happened to her.

None of it was quite real yet; she had to get used to the idea of a baby in her life before telling the world of her secret. She would wait till after Otto's Ceilidh, by then she wouldn't be able to keep her condition from anyone, far less Jon. Already she was growing bigger, her clothes were becoming tighter – and that sensation of butterflies in her stomach was strengthening and quickening – only it wasn't butterflies, it was a baby, and as if to prove it was real and living it suddenly moved strongly within her, making her stop and hold her hand to her mouth in a gesture of childish delight.

On the morning of the McKinnon Clan Gathering, Rhanna woke to overcast skies and drizzling rain that blotted out the hills and the sea in dismal blankets.

'Och, would you look at it!' Kate pushed aside her curtains to glare with animosity at the dripping scene outside. 'After such good weather too, the bugger has been saving itself for this particular day. Otto will be fair scunnered and after him going to so much bother too.'

'It will clear by midday,' Tam forecast knowledgeably. 'Sometimes the best days of all start off pissing and grey.'

And he was right, by early afternoon the clouds had melted away, allowing the sun to shine hotly on the refreshed countryside. Banks of mist unfurled from the hills to rise upwards and wreathe the purple peaks in gossamer scarves. Gradually the haar rolled back from the sea to cling mistily to the horizon so that it merged with little blue islands and gave everything an ethereal, magical quality.

Otto had arranged for a party of caterers to come over from the mainland and by two o'clock a huge marquee had been erected on the stretch of machair that skirted Portcull. Fragrant steam rose from urns of tea and soup. Plates piled with salads, sausage rolls, pies, and sandwiches, cold meat and rolls, filled one table; another groaned under an assortment of cakes and biscuits, jellies and trifles. Several enormous whole cooked salmon, with all the trimmings, were temptingly displayed and when Jim Jim saw them he wondered if they were meant to be eaten or were just there to be admired.

In a smaller marquee stood barrels of beer and a table whose surface was hidden under an array of spirits the like of which Tam said he had only ever seen in fantasies.

Prominently displayed were a dozen bottles of schnapps. When Fergus eventually set eyes on them he grinned wryly and told Otto it was whisky for him or nothing as never again would he risk a repeat of 'the night of the schnapps'.

'My friend,' Otto laughed, 'that was in another age. Since then I have acquired a taste for the *Uisge Beatha*; it is very refreshing – like the tea you are all so fond of.'

'We'll see if you can sup it like tea,' Fergus returned dryly, determined to get his own back on the big Austrian. 'There's a long night ahead o' us, no doubt we'll each have more than just a few drams – and may the best man still be able to say 'it's a braw bricht moonlicht nicht, the nicht' when the clock has struck midnight.'

Shona took his arm and drew him away. 'Och, Father,' she scolded, 'as if Otto could say that, even when he's sober – besides, it isn't fair to make him feel he has to keep up with you in that way, you know you've aye been able to hold your whisky; he's a novice compared to you.'

But Fergus was unrepentant. 'He has to learn sometime; he's built like an ox and ought to be able to keep up.'

Shona looked back at Otto and frowned. 'He *was* built like an ox, I'd say he's got thinner – even since I last saw him with his cat, he looks – frail somehow.'

'Frail! Otto! Havers!' scoffed Fergus. Nevertheless he too looked back at Otto and wondered if there was something in what Shona had said. She had always been perceptive, she seemed to sense things before anyone else, but the next minute he pushed his doubts away when he saw the man in question throwing back his head and laughing at something Jim Jim had said, and to Fergus he looked the picture of good health and high spirits.

The islanders didn't descend on the scene in droves, it was against their natural dignity to do so, but come they did, from all over the island: full-blown McKinnons, vaguely related McKinnons, uncles and aunts, cousins and friends of cousins, nephews, nieces, anyone who had any clan connections, no matter how vague, together with those who had no connections at all but just gatecrashed the scene to mingle with the crowd, including a few of the tinks who weren't going to miss the fun for anything.

'Hmph, would you look at them, they'll go anywhere if it means getting free food and drink,' Behag intoned heavily, fussily and pointedly adjusting the McKinnon tartan ribbon she wore on her frock. She had bought the ribbon just recently from a door hawker who had hastily parted with it for twopence after she had asked him if he held a vendor's licence and had hinted that she would report him to the authorities if he didn't. Behag was a great one for flaunting government bodies to anyone she suspected of unlawful dealings, it had always worked wonders for her: half the ironmongery in her kitchen had been acquired cheaply from travelling salesmen who had no wish to tangle with the authorities Behag spoke about so glibly, even though she couldn't have told one from another.

'I don't see anything wrong wi' the tinks,' Kate said, following Behag's gaze before bringing her own back to stare meaningfully at the ribbon pinned to the old woman's scrawny bosom. 'At least they didny buy their tartans at the door and pretend to be something they aren't.'

Behag's lips tightened but she said nothing more on the subject, certainly not to the formidable Kate, but when she saw Rachel welcoming the tinks she couldn't resist saying to Sorcha in meaningful tones, 'Have you noticed how she canny keep away from them? For all we know she might easily be one o' them seeing as how her mother couldny keep away from them either when she was young.'

257

Sorcha had been in such a hurry to get out of the house she had forgotten to insert her hearing aid and, moulding one ancient lug into a mottled brown trumpet, she shouted, 'Eh? What was that? Rachel a tink? You'd better no' let Kate hear you saying that.'

Kate turned round; the look she threw Behag was venomous in the extreme. Behag scuttled away with agility, her eye falling on Elspeth who was strolling haughtily towards the marquee on the arm of Captain Mac. Behag's eyes immediately sparkled with interest for despite her mournful demeanour she had had a wonderful time that summer: there were so many interesting things going on in the island, but best of all had been the affair between Elspeth and Captain Mac. Behag had noted that the display of luscious lingerie always appeared on the line after Captain Mac had taken himself off on one of his sojourns and the ex-postmistress's imagination had worked overtime. Everyone else had grown rather tired of the subject, the novelty of teasing Elspeth had begun to wear off, but for Behag it would never fade and in her mind she had called Elspeth everything from a hussy to a Jezebel.

Unlike Kate she had a healthy respect for Elspeth's able dialogue and had never dared to say anything that would incur a tongue-lashing, but her innuendoes, her tight-lipped, disapproving silences, had said it all and a little bit more besides.

To her complete and utter surprise Elspeth greeted her warmly and invited her to accompany both her and Mac into the beer tent as it was such a thirsty day.

'The beer tent!' Behag was shocked. So she had been right about Elspeth all along! All that so-called aversion to strong drink was just another front and those rumours about her being a secret tippler must be true. For all anyone knew she and Mac might be indulging in drink orgies and God alone knew what other debauchery.

'Ay, the beer tent.' Elspeth's own lips were very subtly beginning to tighten. 'There's more than hard liquor in there: I've been told there are soft drinks as well, though I might just have a small sherry to wet my thrapple.'

Behag hesitated; a small sherry was respectable, even ministers didn't turn up their noses at sherry, though of course Mark James couldn't even take that, not with his problem – but that was another story and one on which Behag held very firm views.

'Well, just a wee one to keep you company, Elspeth,' she conceded, and wondered why the other woman's eyes gleamed with something that might be called amusement.

By this time the scene was a mosaic of colour and life as half the island congregated on the green in front of the village of Portcull. Magnus of Croy arrived in style, driven by Todd the Shod who had at last learned to drive after years of claiming he would never sit behind a wheel of any sort after a lifetime of dealing with horses. He had spent a whole day cleaning and polishing his beautiful Rolls Royce and now it winked and gleamed and caused many a head to turn and smile at the sight of Magnus, sitting in the back, nodding and waving in a very regal manner.

As soon as the car stopped, Otto was there to help his grandfather alight and lead him away to the refreshment tent as he had expressed a desire to 'wet his whistle'.

'Neither o' them are wearing the kilt,' Kate observed in some disappointment. 'I had thought, wi' this being Otto's official introduction to the Clan McKinnon, he would have appeared in full Highland dress.'

'Ay, everyone else has made the effort,' said Isabel. 'I thought he went to Glasgow to buy an outfit for himself and Magnus – surely he's no' going to let a chance like this slip by him.'

'Ach, give the man time,' said Todd the Shod. 'He'll maybe surprise us all before the day is over.'

'Are you knowing something we don't?' Mollie questioned suspiciously but her husband merely threw her a knowing wink and went to join his cronies who were already making merry in the beer tent.

Halfway through the afternoon Dodie appeared on the scene, shining and scrubbed, thanks to Mairi's administrations on his

259

person. At the time he hadn't been too appreciative of being dumped in the tub in order to receive a thorough overhaul by Wullie, who, armed with a large loofah and an even larger sponge, had scoured every inch of Dodie's skin till he said he hadn't any left and cried out for mercy. But afterwards, when Mairi had smothered him in body lotion and talcum powder and had cut and shaped his baby-fine hair, he had gazed at himself in the mirror for fully five minutes with a smirk of pure vanity widening his mouth.

She had also sponged and pressed his best suit and on the lapel she had fixed a large rosette of McKinnon tartan ribbon because she told him his mother had been of that clan and he had every right to wear the colours. In truth she didn't really know what his mother had been, but Dodie had taken her at her word, and was so pleased with himself he forgot to be awkward and shy in the midst of the large gathering and went immediately to seek out Otto who was sitting outside the marquee talking to Rachel.

Without any of his usual hesitation, Dodie presented Otto with one of his hand-painted stones, stuttering a little in his efforts to utter some appropriate English salutation that would be understood by 'the furrin gentleman'.

Dodie had been one of the first born and bred islanders that Otto had met on his arrival on Rhanna, and ever since the unique ride in Megan's car, shared by Dodie and his twin lambs, Otto had taken an interest in the old man and had endeared himself still further by always asking after Curly's welfare. In Dodie's estimation, Otto was a man of greatness and goodness, and in Otto's eyes, Dodie was a gentle, special creature whose simple beliefs and often staggering insights placed him in a category that was all his own.

Otto's greeting was therefore genuinely warm and he received his gift with pleasure, turning it over in his hand, something queer and sad touching his heart when he saw painted notes of music drifting into a blue and heavenly sky and the motto *Mac nan Èilean* painstakingly scrawled round the edges.

'How appropriate,' he murmured softly. 'How very appropriate, almost as if . . .'

He looked into Dodie's dreamy grey-green eyes. 'You're a genius, Dodie, in your own way, you're a genius, and this calls for a celebration.'

Throwing his arm around the old man's stooped shoulders he led him away to the beer tent and thereafter to the food table where he personally saw to it that Dodie's plate was well filled with the choicest and tastiest of fare.

It was a wonderful day for everyone: the sun continued to shine warmly, Otto had paid Erchy to run a special shuttle service and many of the old ones, who hadn't been outside their own little corners for years, were able to meet up with one another and catch up on all the little snippets of news.

Otto hadn't forgotten the children, in fact he was like the pied piper that day with the youngsters following him around and hanging on his every word. He had arranged games and amusements to keep them happy and half the time he joined in their fun, making them shriek with laughter at some of his antics.

'Ach, would you look at him,' said Tina, gazing fondly at the big man. 'He's so good wi' the bairns, it's just a pity he never— ' She came to an abrupt stop, reddened and turned away, leaving some of the womenfolk to wonder to each other what it was she had been about to reveal.

When it came time for the children to go home, Otto personally presented each of them with a wooden plaque bearing the McKinnon coat of arms and the inscription: *McKinnon Clan Gathering, Island of Rhanna, 1967*, and even though one lad told his friends, 'The last McKinnon in our family was buried fifty years ago,' he went rushing off, carrying his trophy with pride, impatient to show it to his mother who had conjured a very dusty McKinnon out of an equally dusty diary she had just recently found in an old trunk in the loft.

The food and drink had rapidly disappeared during the course of the afternoon, and by five o'clock everyone was beginning to disperse back to their homes to get themselves ready for the concert that was being held that night in the Portcull village hall.

Magnus and Otto repaired to Tigh na Cladach to rest and partake of a meal cooked by Tina.

Otto was very glad to go up to his bedroom and close his eyes; Magnus contented himself with the comfortable armchair in the sitting room; Tina busied herself laying out the clothes both men would wear that night. She beamed with pride as she gazed at the colourful array. 'You'll make a right bonny pair,' she said softly and went to get a clothes brush just in case she had missed anything when she had taken the garments out of their wrappings to air them.

Behag emerged from the beer tent, supported by Elspeth and Captain Mac. Her eyes were glazed, her spindly legs unsteady and she was thankful to have Captain Mac's strong hand under her elbow. Elspeth had mixed her a Mickey Finn and Behag, her palate receptive after three glasses of sherry, had drunk it down without so much as a grimace.

'You'll no' let anybody see me,' she pleaded with Elspeth. 'I canny think what's happened to me, I was fine for a whilie then something just seemed to hit me. My head feels gey queer and my legs are like jelly, but I'll be fine once I'm home wi' a good strong cuppy inside me.'

'I'll no' let anybody see you,' promised Elspeth and promptly steered the inebriated old woman into a hotbed of gossiping crones who stared at Behag with disbelieving eyes.

'She's drunk, the old hypocrite!'

'Ay, and after all her talk about the weaknesses o' the flesh!'

'Years o' it, aye looking down her nose at anybody who takes an innocent wee dram! She's a disgrace to the island.'

So the comments followed in the wake of Behag's erratic course. Because Elspeth made sure they bumped into everyone in their path, her mouth quivering all the while as never had she enjoyed herself more. She had waited for a moment like this for years and now that she had Behag quite literally in the palm of her hand she was going to make the most of every second.

Holy Smoke was bearing down on them. At sight of Behag he stopped dead in his tracks, eyed her with self-righteous disapproval and exclaimed, 'Miss Beag! Is it really you? I never thought to see such a thing in all my born days! May the good Lord have mercy on your soul.'

His droning, mournful tones penetrated the fog that was choking Behag's senses, and even in her stupefied state she tried to make the effort of escaping the one person she never had any desire to meet, be she drunk or sober. Wriggling out of Mac's supportive grasp she took two steps forward, her knees buckled, and she would have fallen had not Holy Smoke himself darted forward to catch her.

'No,' she moaned, 'Leave me be, Sandy McKnight, I want to go home, I can manage fine if I just take it slowly. It's the heat, too much . . . I canny stand noise and heat . . .'

'Ach, the sowel,' Elspeth intoned, sadly shaking her head. 'She'll no' face the fact that she's had one too many – it would be too much to expect her to admit to being human like the rest o' us.' She turned an innocent face on Holy Smoke. 'Isaac and myself have things to do, Sandy, would you make sure she gets home safe and sound? I know I can trust you no' to breathe a word o' this to another living soul, for Behag has aye been a body who prided herself on abstinence.'

Holy Smoke, brimming over with Christian duty, nodded his agreement and firmly led the protesting Behag away. Elspeth clapped her hand to her mouth, it was the final triumphant feather in her cap and she almost smothered in her efforts to keep back her laughter.

'We'll no' see her at the concert the night,' said Mac with a grin as he gazed after the unlikely pair. 'Mind you, I feel a wee bittie sorry for her, it's no' like Behag to let herself go like that, and it just shows how unused to alcohol she is when three wee sherries knocked her for six.'

'That's what she gets for meddling, Isaac.' Elspeth's chin tilted and she sniffed. 'She has spent the summer watching us through her peepscope and I for one am no' sorry to see her getting her comeuppance.'

She took his arm. 'We have better things to do wi' our time than stand here discussing Behag. I have my frock to press for tonight, I have a meal to serve, and you know how long it takes you to get yourself into your kilt and gear.'

He allowed himself to be led away, quite happy to be seen with her arm linked through his, for truth to tell he had spent a very contented summer with Elspeth: she was surprisingly good company, she kept a tight ship, her cooking was excellent, above all she hadn't nagged him once, and anything was better than smelly old Gus with his wind and his wireless, and his disgusting cronies with *their* wind and their other bad habits, not to mention their fondness for that awful brew that tasted like cat's piss and which they had the gall to call rum.

The village was quiet again, except for the notes of 'Onward Christian Soldiers' drifting faintly on the breezes. Behag was keeping her end up, it was the only thing her fuddled mind could think of that might convince the world she most certainly wasn't drunk but just as happy as anyone else that day and was singing to the Lord to prove it.

Chapter Twenty

Jon had never seen his mother so excited about anything as she was about Otto's concert. At last, she had declared, she was going to see some culture on an island where social activities confined themselves to ceilidhs, where everyone seemed to speak in that strange Gaelic language and entertained themselves with singing and music that had no place in modern-day life.

Patiently Jon had tried to explain that the music and language of the highlands and islands was a matter of tradition and that the culture of these lands was uniquely different and special, but she hadn't listened and in the end Jon gave up, hoping that, in time, she would come to realize it was a privilege to live among a people who were as natural as the hills and as unfettered as the very air they breathed.

Mamma hadn't attended the afternoon festivities, pleading a headache but in reality getting herself thoroughly glamorized for the evening concert.

She had gone to Mairi's the day before to have her hair and nails done, expecting to find a proper hairdressing premises, but instead she found a notice pinned to the crofthouse door which read: MAIRI'S SALOON, PROFESSIONAL HAIRSTYLING AND BEAUTY TREATMENTS – INCLUDING FACE MASKS, PEDICURES, OLD AGE PENSIONERS, (AND NAILS) HALF PRICE, EVERY WEDNESDAY.

There followed a list of prices and opening times with an extra proclamation added at the bottom: *Never on the Sabbath – under any circumstances – except for funerals and christenings if completely necessary*.

When a puzzled Wullie had asked why she had made a concession for these two events she had said in her kindly way, 'Ach well, some o' they young mothers would forget their heads if they wereny screwed on and might be wantin' a hairdo at the last minute, and if someone goes and dies on you at the weekend, Sunday would be the only day they might have time to spare.'

'But, if they're dead, they would have no time for anything and couldny very well get up out their coffins to get their hair done.'

Mairi shook her head at her husband's lack of understanding. 'Och, Wullie,' she chided gently, 'I mean the relatives, of course: a dead body wouldny be caring if they went to their grave lookin' like a scarecrow, would they now?'

When Mamma, whose grasp of written English was as halting as her speech in that language, had finally absorbed the contents of the notice, she gave a snort of derision and, without so much as a warning knock, pushed open the crofthouse door and marched in . . . only to see a baldly naked Wullie in the lobby as he emerged from the kitchen tub to make his way up to the bedroom to dress.

He let out a nasal shriek of surprise; Mamma also let out a shriek, only hers was a mixture of shock as well as surprise, to see a man as thin as Wullie so well equipped in the luggage department.

With bulging eyes she stared – and stared – while Wullie strove to shield his private parts with the inadequate coverage of his hands before darting like a bullet upstairs.

Mairi appeared in the hall to welcome Mamma with a fondly shy smile then led her into the room that had been converted some years ago for the purpose of beautifying the island's population.

Frau Helga Jodl was less than pleased by what she saw: a tiny, cramped space containing a few kitchen chairs; a pulley strung from the ceiling hung with an array of towels; two hairdryers that looked as if they might have been rescued from the Ark; one badly marked mirror; a small table that groaned under a pile of magazines, together with copies of the *Oban Times* dating back twenty years; and a trolley spilling over with rollers, curlers, tongs, hairgrips and nail polish.

In the midst of this motley assortment was the washbasin, standing over by the window, the only modern piece of equipment in the room. Powder blue, pristine clean, presided over by two gleaming chrome taps with a little plaque above them which read: *This saloon was officially opened in 1964 by Scott Balfour, the Laird of Burnbreddie.* Opposite the hairdryers was a handwritten notice which joyfully instructed: *Rest, linger, enjoy being pampered. Free tea to all friends and visitors, home-baked scones twopence each, except when the coal lorry is late.*

Mamma did not appreciate the promise of free tea. Tea! Pah! She had drunk tea till it was coming out her ears! No one here seemed to have heard of coffee – as for resting and lingering, she wouldn't stay one moment longer than necessary in this disgraceful travesty of a hairdressing salon.

Turning to the beaming Mairi, who was watching her with expectant interest, she said with cutting sarcasm, 'My eyes, they are deceiving me; I look but I do not believe. I think it is the comedy! Money you cannot expect from people coming here! You should pay them for having the courage to set a foot inside your house!'

Mairi looked as if she had been struck, her guileless brown eyes filled with tears and she turned away on the pretence of folding a clean pair of towels that were already neatly folded and laid ready beside the washbasin.

But that had only been the beginning of Mamma's reign of domination over the little sanctum that was Mairi's pride and joy. She had gone on to ever greater heights of wounding criticism, she had been bossy, imperious, loud and demanding, completely unnerving poor Mairi, draining away her confidence so badly that very soon she had none left. She had become flustered and unsure; gradually but surely her reflexes grew slower, like a clock slowly unwinding till it was only just ticking and no more.

In the end she had dithered about so much she had spilled hairgrips all over the floor and when she bent to pick them up she had bumped her head on the washbasin which made her brain whirl and slowed her down more than ever. A mass of fingers and thumbs, her eyes watering, her head spinning, she had had quite enough of Frau Helga Jodl and told her so in no mean terms.

For placid, kindly Mairi to get angry was, in itself, an almost unheard-of happening; for her to lose her head altogether went against everything that made up her simple, tolerant nature – and the result was disquieting.

With terrible, frightening calm, she bent down, glared into Mamma's startled face and gritted, 'Just you be listening to me, you ugly, bossy, big bitch! I'll tell you what I'm going to do to you so that you will never again speak to me as if I was a bit cow dung brought in from the midden. First I'm going to tear every last hair from your fat, swollen head, then I'm going to hold it under the taps and laugh while I watch you drowning!

'After that I'm going to sit back wi' a good strong cuppy and wait very calmly for Clodhopper to come and take me away. I don't care if I rot in jail for the rest o' my life, it will have been worth it just for the pleasure o' getting to kill you wi' my own bare hands!'

So saying, she set about tearing the curlers from Mamma's head. Mamma shrieked in pain but the relentless attack went on – and on – and on – and the odd thing was, although Mamma was built like a battleship, she was no match for slim little Mairi whose fury lent her the strength of a bull.

Tears of rage running down her face, her arms working like pistons, she went on wrenching, tugging, pulling, till the curlers lay in hairy heaps all over the floor, as quite a considerable amount of Mamma's hairs had come out with them.

If fate hadn't intervened, in the shape of Kate McKinnon herself, Mairi might well have carried out her threats, for she had worked herself up into such a state she was quite simply beyond all control and was just itching to get Mamma's wildly disarranged head into the washbasin.

Kate, who had the next appointment, came in breezily, but stopped dead in her tracks to take in the scene of carnage with bulging eyes, before rushing forward to wrest her daughter-in-law away and fold her into her strong, capable

268

arms, where, her anger suddenly spent, Mairi lay, sobbing helplessly.

Mamma, her hair a knotted tangle, stared at the pair of them with horrified eyes. She had already met her match in the able Kate, now it seemed the daughter-in-law was tarred with the same bristly brush and Mamma was genuinely scared, upset, and only too eager to try and make amends.

'I go, I make the cuppy,' she blabbered, and rose to her feet, causing a stray curler to roll from her shoulder and bounce on to the floor. 'Tea, it is the Scottish cure for everything . . . even attempted murder,' she added with what might be described as a touch of humour.

But Kate pushed her back into her seat with a heavy hand. 'I'll make it,' she said disdainfully, 'you wouldny know how to make a decent cuppy – and I'll tell you this, Frau Helga Jodl, I've known Mairi all o' my life and never, never have I seen the poor lass in such a state. You have a knack of instilling rage in the mildest o' souls, but, as you've seen for yourself, even a body as gentle as our Mairi has its breaking point, and if she ever has reason to kill you again – I'll no' stop her – I'll help her.'

So saying she flounced away to get the tea, returning to the sight of Mamma meekly sitting beside Mairi, talking to her in soothing tones and actually patting her shoulders, albeit awkwardly.

The three of them sat sipping their tea in silence until, revived by the brew, they very gradually began to talk. Half an hour later a feeling of camaraderie existed between them, with Kate at her best describing some amusing incident concerning Holy Smoke before going on to congratulate Mamma for having outwitted him over the question of money.

Mairi listened, clucking and clicking in her usual mild way, Mamma laughed as she hadn't done since her meeting with Merry Mary and Aggie, and for the second time in her life knew the uplifting experience of participating in island gossip instead of being on the outside, just listening.

Eventually, her good humour restored, all idea of revenge forgotten, Mairi rose and proceeded to tackle Mamma's hair, earning an extra pound at the end of the day from one grateful and thoroughly chastened customer.

Todd had insisted on collecting Otto and his grandfather from the shorehouse, even though they said they could easily walk the short distance to the hall.

'Na, na,' beamed Todd, 'everything must be done in style tonight, it is a very special occasion and I didny spend all day polishing my motor just to pick Magnus up from Croy – though of course I was honoured to do that,' he added hastily.

He was looking very swish that night: Mollie had mended the moth holes in his kilt and had bought him a sparkling white evening shirt for the occasion. He had managed to remain reasonably sober despite the temptations of the beer tent that afternoon, and now he stood by his Rolls Royce, resplendent in his finery, opening the doors with a flourish when Otto and Magnus came down the path, Tina having gone home to get herself ready after she had seen to the menfolk.

At sight of the two men, Todd beamed and rubbed his hands together. 'My, my,' he greeted them, 'you are a sight for sore eyes and no mistake, and a credit to clansmen everywhere, no matter their tartan.'

As soon as he brought his motor to a halt outside the hall he extricated his bagpipes from the back seat and went rushing away, in his hurry forgetting his manners so that his two very important passengers had to make their own way out of the Rolls and forward into glory.

Todd, breathless after his rush, hoisted his pipes to his chest, raised the chanter to his lips and waited for the appropriate moment, glad of a respite that he might fill his lungs with air before filling his bagpipes with the air from his lungs.

On the other side of the door, Torquil Andrew McGregor, gold medallist at Highland Games, big-muscled, ruggedly handsome in the McGregor tartan, having tuned his pipes in readiness, now waited impatiently to get started.

Magnus and Otto approached, Todd and Torquil looked at one another, nodded and struck up at the same moment. At first the drones were all that could be heard, then the opening tune came, skirling and spilling forth, and to the stirring blast of 'Highland Laddie', Magnus and Otto were piped into the hall in style.

As one, the packed hall turned to stare, murmur and admire, for Otto had spared nothing when he had gone to Glasgow to purchase his very first Highland dress. He had the build, the bearing and the dignity for such garb, and, more importantly, he had the right to wear it. His McKinnon tartan kilt was of the very best quality, his white evening shirt sparkled against his black Argyll jacket with its triangular silver buttons, the amber Cairngorm stone in his sgian-dhu shone and winked in its silver setting, his silver kilt and tie pins bore the McKinnon crest and altogether he was a splendidly proud figure.

Beside him, Magnus of Croy, his devoted grandfather, was also an eye-catching sight. Otto had treated him to an entire new rigout, his blue eyes were snapping with excitement in his lively brown face, his head was held high, his back ramrod straight and, for a man of his years, he was altogether a credit to himself and his clan.

A burst of applause broke out. Otto acknowledged it with shining eyes, his heart brimming over with emotion in this, the proudest moment of his life.

The islanders had made a fine job of the hall: balloons and streamers hung from the rafters and walls, and strung across the ceiling was a huge tartan banner bearing the message: '*Ceud Mile a'Fàilte, Mac nan Èilean*', meaning, 'A Hundred Thousand Welcomes, Son of The Island'.

Scott Balfour, the laird, came over to personally shake Otto by the hand and fifteen minutes later, when all the noise and fuss had settled down, Scott climbed up on the platform to officially welcome this notable McKinnon to the island, going on to say a few appropriate words before beckoning Otto to come up and join him.

He stood beside the laird and looked down with affection at the faces he had come to know so well these last few months. They had made him feel welcome and wanted, they had befriended him and had very quickly made him feel as if he had belonged here on Rhanna all of his life, and something sore and sad tightened his throat in the knowing that the years were rapidly coming to an end for him and that too soon he must relinquish this land and these people that he loved so well.

The ache inside him misted his eyes and hushed his voice when he thanked the laird and looked straight at the gathering to say simply, 'All of my life I have waited for this moment, all of my boytime in Austria, I listen to my grandmother's voice telling to me the tales of her Hebridean childhood and of all the places she loved and never forgot to her dying day. Through her words I have seen the skies and the seas, I have walked on the moors and beside the ocean, I have heard the birds and listened to the beat of the waves breaking on the shore, the scents of the wildflowers were the perfumes I smelt in my dreams, and I hugged it all to myself and could never get enough of her memories.

'But the best was yet to come – the chance to see and hear all of these things for myself – and in my wildest dreams I could never have imagined the reality to be so breathtaking. I came here as a stranger, but when the time comes for me to go I know I will leave with the knowledge that I didn't just find friends on my island of dreams, I found my family as well and discovered for myself the true meaning and the joy of having kin I could call my own.'

He gazed at his grandfather down there at the edge of the crowd. He extended his hand. Magnus went up to him, grandfather and grandson looked at one another for a long time before they shook hands and embraced, Magnus a bit red in the face, Otto delighted and obviously enjoying every second.

'Ach my, are they no' lovely just?' Kate furtively searched for her hanky and blew her nose hard. 'Tis proud I am to be kin to such a bonny man as Otto, he has such a fine way o' putting himself over and of course, I was the first person on the island to hear about his grandmother and to find out who he was.'

But Kate did not know everything about Otto, as the next few minutes proved. While he was up on the platform Mamma had been watching him with a puzzled frown on her features, it was the first chance she had had to see Otto face to face and she stared at him intently. Her frown cleared and she cried out in a voice that everyone could hear, 'Karl Gustav Langer! The famous pianist! Oh, I have heard your music many times, I attend a concert of yours when you come to Germany, and also in Vienna when I stay with Jon in Austria.'

It was the moment Rachel had dreaded, all along she had known it would happen sometime and in some way, but not like this, in front of everybody, all eyes staring, all heads turning. Frantically she signalled for Jon to do something to shut his mother's mouth but he showed no inclination to do anything that might help a situation which was now beyond saving anyway.

Barra, who had kept Otto's secret well, glared at Mamma and rudely told her to hold her tongue, while Magnus, who had found out his grandson's true identity while they were in Glasgow, was furious with the big loud woman whom he had first encountered at Croy Beag not so very long ago. His recollections of her were anything but fond and he came sprachling down from the platform to take her arm and give her a piece of his mind.

Everyone was looking at everyone else. Word was passed from McKinnon to McKinnon that Herr Otto Klebb wasn't just a long-lost clansman, he was also one of the most renowned pianists in Europe. Many of them had listened to him on the radio, and though none of them had ever seen him, his name was familiar and one to be held in respect. Now there was an explanation for those glorious waves of melody pouring from the shorehouse, and the reason for the beautiful piano being shipped over specially was all at once clear.

Tam and his cronies eyed one another as they remembered that day of sweating and groaning in their efforts to get the Bechstein in through the doors of Tigh na Cladach. Yesterday had seen a repeat of that performance, only this time it was from Tigh na Cladach to the hall as Otto had insisted on having his own piano at the concert. And no one could blame him there, since the hall's ancient old 'wheezebox' had seen better days and those very decidedly in the dim and distant past.

The men also remembered the 'affair o' the Oxo cubes' and the impromptu ceilidh that had followed, with the spirits flowing like water and Otto there at his piano, laughing, joining in the fun, allowing his mask of dourness to slip and letting the warm, generous man to shine through.

'And to think,' Tam whispered breathily in Kate's ear, 'he is one o' us, a McKinnon, the very finest you could get. My, I'm that proud I could burst.'

'Ay, well don't do it here,' returned Kate dryly. 'You would flood the place wi' all that beer you've been drinking and you wi' your reputation to uphold as a first-rate McKinnon.'

Lachlan climbed on to the platform and said a few words in Otto's ear, the next minute he held up his hand and demanded everyone's attention.

The islanders had always listened to him and they listened now. He asked them not to let Otto's identity be known outside of Rhanna. The man was here to have a rest, he told them, the last thing he wanted was for the media to find out where he was, if they did it would be exit Otto, and who among them wanted that on their conscience?

No one, it seemed, was keen for that to happen. A ripple of consternation ran round the room at the very idea, heads nodded, rapid exchanges took place.

Herr Tam, electing himself as spokesman, held up his hand and shouted, 'You can rely on us, we'll no' be telling a soul – and if we hear o' anybody breathing a word you can bet your boots it will be their last.'

Lachlan grinned. 'I hope there will never be any need to go that far. I trust you all, as for Otto, he wants you all to treat him as you've always done, without undue deference or difference – and while he is with us he is Otto, just that, Karl Langer belongs to the world – Otto belongs to us, and while he doesn't want any favours from us, I for one am honoured to have him here on Rhanna and will personally make certain that his stay here will be one that he will remember for the rest o' his days.'

A cheer went up, someone shouted '*Mac nan Èilean*', and before long the affectionate nickname was ringing from the rafters. Otto acknowledged the show of strength with a triumphant fist raised in the air. Lachlan lifted up his own hand and called for 'the show to go on', which had the effect of bringing the gathering down to earth and getting on with the business in hand.

From that night on, the islanders closed ranks. They could be a tight-lipped lot when they liked and vowed to one another that nosy visitors would get nothing out of them, if anyone ever asked about the foreign gentleman they would receive nothing except polite but evasive answers in Gaelic, which was usually a very effective way of dealing with questions that no one wanted to answer.

But for now, it was 'on with the show', which was more in the nature of a dance-cum-ceilidh-cum-concert. The chairs had been cleared to one side of the hall and during the first part of the evening The Portcull Fiddlers, in the shape of Rachel, Lorn and Jon, took the platform to provide music that soon had everyone itching to take to the floor. Torquil and Todd played rousing tunes on the pipes; Magnus gave a stirring solo on his kettle drums and later took up his accordion to provide a medley of feet-tapping airs.

Wild skirls and hoochs rent the air, becoming more pronounced as the evening wore on, with the merrymakers taking full advantage of the bar that had been set up in a curtained-off section of the room.

Fergus and Otto drank glass for glass of whisky till before very long the rest of the menfolk realized that they were witnessing a contest of stamina in the drinking field and, in their enthusiastic way, boosted proceedings by holding their own little 'may the best man win' sessions.

Mamma watched all of this with mounting concern. 'This you call culture?' she complained to Rab who, in his quiet way, was thoroughly enjoying himself. 'Myself, I call it barbaric: the dancing, it is wild, the music is designed to fill the head with primitive behaviour and bring out a madness that is frightening.

But, of course' – she sniffed disdainfully – 'they have never known anything else, they are not people of the world.'

Rab's eyes were calm enough when he looked at her but there was a warning glint in them that promised greater things to come. 'And just what is your concept of worldly people, Mistress Jodl? Your own daughter-in-law is a world famous violinist yet she knows how to let her hair down when the opportunity presents itself.'

'Rachel! We cannot count Rachel, she was born and brought up in this place, the madness was in her right from the start and will always be there, no matter how far in the world she travels.'

'Of course we can count Rachel, and Ruth McKenzie too, she has made her mark in the literary world. Both lassies are a credit to the island, and look at these other youngsters, many o' them attend college in Glasgow, they are educated and they are clever and, of course – they have the good manners on them that makes certain they never deliberately demean other folk.'

Mamma chose to ignore that point. 'Pah! Glasgow! What is Glasgow? It is not the world. If they came to Germany they would know the meaning of culture. In Hamburg— '

'Hamburg?' Rab interrupted, pronouncing it in such a way as to make it sound like 'Humbug'. 'And where in the world is that, I'd like to know?'

'If you do not know where Hamburg is then you too are lacking in the worldliness.'

Rab shook his head, his eyes were now icy cold. In his soft, slow voice he drawled, 'We have a saying here on Rhanna: "You haveny lived till you've been to Glasgow and you haveny been born till you visit the Hebrides." Cities like Hamburg are ten a penny; give me Glasgow or Edinburgh any time, because you see, Mistress Jodl, the people in them are human beings who are known and respected the world over.'

At that Mamma proceeded to have a fit of the 'solkiness' and Rab immediately deserted her to dance with Eilidh Monro who had had her sights set on him for some considerable time and who hated Mamma's guts for having arrived so unexpectedly in the mating ring.

Mamma looked after him with worried eyes; she had made a great effort with her appearance for this man though she wouldn't admit, even to herself, how much she had come to like and admire him. As soon as the music stopped she sought him out, elbowing Eilidh out of the way in her eagerness to make amends with him.

'The apology I make,' she announced to him with an effort. 'You are right, the evening is here to enjoy, but the hall is too hot and I ask of you to get for me the small glass of schnapps.'

Rab's eyes gently gleamed, he went off and returned with the desired drink, which Mamma downed in one gulp before requesting another. When it too had been consumed without a grimace she allowed Rab to lead her on to the floor and show her how to perform a reel, watched by a glowering Eilidh and several other womenfolk whose tongues were soon red hot with enjoyable speculation.

Mamma was not a figure to be missed in any crowd. Mairi had slightly overdone the blue rinse but even so, Jon's mother was an impressive sight in more ways than one and when Rab had danced her to a gasping halt, quite a few of the menfolk jostled for her attention. But she had eyes only for Rab and he, whilst making sure that she didn't monopolize him too much, paid her sufficient attention to make Eilidh retire to the edge of the ring for the rest of the night and join with her cronies in that most satisfying of all female pastimes, that of criticising other females in their choice of dress, hairstyle and footwear.

By nine-thirty everyone had danced themselves to exhaustion and were only too glad to avail themselves of tea and sandwiches before arranging the chairs in rows for the next part of the evening, beginning with the Portvoynachan Ladies Gaelic Choir singing a selection of traditional Gaelic airs, followed by the school choir's eager rendering of popular Scottish and English songs that soon had everyone tapping their feet.

The light shone on the shining cherubic faces; parents hardly recognised their offspring – the immaculate little dresses, the neatly pressed trousers, the clean, glowing skin, the innocent smiles. Neil Black stepped forward to sing a solo in his soaring, sweet, soprano voice, and his parents almost burst with pride and forgot the grimy, untidy ragamuffin Neil in the utter joy of the moment.

Neil received his applause with suitable aplomb and stepped sedately back to his place as little Lorna McKenzie came forward to recite a poem she had composed herself. Ruth and Lorn listened to their daughter with bated breath; Fergus watched his dark-haired granddaughter and squeezed Kirsteen's hand. Lorna concluded her poem, her big, solemn eyes swept the upturned faces, with great restraint she refrained from waving to those members of her family dotted about the audience and she too went back to her place to thunderous applause.

In a spurt of jealousy Margaret Black tugged Lorna's hair and in one minute flat the angels turned into devils. A good going scuffle ensued, parents stormed the platform to rescue, slap, or reprimand their offspring, according to the measure of their misdeeds, while the Portvoynachan Ladies Gaelic Choir rescued the day by singing Brahms' 'Lullaby', which, if inappropriate, successfully filled the gap till order was restored.

It was Jon's turn next. He was a brilliant musician and could have made a notable career for himself, but when he met and fell in love with Rachel, he had buried his own ambitions in order to allow her to pursue hers, for in her he had recognized a talent far greater than his own. But he had never allowed himself to neglect his music and soon Sarasate's 'Gypsy Airs' flowed from his violin, haunting and evocative, filling every corner with trembling ecstatic notes that rose and fell, soothed and excited.

Rachel watched his long, sensitive fingers running over the strings. His thin, gentle face was somehow lost and sad in its repose, making her throat tighten with pain. She knew that she had to make him happy again and she vowed to tell him about the baby that very night. It would bring them together again as nothing else would and when Lorn took the platform to play a gay selection of strathspeys and reels, her spirits lifted with the music and she knew that everything was going to come right between herself and Jon.

With hardly a break the entertainment went on. When Rachel took up her own violin to play Massenet's meditation from *Thais*, an enthralled silence embraced the audience. Mamma looked at her daughter-in-law's lovely rapt face and for the first time she knew the power and the glory of Rachel's talent. She had never been to any of her recitals and something akin to shame touched her, a feeling that grew when, with Otto at the piano and Rachel on the violin, the audience were treated to a soul-stirring performance of the beautiful Poème by Chausson.

Then came the moment that everyone had been waiting for. The platform cleared, Otto seated himself in front of Becky, adjusted his kilt so that he wouldn't sit on the pleats, shrugged his cuffs away from his hands and began, starting with a selection of Chopin's piano solos, including the enchanting Nocturne in E flat, which Otto finished with a great flourish before going on to the exalted and stirring Polonaise No 6 in A flat.

'This is what I wait to hear,' breathed Mamma, going into such vocal raptures that Barra hissed at her to be quiet and let everyone else enjoy the playing. And enjoy it they did, many of them had never paid much attention to such music before, but then, none of them had had the opportunity to hear a live performance from the hands of such an accomplished maestro, and the excitement of it carried them away on wings of fantasy as crescendos of wonderful sound poured and crashed, thundered and reverberated, till the very rafters seemed to tremble and the foundations shake.

Otto gave of his best, his hands flying, his face bathed in sweat. He was in another world, and when he at last jumped to his feet to spread his arms wide and bow to the audience he was Karl Gustav Langer, revered throughout Europe, wildly hailed by other nations over the sea, expecting worship and receiving it, for as one the hall had risen to its feet to cheer and whistle and applaud in wave upon wave of unstinted appreciation.

Tam nudged Fergus and told him, 'The man can hold his

whisky as well as he can the Schnapps. Just look at him, McKenzie, you would think he had drunk nothing stronger than tea, you'll no' get your own back on a man wi' his build and stamina.'

'Ay, well there's aye a next time,' returned Fergus who was himself feeling the effects of his indulgences but would never admit to it. 'It could easily hit him suddenly, I've seen stronger men than him felled at the end o' an evening's drinking just when everybody was thinking they'd drunk themselves sober.'

The performance had exhausted Otto but his adrenaline was flowing, somehow keeping him on top of fatigue and pain so that he was able still to smile and be thrilled when the laird presented him with a framed illuminated scroll, beautifully inscribed in copperplate and bearing the words, '*Otto McKinnon Klebb of Croy, Friend and Kinsman, McKinnon Clan Gathering. Island of Rhanna, 1967*', and at the bottom the by now familiar '*Mac nan Èilean*'.

Officially, the most wonderful concert the island had ever known had come to an end but no one was letting go that easily, the musicians didn't need much persuading to take to the limelight once more and this time everyone joined in. 'Song of Rhanna' had never been sung with such enthusiasm, then 'Amazing Grace' with Torquil and Todd on the pipes and Torquill as the solo piper at the end. Song after song, melody after melody, hit the roof.

Otto sat down once more at the piano, the flowing, infectious music of Johann Strauss II came tumbling out: waltzes, marches, polkas.

Rachel, as carried away as everyone else, turned to look at Otto and realized suddenly that he was at the end of his strength, only his indomitable will was keeping him going and she was thankful when he came at last to a halt and all that remained was for 'Auld Lang Syne' to be sung before everyone went home.

But it wasn't the end: someone, it might have been Fergus, began singing 'Vienna, City of my Dreams'. It was seized upon, taken up, those that didn't know the words hummed the tune till before long a swelling vibrancy of melody rose up to make for an enchanting finale to the evening.

Otto stood by his piano, shaking his head, so moved by the tribute that tears filled his dark eyes as the evocative words filled every space inside his head.

> Farewell Vienna mine,
> I'm in the spell of your charms divine,
> Dressed like a queen with lights so gay,
> You are the love of my heart today . . .

Otto swayed, his legs crumpled beneath him, blindly he felt for the piano stool and sank on to it, his face deathly white.

Tam and some of the other men grinned and told Fergus, 'You were right, McKenzie, the *Uisge Beatha* has played its trump card, Otto has had it by the look o' him and might need some help to get home.' There was a move forward but Rachel, who was still up on the platform with Magnus and Otto, got there first.

Rushing to Otto's side she saw that he was in great pain and immediately she looked around for Jon to help. But he had disappeared into the crowd and was nowhere to be seen and it was as well that Mark and Megan had noticed Otto's distress and were first up on the platform, to be seized upon by Rachel who frantically tried to convey to them that she needed help to get Otto outside.

Without hesitation they each put a shoulder under his armpits and got him as quickly as they could out of a side door and down to Todd's car, followed closely by Rachel and Magnus.

Somehow they bundled the big man into the back seat and got in after him. Todd had left his keys in the ignition, Mark started up the engine just as Todd reached the scene to peer in the window with enquiring eyes.

'We're taking him home,' Mark quickly explained. 'All he needs is a gallon of strong tea to sober him up. McKenzie o' the Glen has won this round by the look o' things.'

Todd beamed in complete understanding and stood back to watch his gleaming Rolls disappearing off into the night, only too happy to help *Mac nan Èilean* in this, his hour of need.

As soon as Otto was safely settled on the sitting-room sofa, Rachel took Megan's hand and led her up to the bedroom. She couldn't keep this terrible thing to herself any longer, her heart was leaping in her breast with the dreadful strain of the last few minutes, and she didn't pause once when they reached the bedroom but went straight to the little bedside cabinet to pull open the drawer and reveal its contents.

Megan stared, one by one she picked up the brown bottles to look at the labels, and her hazel eyes were serious and sad when she said with a strange little catch in her throat, 'Rachel, how long has he been taking these? There are dozens of them, he certainly must have brought a good supply with him but most of them are now empty. Can you tell me, please, just how ill is he?'

'He is dying.' Rachel's lips formed the words, gently Megan took her arm and made her sit on the bed.

'You've known this for a long time, haven't you, Rachel?'

The girl nodded, the miserable dull ache in her heart forcing her head down to her breast so that the other woman wouldn't see her eyes. But she couldn't stop the tears from springing; she had locked away her pain for too long, and once the flow started it wouldn't be stemmed, and with a cry of sympathy, Megan folded her arms round the slender body and held on tightly till the trembling gradually ceased.

Only then did Rachel raise her swollen face. She had never felt more frustrated by her lack of speech, she wanted to pour it all out, so much to say and no voice to say it with, her head pounded with unspoken emotions, her silent screams of heartache reverberated inside her skull, her swimming eyes were blinded by weepings and wantings, and all she could do, all she could ever do, was wave her hands about in wordless speech that might or might not, be understood.

She clenched her hands into fists, her turbulent black eyes looked at Megan, once more her lips formed words. 'Help Otto.'

Megan squeezed the girl's hand. 'Of course I'll help him, he's going to need a lot of medication, I'll send for some stuff right away but for now I must get over to the Manse to see what I have there.'

At the door she turned. 'Magnus should be told,' she said softly. 'He has a right to know: Otto is his grandson. Can I ask Mark to tell him?'

Rachel hesitated, wondering if she had the right to take on that kind of responsibility. Otto should be consulted first – she thought of her beloved stranger – he was strong, stubborn, wilful – the last thing he would want was for people to make a fuss and tell him what he should and shouldn't do.

But he was so alone, so vulnerable; he needed love and comfort at a time like this and Magnus of Croy was the last man on earth to make an issue of anything – even death.

She nodded, Megan inclined her head in acknowledgement and went quickly downstairs to seek out Mark. She was remembering that night of the ceilidh in the shorehouse – Otto's eyes, something about them that she couldn't quite fathom. She of all people should have known, Mark had said it was the drink but she had felt there was more to it than that and tonight she had found out what it was. Drugs! The black pupils had been glazed with them and all the time only Rachel had known the lonely secret of a dying man . . . and had carried the burden of that knowledge as only a young woman of her discipline and devotion could.

Magnus sat alone in the armchair by the fire. Otto was in bed, helped there by Mark and Megan after she had given him something to ease his pain. They had gone home, leaving Rachel up there with him. She would stay till he fell asleep and maybe longer, Rachel was a good person to have at a sick bed, something about those hands of hers: she had the touch, the power to help the ill, soothe the dying.

But Otto wasn't dying yet; someone, Magnus couldn't remember who, had said he still had some time left, weeks, months, it was difficult to know for certain in cases like these.

Magnus gazed into the fire. A few months. That powerful, vibrant man, that musical genius, a few months. Magnus felt as if his heart had turned to stone within him, he felt nothing, only the homely things, like Vienna warm and purring on his knee, the heat of the fire burning his legs, the safe, tranquil cosiness of the chintzy room, the clock, tick-tocking the minutes away.

Minutes, hours, days . . . months. The last few months; summer; sweetness; sun; wind; rain; a big, black-bearded bear of a man coming to him out of the blue to relay the news that he came as one who had sprung from Rhanna soil, grandson of Sheena and Magnus of Croy . . .

Sheena . . . A mist blurred the old man's vision. Sheena of the summer shielings, Sheena whose feet had trod light and sure over the heather braes, whose laughter had rung in the corries, soared among the bens. He could still hear the echoes of it, for him it would always live in his heart . . . and her lips, soft and sweet as a wild rose, tasting of nectar and dewdrops, driving him crazy, so crazy with his love for her . . .

And then she had gone, and there had been nothing, no one, only the emptiness of spaces. Gone were the shielings from the hills, wild grew the heather, cold blew the wind, untouched sprung the sweet briar on the hedge; no one to share the quiet joys of lonely places; lonely; lonely; only the memories, the sad echoes of love, reaching far over the sea, seeking but never finding, mortal joys, gone forever . . .

Until Otto, a man who came as a stranger but who had soon become a beloved friend, a man who had known and loved Sheena, who had heard the ring of her voice, who had listened and had listened well. Through her font of memories he had known the call of the islands, he had breasted the ocean . . . that same ocean that had taken her away all those years ago . . .

Otto, his and Sheena's grandson.

The old man's hands tightened in his lap . . . his snowy head sunk to his breast, the cat purred, the clock ticked . . . a few months . . . The stone in his breast melted . . . he put his head into his hands – and he wept.

Chapter Twenty-one

'It isn't mine!'

The statement was brutally terse and Rachel stared at her husband in horror, hardly able to believe the evidence of her own ears. She had buoyed herself up for this moment, she had felt the time was now ripe to share her wonderful news with her husband, an excitement had mounted in her as she had visualized his face, anticipated his reactions – in her blackest of nightmares she could never have imagined that he would turn on her like this, say the things he was saying.

Everything in her, all the love, the joy, the life, drained out of her body, dispersing like dust in the wind, leaving her feeling fatigued and miserable beyond measure. This should have been the happiest moment of their lives, they had waited so long to have a child and over the years they had discussed with one another how it would be when the longed-for day actually came.

He couldn't mean what he had just said. Frantically she spoke to him with her hands but he wouldn't look at her and a sob of sheer frustration bubbled in her throat.

'It isn't mine!' he repeated forcibly. 'And you're not going to deceive me again, Rachel, we both know who the father is! I've watched you with Otto, you can hardly keep your eyes off him – just like you couldn't keep your eyes off Lorn McKenzie not so many years ago. I tried very hard to forgive you that time, I knew I was no match for that particular young McKenzie. I told myself that it wouldn't happen again and fooled myself into believing it. But I was never a match for those other men in your life. I'm too tame, too serious, too easily taken in!'

She had never heard him speak like this before, his voice throbbing with emotion, filled with such terrible deep conviction that when he at last turned to face her, it seemed as if a wild beast looked out of his eyes, those eyes that had always before regarded her with gentleness and love.

Jon! Her fingers were a blur, forming words, trying to make him see how wrong he was, but it was no use.

'It's the last straw, Rachel,' he told her angrily, and something cold and hard replaced the feverish expression in his eyes. 'After all this time you tell me you are expecting a baby and try to make me believe it is mine. You're so obsessed with Otto you can't even bear to have other people see his faults or his human weaknesses. I was watching you last night trying to cover up the fact that he was so drunk he couldn't even make it outside on his own. You went home with him, didn't you? And you came creeping back here at some godforsaken hour of the morning. Was he as good in bed drunk as he is when he's sober? Why don't you tell me about it, I might be able to pick up a few hints. As for trying to pass this child off as mine, you can forget it, I'm leaving Rhanna, I've had enough, tell your wonderful Austrian lover that you're expecting his child, or are you afraid that he'll want nothing more to do with you when he's faced with that kind of a burden?'

She felt as if icy fingers were clutching her heart, Jon, her wonderful, kindly Jon, speaking to her as if he hated the very sight of her, looking at her as if she was some sort of fearsome stranger instead of the wife he had always cherished with such selfless love.

He would have to know about Otto, she should have told him long ago but it wasn't too late, it wasn't . . . But even now something held her back, anger flooded her being, she told herself she shouldn't have to use Otto's illness as a lever to make things right between herself and her husband. Her head went back, her chin tilted, wilful pride, black resolution filled her breast. Let Jon think what he would, she wasn't going to beg or bargain for any favours. He could leave Rhanna if he wanted, he could go to hell for all she cared, but one thing was certain, wherever he went she wasn't going with him, she was staying here on Rhanna till her baby was born – and no one – nothing – was going to change her mind on that score.

There was nothing more to be said, Jon had said it all in just a few short minutes, and turning on her heel she ran out of the house, down to Mara Òran Bay where the sea sighed over the pebbles and the wind rustled the seed pods on the whins. She could hardly see where she was going for tears, her head ached with weariness after a night spent at Otto's sickbed, her heart was heavy and sore in her breast. Everything that she had ever hoped and dreamed of was crumbling about her ears, and she was too unhappy in mind, body and spirit to see how unfair she was being to her husband in not letting him know the reasons for her unswerving allegiance to Otto, not only last night, but all the other nights and days she had spent away from the one man who had devoted himself to her, every minute of every day of all of their years together.

Jon watched her go, she who had been his whole life, who had made his world a wonderland of music and light, laughter and love, excitement and adventure. Ever since the day he had met her on the road with Ruth, Lorn and Lewis, he had been fascinated and bewitched by her. He had come as a tourist that warm spring of 1950, complete with rucksack and maps, looking for Croft na Ard, the home of his former commander, and once the children had gotten over their initial shyness, they had been only too willing to help, especially Lewis, who, with his brown limbs, black hair, and mischievous smile, was the epitome of health and youthful beauty.

He had been the leader, there was never any doubt about that, an aura of great authority emanated from every gesture, every laughing glance – and he had only been nine years old, approximately the same age as the others who had all been born in the same month of the same year.

Of them all, Lewis had seemed the strongest, the most robust . . . the most passionate. He had been Rachel's first great love. They had been wild together – untamed – each of them a free spirit that had laughed at life and had taken everything it had to offer. And then Lewis had died, his magnetism, his greedy delight of life, all gone in just one swift burst of tragic illness. In the end he had died on the beach after falling off his horse, his dying eyes had seen the skies and the seas that he had so loved, before they had closed forever on the wonder and the beauty of his world.

But by then Rachel belonged to Jon . . . or had she? Had that golden-skinned gypsy ever really belonged to anyone? No, he decided as he stood there at the window, the visions of the past floating through his mind, Rachel was an entity unto herself and always would be. Sometimes he was lulled into believing that she was really his and then something, or someone, would enter their lives to shatter his illusions and make him aware of how fragile his hold was on her.

Lorn had been the next of her tempestuous affairs. It had been a brief infatuation, lasting only a summer, but inflamed desires and intoxicating passions had consumed them both till the fires had been quenched and they had returned to the reality of how much hurt and harm they had caused. Ruth and Lorn had nearly split up because of it but Jon had forgiven and had tried to forget, though he couldn't help feeling threatened by the presence of the many men who surrounded her in the course of her existence.

Now there was Otto, out of nowhere it seemed, a man of great charm and mystique, one with similar talents and interests as her own, one furthermore who had the same alluring qualities as herself: power, personality, a passion and a thirst for life that made everyone else look impassive in comparison. She was obviously bedazzled by him, she had spent every minute she could with him. Without consideration of what her actions were doing to her husband she had openly, and for all the world to see, paid court to a man who had pretended friendship with her husband when all the while . . .

Jon raised a trembling hand to his eyes, he removed his glasses to clean them but still a mist blurred his vision. His tormented emotions tugged him this way and that, insecurity tightened his nerves. He shivered and wondered if he could ever really leave the girl who had infused his timid world with inspiration ever since that fateful day, long ago, when a curly-haired child had captured his heart forever with the radiance of her pearly smile . . .

He came out of his reverie with a start – that child had grown into a woman – one who had just told him she was expecting a baby . . . a baby. How he had longed for such news, how often they had both imagined what it would be like when the gift of a child came to them at last. But it wasn't his. She had robbed him of everything that had been good and sweet in his life and he could hardly bear the hurt of her final betrayal.

He turned away from the window. Let her go to *him*, let her stay here on Rhanna and have another man's child. She could go to hell for all he cared . . .

The years of his devotion were done with – it was finished.

Only a few people knew of Rachel's pregnancy; she was easily able to hide it since she was still at the stage when nothing much showed, except when she ran her hands over her belly and felt its taut roundness. She had always walked tall, her figure was superb, a flowing blouse was all she needed to deny her condition to the world and deny it she did. Jon's rejection of his own child had done that to her. If he had accepted it as joyfully as she had imagined, everyone would have known by now; as it was she felt no exuberance and had decided to allow the passage of time to tell its own tale.

Ruth only found out by accident from Phebie when they met one day in the village. 'You and Rachel will have more in common than ever now,' Phebie had said in a burst of cheery impulse. 'It will be nothing but baby talk and, of course, wi' you being an experienced mother, you'll be able to give her a few handy tips nearer the time.'

She saw the look on Ruth's face and her own fell. 'You didn't know about it? Och, Ruth, I'm sorry, I should have held my tongue. Lachy did warn me to keep quiet and let Rachel blow her own trumpets but I thought – wi' you being her friend . . .'

Ruth had gone home to pour her indignation out on Lorn, so

incensed by the fact that she had learned the news from someone other than Rachel she was beside herself with temper and in a mood to battle with anyone who got in her way.

As it was she wasted no time next day in making tracks for An Cala. If Lorn had been there to make her sit down and talk things over in a logical manner she might never have made the move she would later live to regret, but Lorn was working with his father in Laigmhor's fields, the children were with Shona at Mo Dhachaidh, and Ruth, with more time on her hands than usual, was in a mood to spend it dangerously, particularly since she had seen very little of her friend these last few weeks.

And no wonder, she fumed to herself as she started up the little car Lorn had bought her to celebrate the publication of her first novel, she's been too busy elsewhere to spare much time for the likes of me!

An Cala was empty but for Rachel, Mamma was out, so too was Jon, the way was clear for Ruth to say what every unreasoning emotion forced her to say the minute she stepped over the threshold.

Rachel looked up with a start at the suddenness of the unexpected intrusion. She was about to offer the usual hospitable cup of tea but got no chance to do so as Ruth, her fair face flushed with purpose, her violet eyes big with bottled-up indignation, went into the attack right away.

'I finally heard about the baby' – she said it like an accusation – 'from someone who thought I must already know and was quite shocked to learn that I didn't. In the normal way o' things I would be the first to congratulate you, Rachel, but this isn't the normal way o' things and I think I know the reasons for your secrecy. I've seen how you've behaved wi' Otto, how you run to him at every turn, leaving Jon to his own devices like you've left everyone else this summer. You've never even spared the time for your own mother. You never come to see us anymore, it's always Otto, isn't it? Right from the start it was Otto!'

For answer Rachel merely stared in total amazement, so taken aback she could do nothing to defend herself and Ruth, taking the reaction as an admission of guilt, slowly nodded her head.

'How could you, Rachel?' she cried aghast. 'How could you do this to Jon?'

'How could you with Lewis?' Rachel countered, her fingers spelling out the words, her eyes like black coals in the deathly pallor of her face.

'That was different!' Ruth flashed back. 'Lewis was dying!'

'So is Otto.' Rachel swiftly relayed the message before her hands went still, fluttering to her lap like spent butterflies. She was appalled at herself for giving away such a confidence, furious at Ruth for having dug below the surface of her defences with just a few cryptic words.

Stepping back a pace she sunk into a chair and covered her face with her hands, too overwrought to weep, too sick at heart to even be angry.

There was a stunned silence in the room. Ruth stood there, hating herself, deflated and uneasy, horrified and afraid.

'Oh, Rachel,' she whispered at last, 'I know it's too feeble to say sorry but I am, truly I am, I . . . I don't now what came over me. I know I'm guilty of being too quick to pass judgement, Shona pointed that out to me and though I was mad at her I saw later that she was right – also – I think I was jealous of the time you spent with Otto – I thought . . .'

She stammered to a halt, unable to go on, Rachel looked up, and her eyes were black, and hard, and cold, 'You can think what you like about me, Ruth,' wearily her hands moved, 'but never, never, must you tell anyone about Otto – not even Lorn. Otto plans to go back to Vienna to die but while he is here all he wants is peace – and peace is what he will have or you'll have me to reckon with.'

Desperately Ruth tried to make amends but it was no use, Rachel had withdrawn into herself, her whole demeanour was of one who had retreated into some inner world where no one could follow. She looked very alone sitting there and somehow so vulnerable Ruth wanted to rush forward and comfort her. But she didn't, she was too afraid of rejection, too horrified at her own folly to even begin to forgive herself, let alone expect Rachel's forgiveness.

Turning on her heel, she walked out of An Cala, her foot dragging so badly she tripped and had to hold on to the gate to steady herself.

She glanced back at the house. It looked empty somehow, as if no one lived there, neglected and sad and abandoned. It was only fancy, of course, but in her heightened state of awareness Ruth imagined that the spirit of life had left it, leaving it comfortless and bare where before, the very aura of Rachel's presence had enfolded it in a vibrant shroud of light.

'Oh, Lorn!' she cried when he got home that day and found her sitting by the empty grate in the parlour. 'Rachel and myself have had a terrible row! I think she might never speak to me again.'

Lorn was weary after a day spent in the fields and was in no mood to listen to details of an argument that had taken place between two battling women. Ruthie had been temperamental that summer. She was always restless and keyed up when Rachel was on the island, as if she expected exciting happenings to occur every minute of the day, but this time she had been more than usually tense and he sighed and wondered if the water was hot for a wash and if his tea would be late with her in her present mood.

'Where are the bairns?' he queried, ignoring her look of tragedy. 'I thought you were picking them up from Mo Dhachaidh.'

'Shona said they could stay and have tea wi' her . . .' She eyed him in some annoyance. 'Did you hear what I said, Lorn? Rachel and me . . .'

He ran a hand through his black curls and sighed. 'All right, what was the row about – this time?'

She wasn't slow to pick up his rather sarcastic tone and her golden head tilted stubbornly. 'I'm sorry, I canny tell you, it's something between her and me. One day you'll know, one day everyone will know but for now I canny say.'

'Women!' he cried in exasperation. 'What you really mean, Ruthie, what you aye mean when you're like this, is you could say but you won't.'

'No, Lorn, this isn't like that, it's – well – it's a matter o' life and death – and could easily be my death if Rachel ever found out I had breathed a word to anyone.'

Lorn bent to pull on his slippers, having left his mud-caked boots in the porch. His stomach was rumbling, his hands were callused from hoeing turnips all day, he wanted only to sit down and allow every tired limb to relax, but there was no chance of that or anything else till Ruth had had her say.

Reaching out, he lifted her hair and let the silken strands slide through his fingers. 'Ruthie, if it will make you feel better you can tell me what ails you, I'll be very quiet and attentive and won't interrupt once and nothing can be as terrible as you make out.'

She shook off his hand and sat forward in her seat, her pupils huge and black with the enormity of the dark deeds she had done that day and which nothing she said or did could ever take back. 'I'm sorry, I canny tell you, Lorn: Rachel made me promise not to breathe a word, no' even to you – and you especially should know how frighteningly intense Rachel can be when she has a mind.'

Resentment was in the glance she threw at him. She knew she was being unfair but she couldn't help it, she was hating herself, hating everything she had done, and she was unable to stop herself transferring some of that feeling to her husband who had done nothing but just be there in the firing line.

His eyes were on her, suspicion darkening them till they were just as black as her own. 'This wouldny have anything to do wi' Rachel's baby, would it? Ruthie, I'm asking you a question and you're avoiding my eyes which means you're feeling guilty about something. You were in a funny mood when I left this morning, as if you had a burden on your mind and couldny rest till you had unloaded it on to someone.'

'Ach! You McKenzies! You're all the same! Too full o' fancies for your own good and I haveny the time to listen to your blethers. There's coal in the bucket, you can make yourself useful for a change and light the fire. If it wasny for me this place would go to rack and ruin and you would do nothing but stand back and watch it falling about your lugs!'

She sounded exactly like Morag Ruadh, her red-haired religious fanatic of a mother, who had ruled her with a rod of iron, and who had finally taken to her deathbed in mortal fear of what the Lord would do to her for having indulged in 'the sins of the flesh' when she had conceived her daughter in a fit of drunken lust, and ever after had never been sure who had fathered her child.

Ruth got up, she flounced away through to the kitchen, murmuring something about making the tea, adding under her breath that she was just a 'skivvy' who had no life of her own and it was a wonder she ever managed to find the time to write books.

Morag too had believed herself to be indispensable and Lorn stared after his wife with apprehension clouding his face. But he knew he was being silly, Ruthie could never turn out like her mother, she was too soft and sweet, and romantic – except during times like these when he could gladly have taken her across his knee and given her a good skelping.

'Home!' Mamma's face fell, she was thoroughly enjoying herself on Rhanna and had visualized a few more weeks on the island.

'Yes, Mamma, home.' Jon spoke firmly, the mood that had beset him since the row with Rachel had grown blacker and deeper with the passing days, leaving no room for him to easily deal with unnecessary trivia or to placate his mother in his usual patient manner. 'Though when I say home I really mean London. I have much business to catch up on, I have also applied for a teaching position at the Royal Academy of Music and want to be on hand for any likely interviews. You could always stay here with Rachel, of course, she won't be coming with us, she feels the need to remain on Rhanna for the foreseeable future, hence my reasons for wanting to take up teaching again.'

Mamma looked warily at her son. He hadn't told her about the baby, she only knew that all was not well between him and Rachel. The atmosphere had been very tense in the house and she had made herself as scarce as possible since all her old enjoyment of picking fault with her daughter-in-law had deserted her of late.

Nevertheless she had no wish to remain at An Cala without Jon. His news of seeking a teaching post in the musical world had taken away some of the sting of having to leave Rhanna and waving a nonchalant hand in the air she said graciously, 'With you to London I will come; Rachel has no need of me here but you, Jon, you must have someone to look after you. Rachel is not the type of woman to feel the obligation to carry out wifely duties, so I, your mother, will be happy to take them upon myself as I do not wish to go back to Hamburg, knowing you have need of me.'

Her slightly martyred air didn't fool Jon for one moment. He had seen a big change in his mother that summer: no more did she fret and whine and complain, she spent more time out of the house than in, she was cheerful, buoyant and happy, in fact her entire attitude and outlook on life had undergone a complete metamorphosis and sometimes Jon had to look at her twice to convince himself that this really was the same woman who had spent her entire life bossing people about and making things difficult for those who were nearest her.

She not only behaved and sounded different, her appearance had altered too. Her eyes held a new sparkle, her face glowed, her downcast mouth smiled more often, she laughed readily and he had discovered in her a sense of humour that had hitherto only manifested itself in a somewhat satirical way. She had always been a handsome woman in a rather hard and mannish fashion, now she was softer, more feminine, more attractive altogether; she spent a good deal of her time in front of the mirror and she made regular trips to 'Mairi's hairdressing saloon'. She had even gone to the lengths of ordering some fashionable clothes from Aggie's mail order catalogue, though oddly, and here even Rachel had to smile, along with all the finery had come a stout pair of wellington boots and a voluminous oilskin jacket, both of which items she had hastily explained away as being the only kind of apparel to wear in a place where it rained most of the time and 'even when it stops it forgets to be dry'.

That, of course, was only bluff. In due course the real reasons for the boots and the jacket became known, via that most reliable of communications, Highland Telegraph: quite simply, word of mouth – many mouths, all flapping away, exaggerating, elaborating, enjoying hugely anything and everything that held the merest whisper of interest.

No one escaped, particularly visitors, who were always a great source of curiosity, and Mamma, with her reputation for doing and saying outrageous things, demanded an even greater scrutiny than most. And Eilidh Monroe, incensed beyond measure at Frau Helga Jodl's monopolisation of Rab McKinnon, made very sure that the tongues were kept piping hot with conjecture.

But it was that ubiquitous personage Erchy, in the course of his innocent travels, who saw, with his very own eyes, the incongruous spectacle of Mamma, 'wrapped to the lugs in waterproofs', over there at Croft nan Uamh (Croft of the Caves), helping Rab bring the cows in for milking, or rather, ostensibly helping him, since, like all good cows everywhere, they didn't need much coaxing to plod through the gates into the byre to wait patiently for their udders to be emptied.

'Hmph, as if she could ever be any good on a croft!' was Eilidh's verdict when the news filtered through to her ears. 'Just wait till she has to help wi' a difficult calving or has to put the fork to a steaming dung midden in the rain. She'll no' look so smart then wi' her new welly boots covered in glaur and pig shit.'

It was amazing enough for Frau Helga Jodl to have actually participated in menial croft work, but it was a miracle that she had actually done so on land situated high on the machair above a group of awesome caves known as Uamh na Mara, (Caves of the Sea). At high tide the ocean spumed and roared into the fearsome caverns and local legend had it that once, long ago, during an almighty storm, the ground above the caves had trembled so much with the boom and might of the waves that the very crockery inside the croft had rattled about as if in the grip of an earthquake.

Despite all, Croft nan Uamh had managed to remain intact

on the same spot for the last hundred years and more, and was so sturdily built it looked as if it could easily still be standing with the passing of another century.

But that wasn't all that Mamma had endured and enjoyed that fateful summer, there had been sightings of her all over the island – rattling along in Rab's uncle's old motor car, parked on the cliffs, the moors, the machair – anywhere and everywhere off the beaten track, though never far enough off it not to be espied by somebody.

That was the thing that really had the steam coming out of Eilidh's ears and she fumed and fretted and wished for the day when it would be exit Frau Helga Jodl from the island.

Now that day was almost here and no one was more surprised than Jon when, on the eve of their departure, his mother confided some of her most personal feelings to him. 'I speak to you first of Rab McKinnon,' she began, an uncharacteristic hesitancy in her voice and a blush on her cheeks. 'All of my life I look for a man like him, he does not let me have too much of my own way, the authority I like, the strong silence I respect, he tells me to be quiet when I have the verbal diarrhoea, if I show the solkiness he tells me he has no use of women with the moods and so I do not have the solkiness anymore.'

Verbal diarrhoea! Mamma's vocabulary was certainly expanding and Jon looked at her with a new light of affection shining in his eyes.

'I have many good friends here on Rhanna,' she continued, the revelations pouring out of her. 'I was lonely when I live in Hamburg, here I am never alone unless I seek the solitude. Aggie has been kind to me, she befriends me when I think I have no friends, after that I find friendship with many people. At first I think they come from the moon, they have the strange language I do not understand, but then I see I also have the strange language and cross the bridges I must. Happy Mary always has the smile for me, Mairi is always ready to help and with her and Kate McKinnon I drink the tea and even grow to like it. Herr Holy Smoke never tries to cheat me anymore and always he gives me the cheap meat for my cat, on the road Erchy waves to me from his post van or his dreadful bus and I even forgive him for the knots I tie in my stomach when he took me to find the city of Croy that was not there. Yes, Jon, the people here I like very much.'

'But, Mamma,' Jon said with a smile, 'you don't have a cat, you don't even like cats! How can Holy Smoke . . .'

He saw the sparkle of humour in her eyes, he suddenly liked his mother very much and throwing his arm around her shoulder he gave her one of the most affectionate hugs he had ever given her.

Before she left, Mamma paid her daughter-in-law a surprising, if offhand, compliment.

'I have always liked one thing about you, Rachel,' she said nonchalantly, making Rachel think: at least one thing is better than none. 'You have the honesty, always you show to me the truth, you never hide your feelings from me like an actress. We have not always seen one another's eyes but in many ways, I like you.'

Rachel stared; she thought: if I was able to speak I would be so dumbfounded I wouldn't be able to speak. She smiled and Mamma, imagining the smile was for her, beamed back and with abrupt suddenness she took the girl to her mighty bosom, almost crushing the life out of her.

'You must not allow Jon to be too long on his own.' Embarrassed by her own display of affection, Mamma quickly reverted to her old self. 'It is not good for a husband and wife to be apart like this.' She frowned. 'For some time now I have not been able to speak to Jon, he has the anger in his chest that I do not understand but I will not interfere, you are his wife, you and he must arrange your lives between yourselves and sew up your disagreements.'

This was almost too much for Rachel, she had grown accustomed to dealing with a bellicose, interfering mother-in-law, and this vastly changed woman, who was regarding her with an expression that bordered on benevolence, was an entirely new departure and would take some getting used to – if Mamma continued along her present path – which Rachel very much doubted.

Even so, it made a pleasant change from the domineering matriarch, and Rachel, her senses lulled into peaceable lines, wondered if she and Jon were doing the right thing keeping quiet about the baby. They had discussed the matter, clinically and coldly, and had decided that it would be better if Mamma didn't know, considering the present set of circumstances.

'It will only make things more unpleasant,' Jon had said, not looking at his wife. 'She will start asking awkward questions and there's enough bad feeling in the air without her adding her voluble contribution. She'll find out soon enough when the baby comes and will have to learn the truth, till then it will be better for us all to keep everything on an even keel – the boat will inevitably rock and which of us goes down first remains to be seen.'

An even keel! Rachel's face reddened as she thought about that conversation, there had been something very final about it. She couldn't believe, even now, that it had ever taken place, but she wouldn't let him see, she wouldn't let anyone see, how much it had hurt her, and unconsciously her head went up in a gesture of proud defiance of everything that ached and burned in her heart.

For a moment she felt sorry for Jon's mother. Poor Mamma! She who had so longed for a grandchild, who had fumed and fretted and fussed when none were forthcoming over the years. All for nothing, the weeping and the wailing were done with— Rachel started. Was this the last time she would ever see Jon's mother? Was this the end of all the hints, the innuendoes, the arguments?

Rachel shuddered, she felt oddly sad at the thought, yet not so long ago she would have given a great deal of what she owned to see the back of this loud, demanding monument of a woman.

But Mamma had one or two trump cards up her sleeve and over the next few minutes she played them so cunningly that a flabbergasted Rachel was left wondering if her mother-in-law knew more than she was making out.

Looking beyond the window to the glistening ribbon of the sea she delivered her bombshell. 'I am glad I came here, Rachel, now I know why you and Jon like this island so much, the friendliness, it is all around, the freedom is like a good wine, it makes you want more of it. With Rab I have been to many places – much to my surprise, the car, it was not reliable, always it breaks down, everywhere, anywhere – and no one to come and help us to get started. The experiences, they were not good.'

Her tone belied her words, Rachel looked at her, her handsome face was glowing, her eyes were sparkling, she looked positively radiant.

Rachel drew in her breath, Mamma and Rab, it was impossible, it couldn't be – yet – those stories that had been flying around, Rachel had thought it was just gossip, built on flimsy ground, but occasionally these fables were woven from the fabric of fact.

Mamma's next words confirmed that there was more than a hint of truth in the tales. 'The ocean I will cross again,' she said almost dreamily. A promise or a threat? Rachel thought grimly. 'I come back to Rhanna when the snow is on the hills – at Christmas time. Rab will need someone to cook him a good dinner and Eilidh Monroe knows only the rabbit stew and the stodge. I make the German meal, the hams and the cooked meats, the spicy sausage, the apfelstrudel, the chocolate gateau, the baked apple stuffed with cinnamon and raisins . . .'

She went into raptures over the virtues of the food she would make, the festivities she would arrange, while Rachel thought: Christmas! When a child is born! Her child. Hers and Jon's, Mamma's grandchild – and she would be here after all, though by that time whether she acknowledged it as hers would be another story.

'Perhaps Karl Gustav Langer will still be here.' Mamma was enthusing, bringing Rachel back to earth with racing heart. 'He could give a concert, a Christmas concert. Oh, *wunderbar*! Never did I think I would meet such a great musician when I came to Rhanna.'

Then Mamma did a strange thing, for the first time ever she

was making a sign in the dumb language. She could have said aloud what she had to say, but in her uplifted mood she was letting Rachel know that she could converse with her perfectly well when she had a mind to do so.

Rachel stared fascinated as the be-ringed, somewhat stubby fingers, moved clumsily. The message read: 'I will take good care of Jon till you come back to him. He will put up with me because he is my son, but always it will be you on his mind. We cannot get rid of you so easily – we have to learn to put up with you – the Jodls are a very brave family.'

Despite herself Rachel smiled, Mamma was herself again, and oddly, Rachel was glad: the other Mamma was a stranger, she could cope better with the old one – for as long as she had to.

Part Four

AUTUMN/WINTER
1967/68

Chapter Twenty-two

It had been a golden summer, one that was unwilling to relinquish its hold on the land. The dawns, the days, the suns, the moons, rose and set as vigorously as ever but each of them wove their changes into the seasonal arrangement of things so that gradually there was a sharpness on the breath of morning. The berries ripened on the rowans; the grass on the hill became shaggy and coarse; the bracken was gold in the sun while the pearly mists of autumn lingered in the corries and banners of peat smoke hung suspended in the mellow air.

On the Muir of Rhanna the purple of the heather covered the land in a springy, thick mattress, interspersed by mounds of peat that had dried to brick-like hardness in the summer winds and would soon be ready to fuel winter fires throughout the island.

Gradually the visitors were leaving and in their camp over by Dunuaigh the travellers were thinking about leaving also, though for them it was an unhurried process. The autumn tourists had still to be met coming off the boat and persuaded to buy bunches of 'lucky heather' and never mind that there were acres of the stuff growing wild all over the place, the travellers picked it while it was still in bud and able to be passed off as the white heather so coveted by superstitious romantics of any age.

As the days shortened and the pace of life slowed for both man and beast, so too did a quieter tempo beat for Otto and Rachel, ruled not by the seasons but by the changing ebb and flow taking place within their own separate spheres.

Rachel knew the quickening of eager new life inside her own body, while for Otto the stream of his life was draining slowly but surely away. The time was coming for him to go back to Austria and it seemed to Rachel that everything that had been precious and good in her world was drifting off like smoke in the wind. He was dying, yet he was her strength; every day she saw some slight change on his wonderful face, but even as he grew thinner and weaker his spirit seemed to grow and expand till it filled her whole world with its light.

Hurt and alone after Jon's departure, she had turned more and more to Otto, and the solace they found in one another's company was a shining thing. He had been delighted when he found out she was expecting a baby.

'I told you it would happen for you, *liebling*,' he had said, taking her hand to hold it to his mouth and kiss it. 'But why has Jon deserted you at a time like this? He should be the happiest man in the world just now and certainly one of the luckiest.'

She had told him that her husband was busy, that he had gone to London to seek a teaching post and that she had opted to remain on the island for as long as she could and even try to have her baby here if it was at all possible. But she didn't fool Otto in the least. After that he was more attentive to her than ever and inevitably the tongues started wagging, especially with her in her 'condition' and no Jon there to keep an eye on her.

But the crones and the coteries didn't bargain on Tina, no one could have imagined that such a placid creature as she could be so tough and aggressive but, fiercely loyal to both Rachel and Otto, she protected them with such a might of verbal power she only had to be seen approaching a gossiping group to send them scuttling guiltily about their business.

Tina knew about Otto, she had been with him at Tigh na Cladach from the start and he had come to cherish her tranquil presence in his home. His trust in her was infinite and one day he had made her sit down on the couch beside him, had taken her hand in his and in a quiet, gentle voice had told her he hadn't very long to live.

She had reacted in a typically Tina-like way, first of all burying her face in her hands to have a 'good greet' before straightening up to scrub her face with his proffered hanky while at the same time endeavouring to capture loops of flyaway hair and confine them into kirby grips.

'Ach, Mr Otto,' she sighed, shaking her head, her brown eyes glazed with sadness, 'I knew fine something was ailing you. I've watched you growing thinner and more wabbit with each passing day but – I never thought – I canny believe . . .'

She was off again, her plump shoulders trembling with heartrending grief that alarmed Otto so much he enfolded her into his arms and crooned words of solace into her ears.

'Och, I'm such a fool,' she chided herself, emitting several watery sniffs before blowing her nose hard and handing the soaking hanky back to him. They looked at one another and laughed. She snatched the hanky back with an apology and a promise of rinsing it under the tap later, before collecting the hairgrips that had descended on to the couch and viciously jabbing them back into her hair. 'I'm the one who should be comforting you, Mr Otto, and I will, you can bet your boots on that. I did the same when I lost my Matthew, I just cried and cried for days then one morning I woke, collected myself up, and just got on wi' my life. Ach, but it's terrible just, a bonny big chiel like yourself, all that music and talent going to waste, but the angels will welcome you to heaven, I'm damty sure o' that, and you'll still get to play your music, and though they might no' have a piano they'll let you play their harps and anything else connected wi' life beyond the grave.'

Her simple philosophy cheered them both immensely, and after that day Tina 'collected herself up' and got on with life, devoting herself so wholeheartedly to 'Mr Otto' she was more often at Tigh na Cladach than in her own home, cleaning, cooking, tending fires, doing it all in her own unruffled fashion. But that was how Otto liked it: in Tina he found a sweet and undemanding companion, a comforting presence who could be as silent or as entertaining as the occasion warranted.

Tina knew that something momentous had happened between Rachel and Jon but she never pressed the matter. It would all sort itself out in its own time, she told herself, meantime she saw to it that both Rachel and Otto received as much care and attention as she was capable of giving. She encouraged them to spend as much time together as possible because in her uncomplicated way she recognized their need for one another in their separate experiences of lonely waiting, one about to part with life, the other preparing to give it.

October came with a mellow sweetness that filled the air with the tangy scents of ripe apples and bramble berries, heavy and black on the bough . . . and Otto could wait no longer, if he didn't go back to Austria now he never would and he began to prepare for that departure with a torpid unwillingness, every fibre in him fighting against the decision he had made while he was comparatively strong and very much a stranger on Rhanna.

But he was a stranger no more, he had become part of the very fabric of the island. He knew and loved every contour of the hills; each bend in the road was as familiar to him as the palm of his own hand; he had walked the shores of Burg and had listened to the might of the waves; from his window he had watched the summer sun bursting above the hills; from his bed he had witnessed the blazing hues of sundown setting fire to the ocean before the moon's cold luminosity quenched the flames and replaced them with silvery spangles of light that spilled into the sea and flooded the world with mercurial beams.

He had seen it all and he had treasured everything and had felt regenerated with the beauty of an island that was, and always would be, his spiritual home.

'You don't have to go, son,' Magnus had said, his voice gruff with emotion. 'Bide here wi' me, it might no' be very fancy or sophisticated but it's homely and warm and it has everything in it to keep a body occupied. You'll never grow weary wi' books and music to hand and a fine view o' the sea when you want only to sit back and do nothing for a whilie.

'And just think o' this, son.' Magnus looked away so that his grandson wouldn't see the mist that shrouded his blue eyes. 'This is your home, if Sheena and me had wed, your mother would have been born here and you too when it came your turn, for that's the way we do things in the Hebrides: families stick together, they look after one another, and they do it in humble surroundings like these. It might only be a bit thatch and four thick walls but I've managed to thole it for ninety-seven years so it canny be that bad – and besides, you'll have me to keep you company till the end o' your days. I would see to it that you were well looked after, you wouldny want for anything, by God, you wouldny.'

'Magnus,' Otto took his grandfather's frail body into his arms and kissed the top of the snow white head, 'I could never lay such a burden at your door, but it would be heaven, to be here with you, to talk ourselves back over the lost years, to have my last rest in a place that I feel I've known all of my life – and with you here at my side, my flesh, my blood – and in the end, my last memory of what it was I glimpsed so briefly but held with such joy.'

'Then stay, Otto, stay,' urged Magnus. 'It would be an honour to have you here, folk that you love can never be a burden and I've had such a short time wi' you after a lifetime o' empty hopes and dreams. The twists o' life are cruel, to take you away after just finding you . . . and if you leave Rhanna now I'll never see you again – and I might as well be dead too.'

The memory of that conversation with his grandfather both tantalized and tormented Otto. Even while he knew that he could never seriously consider the offer, it would be too much to ask of anyone, never mind someone of his grandfather's great age; even so, Otto imagined what it would be like to spend his last days in the undemanding peace of Machair Cottage.

In the end it was Tina who made up his mind for him. 'You've already said your farewells to Vienna,' she told him with quaint simplicity, 'so what way would you be wanting to repeat yourself when all your friends are here on Rhanna? It might be a lot fancier to bide in a place full o' luxuries but it would be an awful lot lonelier – and just think, you wouldny have me to look after you. I'll come over to Machair Cottage, Magnus has plenty o' room and I'll bide there for as long as I'm needed. Eve is able and willing to look after herself and Donald, so just you gather up your bits and bobs and your cat and we'll get Bob the Shepherd to take them over to Croy in his van.'

'Tina, what would I ever have done without you?' he said huskily, hugging her with such affection she giggled girlishly and rescued a few errant hairgrips from the hairy tweed of his jacket collar.

When Rachel heard the news she went rushing over to Tigh na Cladach to throw herself at Otto and Tina and kiss them both in a passion of delight. She had been growing more and more depressed lately: Jon had left her, Ruth had rejected her, the thought of losing Otto as well had been almost too much for her to bear and she had halfheartedly toyed with the notion of going away from Rhanna to nurse her lonely grief in some place that held no evocative memories.

Now her beloved stranger was staying after all and she was so filled with relief that, after the first euphoric reaction, she ran home to sit down and simply burst into a flood of tears that unleashed every unhappy emotion from her heart and made her feel so much better she was able to burn her incense, switch on her music, and dance round the room in a swirl of gladness.

But just when it seemed that an element of joy had entered her world, fate took another cruel hand in things and dealt her a further blow. Ever since Jon had left Rhanna she hadn't had the heart to even look at her violin, but now, in a mood to pour out her feelings in music, she went to get her violin only to discover it wasn't there. She searched the cottage high and low but it was a fruitless effort, the case containing her beautiful Cremonese had simply vanished, only the key remained, affixed to the gold chain round her neck where she always carried it for safety.

It wasn't long before the news of Rachel's loss swept through the island.

'I'll kill the bugger who did this to the lass!' vowed Kate grimly. 'She's had more than enough to put up wi' this whilie back without this happening as well!'

'Ay, she's treasured that violin ever since old Mo gave it to

310

her,' nodded Tam. 'But it canny just have got up and walked away by itself.'

'Ach no, some thief has stolen it,' decided Annie with conviction. 'Och, it's a shame for my bonny Rachel, she's been looking peekit this whilie back but she'll no' even tell her own mother why Jon left her the way he did.'

Kate glowered at her youngest daughter. 'She'll no' tell you for the simple reason that you've never listened to anything she has to say. You haveny even bothered very much to learn her sign language and never even gave a wee celebration ceilidh when you heard she was expecting your first grandchild.'

Annie's nostrils flared. 'My house isny grand enough for the likes o' Rachel! She looks down her nose at everything when she deigns to visit once in a blue moon and I'll no' stand for that from my very own flesh and blood!'

'The flesh and blood you never wanted to acknowledge,' Kate flashed back. 'And she doesny look down her nose at your house – though I wouldny blame her if she did – the state you keep it in. Na, na, Annie, my girl, why can you no' face the truth, you could never accept that you gave birth to a lass that didny have all her faculties – except of course when she became famous and you just wallowed in the fame and the money . . .'

Annie's hackles rose at this. 'I never heard the likes! Me take money from Rachel! I never even let her buy me a house when she wanted to, just so's the likes o' you wouldny have anything to talk about!'

'Oh no, but you canny deny that she sends you money which you are busily stashing away in the bank. I'm no' daft, Annie— '

'Och, be quiet you two,' interrupted Nancy, Kate's sweet-natured eldest daughter. 'We're no' here to argue about money, I thought we were trying to help Rachel discover who took her fiddle. Father's right, it didny just walk away by itself, so where on earth is it? If it doesny turn up, Clodhopper will have to be called in, and a fine to do that will be, he'll start raking up all kinds o' dirt and you haveny renewed the insurance on your lorry, Father.'

Tam blinked and went into a panic at the very idea of Clodhopper roaming round the island looking for trouble, and he immediately set out to visit his granddaughter to try and persuade her 'no' to call in the law till he had a chance to insure his lorry'.

But for the moment, Rachel had no intention of alerting the police, as she was hoping to resolve the matter in her own way. She had remembered Mamma telling her about Paddy's suspicious behaviour the day he had wangled his way into the house on the pretext of wanting a cup of tea.

'It was not the tea he was looking for,' Mamma had said decisively, 'he was – how do you say it? – a snooper. And yes, he was snooping through the house the minute I turn myself. The unpleasant person he was, the others – they were kind to me – but him – he was rude.'

Tam wasn't the only one to be worried by the threat of a visit from Clodhopper, the travellers themselves, almost but not quite ready for the road, heard the news with dismay, and, wishing to keep several little misdemeanours under wraps, had every reason to avoid the law. It was therefore with great energy that they set themselves the task of searching for the missing instrument.

'Bejabers and bejasus!' Aaron said to Rachel. 'I never minded you havin' me brother's fiddle. I would just have sold it for a few bob and spent the money on booze. It was meant for you, me fine lass, and by the blessed St Patrick, you can indeed be certain we'll do everything we can to find it for you.'

And he was as true as his word, every traveller worth his salt helped in the search, Little Lady Leprechaun proving to be a great asset since she managed to get into the smallest spaces. The Abbey ruins, derelict cottages, barns, haysheds, peatsheds, even the very caves on the shore were given a thorough going-over, but to no avail. In the midst of all this Paddy surprised everyone by putting on a great show of willingness as he scrambled into the most unsavoury places, though he didn't fool Aaron in the least

Paddy had always grumbled about old Mo's foolishness in

giving his violin away to a girl who wasn't even remotely connected to the family, and by that he meant the group of itinerants who habitually travelled the roads together. But Aaron had never liked or trusted the rough-speaking Irishman and felt uneasy every time something unpleasant like this happened. Aaron was almost certain that Paddy was the culprit in this latest incident but he could prove nothing and could only hope for the safe return of Rachel's violin before the law had to be consulted.

Shona sat bolt upright in bed, wide awake and sparkling-eyed, even though she had just emerged from the land of dreams.

'Of course,' she breathed, 'the cave! Over there by Dunuaigh! That's where it will be, I can feel it in my bones.'

Niall's ruffled head erupted from the blankets. 'Eh?' he demanded in startled tones. 'Bones! You're dreaming, *mo ghaoil*, go back to sleep, it's too early to be awake, you'll rouse the bairns and I don't want Joe crawling all over me at this time o' the morning.'

'No, Niall, listen,' she spoke imperatively into his ear, 'I've had a marvellous idea, call it an inspired guess if you like. Och! Don't go back to sleep, I want you to hear me out, if you don't I'll tickle and torment you till you beg for mercy – and that's a promise.'

'Oh, all right,' he grumbled, hoisting himself half up on his pillows. 'Fire away, but not too loudly, I canny bear too much noise first thing and I certainly don't want to hear about bones, I see enough o' that sort of thing in my job.'

'Daftie, it isn't about bones, it's about Rachel's fiddle. I've been wondering where on this island anybody could safely hide a valuable instrument. All the obvious places have been searched but what about somewhere near the travellers' camp itself? If Paddy is the culprit as everyone seems to think, he would hide it near to hand so that he could easily collect it just before he leaves. And, listen Niall, what about our cave? The one over by Dunuaigh. It would be a perfect place, it's so well hidden yet easily accessible once you know it's there.'

Niall barely allowed her to finish. With a martyred groan he slid back down into the blankets and snuggled into her soft thighs. 'You're havering, Mrs McLachlan, all this talk about bones and caves has gone to your head, but since we're awake we might as well make good use of the time, so just you coorie in close to me and I'll show you one bone that will never need a splint.'

'Niall McLachlan! You dirty bugger!' she cried, letting out a snort of laughter. 'But you're no' getting away that easily. Come on, up! We'll get the bairns ready and go over to Dunuaigh.'

'What? Now?'

'Ay, now. I'll not rest till I've seen and searched our cave for myself.'

'And no one else will be allowed to rest either,' he grumbled but he had caught some of her mood and got out of bed willingly enough to throw on his clothes.

It was strange to go back to the cave at Dunuaigh after all these years, though it was so overgrown with thorns and ferns it took them some time to find the entrance. The October moor was a sea of amber and gold mingling with the purple of the heather and the bright red splashes of rowan berries.

A hazy sun had broken through the early mists, warming the hollows, bringing out the tang of the brambles that grew in abundance along the rocky face of Dunuaigh, the Hill of the Tomb. It was these same thorny bushes that made the finding of the cave so difficult, but they were guided by the birch tree that they had planted on this spot when they were just children. Somehow the sapling had survived the wild winds that swept over the moors, and even though it was cruelly twisted and warped it had kept its tenacious hold on life, and it was the little golden leaves on the bleached branches that caught Shona's eye and guided her footsteps forward.

As Niall pulled back the bracken and the brambles, the children stared fascinated, thinking this was some new kind of game, thoroughly appreciating parents who did some pretty daft things sometimes and were often like children themselves with their fun and their laughter and their willingness to join in childish games.

'Look, Niall,' Shona said wistfully. 'It's just as we left it all these years ago, the cruisie and the candles, even the sheepskin rug on the ledge. Oh, I want to cry, it brings back so many memories.'

Taking her hand, he squeezed it and kissed the tears from her eyes, much to the amusement of little Ellie Dawn who clapped her hand over her mouth and went into a fit of the giggles.

It didn't take them long to search the small enclosure. In minutes they found the violin, carelessly hidden in a fissure behind the stone 'fireplace' where, as children, they had made smoky tea while pretending to be man and wife living together in their own small world.

'I always said it!' Niall exploded, gazing in disbelief at the leather violin case. 'You're a witch, Shona *mo ghaoil*, how did you do it? Was it a dream, or a vision, or what?'

'Just an educated guess,' she said rather smugly. 'Some o' us were born wi' brains in case you didn't know, but of course, you were aye the glaikit one o' the family, so we have to make allowances.'

He chased her outside into the sunlight, brandishing the leather case, the children dancing and laughing behind them and asking if they could come back here tomorrow to play more games.

It was sleepy and quiet at the travellers' camp with everyone sitting round a smoky fire, drinking tea while they discussed their departure date. They hailed the visitors with surprised pleasure and proffered the teapot, but when they saw what Niall carried everything else was forgotten as they crowded round, all talking at once. Shona looked over Stink's head. Paddy was scowling and making ready to skulk away, all too plainly betraying his guilt but given no chance to go anywhere since he was soon apprehended and brought back to explain himself.

Niall and Shona left them to it and went back to where they had parked their car, getting in to drive post-haste to An Cala where they deposited the violin, along with an explanatory note, as Rachel was nowhere to be seen.

'A good morning's work, Mrs McLachlan,' Niall said approvingly on the road home. 'And now, please can we sit down to a proper breakfast? All together like a normal family, with no more of your weird premonitions to disturb the peace?'

'Only if you say you recognize the fact that you married a genius and remain very humble and polite for the rest o' the day.'

'I give in: I married a genius, I will kiss your hand humbly, I will be unnaturally polite for at least a week, I will not demand anything of you that will upset your brilliant thoughts – but would you mind if I have two eggs, six rashers o' bacon, one of Holy Smoke's black puds all to myself, not forgetting a mountain of toast and a gallon of tea to wash it all down, all for the purpose of keeping up my strength in order to do all the things that you ask o' me.'

She burst out laughing, the children clapped their hands and giggled, the McLachlans went home in fine fettle, well pleased with themselves and hoping that Rachel would be pleased with them also.

Rachel read the note, she opened the violin case and stared at the instrument reposing in its blue velvet nest. It wasn't hers, it was Jon's! Paddy had stolen the wrong one – then a terrible thought struck her, what if he hadn't, what if he had taken the two of them and had hidden this one in a place where it was sure to be found in order to put everyone off the scent of the real thing?

Devastated, she sank into a chair, wondering wildly what to do. Her beautiful Cremonese, still missing, perhaps never to be found. Paddy could easily deny all knowledge of it and come back to the island to collect it at a later date when the heat had died down.

She felt sick, frightened and very alone; everything and everyone seemed to be conspiring against her and depression settled over her like a black cloud. She had never visualised any of this when she had come so blithely to Rhanna and it had only been thoughts of her unborn child that had kept her from sinking to the bottom of the deep, dark, despairing well of her innermost being.

Erchy was coming through the gate, whistling cheerily, avidly examining the letter he held so that he could tell Rachel who it was from. He knew nearly everyone's handwriting by this time and was apt to be deeply disappointed and mad at himself if by chance he got it wrong. But this morning he was full of confidence in his abilities and could hardly wait to open Rachel's door and shout, 'A letter for you, lass! From Jon by the look o' things, it's the way he strokes his t's, they just about fly off the top and that indicates a very ambitious person – I was readin' about it in a book,' he finished lamely when he saw that Rachel wasn't in a mood to appreciate his knowledge.

She took the letter, her hand shaking slightly. 'He'll be coming back soon, lass, never you fear,' said Erchy kindly before taking himself off with all haste. Sometimes those black eyes of Rachel's could look right through you and besides – he didn't fancy that tea she made, all funny and spicy and not at all like the good homely brews he enjoyed in other houses in the course of his rounds.

Rachel didn't know what to expect when she opened the letter but her heart had leapt with hope when she had heard Erchy shouting Jon's name.

The piece of paper she withdrew from the envelope could hardly be called a letter, it was more in the nature of a note, a curt, cold little message that simply said:

Dear Rachel

Just to say I took your violin by mistake, your case is much like mine and I was in a hurry when I left. Since you haven't been in touch about it I assumed you haven't been getting in any practice, unless of course, you have used mine. I got the post at the Royal Academy and have been playing the other violin we left here at the flat. Next week, however, I am giving a recital and wondered if you would mind very much if I used the Cremonese. The case is locked, you have the key, you don't owe me any favours but I want to make a good impression next week and know you will understand this.

If you need anything, let me know and I will arrange to have it sent. Mamma is well and enjoying London. I hope you are all right and managing to pass your time on Rhanna.

Yours, Jon.

Rachel screwed the paper into a tight ball and threw it into the fire. A flush of anger burned high on her pale cheeks and her eyes were too bright.

Oh yes, she was managing to pass her time on Rhanna, and her treasured violin was safe. That was all that mattered – with the exception of her unborn child – and Otto, of course.

Jon was the stranger now, and the way she was feeling he could remain so forever – him and his precious Mamma!

Chapter Twenty-three

Rhanna was quiet again: the tourists and the travellers had departed, the latter preceded by Paddy who had left with his tail well tucked between his legs, having been all but banished from the group till he could prove that he had mended his unsavoury ways.

Silence settled over the land, that special sort of tranquillity that always brought with it a sense of repose from the bustle and life of summer. The gossamer days were done with, the short perfumed nights were only a memory, the slumbering earth yielded less of its bounties and in so doing afforded rest to those who worked its soil.

But even so there was still work to be done to ensure a warm winter. The peats had yet to be gathered and both Ranald and Tam had a profitable time hiring out themselves and their respective lorries to those beings who were able to afford such a luxury – if such a term could be applied to ancient machines with a distinct penchant for sinking into bogs and potholes, which meant long, grumbling delays while they were pulled out again by tractors or, if these weren't available, by the sheer might of human muscle.

The remainder of the population trundled to the moors by other available means but, whatever the mode of transport, it wasn't long before peat stacks had sprung up in back yards everywhere. And then came that most distinctive of island scents, that of peat smoke, puffing lazily into the chilly air of morning, invading the senses with agreeable enjoyment, bringing also a quiet pleasure in the picturesque harmony of hill and moor, ocean and shore, the little villages with their white sugar-loaf houses, the islanders going peaceably about their daily lives.

Everything moved at a slower beat, even the very clocks on the wall seemed to tick at a more leisurely pace and it was good to sit back and survey the harvests of a summer well spent and to look forward to the comforts they would bring in the long, winter days ahead.

For Otto, it would be his last summer. He had spent it well and had done all the things he had wanted to do in those final months of his life, even so, he couldn't help wishing he had known this enchanting island sooner and he took to sitting at his window, gazing, just gazing, at the silent hills; the sylvan fields; the beaches; the sea; the people passing by with cheerful smiles and waves, for they had heard that he was staying on in the island and expressed their approval in many different ways.

Kate often popped into the shorehouse for a crack and a cuppy, bringing with her the home-made bannocks and tattie scones for which she was famed. Tam also came, for a game of cards, a dram and a blether, and on one such visit, with the time fast approaching for his departure from Tigh na Cladach, Otto said rather wistfully to Tam, 'I'm going to miss you, Herr Tam. Soon I go to stay with my grandfather, I won't be coming back to Portcull.'

'Och, but surely Mr James will let you have that old motor o' his a whilie longer. I will aye be pleased to see you and you know fine what Kate's like, she would be black affronted if she thought that the best bloody McKinnon yet wasny for stopping by for a strupak.'

'Herr Tam.' Gently Otto laid his hand on Tam's shoulder. 'It is not to be, my days, they are counted, that is why I go to live with Magnus, we wish to be together for all the minutes that are left. It is my dearest wish to be with him. Tina is right, I have said my farewells to Vienna, all my friends and family are here on Rhanna. It is right that I should live for a while in the home of my grandfather; it is right that we share with one another the talk of the old days when he and my grandmother Sheena walked together through the summer shielings of their youth. I will be surrounded by love and in that way I will not be alone when I die.'

For quite a few minutes Tam didn't comprehend the meaning of Otto's words, then his homely face crumpled and so overwhelmed by emotion was he that all he could say was, 'Oh ay, we'll visit you, Mr Otto, you can be damty sure o' that,' before he stumbled to the door, the drams, the cards, forgotten in the trauma of the moment.

Before Otto left Tigh na Cladach he walked with Rachel on the shores of Burg, his eyes devouring the ocean, the cliffs, the great sweeping curve of the silvery bay, everything that he had loved and treasured so well.

His arm was around Rachel's shoulder, her head was on his chest, she knew the warmth of his body, she could hear the beat and surge of his big, warm heart, beat, beating, strong, mesmerising, compelling, filling her own heart with a pain so great she felt the tears welling in her eyes and was glad that he couldn't see them because she wanted these last precious minutes on Burg Bay to be happy ones for him.

But as always he knew what she was feeling and raising her face to his he kissed her tears away and said huskily, '*Liebling*, these moments here with you mean so much to me. Whenever I think of this place I will remember how it was with you, sharing so much of my thoughts, my emotions . . .'

He paused to study her upturned face, struck anew by her dark, vibrant beauty, by the compassion and life blazing out of eyes so black and deep he felt as if he was being pulled into the very depths of her soul, and he knew an enchantment and a love for her that he had never known with any other.

It had always been there, from the start, but he knew he had no right to her, and he had pushed the knowledge of it away from him because to have succumbed to that kind of ecstasy would have been the beginning and the end of the very special relationship that had sprung up between them. They were the richer for having denied themselves the earthly joys of the flesh; their hearts and minds had remained pure and guilt-free; she would go with him to the very end of his earthly existence and she would remember him with gratitude when all that was left of him were memories.

'Rachel,' he pushed wings of dark hair away from her cheeks and kissed her very gently on the mouth, 'you are a unique and wonderful young woman. Your loyalty to me has been a joy, it was happiness enough to come to this island and to have found everything I hoped to find, but you made it so much more for me, you enriched my days with your devotion, but now you must think of yourself and your own life – your life with Jon and the little one soon to be born. You aren't happy, I see it in your eyes; you and he should be together at this time. If you argued because of me then I am sad, but I also understand why Jon would be jealous of us. You gave me much of your time, now you must make it up to him, he is your husband, you need him as much as he needs you. I hope you told him why you were kind to me, if not you must do so right away and I want you to promise me that you will write to him and tell him how much you love him and miss him.'

Rachel took a deep breath. She knew the sincerity and the wisdom of his words, at first she had been very hurt by Jon's desertion of her, hurt had turned to anger, then bitterness, back and forth her emotions had swung, like a relentless pendulum, never giving up, never slowing down, but now she was angry again and though she recognized that much of Jon's behaviour owed itself to misunderstandings, she wasn't going to give in so easily, her wilful, stubborn heart wouldn't allow it.

She didn't need him! She was perfectly capable of making a life for herself and her child without him! Let him sulk and mope and stay in London forever, if that was what he wanted, but she wouldn't go to him, she would stay here on Rhanna and have her baby and if any of those gossiping crones wanted to make something of that – let them. She had always been able to stand up for herself, from early childhood she'd had to and now that she was grown she was more able than ever . . . just like Grannie Kate.

She smiled at this. Otto took her look as an acceptance of his words, he hugged her to him and urged her footsteps on and she allowed herself to go, not looking forward, not looking back, just letting herself drift with the order and inevitability of events.

Captain Mac was as furious as he could ever be, his eyes blazed, his snowy white whiskers bristled, his jolly, bulbous red beacon of a nose grew redder still as he faced Elspeth in the cosy warmth of her orderly kitchen.

Mac had had a very pleasant time of it since coming to live with Elspeth. Whenever he had felt like it he had gone off on his various pursuits and never a word of protest had she uttered; he had expected a lot of teasing from the local menfolk regarding his changed lifestyle but oddly enough Tam and the others had exercised a great deal of restraint in the matter, so much so that Mac had often wondered if he was missing out on something he ought to know.

On this particular morning the bombshell had dropped: he had been away on one of his fishing trips but because of a storm warning the trawlers had put into port earlier than expected. Tam and Robbie had been there at the harbour, the latter winking at him in a most meaningful manner while Tam smirked and said, 'Tis yourself, Mac, back from sea for more nights o' passion, a mite too soon for Elspeth because I passed her washing line just two minutes ago and all her frilly bits are still hanging out to dry . . .'

He got no further, Mac's welcoming smile faded, he demanded to know what Tam was on about but that worthy, realizing he had said too much, stuttered out some excuse and with Robbie on his heels he deserted the scene with alacrity.

A short walk from the harbour soon put Mac in the picture and he stared with incredulous eyes at the display of silks and satins gaily flapping about in the wind.

'Katie's birthday things,' he muttered in disbelief, shock blanching the colour out of his face as the full import of Tam's careless words slowly began to dawn on him.

Now he expressed his feelings to Elspeth with none of his usual economy of words. He told her she was a fallen woman with

323

nothing more on her mind than sex and sin. He had trusted her, he had relied on her, he had truly believed that she had invited him to stay at her house with nothing but good intentions on her mind when all the while she had just been using him to exact revenge on other gossiping crones of her like. She had made him the laughing stock of the place but it was for the last time. He would never set foot inside her door again, even supposing he had to go and live in a cave for the rest of his days.

'And here was me, all this time, thinking I had never been happier since my Mary went and died on me! I should have known it couldny last. You were aye a silly woman, Elspeth, wi' naught in your head but cunning and bitterness and tis no wonder poor old Hector went the way he did, you likely drove him to drink – maybe to his death for all we know. Well, I'm no' for having the same thing happenin' to me so you can just bide here, alone and bitter to the end o' your days, for I want nothing more to do wi' you.'

With that he barged out of the house, never stopping to collect even his pyjamas, back to the bed that 'aye waited for him at Cousin Gus's – fleas and all'.

The door banged shut, Elspeth sank into a chair, her eyes wide and staring, her gaunt body trembling with reaction. She had lost Mac, through her own childish stupidity she had lost the one man who had ever brought any meaning into her lonely life. Her shoulders shook, the slow tears trickled unheeded down the deep seams of her face, the grey ashes of her life piled up in front of her mind – and made a far greater mound than the little heap of peat ash that had spilled out of the fire on to the gleaming hearth.

Ruth's heart was beating rapidly in her breast as she steered her car in the direction of An Cala. Ever since the row with Rachel she had had a miserable time of it, she had moped, she had mooned about, her conscience pricking her so badly it had been almost a physical pain. She had needled at the children, she had sulked with Lorn – in the end he could stand it no longer and had finally given her an ultimatum.

'Go to Rachel and apologize; if no' I'll take the bairns to Laigmhor and bide there with them till you come to your senses. I mean it, Ruthie, if I stay here wi' you a minute longer I might just be forced to take you over my knee and give you a good skelping.'

His anger had shocked her out of her self-pity. She didn't dare be angry back because a determined Lorn was a Lorn to be reckoned with, and after an agonizing night of indecision she had finally made up her mind and had run out to her car before her courage failed her.

Saying sorry didn't come easy to Ruth. When she was younger she had always apologized, mostly for innocent actions that her mother had chosen to interpret as sins, but in the end she had rebelled at having to be sorry for everything, even she sometimes felt, for her very existence, with the result that now she could hardly bring herself to utter that familiar expression of humility, even when she knew she was at fault.

This, however, was different. She had greatly wronged her dearest friend with her blind accusations and knew that nothing could ever be right between them again till she had made amends. But such actions took courage and Ruth's traumatic upbringing had very effectively quelled many of her natural strengths, allowing some of her weaknesses to push through in the process. Marriage to Lorn had certainly given her a lot of confidence, even so, the very idea of having to face the vibrantly powerful Rachel was almost too much for her and she gulped with nerves when the peacefully smoking chimneys of An Cala hove into view.

She needn't have worried, Rachel was delighted to see her and made no attempt to disguise her feelings. Ruth was so overwhelmed with relief she burst into tears, so thoroughly ashamed of herself for the way she had treated everyone these last few weeks that it was all Rachel could do to make her stop crying and accept a brew of her 'strange-smelling tea'.

Ruth dried her tears, she laughed instead, and clasping her hands round the cup she gulped down the liquid, never minding the taste, something in her romantic soul making her see it as an offering of peace from a girl who could have thrown her apologies back in her face but who was far too big-hearted to be so petty.

Ruth couldn't wait to catch up on all the lost weeks of separation. She remained at An Cala for hours, and they talked and talked, Rachel's hands flashing, Ruth's face a study of animation. No holds barred, they brought everything out into the open and drew closer than they had ever been been since the golden days of innocent childhood. Rachel confided her innermost thoughts to her friend and Ruth wriggled uncomfortably when it became clear that Jon had left Rhanna, thinking the exact same things about his wife as Ruth had done.

Determined to make up for her hasty judgements, she offered to drive Rachel to Croy Beag whenever she could, and Rachel, who had been in a quandary wondering how she could get to see Otto, jumped at the chance with such eagerness Ruth threw back her fair head and laughed, her violet eyes shining in a face all at once happy and carefree.

With a very determined expression on her face, Nellie, having just arrived from Hanaay on the steamer, made her way to Cousin Gus's house looking for Captain Mac.

Ever since her brother had lost his wife, Nellie had maintained a fairly firm hold on his affairs but she hadn't seen him for some considerable time and might have left it like that for another few weeks had not a rather disquieting rumour reached her ears. She was therefore in quite a state of self-righteous indignation when she presented herself at Gus's door and was no sooner over the threshold when she demanded to see Mac at once.

'He doesny live here anymore, Nellie,' Gus explained rather fearfully, endeavouring to rub away a dinnertime soup stain on the greasy lapel of his ancient tweed jacket whilst he spoke.

Gus had a great respect for Nellie who never minced words, as far as he was concerned, and always gave him a biting piece of her mind whenever their paths crossed.

Nellie wasn't exactly a formidable figure: she was plump of

face and rotund of figure, her salt-and-pepper hair was rolled into a tight sausage round her head, her untidy skirts revealed dimpled knees on otherwise shapeless legs, her splayed feet, which Mac said reminded him of a pregnant duck, were stuck into stout brogues, and altogether she was a quaint figure to behold. But a perpetual frown on her round, jutting-jawed face belied her kindly nature and Gus never dared take any cousinly liberties when in her company.

At his words her nostrils flared. 'I'm no' surprised,' she snorted, glancing round her in disgust. 'The place is a piggery, no' fit for a dog, never mind a decent man like Isaac!'

Gus bristled a bit and jutted out his own jaw in some defiance of her criticism, but she was calling her brother by his 'Sunday' name, which meant she was really on her high horse, so Gus knew to go warily. 'Maybe no', but Mac *did* bide here for a good whilie, so it canny have been *that* bad. And as a matter o' fact, he turned up here the other day lookin' for a roof but went away again, just before you arrived . . .'

Gus stroked his beard as he recalled his cousin's parting words, 'It's no' possible to live here wi' you again,' had been Mac's biting assessment of his short-lived stay. 'No' after Elspeth and her clean and decent ways. You're just no' fit to bide under the same roof as another human being. You pick your nose; you rift and fart like a horse wi' the colic; you do awful things wi' your beard behind your newspaper and yon stuff you call rum would make a pig sick for a week. I've shat bricks for two days because o' these damt ferrets o' yours! I canny thole it any longer and if Elspeth will have me back then, by God, I'll never leave her again for she's a woman in a million and that's a fact!'

'And that's gratitude for you!' Gus had retaliated hotly but to Mac's receding back – he had left the house and was already hot-footing it down the brae to the village.

'And just where has Isaac gone?' Nellie demanded, in a tone that suggested she knew the answer but wanted to hear it spelled out.

Gus looked surprised. 'To that cailleach, Elspeth Morrison.

He's been livin' wi' her all summer, I thought you would have heard.'

'No! I didny hear! At least, no' from him!' snapped Nellie, her face turning a bright crimson. 'The bodach never breathed a word to me about it – and wi' that dried-up besom too.' She stomped to the door.

'Will you no' stay and sup a cuppy wi' me?' Gus offered in an attempt to ingratiate himself with her.

'Gus McIntosh! The last time I supped tea in this house *was* the last time! The cup was thick wi' tanning inside and black wi' dirt on the outside! The rim was chipped and cracked and was so full o' germs I had food poisoning for a week and skitters for a month, so just you keep your damt tea and put it where it will do the least harm – and if you don't know where that is ask the doctor and see if she'll risk showing you!'

Gus was hurt, mortified, and furious. Raising two fingers, he viciously prodded the air with them and shouted to the closed door, 'And that's to you, you po-faced hag! At least the doctor could find my backside – yours healed up years ago and two fingers in the air is about all you'll ever get from a man for he wouldny know where else to put them!'

At that precise moment, Mac stood facing Elspeth in her cosy kitchen, shamefaced and apologetic, his big red fingers worrying the pom-pom of his knitted woollen cap which he had removed in a most mannerly fashion on entering the house.

'Ach, lass,' he said kindly, noting the hurt and embarrassment on her gaunt face and the puffy eyes which denoted plainly enough a woman who had cried a lot in recent days. 'I'm sorry for all the things I said to you. I wasny thinkin' straight at the time and cared more for my own feelings than yours. Who gives a sow's erse if all the world talks about us? When I had time to think about it I pictured all the shocked faces and had the best bloody laugh I've had in years. I bet Behag nearly peed her flannel breeks at the sight o' all the satin knickers on your wash line. She will maybe have a permanent ring round those beady wee eyes o' hers from all her peekin' through her spyglasses, just like one o' they spotty dogs you see wi' floppy lugs and hair specs.'

Elspeth's lips twitched, a strangulated sound escaped her tightly held throat. She sniggered, she snorted, she threw back her head and broke into skirls and cacophonies of pure unadulterated laughter. Mac joined in, the two of them held on to the back of the couch and simply screeched with unrestrained merriment.

Mac wiped his streaming eyes with his woolly cap, his brimming brown eyes regarded her fondly. 'Ach, tis good to see you happy, lass, and I'm going to tell you something to make you even happier, how about you and me going to Oban on a shopping spree? We'll get Katie some new things for her birthday and at the same time I'll buy you the finest set o' underwear that any woman ever had. Anything you like, see-through, pee-through, the treat's on me, for your Christmas when it comes, the best bloody Christmas for us both in years.'

Elspeth's eyes were wet again, but this time she wept the tears of disbelieving happiness, her thin shoulders shook, her head trembled on her scrawny shoulders, with a wail of impatience she scrabbled in her apron pocket for her hanky, but before she could withdraw it Mac folded her into his hairy strong arms and gently wiped away her weepings with the corner of her apron . . .

And at that inopportune moment the door opened to admit Nellie who stared at the tender scene before her with tightly folded lips.

'I knew it! I knew it!' she snorted with thinly disguised disapproval. 'I heard that the pair o' you were up to no good but I didny realize that things had gone this far.'

'Nell.' Mac let go of Elspeth and steered his sister into the parlour. 'You have no right to speak like that in front o' Elspeth,' he continued as soon as he had closed the door. 'She is a respectful and decent woman and deserves some o' your respect in turn.'

'Oh ay, it's clear to see she has you well and truly fooled but it beats me how a sensible man like you can have allowed himself to be taken in by the likes o' that sour prune out there.'

'But, Nell,' protested Mac, 'I enjoy biding here wi' her, she's no' the targe everyone thinks, she and me get on fine, she's a kindly body and has never nagged me once.'

'No' yet, but wait you, she will. She'll dig her clooks in deeper and never let go – and of course – anything is better than livin' wi' that dirty old bodach of a cousin wi' his cracked cups and his soup stains. You had best come back to Hanaay wi' me, you know you aye have a clean bed and a full belly at my house.'

Mac's jolly countenance took on an unusually stubborn expression. 'It's no' the same, Nell, you've looked after me well, I'll grant you that, but you're my sister; Elspeth – well – she's . . .'

He faltered and came to an abrupt halt, leaving the way clear for Nellie to take up the cudgels. 'Ay, you've said enough, Isaac, we all know what Elspeth is and I'll no bide another minute under the roof of a pair o' – o' shameless sinners who are old enough to know better!'

With that she marched ben the kitchen where Elspeth was making tea, her shaky hands belying her calm demeanour. She had heard most of what had transpired in the parlour, simply because she had kept her ear glued to the door for most of the conversation, the result being that her first instinct was to make some cutting remarks to Nellie. But with an effort she stayed her tongue – she wasn't going to spoil things now – not when she had Mac just where she wanted him.

So she was polite to the visitor, she was the epitome of good manners and consideration. Graciously she invited Nellie to stay, with admirable efficiency she set about preparing a meal which later proved to be so palatable that even Nellie was moved to giving it some grudging praise.

'Of course, the pork could have been doing wi' a bit more crackling,' she added, 'and the carageen pudding needed a wee bit nutmeg to give it flavour but otherwise it wasny bad – no' too bad at all.'

Over her head Mac winked at Elspeth and it took him all his time to keep a sober face when she promptly and boldly winked back.

* * *

That night Mac sat happily back in his favourite chair, wiggling his stockinged feet on the hearth while he waited for the poker to grow sufficiently hot that he might plunge it into the tot of rum at his side. He thought about his life here with Elspeth and how easy she had been to live with, and even though she made him bathe twice a week and change his drawers every other day it had been a small price to pay for everything she had given him in return.

Picking up his glass, he watched the reflected light of the fire dancing like ruby-tinted nymphs in the liquid, and then he peeped at Elspeth over the rim. She had declined to join him in a drink, even though it had become an enjoyable habit of theirs to sit by the fire of an evening, savouring their drinks, the smell of burnt rum pleasurably invading their nostrils. He suspected that she was doing all in her power to impress Nellie with her restraint and he smiled to himself at the sight of the two women, sitting side by side on the couch sedately sipping cocoa.

With slow deliberation Mac pushed tobacco into the bowl of his pipe with a horny, tar-stained thumb, lit it and sat back, puffing the smoke into the air, watching it drifting and curling up to the ceiling.

'Oh, by the way,' removing the pipe from his mouth he spoke very casually, 'I meant to tell you, Nell, but wi' all the talk and pleasure o' seeing you again it just slipped my mind. Elspeth and me are to be wed in the spring, just a quiet affair wi' maybe one or two o' the family present. Oban, ay, it will likely be Oban, a registry office, seeing as how both Elspeth and me have been married before.'

Both women choked into their cocoa, coughing and spluttering so badly that Mac had to rush over and thump each one on the back in turn. Elspeth glanced up with streaming eyes, her expression was a study of bemusement and disbelief – and it was more than just the cocoa that had induced her wet eyes – for the second time that day she wept the tears of pure happiness – and this time she made no attempt to wipe them away.

Chapter Twenty-four

Otto was never short of visitors, every day there was always someone popping in for a 'crack and a cuppy' and very often an impromptu ceilidh would get going, with fiddles and 'squeezeboxes' providing the music; poetry from the island bards; Magnus or old Andrew drawing on their store of magical tales, traditional myths and folklore which had improved with age and which had never been written down but had been passed on orally from one generation to the next.

As more and more modern influences intruded into island life the days of the Seanachaidh were fast disappearing, therefore it was a precious thing indeed to listen to these old men with their seamed, wise faces and their air of authority. The hushed respectful voices of them stirred the imagination and mesmerized the mind till it really seemed that the witches and hobgoblins of yore came leaping, prancing, and skirling into the present day, thrilling and terrifying the listeners till, with expert ease, the senses were soothed by gentler stories of water kelpies that haunted the lochs and snow bochdans that roamed the hills in search of the spirits of children who had departed earthly life but still liked to come back now and then to play in the ice caves high on the corries.

Children who were very much alive and kicking loved these old men and their shivery tales and Otto encouraged them to come and visit and join in the ceilidhs, though they didn't need much encouragement, having grown to love the big Austrian as much as the grown-ups did.

Machair Cottage had a perfect atmosphere for such simple pastimes, its thatched roof and deep windows, its warm hearth and its booklined walls, even the very cobwebs in the corners, all combined to give the impression of a past era that had somehow survived into modern times.

And with Tina in charge there was no danger of the spiders or their webs being disturbed, since she was kept too busy cooking and cleaning for 'her menfolk' to bother her head with such harmless creatures as spiders who, in her opinion, had been put on the earth for a good reason and earned their place by catching flies and midgies and other pests.

'Though, mind,' she said once, 'if one o' they big hairy tarantulas came creeping in I would be the first to drop my duster and go screaming outside with everyone else!'

Her refreshing presence in Machair Cottage was a continual source of comfort and joy for both Otto and Magnus. Without her they could never have managed to cope, even though Otto's bed was in a recess in the kitchen so that he could be right there in the heart of things instead of being tucked away in a part of the house where he could see or hear very little.

Megan and Babbie were regular visitors, the one administering the drugs and the painkillers that kept Otto going, the other attending to his personal comforts, which also kept him going but which involved procedures that had embarrassed him so much in the beginning Babbie had been moved to cry out in exasperation, 'Och, for heaven's sake, you're no' the first man in the world I've had to bathe and you'll certainly no' be the last! I've seen hairy bums, pink bums, fat and thin bums, and bums with rashes and pimples that were often bigger than the bums they were on! So just you lie back and let me wash *your* bum and if you're very good I might even use hot water to do it with!'

At that Magnus had collapsed in his chair to chortle and wheeze in a gluttony of mirth that was so infectious both Babbie and Otto joined in, the former ending up so winded it was all she could do to wash her patient, who by that time was so exhausted himself he succumbed meekly to her tender mercies.

From that day forth he was never too ashamed to 'bare his bum' to her and indeed even began to look forward to her visits for, with her wonderful green eyes, red hair, and wide smile, she seemed to bring sunshine into the room and was never too rushed to spare the time for a cup of tea and a good chin-wag.

Ruth, as good as her word, brought Rachel to visit as often as she could and in so doing, the young writer with the poet's heart and romantic soul, found a treasure trove in Magnus's house that totally enthralled her from the moment she stepped over the threshold. The place was a paradise for musicians, artists and writers. Books on every subject under the sun were there for the taking; Magnus's own personal jotters, filled from cover to cover with the writings of a lifetime, were a particular joy for Ruth and she never wearied during her visits, rather she looked forward to them with a zest that almost matched that of Rachel and could never get over fast enough to Magnus and his 'magical house'.

From his bed Otto could see the ocean from one window and the moors from the other, and he loved just to lie there, watching the calm or the rage of the sea, the cloud patterns moving over the shaggy wilderness of the great amber plains, in his mind smelling the perfumes of summer and the lark song high in the heavens.

Tina sometimes sang to him in her sweet, clear voice, slightly off-key, but something so poignant in the tremble and tone of it, he would find a lump in his throat, and taking her hand he would squeeze it and urge her to carry on singing, making her cry inside of herself for her 'dear Mr Otto' who watched her with dark eyes that were weary yet hungry for everything that was still good and precious in his life.

But the hands and the eyes that soothed him most were those of the girl who had come to him out of nowhere it seemed and who still came to him out of a deep wild sea of forbidden dreams. She haunted his sleep, she disturbed his awakenings, but only when she wasn't there. The reality of Rachel was like balm on a deep, raw wound. She sat by his bed, so soothing in her silence, the voice that could never speak finding expression in her eyes and in her hands, healing hands that caressed his brow with a tenderness that brought him comfort beyond compare and a conviction that the heartbeat of his life would never fade or falter as long as she was there by his side.

Whenever she came he often felt so good he would get up and get dressed and together they would slowly walk over the machair to the cliffs, each of them heavy and waiting, both of them content to sit there on the edge of the world and watch the ocean tossing in its restless bed far below.

One day he took her hand and held it tightly. 'How long now, *liebling*?'

'Three weeks – round about Christmas.'

He frowned. 'Jon must come soon,' he said sternly. 'He should be here now, sharing this time with you, giving you his support.'

The wind was springing up from the sea, cold and penetrating; she huddled herself further into her jacket and made no reply. Her anger, her bitterness was spent; she wanted Jon to come, she longed to see him again. Perhaps he would relent at the last minute, she thought forlornly, and knew a pang of fear at the thought of having her baby without him there at her side.

Megan, on one of her routine visits to An Cala, was stressing to Rachel the importance of having her baby in a mainland hospital. Rachel had been burning incense, the house reeked of it and Megan thought the tea reeked of it too as she sat sipping the brew that Rachel had courteously made for her.

Despite a flash of annoyance in the girl's dark eyes, she managed to remain polite when Megan, continuing the conversation that the arrival of the tea had made her break off, said that she would make all the necessary arrangements with the hospital and it might be wise to go a week or so earlier just in case the weather turned nasty.

But Rachel was having none of that: she wanted her baby to be born on Rhanna, she had set her mind on it and nothing was going to make her change it, and she conveyed this to the doctor by means of pen and paper and any other means that would stipulate she meant what she said.

Reluctantly Megan agreed, but only on condition that the girl came to live at the Manse till after the birth. Again she came up against fierce opposition. Rachel's chin jutted, her mouth set itself into determined lines and, grabbing pen and paper once more, she insisted that she wanted to stay on at An Cala till it was all over.

'But you don't even have a phone,' Megan pointed out. 'You are all alone in the house and might easily go into labour in the middle of the night with no one to turn to for help. Also' – at this point she groped for the right words to say – 'as this is your first child it's only fair to give it a good start. You are young and strong and healthy but supposing something went wrong? Some babies suffer from birth defects that could easily have been prevented if the mothers had been in hospital at the time.'

Rachel knew what Megan was trying to say and she flushed with anger but couldn't express how she felt to someone with only scant understanding of her sign language. But Ruth was an expert on the subject, she had learned to read that particular language almost from the moment Jon had taught it to Rachel and, arriving in time to hear Megan's arguments, she immediately took up the cudgels on her friend's behalf.

'Ach, Doctor Megan,' she chided softly, 'neither Rachel nor myself got our wee bit flaws at birth, they were caused by our mothers' having had German measles when they were carrying us. They canny be passed on because they aren't what you would call congenital. Lachlan explained everything to me before I had my two and no doubt he did the same to Rachel.'

Megan flushed. 'I see you're well up on the subject, Ruth, and of course I know that what happened to you and Rachel can't be passed on, the fact remains, however, that she is all alone in this house, unless . . .' – she turned to Rachel – 'your mother or grandmother could come and stay here with you.'

Rachel looked horrified at the very idea of her untidy mother making An Cala into a replica of her own disgracefully muddled house, and though Grannie Kate was a cheerful and welcome presence in most circumstances, it was too much to visualize her loud and boisterous intrusion at the birth of any child, even that of her very own great grandchild.

'I'll come.' Ruth made the decision quickly and was well rewarded by the expression of relieved gratitude on her friend's face. 'I would love to do it, I'll ask Shona or Kirsteen to take the children' – she giggled – 'They can halve them between them if two is too much for one, if you see what I mean, and Lorn can stay at Laigmhor. I'll go home right now and ask him.'

Lorn wasn't exactly over the moon about the arrangements. He hummed and hawed and permitted himself one or two grumbles but gave in eventually as he knew Ruth wouldn't be happy until she did this for Rachel to further atone for her earlier misjudgements.

'If only Jon would come back,' she said unhappily. 'It's terrible to see Rachel alone at a time like this. I know fine she waits for Erchy to bring some word from Jon but he never writes and soon it may be too late for both o' them to ever make up.'

Tina was thinking the exact same thing and on one of Ruth's visits to Machair Cottage she took her aside and asked her outright if she had any idea what had happened between Jon and Rachel to have caused such a rift in their marriage,

Shamefaced, Ruth told her that Jon believed the baby to be Otto's – as she had done – he hadn't known then about Otto's illness and by all accounts he didn't know now. If he had, things might have been different but the damage had been done, and with Rachel stubbornly refusing to write and tell her husband the truth, the future looked bleak for them.

In response, Tina clicked her tongue loudly and gave vent to such an uncharacteristic tirade of rebuke, Ruth felt her ears growing hot and her face turning crimson.

'How could you, Ruth? You've aye been a mite too ready to believe the worst o' people!' Tina scolded, in her agitation prodding loose hairgrips into her skull with such viciousness she hurt her own scalp and let out a yelp of pain.

Ruth felt very glad it wasn't *her* scalp that was on the receiving end of such treatment and she was only too willing to supply the older woman with Jon's address when she demanded it.

'Right,' Tina glared at the scrap of paper in her hand, 'just you leave this to me, my girl. But for now, away you go ben the kitchen, you'll be safe there, for the way I'm feeling right now my hands are itching to skelp somebody's erse and if you bide in here a minute longer it might easily be yours!'

That night, when the house slept and she could at last be alone, Tina took a pen, a notepad and an oil lamp to the kitchen table and sat herself quietly down, her gaze roving every so often to the quiet bed in the corner where Otto breathed deeply in his drugged sleep.

Ach, my poor, dear man, she thought, you are a gentleman just and I'd kill for you, that I would. If any other bugger tries to tarnish your good name they'll have me to deal with – and may the Lord forgive me for such harsh thoughts – but I canny seem to help myself these days. I'm seeing a side o' myself I don't like very much but I'd do anything for you, Mr Otto, and right now I'm going to clear your name o' blame – if it's the last thing I do.

But it wasn't so easy to find the words she wanted to write and she sat there at the kitchen table, lost in thought, her hands folded tranquilly in her lap, her languorous brown eyes surveying the night shadows on the walls without really seeing them. The halo of light from the lamp blurred all the surrounding edges so that she felt as if she was in a small sphere of peace that was all her own. Just her and Mr Otto, alone together in the room but separate, he from her by sleep and dreams, she from him by wakeful ponderings that wouldn't let her rest till she had done what she had to do.

She shrugged herself out of her reveries and smiled. Mr James was always telling her she thrived on romance and nonsense and he was right enough in that respect – and at her age too! But och, she never did anyone any harm by just dreaming and she would never get this damty letter written if she didn't focus her mind on it.

Nevertheless she deliberated for another ten minutes before she seized her pen with a decisive gesture and began to write purposefully.

Christmas was just three days away and it was Rachel's birthday. Ruth, determined to make it as happy an event as possible in the circumstances, had baked a little cake covered with pink icing, which she had decorated with a little chocolate violin and one single red candle, which was all Merry Mary had in the shop at the time as she had been cleaned out of such frivolities because of the festive season.

But Rachel had been delighted anyway. Kate and Annie and a few others had come, bearing little gifts. Lorna had made a squinty Chinese lantern in school and had proudly presented it to her adopted aunt while little Douglas handed over a crumpled bag containing chocolate drops which he had promptly devoured when no one was looking.

At dinnertime everyone departed, including Ruth who wanted to get some supplies at the shops before taking the children back home, Douglas to Laigmhor, Lorna to Shona at Mo Dhachaidh.

The house was quiet again. Rachel stood at the window, watching the steamer coming round Mara Òran Bay as she had watched it so often since Jon had made his hasty departure from Rhanna – but he had never returned – and she had given up wishing and praying for the boat to bring him home again.

She sank into a chair, glad to be alone for a little while. She was feeling lethargic and fretted that she hadn't been able to visit Otto for some days now, but her time was very near and Megan had made her promise not to leave the house unless it was strictly necessary. She was also suffering from nostalgia. Her birthday – and Jon hadn't sent so much as a card to mark the event when in days gone by he had showered her with gifts and had made it altogether a special occasion.

Jon. She spoke his name in her heart, please come back to me, I love you, I miss you . . .

She was totally unprepared for the searing pain in her lumbar region and she gasped, gripping the arms of her chair till the moment passed.

She closed her eyes. The waiting was done with, the day she had longed for had come at last – and Jon wasn't here to share it with her . . . She wept, for all the things in her life that had been precious and sweet, for Jon, for Otto . . .

Poignancy swelled in her breast, her heart pulsed in her ears, deafening her, pounding through all of her body till it seemed the whole world was just one big heartbeat with herself trapped in the echoing roar of it. She didn't hear the opening of the door but some separate sense made her open her eyes and turn her head to see Jon framed in the doorway, like some impossible vision without substance.

But it was Jon, all right, very much alive, bounding towards her to take her in his arms and crush her to him, warm, whole, real, kissing her tears away, murmuring words of love into her hair, her face, her neck. The light from the window poured over his face, it was thinner than she remembered, he looked as if he hadn't slept properly in months. Her heart turned over and she knew then how much she had wronged him by not taking him into her confidence, the one person in the world who deserved her honesty and had failed to get it.

Jon. Her lips formed his name, her fingers traced the contours of his face as if to reassure herself that he was really here, her mouth nuzzled his, she fought down another spasm of pain because she couldn't bear anything to interfere with those precious moments of reunion . . .

And then she looked over his head and saw Mamma Jodl coming into the room, burdened down with an enormous suitcase that Jon had dropped in the porch in his anxiety to get inside.

Rachel's heart fell. Mamma had kept her word, she had said she would be back for Christmas and she had certainly meant what she said.

Then Mamma did a surprising thing, she swept over to her daughter-in-law to take her to her bosom in a mighty hug. Her eyes were alight, her face was glowing, she looked really pleased to see Jon's wife and wasn't slow to express herself.

'For Christmas I come, but more than that I am here for the birthtime of my grandchild. Jon tells me this only last week; the shock to my heart was not good. I scold Jon for not telling me sooner. My son! Leaving alone his wife to carry the burden of his child. No argument is worth such selfishness and this to him I tell.'

Rachel stared. Had Mamma been the instigator of Jon's change of heart? Had she taken leave of her senses altogether? Scolding Jon! Sticking up for her daughter-in-law! All at once Rachel realized that she was really quite pleased to see her mother-in-law and, with a small glow warming her heart, she returned the crushing embrace with a more restrained one of her own.

Mamma straightened, she gazed around her with pleasure. 'To my room I must go,' she announced. 'I have pictured the scenery in my mind, now I will look at the real thing from my window. Portcull will be there in the distance, soon I will see Happy Mary and Aggie and all my other cronies, I will listen to the gossip and the cleck, Mairi will give me tea, Kate will give me her worries. I have much to do while I am here – and Christmas to make for Rab McKinnon.'

She disappeared upstairs, they could hear her clumping about, familiarizing herself once more with the house. She hadn't forgotten anything or anyone it seemed, her mode of speech had been liberally sprinkled with quaint local expressions, she had spoken with great fondness of 'her cronies', she had remembered the landscape vividly and obviously couldn't wait to see it all again. Mamma had very definitely changed her first opinions about Rhanna and had vigorously returned to re-acquaint herself with everything.

Jon and Rachel gazed at one another, shy suddenly, too filled with the wonder of the occasion to trust themselves to express their feelings.

Wordlessly Jon withdrew a letter from his pocket and handed it to his wife.

It was from Tina, beautifully written in a style that was almost copperplate, but the lovely and unique thing about it was that Tina wrote with her pen in the same dialect as her tongue, which gave the impression that she had whispered the words as she was writing them.

Dear Jon,

You might be thinking this is none o' my business but when Ruth told me that you thought Mr Otto was the father o' your child then I just made it my business, since that thrawn wee wife o' yours would rather die than swallow her pride by writing to you herself.

First of all, the dear good man I have come to love like a brother has only a short time left to live. Rachel knew this almost from the start and kept the burden of it locked away tightly in her staunch little heart.

He didn't want folks knowing and maybe pitying him and she made sure it remained a personal matter till he himself knew he couldn't keep it a secret any longer.

Maybe they did start off loving one another as man to woman, but he is a gentleman just and would never take what isn't rightly his. After that, he and Rachel shared a rare kind of companionship, a sort of understanding o' souls, it was a beautiful thing to see, they were like a a pair o' children, innocent and relaxed together, and I sometimes had a wee greet to myself just watching them. I was there every day and special friends was all they ever were, dear, good friends who understood one another and found so much to share and laugh about.

He was so happy for her when he found out she was expecting a baby. Mr Otto could never have children of his own, that was one o' the reasons that he and his wife separated. He told me this in confidence and now I'm telling you in confidence, trusting you will hold your tongue in the matter.

I know fine you love Rachel as she does you. I hope this letter brings you both to your senses, if no' I'll personally take the pair o' you and knock your silly heads together.

When my Matthew died I realized how privileged I was to have had a good man, the amount o' years we had together wasn't the important part, it was how we spent our time that counted, loving and caring for one another and trying to live wi' the faults we both had. Since his death I have never had a moment's regret, for we treated each other kindly, Matthew and me, and I will never look back in sorrow and anger for things left undone.

Your baby will soon be here, the one you have both been waiting for, so just you catch the next boat or the bairn will arrive before you.

I remain yours respectfully,
Tina

Rachel crushed the letter to her breast, her eyes were glazed with unshed tears. God bless you, Tina, my dear, dear friend, she thought. Reaching for Jon's hand she held on to it tightly. Her pains were coming faster, growing more intense, little beads of sweat glinted on her brow and Jon gazed at her anxiously. He had come armed with birthday gifts and had been looking forward to seeing her opening them but all that would have to wait.

Rachel had gone into labour in earnest and it was thanks to Tina that he had come when he did or his baby might well have arrived before him.

The trauma of not being able to express her pain vocally would live with Rachel forever. Racked with the torture of childbirth, she writhed and tossed in a silent agony of endurance, feeling at times that she was sinking into a deep red pit of oblivion which never totally engulfed her even though she prayed for the relief it would bring.

Out of one nightmarish trough after another she climbed, clinging to Jon's hand, vaguely hearing his voice as he spoke to her and encouraged her and suffered some of her ordeal with her.

She knew Mamma was there too, bathing her brow, speaking soothing condolences in broken accents that were oddly comforting because they were familiar sounds in a frighteningly unfamiliar situation.

And even in the midst of her suffering she wondered how she could ever have hated Mamma and wished her out of the same vicinity as herself, for the hands that touched her were gentle and the voice that spoke her name was sincere and caring.

She liked Mamma Jodl in those tormented moments and she knew that no matter how much her mother-in-law might anger her in the future, she would never dislike her with quite the same intensity as she had done in the past.

Minutes, hours, days – she had no idea of the passage of time, for her, each pain-filled second was endless, each hour eternity that had no dusk or day.

In fact, it was a short, if violent, labour. It ended in an explosion of sensations: pain, relief, exhaustion, an eruption of trembling emotions, a baby's cry, Babbie's wonderfully sane voice, bubbling, laughing.

'Happy birthday, Rachel, she's all yours.'

She put the baby into Rachel's waiting arms, a tiny daughter with a mop of black hair and a voice that almost deafened everyone in the room. To Rachel it was the most beautiful sound she had ever heard and both she and Jon gazed at the tiny screwed-up face with utter wonder on theirs.

Mamma was beside herself with delight. She had been a good help to Babbie and Megan, she had fetched and carried, she had administered to Rachel, she had tried to domineer Ruth in the kitchen, but had soon discovered that the fair-haired, slightly built girl was stronger than she looked and was having none of Mamma's bossiness. After that she had tucked in her horns and had set about helping Ruth in every way she could, including keeping the big kettle boiling on the stove all afternoon. Hot water was an essential, endless 'cuppies' even more so, but Mamma was growing used to the Scots' thirst for tea and had herself sat with her feet on the fender to drink two steaming cups, one after the other, during a lull in proceedings.

Despite her busy day she didn't look in the least fatigued; she held her new granddaughter, she beamed, she crooned. 'The next will be a son,' she said in her incorrigible way, and seeing a pair of headlamps coming down the road from Portvoynachan, she rushed to put on her hat and coat in order to go outside and stand waving her arms in the middle of the road.

It was Erchy, coming back from his Christmas deliveries, and he was easily persuaded to take Mamma to Rab's house when he heard the news about Rachel's baby.

'A wee lass, eh?' Erchy slapped his knee, as tickled pink as Mamma herself. 'Rab will want to wet its head so I'd best come in wi' you to make sure he does the job properly.'

'Wet its head?' queried Mamma in puzzled tones.

'Ay, it's a Scottish tradition,' Erchy explained happily. 'A way o' welcoming a new bairn into the world – it doesny have to be there, of course, we leave it to the minister to do the real thing at the christening, but as long as we wet our own thrapples wi' a good dram o' whisky the bairn will have all the good luck it ever needs to start it off in life.'

Erchy wasn't the only one to be 'wetting his thrapple'. Babbie, Megan, Ruth, Jon, all drank a toast to the new baby while Rachel drank a well-earned cuppy, a wonder in her that only that very morning she had wakened alone in her bed and had risen to face a birthday without Jon. Now she was a mother, Jon was a father, all in the space of a few short hours – and it was still her birthday, complete with the most precious gift she could ever have wished for.

At last she and Jon were alone in the room with their new daughter. He stood there at the bedside, gazing down on the small, red face, quiet now, one tiny fist jammed into the pink little blubber of a mouth, the other clenched beside one paper-thin ear as she slept the deep and dreamless sleep of the newborn infant.

'Let's call her Karla,' Jon said quietly, 'Karla McKinnon Jodl.'

Rachel looked at him quickly: surely he wasn't still thinking that this was the child of Karl Gustav Langer! But the quiet brown eyes that sought hers were innocent of guile as he went on, 'I want us both to always remember a great man. If you agree then she will have a name to be proud of, Karla for him, McKinnon for you, and Jodl for me, it seems as if it was meant for her.'

The name rang inside Rachel's head like a melody, Karla McKinnon Jodl. It was beautiful, it was perfect. With tears in her eyes she held her arms out to her husband and he went to the breast that had newly suckled his baby to kiss the creamy skin and nuzzle the warm flesh before curling up beside her, holding her close till she fell asleep in the safe stronghold of his loving arms.

Christmas came on the teeth of a sou'westerly gale that shrieked over the island, whipping the trees into frenzy, lashing the shores, rattling the chimney pots, wailing at windows and doors as if all the witches of hell had been let loose and were trying to gain their demented footholds. But the stout walls held firm; doors and windows remained grimly closed; hardly a soul ventured out of doors but were quite happy to remain by cosy hearths where Christmas lights twinkled and tables groaned under festive fare.

Mamma had never been happier. She organised, she arranged, she cooked, baked, sweated, and produced enormous amounts of food, not just for Rab but for everyone: great smoked hams, mouthwatering cheeses, batch upon batch of apfelstrudel, pastries stuffed with cream, buns bulging with raisins, puddings rich with spices, gateaux dark with chocolate, cakes thick with almonds.

Rachel was very glad to let her mother-in-law take charge, though all the time she fretted, not because Mamma had taken over her kitchen, but for her enforced confinement to the wind-battered house. She had quickly recovered from the birth of her baby and her desire to be up and about was imperative: every minute, every hour, brought Otto closer to death. She had heard that he was failing fast and his last words to her had been a request to see her baby.

So Rachel wouldn't allow herself to rest. Much to Megan's dismay she arose from her bed only hours after giving birth in it, and she refused to sit still for any length of time but insisted on wandering about the house 'like a demented spook', to quote Annie who had arrived expecting to find her daughter in bed but had instead found her up and fully dressed, going about as usual.

Megan thought the description was apt enough. She had come to know Rachel well in the last year; in the girl's turbulent dark eyes she recognized a yearning soul and knew that nothing would bring her appeasement till she could visit Otto for the last time and let him hold her baby in his arms.

The little thatched house that overlooked the sea was quiet and peaceful when Jon and Rachel at last took their baby to see Otto. Tina had decorated the kitchen, a tiny tree stood on a table near the window, a row of squinty paper stars were strung across the room, dozens of Christmas cards filled every available space. The homely smells of baking and cooking hung agreeably in the air, a large tray of spicy buns stood cooling on a shelf, presided over by Vienna who was addicted to cakes and pastries and would do anything to sink her fangs into them, while Tina in her turn would do anything to ensure that the 'big, sleek brute o' a cratur' never so much as tasted the reek o' a scone'.

But she didn't mean it, even though cats had never rated very highly with her, she put up with them and treated them well because the menfolk in her life appeared to dote on them. Mark James had three 'sly sleekit brutes' as she called them; they sized her up, tripped her up, stole food from the table, left bird and mouse corpses in the living room and 'frightened the shat out o' her' by leaping at her from dark corners when she was least expecting it.

But Vienna was special because she was Mr Otto's cat, and Tina was feeding her a piece of spicy bun when she heard the visitors and turned to welcome them. She had been crying, her eyes were red and dull with sadness. She smiled at the baby, indicated the chairs by Otto's bed, and took herself ben to the little parlour that led off from the kitchen.

Otto's condition had greatly worsened since Rachel's last visit, he was gaunt and pale, the shadow of death lay over him, and it was difficult to believe he was the same big giant of a man who had arrived on Rhanna not so many months ago.

Even so, his eyes were bright and eager for life; he was delighted to see the visitors and immediately stretched out a hand to pull away the shawl from the baby's face.

'This is Karla,' Jon spoke in a low voice, 'Karla McKinnon Jodl.'

'Karla.' Otto repeated the name in disbelief. He sank back into his pillows as Jon placed the baby in his arms. 'Karla.' He stared at the tiny, sleeping face. 'How perfect she is, such miraculous perfection, you must have more like her, I would have had dozens but it was not to be – my wife left me because of it.' He gripped Jon's arm. 'My friend, I thank you for bringing her here – and also for honouring my name in such a generous way. You are a good man and I'm happy to see you all together – my life is complete now and I will die in peace.'

Jon took the baby and stumbled out of the room, hardly able to see where he was going for the mists that blinded him.

'Rachel.' Otto reached out and took her hands, his were thin and frail, those once-strong, beautiful, pianist's hands with their long, slender fingers. 'Soon it will be goodbye, *liebling.*'

A sob tightened her throat, she who had once run to him on effortless feet couldn't bear the pain of being with him any longer.

She drew her hands away, briefly her fingers whispered over his face, lingered on his mouth, their eyes met and held . . . moments passed, laden with a million unspoken dreams and longings . . . then she stepped back from his bed and went quickly away.

*　　*　　*

Death came gently and kindly to Otto. He went with the night that rolled slowly back from the shadowed horizon and he never saw the promise of day silvering the purple-black clouds. Dawn came, rosy and sweet above the sea, chasing the quiet shadows from the hills, spreading light on the sleeping bens, stirring the herds and the flocks in the fields, glinting on the ice-cold burns tinkling over the stones.

The kitchen was quiet when Magnus arose, he knew before he looked at his grandson that he had lost him and he went outside, into the cold morning, feeling the peace of lonely places enfolding him, that special peace that he and Otto had often shared without either of them losing anything of its quality.

Tina looked from the window and saw the old man there, alone on the cliffs, his thatch of white hair blowing in the wind. Her heart went out to him; she followed him outside, but being Tina she stopped first to take his jacket down from its peg, her hand trembling, her tears spilling.

'Ach, Tina,' Magnus murmured huskily, allowing her to tuck the jacket round his shoulders, 'did I do right? Bringing a fine gentleman like him into my humble home?'

'Where else would he have died so peacefully?' Tina said gently. 'He was loved to the last, surrounded by family and friends. I know fine he enjoyed every minute for he told me so himself, also he was honoured to have shared the last part o' his life here wi' you, his very own grandfather. You yourself have lived here all o' your days and there is no gentleman in the land as fine or as wise as our very own Magnus o' Croy.'

It was January, the snow was on the hills, Rachel walked quickly along the road from An Cala. She, Jon, Mamma and the baby, were leaving the island next day but she couldn't go without saying her last farewells to Otto. Her footsteps slowed when she reached that lonely grave on the Hillock with the sea and the sky and the silent bens all around.

The inscription on the gravestone was deceptively simple, in

349

days to come it would mystify the casual observer though the people of Rhanna would always know what it meant;

KARL GUSTAV LANGER,
WHO CAME TO THIS ISLAND
AS OTTO KLEBB,
AND DIED A McKINNON.
NEVER FORGOTTEN.
MAC NAN ÈILEAN.

He had been a very generous Son of the Island. He had gifted his beautiful Becky to the village church hall and had set up a trust fund for talented island youngsters. Tina had been left five thousand pounds, various McKinnons had also benefited, the coffers of the Church Fabric Fund had greatly swollen, baby Karla would one day be a rich young lady, and not even Vienna had been forgotten, but it was Magnus who had received the bulk of his grandson's fortune.

'Buy a new house,' he had been urged, but he had just shook his head at that and, smiling his beguiling one-toothed smile, he had said firmly, 'Na, na, this cottage has done me fine all o' my days and I'm no' going to move now, though the money will come in handy and will see me into my old age.' He had finished with a chuckle which might have fooled some but not those who knew how much he grieved for his grandson.

The world beyond Rhanna had learned of Otto's death and the reporters had come snooping, but the islanders had closed ranks. Magnus had told them as little as he could but even so there had been splashes in the newspapers about the famous musician spending his last days in the humble thatched cottage of his maternal grandfather.

But all that was past now, the kirkyard on the Hillock slumbered once more, the silence of it shrouded Rachel as she stood there alone, remembering.

But it was too quiet, too sad. In life Otto had known the freedom of wide, wild spaces, she raised her head and gazed towards the great bastion of Burg and she knew where she had to go to find him.

She walked away from the kirkyard, through the gate and down the Hillock. Kate was coming along, her face like thunder. 'That Tam!' she exploded. 'I told him I wanted a washing machine for Christmas, ready for the day when the electrics came to Rhanna. He said he had sent for my present; it came this morning. You'll never guess what the mean bugger gave me! A scrubbing board! The bodach, he'll never move wi' the times, and it wasny even here in time for Christmas!'

Rachel's lips twitched, Kate's own generous mouth widened and she gave a snort of laughter, then she sobered and laid her hand on the girl's arm. 'Life goes on, *mo chridhe*, life goes on,' she said gently and went on her way, pensive and quiet, throwing over her shoulder, 'You'll bring the bairn to see me before you go away, Rachel, I'll be looking out for you.'

Rachel nodded, she too went on her way, her steps taking her along one of the many sheep tracks that led to Burg Bay. There she stood, surrounded by the soar of the cliffs, the tumble of the ocean, and in her mind Otto came to her, striding along the sands, a smile lighting his face, crinkling his eyes. Glancing up she saw Tigh na Cladach and just for a moment she imagined that a spark of light illuminated the windows, reminding her of that day when waves of music had come pouring out, soaring, soaring, filling her world with power and gladness.

This was where Otto was, where he would always be; never again would she walk the shores of Burg without seeing him and hearing him and sensing that his soul touched hers as it had done when he had filled her life with his joy and vitality.

His spirit was here, whispering to her in the wind, caressing her heart with love and beauty. He would never die, never! She spread her arms and threw back her head, she wanted to shout his name but her lack of speech didn't matter anymore. His own words, spoken before he died, came to her as if on the breath of the breeze: 'I have never heard your voice but you have no need of it, I have always known what you were feeling and thinking, always it will be so.'

Always, always, now and forever!

Mac nan Èilean! The joyous benediction rang inside her

head, and as she stood there she seemed to hear the echo of it, springing out of the sea, tossing up from the waves, reverberating against the cliffs, over and over, like the notes of a great symphony pulsing and throbbing, drifting free and unfettered over the clean wide spaces of the shores of Rhanna.